TRIPTYCH

Selected Fiction of P.K. Page

TRIPTYCH

SELECTED FICTION OF

P.K. PAGE

edited by Elizabeth Popham

The Porcupine's Quill

Library and Archives Canada Cataloguing in Publication

Page, P. K. (Patricia Kathleen), 1916–2010
[Works. Selections]
    Triptych : selected fiction of P. K. Page / edited by Elizabeth Popham.

Novel and short stories.
Sun and the moon originally published in 1944 under author's
    pseudonym, Judith Cape.
ISBN 978-0-88984-408-7 (softcover)

    I. Popham, Elizabeth A., editor II. Cape, Judith, 1916–2010. Sun and
the moon. III. Title. IV. Title: Selected fiction of P. K. Page.

PS8531.A34A6 2017   C813'.54   C2017-905463-5

Published by The Porcupine's Quill, 68 Main Street, PO Box 160,
Erin, Ontario NOB 1TO. http://porcupinesquill.ca

Represented in Canada by Canadian Manda.
Trade orders are available from University of Toronto Press.

We acknowledge the support of the Ontario Arts Council and the Canada Council for the Arts for our publishing program. The financial support of the Government of Canada is also gratefully acknowledged.

Canada Council   Conseil des arts
for the Arts   du Canada   Canadä

ONTARIO ARTS COUNCIL
CONSEIL DES ARTS DE L'ONTARIO   Ontario
an Ontario government agency   Ontario Media Development
un organisme du gouvernement de l'Ontario   Corporation

A Note on the Collected Works of P. K. Page

Triptych: Selected Fiction of P. K. Page is the fifth in a series of volumes being published by the Porcupine's Quill as a complement to the online hyper-media edition of the *Collected Works of P. K. Page.*

The online edition (digitalpage.ca) is intended as a resource for scholarly research, while the print volumes are intended as attractive and inexpensive reading texts, edited to the highest scholarly standards but without the extensive textual apparatus which can be more effectively presented in a digital edition.

CONTENTS

INTRODUCTION

In her 1970 essay 'Traveller, Conjuror, Journeyman', P. K. Page describes herself as 'a two-dimensional being', saying 'I live in a sheet of paper' ('Traveller', 44):

> At times I seem to be attempting to copy exactly something that exists in a dimension where worldly senses are inadequate. As if a thing only felt had to be extracted from invisibility and transposed into a seen thing, a heard thing. The struggle is to fit the 'made' to the 'sensed' in such a way that the whole can occupy a world larger than the one I normally inhabit. The process involves scale. Poetry or painting is a by-product. ('Traveller', 43)

She goes on to describe artistic media as 'vehicles' of spiritual exploration ('Traveller', 44). In the sonic and verbal medium of a poem, she seeks to embody the tension between what is 'sensed' and what can be 'made', while in visual art she attempts to manifest—as far as possible—the 'sensed' thing in material form. And I would argue that, in her fiction, the temporal dimension of narrative provides her with the scope to explore the 'process' of 'remembering, re-membering, re-capturing, re-calling, re-collecting …' that is essential to her search ('Traveller', 44). However, in her essay—the closest thing she produced to an artistic manifesto—references to fiction writing are noticeably absent.

Here and elsewhere it is evident that P. K. Page did not think of herself as a fiction writer. In her 1986 'Afterword to *A Flask of Sea Water*' (the first of three linked parables in 'The Sky Tree' trilogy), she writes about the distinction between poetry and prose fiction:

> … the trouble with a story—as against a poem—is that it needs an idea. Where a poem begins with a rhythm or sound, a story begins with an idea. And not just any old idea—but a charged idea, as evocative as the rhythm that starts a poem.

9

Had I been strong on ideas, I might have been a fiction writer. As it is, I have always had to wait patiently for any that have come my way. ('Afterword', 48)

Despite this disclaimer, Page wrote a surprising amount of fiction throughout her seventy-year career. She published a novel, over thirty short stories in journals and three collections, and a volume of linked short fiction—and there are completed drafts of over twenty more stories and an unfinished novel in the P.K. Page fonds housed at Library and Archives Canada. As one familiar with her poetry and autobiographical writing (*Hand Luggage: A Memoir in Verse, Brazilian Journal, Mexican Journal*) would expect, her fiction is characterized by extraordinarily insightful and provocative explorations of 'ideas' about perception, imagination and identity, the environment, metaphysics, morality, and art. And, as always in her work—whatever the medium—it is grounded in vividly recalled experience, the 'mingling of the personal and universal' (Pollock, 'Introduction', *The Filled Pen*, xvi). For P.K. Page, poetry, painting, memoir, fairy tale, prose fiction—all the many ways in which she engages with the page—are 'alternative roads to silence' ('Traveller', 47), to an inexpressible truth.

While *The Digital Page* edition of P.K. Page's fiction will document the genesis of her novel and short stories from preliminary notes to polished prose, this volume is designed to provide a sense of her development as a writer of fiction. Therefore, it is presented as a 'triptych', opening with her first major publication, the novel *The Sun and the Moon* (1944), out of print since 1973, and closing with *You Are Here* (2008), very much the author's valedictory address to her readers. The middle section consists of representative short stories—some of the best produced in her long career.

* * *

During her early apprenticeship as a writer, Page did not define herself exclusively as a poet. As she explained to her biographer, Sandra Djwa, her early models—literary and personal—were Virginia Woolf and Katherine Mansfield, both predominantly writers of fiction. She read and annotated Woolf's *A Room of One's Own* and Mansfield's *Letters* in the late 1930s, and was deeply influenced by the sensuality of Woolf's prose and by Mansfield's 'minuteness' of detail (P.K. Page interview, 26 June 2001; Djwa, 54). Like them, she aspired to write out of personal

10

experience, capturing and communicating 'light, bright, intense glimpses' of life (Djwa, 54). Her earliest stories are modelled on Mansfield's, reflecting life in rural New Brunswick ('"Sploring', 'The Harp', 'Easter Pie', 'A Winter Picnic'), her experiences as a child in a military family ('The General's Daughters', 'Mother's Psychic Fear'), interactions with the artistic community in Rothesay and Saint John ('The Christmas Present'), incidents from her life as a 'working girl' ('The Little Man') and critical assessments of upper middle class 'society' ('This Happiness', 'Herbie').

She submitted her stories to numerous magazines, including *Saturday Night* and *Maclean's*, but none were published. A foreshadowing of her later spiritual seeking is evident as early as 1940 in a stylized fairy tale titled 'The Laughing Boy', which elicited this reaction from the literary editor of *Mademoiselle: The Magazine for Smart Young Women*: 'Sorry, but this is not for us, the fantasy, coupled with Plato and Buddha (or is it Yoga?) makes strange fiction!' (P.K. Page fonds, 4.37.10). But she also emulated the sophistication of New York magazines in stories like 'This Happiness', which won a prize in 1940–41 in the *Atlantic* Short Story Contest. Her chief accomplishment during this period was her novel, *The Sun and the Moon*, begun in New Brunswick in 1940, but revised in Montreal in the summer of 1941 and again in December 1942 in the first months of her long love affair with F.R. Scott.

The inexperienced heroine Kristin Fender, born during a lunar eclipse, is viewed by her family as 'queer' because of the extreme empathy which allows her 'to become a rock ..., knowing nothing but the sun and the wind and the sea ..., to know the static reality of inanimate things—the still, sweet ecstasy of change in kind' (23–24). With her strange disconnection from other people and her instant recognition of a kindred spirit in the visiting artist, Carl Bridges, himself so clearly out of place in the artificial social setting in which her parents and their friends are so invested, Kristen may be a stylized surrogate for the young Pat Page. No drafts of the novel survive, but in the version revised for publication, the male protagonist, painter Carl Bridges, twenty years Kristen's senior, with his angular frame, 'upward-pointing' shoulder (27) and passion for the landscape of the Laurentians, resembles Page's lover F.R. Scott. For Kristin, love of Carl becomes a 'sweet terror', a 'terrible joy' (34) when she discovers she has the power to possess him, to sap away the talent that defines him. Carl Bridges is the first of several painters, sculptors, conceptual artists who populate Page's fiction, acting as conduits for her exploration of aesthetics, vocation, and the potential and limitations of art for self-actualization and spiritual growth. And Kristen Fender is the first of many characters exhibiting abilities of empathy and synaesthesia—heightened perceptions and a profound identification with the natural world. Kristen and Carl split the persona of the artist between them, and are forced into competition for survival.

During the delay between the novel's acceptance by Macmillan Canada in 1940 and its publication in 1944, Page moved to Montreal to pursue writing as a career. There she was introduced to the sophisticated ideas of the *Preview* group and was tempted to disavow the book, eventually deciding to publish it under the pseudonym Judith Cape. However, despite her uncertainty, the story has a great deal of the acute psychological insight and wit that characterize Page's mature writing. As Margaret Atwood observes in the foreword to the Anansi edition (1973), it offers a distinctly modern—and Canadian—take on the conventions of Gothic romance (Atwood, iii), in which the setting is 'no lonely house on the moors' (Atwood, iv), but upper-middle-class 'society' in New Brunswick, with its cocktail parties and pretensions. To that, I would add that Page has reversed the polarity both of Gothic romance and of the still older tradition of Petrarchan rhetoric, in which the desired woman is depicted as a besieged city. In *The Sun and the Moon*, it is the woman who is the unwilling source of aggression and power:

The invader marched in, stormed his defences, hoisted the invading flag, took possession smoothly and entirely. The city that was Carl knew foreign leadership; foreign colours waved from the ramparts; foreign primitive workmanship ousted the easy-running talent. Night fell on the city that had been Carl, dark and still—a silent abyss—but the fingers moved on relentlessly, unwittingly. (97)

Kristin is a contemporary of the seemingly fragile blonde heroines of Alfred Hitchcock's films, and like them is uncanny, dangerous. The hero is drawn in, almost against his will. In the films, the heroine must be rescued, but here for most of the narrative, the story is told from her perspective, and in the end she sacrifices herself—becomes inert, inhuman—in what will likely be an ineffectual attempt to rescue the hero.

* * *

As a member of the modernist *Preview* group, Page worked to establish herself as a professional writer and refined her aesthetic. Although principally known as a poetry magazine, *Preview* spanned genres, and Page contributed twenty-four poems, nine stories and two essays over its four-year run (Precosky). The claustrophobic experience of rooming house life that is transformed through the surrealist lens in Page's well-known poem 'The Landlady' is explored at length in a series of short stories ('Room and Board', 'The Glass Box', 'The Green Bird', 'Neighbours', 'Looking for Lodgings', 'George', 'The Midgets'). Page's brief time (June to July 1942) working as a clerk at Allied War Supplies (which inspired some of her most anthologized early poems, 'Typists', 'Offices' and 'The Stenographers') is developed in a series of unpublished stories focused on workplace dynamics—the aspirations, petty jealousies and power struggles of the office ('As a Dog or a Flower', 'Heads I Win, Tails You Lose', 'A Man with a Future'). In several stories which were written during and after her time in Montreal, she depicts life on the home front during World War II ('Miracles', 'The Resignation') and the traumatic adjustment of the soldiers' return ('Reunion', 'George', 'The Woman').

In many of these stories, there is only a thin veil between the author and her subject. In some, as in 'The Green Bird', Page gives her narrator/protagonist her own name. And some situations are particularly close to home: in 'Growing Up', a fledgling career woman justifies her desire for independence to her protective father; and in 'The Glass Box', a frustrated young woman evades the surveillance of an interfering landlady to meet with her lover. In other stories, the politics of the *Preview* group take central stage as P.K.—left-leaning, but never explicitly 'political'; sympathetic, but never 'of the people'—tries her hand at social critique ('Leisure Class', 'Under Cover of Night').

In her unfinished second novel, tentatively titled 'The Lion in the Streets', a young married couple pass the time before the husband's deployment in a small French-Canadian village. Luke is conservative, made more so by his military training, but Jessica's experience as a working woman has exposed her to new social and political ideas, and she finds herself in sympathy with the political and cultural resistance of the Québécois to colonization by the 'English'. The polemical stance may have been informed by association with F.R. Scott, who had been villainized for defending French-Canadian resistance to conscription in his essay 'Why Québec Voted No' (June 1942), but Page is clearly uncomfortable with overt political statement. In the portion of the novel published as the short story 'Miracles', the focus is narrowed, and the political statement less direct.

Between 1941 and 1950, Page published nine stories in *Preview* and one in *Here and Now*, and wrote several more. A respectable output. However, then came her marriage to Arthur Irwin and her legendary hiatus from creative writing during her husband's diplomatic postings in Brazil and Mexico. Between the publication of the Governor General's Award–winning *The Metal and the Flower* (1954) and *Cry Ararat! Poems New and Selected* (1967), she wrote journals of her time in domestic diplomacy, redirected her creative energies toward drawing and painting, and began a disciplined intellectual and spiritual search that led her to Sufism as a follower of Idries Shah.

* * *

After her return to Canada in 1964, Page re-established herself as a poet—perhaps the best of her generation. But Margaret Atwood's anthology *The Sun and the Moon and Other Fiction* (1973) also created renewed interest in Page's fiction, and she began (tentatively) to write in that genre again, using prose as a vehicle to process the powerful 'ideas' that had increasingly come to occupy her thoughts. The stories of the 1970s, '80s and '90s mark a middle period in Page's career as a fiction writer during which her work became more consistently autobiographical in inspiration. In part this was a result of critical interest in her work and interviews with her biographer, Sandra Djwa. However, as she explains in 'Traveller, Conjuror, Journeyman', the 're-membering' of the past was also essential to her quest for spiritual enlightenment:

My childhood is a series of isolated vignettes, vivid as hypnagogic visions. Great winds have blown my past away in gusts leaving patches and parts of my history and pre-history. No wonder I want to remember, to follow a thread back. To search for something I already know but have forgotten I know. To listen—not to but for. ('Traveller', 44)

The resulting stories chart a journey of exploration—a merging of Page's early style with Sufi storytelling.

In 'Victoria', two painters who embody the differing aesthetics—surreal and representational—of Page and her friend poet Elizabeth

Brewster, debate the details of their first meeting, and their conflicting memories are spliced together with vignettes depicting the gradual mental and physical decay of the narrator's aunt. A crucial question emerges from the interplay: 'Is imagination perhaps a further, longer memory? A remembering outside of time, beyond space?' (141). Here, and again in 'Birthday', Page explores the possibility that death may be a transition to a new reality, a kind of birth and transfiguration. In 'Unless the Eye Catch Fire', she imagines environmental apocalypse, but also the liberating transition to an ecstatic state of being for those who are able to see a new and emerging spectrum of light.

In 'Mme Bourgé Dreams of Brésil', having recently edited her *Brazilian Journal* (1987) for publication, Page recreates the powerful sensual impact of her memories of Brazil, and in 'Fever', she reconceives memories of the traumatic surgery which left her unable to have children as an unrealized love affair and a death. In 'Even the Sun, Even the Rain', she takes as a starting point a bittersweet meeting with F. R. Scott after several decades apart, and explores the idea that love can evolve with time into an even more satisfying version of the 'old joy'—'"I call it subliming," she said. "Funny that all these years I've never told you."' (177).

Published in 2001, *A Kind of Fiction* consists primarily of stories published in *Preview* between 1941 and 1945, but fiction written since Page's return to Canada fleshes out the collection. In the title story, Page explores her creative process. The narrator, Veronica, encounters an old woman and becomes obsessed by her, constructing a narrative of her life, adding details and becoming increasingly certain of their authenticity:

She had read somewhere that characters in fiction very often took on lives of their own, got out of hand and surprised their creators. She had never quite believed that. But she was in no position to argue now. For that was exactly what was happening. The old woman was a kind of fiction, one she could not erase from her mind, one who was absorbing more and more of her time and thought. (197)

The final revelation—that she herself is 'the old woman'—establishes the pattern for Page's relationship with many of her protagonists in the stories written in the final decade of her life, several of which are anthologized in *Up on the Roof* (2008).

These late stories are less overtly influenced by her studies of Sufi philosophy, but in them Page declares her concerns, influences and aesthetics, and maps her creative process with increasing openness. Interviews with Djwa document connections with defining memories—'isolated vignettes, vivid as hypnogogic visions' ('Traveller', 44)—with which she is coming to terms. Page is, or distinctly remembers being, a child with an extraordinary sensitivity to colour, a fledgling artist like Susie in 'Crayons' who uses her crayons to reclaim the pebbles taken from her by her overbearing uncle. She is Ivan in 'Ex Libris'—the loping basketball player, raised 'from the book'—who, after pursuing the physical fulfillment of sport and erotic passion, reclaims his literary inheritance and creates an atrium of light, a temple to literacy. The atrium is an image from Page's own dreams (Djwa, 306), and the 'most eclectic library' he enshrines there is Page's own, full of art books, science fiction, poetry and philosophy—'the literature of ideas' (216). She is the sculptor C.D. Stone in 'Stone', whose passion for art is lost—stolen from her—and then found again when the 'Egg of the World', a variation on Page's own painting *A Kind of Osmosis* (1960), emerges from a block of marble. She is the conceptual artist whose life story may be a fiction in 'True Story'. In Page's last book, *You Are Here* (2008)—a set of prose sketches or meditations on identity—the spiritual exercise is made explicit with entire sections echoing almost verbatim transcriptions of interviews with Djwa.

* * *

In 1958, Page painted *Triptych*, a startling self-portrait: the artist is present, but not visible except in three distinct reflections in the mirrors of her dressing table—all of which are, and are not, the subject. This multiplicity of identity is a theme that she returned to throughout her life—in every medium, but perhaps she explains it best in the essay 'A Writer's Life':

The fact is, we live not one life but many, and this creature that answers to my name is not single, not simple, but multiple—a crowd. ('A Writer's Life', 4)

In *You Are Here*, the linked prose sketches of a 'day in the life' of a writer named Mimi, her protagonist considers her many names—Mimi, but also 'Margaret, Maggie, Marg, Meg, even', Mrs Richardson—and multiple identities—a wife, a daughter, a friend, a Canadian, a writer, a seeker exploring her 'Buddha nature' (275). The sketches themselves have no clear connection except that they record the thoughts and memories of Mimi as she muses on names and identity, animals and aliens, ophthalmology and second sight, empathy, sexuality, synchronicity and serendipity, life after death. She ends with the declaration, 'No doubt about it. That's me alright.' (276). The concept is profound; the images precise and vivid; the delivery—with its wit and self-deprecating humour—is pure Page. But the origin of what we now recognize as 'pure Page' is identifiable in her earliest prose fiction and is developed throughout her career as a writer of short fiction: thought-provoking explorations of 'charged ideas' grounded in vividly recalled and reimagined experience.

Works Cited

Atwood, Margaret. 'Introduction', *The Sun and the Moon and Other Fictions*. Anansi, 1973. iii–v.

Djwa, Sandra. *Journey with No Maps*. McGill-Queen's Press, 2012.

Page, P.K. 'Afterword to *A Flask of Sea Water*', *The Filled Pen: Selected Non-Fiction*. Ed. Zailig Pollock. University of Toronto Press, 2007. 48–50.

_____. P.K. Page fonds (MG30 D311/R2411), Library and Archives Canada.

_____. 'Traveller, Conjuror, Journeyman', *The Filled Pen*. 43–7.

_____. 'A Writer's Life', *The Filled Pen*. 3–22.

Pollock, Zailig. 'Introduction', *Kaleidoscope*. The Porcupine's Quill, 2010. 7–18.

Precosky, Don. '*Preview*: An Introduction and an Index', *Canadian Poetry* 8 (Spring–Summer 1981) http://www.uwo.ca/english/canadianpoetry/cpjrn/vol08/precosky.htm.

THE SUN
AND THE MOON

PART ONE: KRISTIN

The world throbbed to the excitement of a lunar eclipse. Astronomers and their bastard brothers, the astrologers, worked busily charting the heavens, linked at this moment by a mutual concern for the moon.

In a hospital, a pale pile of yellow brick on the top of a hill, which strove to touch the sky with its longest finger of stone, doctors, nurses and a young mother worked to bring a girl-child into the world.

The sweet smell of ether hovered in the air when the mother opened her eyes.

'It is a girl,' the nurse said, 'I'll bring her to you.'

'A girl,' said the mother, 'she shall be called Kristin,' and shut her eyes again. The electric light hurt them; it was a small pain compared with that of the last hours, but there was no need to tolerate it. It could be borne if necessary, but necessity was no longer a part of suffering. The baby was alive; she longed for the feel of the small creature against her body.

There was no time in this building of births and deaths, where the record of human suffering mounts on its own time chart, oblivious of the convenient man-made clock. It might have been hours or minutes when the light snapped on again, opening the room away from the young mother on the bed; pulling back the walls and reconstructing space, where space had been crowded out. It might have been hours or minutes since that first encounter with light until this one; since the moment she knew it was a girl until this moment when the white nurse held something in her arms that made the mother eager to hold it too. Until this moment when the nurse said, 'Isn't she sweet? Here she is,' and bending down had put her in the bed.

Astronomers forgot in the period of eclipse that human life was being propagated still. Theirs was the world of mathematics; mathematics so vast and inconceivable that even their minds were made dizzy with contemplation. But the astrologers had been busy for weeks turning out articles for the pulps on the subject of birth and the eclipse: 'Was Your Baby an Eclipse Baby?' headed paragraphs leading to founts of evasive prediction.

The young mother didn't care. All of importance lay beside her embodied in the small shape which was her daughter. The resentment she had felt previously, because her husband was away, was a thing of the past. What he had given her compensated for his absence. And as she thought she realized that his present to her was also her present to him and she marvelled at the miracle and smiled to the child at her side.

Kristin was so small. Surely never, never had a child been smaller, her mother thought. And she grew strangely, not with a slow continuous growth, but with sudden spurts and little unfoldings. And she was good. No baby had ever been better. She just lay with her hands curled like shells and her funny long eyes gazing beyond.

When Ralph first came to see her she had felt her love flood through her and she had wanted to say, 'Here she is, our precious, whom I give you.' But she had been afraid then, and it was too late to say it now. For a year was almost gone and the miracle was over though the joy remained. Oh, just to be with Kristin, to know her for her own, that was enough.

Ralph had laughed at the name. 'Kristin!' he had said. 'A little stagey, darling.' But he had let it pass, adding as his contribution, Jane, as a middle name. And secretly she had laughed in return. Ralph knew no escape from what he called the accepted-common-or-garden. Therein lay his security. But she was different; three-quarters of the way she plodded, but she skipped so frantically for the last quarter that the plodding was forgotten.

She would temper the plain Jane in Kristin with her own imagery.

It was exquisite to stand by and watch Kristin grow. The shell hands changed to two stars. Kristin walking, holding out her arms for balance and her hands two little dimpled stars. 'Oh, thank you, Kristin, I had forgotten the grace of children, and their beautiful shy aloofness. I never knew that it is the very young who possess the key to fairyland. I didn't know so much.'

But Grace, the mother, knew a shrinking of delight as Kristin grew older, and a small fear nagged her heart. She and Ralph had produced a queer child, someone who could not have grown from themselves. Grace now began to take refuge in Ralph's conventionality. But Kristin felt nothing of the restraint of her surroundings. Like a dream child, fair and ethereal she walked about the house, talking to people constantly who were not there. People with names and evidently shapes and weights.

At meal times her whole body struggled with the effort of lifting these friends onto chairs so that they too could eat. And she insisted they have their portion of food. The fact that it remained untouched worried Kristin not at all.

Kristin had peopled the house. And Grace grew afraid, not of meeting these people but of perpetually not meeting them. Ralph laughed at her for this. 'All children imagine themselves surrounded by friends,' he said. 'There is nothing extraordinary in it.'

'But,' said Grace, clutching a book in her hands and sitting on the extreme edge of her chair, 'she doesn't *imagine* them, she *sees* them, actually sees them and feels them. She asked me the other day who the funny little old lady was and what she was knitting. I nearly jumped out of my skin.'

Ralph knocked the ashes from his pipe. 'Don't worry,' he said, 'she'll outgrow it.' But as he saw her face he knew Grace needed more practical and immediate comfort than that. It was not enough to predict vaguely for the future, so he added:

'Tomorrow I'll play truant and we'll have a day at the sea—Little Cove—just the three of us. Like to?'

'Oh, Ralphey, yes!' Her face lit up. Already she had forgotten Kristin.

She is very young, he thought. I must be with her more and look after her. He crossed to her chair and kissed her but as he drew away she clung to him saying, 'Kiss me again. Oh, Ralph, don't leave me yet, I want you near so badly.' She ran her fingers against the grain of his haircut and pressed her face to his. Here was a depth in which she could sink and submerge herself.

And so they sat together, both suddenly aware of a new relationship, aware of a new peace; neither knowing the need of speech in this strange calm that lapped over them. Then a tremor ran through Grace and he sensed her fear. She sat upright with a jump and clutched the lapels of his coat.

'Ralph, if it were to rain tomorrow I couldn't bear it.' Her voice was tight with panic and her eyes were wide. 'I could stand everything but that—everything.'

It didn't rain. The morning dawned with no sign of a cloud in the sky. Little Cove was sparkling and clear in the sun—a dream beach that had just emerged from the sea, unspoiled. And Grace lay on the sand, completely content, happiness curled like a cat on her chest.

Kristin, with the sureness of five-year-old fingers, dug through the soft dry upper sand, smoothed it carefully and dug again. She liked the feel of it forcing her nails away from her fingers. She liked the wetness you reached if you dug far enough—the crispness that lay covered until you began to dig. She enlarged the hole and smoothed its edges and sat back on her heels to admire.

'Here,' said her father, joining her. 'If you must be a ground-hog, be a Girl Guide ground-hog and bury the picnic rubbish.' He put the parcel of papers and eggshells into the hole and scuffed sand over them.

'See if you can cover them up so no one could possibly know we've been here.'

Kristin didn't move. He had spoiled it now. It had been so smooth, all patted and beautiful. Now it was just a garbage hole. She didn't want to look at it again.

'Come on, Kristin,' he said. But she had turned. Mummy lifted her hat from her face and raised her head.

'Go along, darling. Do as Daddy tells you. There's a good girl.'

But Kristin didn't hear. The hole was spoiled. It didn't exist for her any longer. She was no more a part of it. Already her interest had shifted. A mass of seaweed caught her eye—deep maroon seaweed swirled around a log at the high-tide mark. Kristin moved towards it slowly, stooped and fingered its crispness. Its touch on her fingers was brittle—a thin, almost forgotten touch. She broke a piece off and held it in her hand loosely. Where the seaweed curled it pricked her palm.

The day had settled to a still weight of heat. The half moon of white sand danced in the sun and there was a haze far out at sea so that the horizon was impossible to find. Kristin followed the mark of the high tide, excitedly finding devil's purses and fisherman's floats and seaweed with bubbles in it that popped if you pressed them hard. And thus, following the flotsam and jetsam at her feet she arrived at the great rock cliff at the far end of the beach. The rocks were pale and large and smooth, and waves lapped at their base and broke into laughing spray that splashed high into the air. She was hot and tired. Far along the beach she could see Mummy and Daddy like two little coloured dots with the sand dancing and wiggling between. She gazed up at the rocks and climbed carefully to a ledge of stone and flung herself down on her stomach. Up there, so high, the sun beat harder on her back, and below—a long way down—the waves broke themselves to powdered glass as they hit the rocks.

Lying there unmoving, Kristin felt something she had never felt before. A change came over her. Slowly she stiffened and became hard and still, knowing nothing but the sun beating on her back. The sun on her back and a sense of rest, nothing more. Nothing more for a very long time. Then suddenly there was movement somewhere and voices talking. But she knew without hearing, for her ears were stone; she knew only as a rock can know, by the vibrations of sound striking an inanimate thing. Then, as gradually as she had stiffened from flesh to stone she melted from stone to flesh and heard then as a person hears and knew as a person knows, that her mother and father were standing over her, worried. And her father bent down and picked her up in his arms and said:

'She's got a touch of the sun.'

And her mother put her hand on Kristin's head and said, 'Darling, darling!'

'Lie still, Kristin,' said her father, 'and we'll take you home to bed and you'll feel quite well again.'

But Kristin didn't feel ill and didn't want to go home to bed. All she wanted was to be left alone on the rocks, forever, and to become a rock again, knowing nothing but the sun and the wind and the sea.

'She's so pale,' said her mother.

'Course I'm pale,' Kristin replied, 'I was a rock.'

'Ssh! dear,' whispered her father shifting her higher in his arms; and her mother ran along beside them, the brim of her large hat flip-flopping in her worried eyes.

They bundled her into the car.

'Sleep, my darling,' said her mother. And Kristin shut her eyes. But she couldn't sleep. The rocks were large in her head, like a magnet drawing and drawing.

The picnic things were stowed away. The car started.

'The day is left behind,' she heard her mother say as the car moved off.

'There, there, Gracie,' her father answered, 'there are other days ahead.'

'She looked so strange,' her mother said, 'as if—as if—she'd been dead. As if she knew something we didn't.'

Kristin lay across the back seat pretending she was on the rocks. Almost she could feel herself tightening to stone again. But the noise of the car and the talk of her parents were with her. They were too close—they held her from the rocks, her rocks. Lying there she knew they were hers as nothing had ever been before.

'She is quiet,' said her mother, one night later. 'Ralph, she won't play with other children. She's not like anyone else. She sits and sits.'

'School will knock it out of her, you'll see,' he answered. 'She'll be a different child when she starts school.'

But as the years drew Kristin taller she wanted more and more only to be alone. Children bounced and ran and yelled and screamed. They bothered her. She hated quick movement, hated to jolt the quietness of her body. Grown-ups were different. At least they sat still, but they talked so, on and on, until their speech was as restless as movement and Kristin, listening, found it necessary to slip away from their chatter and withdraw into the peace of herself.

The rocks had faded for her now only because of more recent experiences. She had only to sit still long enough to know the static reality of inanimate things—the still, sweet ecstasy of change in kind. But this knowledge, this breath-taking communion, she kept to herself. She learned early that to speak of it drew the eyes of her parents back in a sudden fear, resulting in the vigilant supervision of her movements. And that supervision denied her the essence of her life. So she lived in a world of her own, like a pale sprite barely able to touch on a common ground with the people around her.

School was an interlude to get through somehow—an interlude of jarring faces and movement and speech. Her teachers resented her aloofness, her disinterest. But once, unconsciously, she centred attention on herself in the classroom. She had written a descriptive composition on a chair which had been read aloud to the class and later sent home to her parents with this note pencilled in the margin:

'Although the literary style is, in itself, negligible, Kristin has somehow in her immature way made the chair an entity, endowed it with a physical individuality that is quite unusual. It is almost as if the child had actually been a chair herself.'

And of course, she had. She had known the pressure of the molecules in the wood, the massing together of atoms, the feeling of the cleats that hold a chair together and the upward surge within the wooden framework that keeps it a composite thing. It held no mystery for her; she knew with the understanding derived from personal experience.

When Kristin was seventeen she met Carl. He was in town, having been commissioned to paint Judge Lothrop, and the Lothrops were celebrating the occasion with a cocktail party. The picture was finished, the artist was to be there. And Carl Bridges was a name to conjure with.

Kristin, sitting before her mirror, running the comb through her long hair, was annoyed at her lack of calm. She didn't want to go. She dreaded the noise ahead of her, the endless talk which she could never take part in. But her protests had been useless. 'Kristin, darling, this is the opportunity of a life-time. Just think, you'll meet Carl Bridges— *the* Carl Bridges, my pet. You'll regret it for the rest of your life if you don't go.' And so here she was getting ready, combing her long hair back from her forehead, refusing to hurry.

'Kristin, Kristin! We're waiting.'

'Coming,' answered Kristin, picking up her bag and gloves and grimacing at herself in the glass.

She felt stiff in the car on the way over. Her hands in her gloves were numb and there was a vacuum around her heart. Long, slim, shiny cars were drawn up before the Lothrops'. The green of the lawn ran right down to the pavement. Bright beds of flowers lined the path up to the front door. Everything looked so right, so set to its pattern of correctness. Kristin almost laughed. And there was her mother, spike-heeled elegance, slim as a reed. And her father running to paunch, the successful business man, hair beginning to thin. They, too, were of the pattern. They need not question where to walk or what to say. Their pattern carried them where hers didn't. Hers didn't follow this direction. She had walked away from its certainty and was just a little afraid.

The front door was open. Like garlands flung on streamers talk came to them through its opening and Kristin winced at the noise and hesitated on the step.

'Come on, Noisey,' said her father over his shoulder. He was in a party mood already. He called her that when he felt gay—as an apologetic gesture for his daughter. She didn't mind. Her mother waited and slipped her white glove through Kristin's sleeve, leaving a smudge where it had rested. 'Silly baby,' she said. 'This is a party, not an execution,' and then suddenly left her as she caught sight of Mrs Lothrop.

When Kristin turned, her father had gone too. She saw the grey expanse of his back being thumped enthusiastically by a friend.

Poor darlings, she thought, that they should have had me as a daughter, and she brushed the white patch on her sleeve and walked into the dining room.

It was practically empty and unexpectedly quiet. Over by the sideboard stood a friend of her mother's.

'Come here, funny child,' she called. 'Come and let me talk to you.' Kristin crossed to her.

'They dragged you here after all? Your mother said you didn't want to come.'

'No, I didn't,' said Kristin.

'You'll get over it,' said the friend. 'Cocktail parties get in your blood in time. It's just a matter of getting over being shy.' Kristin smiled. She wasn't shy, but she couldn't explain that—not to this woman with her thin mouth and metal eyes—not here where there was no peace.

'I used to be just like you when I was your age,' the woman went on, twirling her empty cocktail glass between pale fingers. 'It's your parents' fault, they should have had more children. I, too, am the product of self-ish parents. I wonder if that shaker's full.' She eyed it, lifted it, beamed and poured herself a drink. 'Oh, and one for you,' she said. 'You'll feel better with a drink inside you—limbers you up.'

'Thank you,' said Kristin. It was clear and golden in the glass—almost the colour of my hair, she thought, and the woman caught it.

'You have cocktail-coloured hair,' she screamed, delighted with her own humour.

'What's that?' asked a man across the room.

'She has cocktail-coloured hair,' she repeated, quite weak with laughter and he spluttered and put up his knee to slap it and turned to tell the phrase to a man at his side.

'You see, people want to laugh,' the woman went on. 'Make them laugh and they'll love you, is my motto. It's easy when you get the hang of it. It just needs courage to start.'

But Kristin wasn't listening. Through the doorway opposite, attended by a flurry of chiffon and little wisps of laughter, came Mrs Lothrop and a thin dark man. Kristin's fingers tightened on the stem of her glass as she watched him. His eyes are like sailing ships, she thought, quite free of his face. And his brown hands are beautifully still. His whole body is still.

'Well!' said the voice at her side with a rising inflection, 'well, our Kristin is not so shy and young that she doesn't know an attractive man at any rate. I've been wasting my time on you, child. But remember, if you want to catch him, make him laugh.' And as she went, her knife-blade body cut the air and sent it off in two folds on either side. But Kristin didn't move. She knew suddenly that she was glad she had come. If she never met him, if she never saw him again, it didn't matter for she had seen him once across a room—a sailboat in a harbour of screaming, bustling little tugs. And he had seen her and in his seeing his body seemed rested. His upward-pointing shoulder had fallen.

They were circling the room. Introductions fluttered before them. They stopped for a minute here, a minute there and came on again. Now they were in front of her. And for the first time she did feel shy, breathlessly shy.

'And this is Kristin,' Mrs Lothrop said. 'Kristin, I want you to meet Mr Bridges so that you can always remember you met a great artist the year you came out,' and they were gone again.

He had swept over her like the sea. Her hand was shaking. She put down her glass and twisted her fingers together. She wanted to go now. Go while she held that moment in quietness within her; go before the encounter was jarred and broken. But still she didn't move. Quite close, in the next room, perhaps, was Carl. She liked the feeling of his being in the same house; she liked the sound of his name—Carl Bridges.

Kristin picked up her glass. She wasn't shy any more. If she did see Carl again, if he crossed to her and said 'Hello' she would not know the silly panic of before.

'Enjoying yourself, Noisey?' Her father was very hilarious. There were drops of perspiration on his forehead and his face was creased from recent laughter.

'Yes, Daddy,' said Kristin.

'What did I tell you?' he said, putting his hand on her shoulder. 'Come into the other room where there are more people.'

'I'd sooner not,' Kristin said. She didn't want to leave this room where she had seen Carl, even for a room where she could now see him. This moment is like the rocks, she thought—new and wonderful. They dragged me away from that, but this time I won't move. Her father had gone again, pushed through the noise to greater noise and left her as she would be left, alone on her island.

And then he was in the room and coming to her, past the table, beside the sideboard and standing in front of her.

'Hello,' she said. His whole body seemed free now—his eyes weren't so noticeable. He was quiet with the quietness of complete freedom. She didn't know what to say to him but it didn't matter. She told him so and he smiled and stared, content in their small silence. And then he lifted a hand to put down his glass.

'Your hands,' she said, and there were tears in her eyes. 'Your brown hands. They are beautiful.' Now, now, she thought, it is no longer enough just to have seen him. I cannot bear that this be the complete experience.

'I am not leaving tomorrow,' he said. 'I had planned to, you know.'

'I didn't know.' How awful, she thought, if I had known.

'I want to stay. I want to paint you—if you will sit for me, that is.' He smiled. 'Please.'

'I will,' said Kristin. Was it only as a model that he was interested? Because he liked the way her hair grew, or because her legs were long and straight, and not at all because she was Kristin? She lowered her eyes, frightened to look at his face, frightened to read there the strict gaze of professional interest.

'But tomorrow,' he said, 'tomorrow we shall have a holiday. You are free, aren't you? You must be free.'

'Yes.'

'Can you walk?'

'Yes.'

'May I call for you at eleven?'

I am going to cry, Kristin thought. This is stupid. But I've never loved anyone before—never—anyone. She stretched out her hand for his brown one, hoping, hoping that he would know it meant the 'yes' she couldn't say.

28

'Darling!' said her mother, pleasure and surprise in her voice. '*Here* you are. So you've been talking to my funny little girl, Mr Bridges, my funny, shy little girl. I hope you realize, Kristin, what an honour this is, when everyone here is clamouring—but clamouring!—to talk to Mr Bridges. You mustn't let her be selfish, Mr Bridges, you really mustn't.'

It doesn't matter, thought Kristin. If she wants to she can talk on and on. Everything is said. The bridge has been built, the bridge that carries today over to tomorrow. She cannot destroy it now. And as she thought, she walked onto it that it might feel her weight and she looked down at the swirling water below her.

'It is I who am being selfish,' Carl said. His voice came out of the water.

'What a sweet thing you are, Mr Bridges. Kristin, tell him what a sweet, sweet thing he is. But I'll leave you now,' and she went.

The bridge was firm under Kristin's feet and she wanted to say to Carl, 'It is safe, we have fashioned it securely; come, step onto it and stand with me,' when he said, 'I'm cheating. I'm half-way across to tomorrow already.'

'It's safe, as far out as that?'

'Yes, it's safe.'

But Mrs Lothrop had borne down. Like a large spider, her fat body in grey chiffon, she had caught him again—her fly. He made no struggle, moving as if he wished to go, smiling as he turned and saying, 'It is only a little way farther,' he had gone.

Kristin trembled and ventured another step onto the bridge. Tomorrow, as she stepped off, he would be there. She felt the strong pull of excitement in her loins. This happiness was an agony. She must escape to suffer it by herself. She moved from the dining room out to the hall where the air blew in from the garden, smelling of late afternoon cool-ness. She and the day were one, settled to stillness. She sat down and the hum of the voices closed about her. Reflections from the living room passed in the mirror before her. Her eyes clung to its surface, watching the light and shade, the kaleidoscopic pattern that broke within its frame. There! Was that Carl now—his elbow jutting out from behind Mrs Lothrop's grey bulk? Or there, the back of his head, leaning towards young Katie Steen? She shut her eyes. She saw him everywhere, in everybody, and she felt, for the first time, part of the world. Carl linked her with humanity.

'Kristin, it is time to go now.' Her mother, brilliantly soprano, sharply black and white, was calling from the dining room doorway. 'Go and say good-bye to the Lothrops.' And her father, his face appearing red and round above her mother's, laughed loudly and added, 'And apologize for making such a racket.' But his face wrinkled and looked puzzled and strange when she smiled at him and said, 'I'll leave the apologies to you; I'll just say the good-byes.'

He nudged his wife as Kristin went. 'That's the first time she's ever seemed like a normal person. Grace, Grace, did you notice? Something has happened to Kristin, she has changed.'

'Perhaps she's growing up at last,' Grace answered.

Alone in the back seat on the way home Kristin was silent. Her parents were gay. Occasionally they tossed words back to her for their amusement rather than hers, as people toss peanuts to monkeys in the zoo. They have had too much to drink again, Kristin thought. They'll both be bad-tempered by dinner-time. But that was incidental. It didn't matter. She could shut herself off from them, stand on the bridge and wait.

I never knew, she thought, that it was possible to lose oneself in a person. I never knew before. And feeling the fire run through her she dug her nails into the palms of her hands and shut her eyes and saw Carl.

'You might have told me, Kristin,' her mother said in a hurt voice, pausing as she arranged the flowers and standing with one large white peony in her hand. 'The least you could have done was to tell me. You know how interested I am in you. Mr Bridges of all people!' her mother went on, cutting the thick green stem of the flower as she spoke and holding the scissors uplifted so that they caught the light. 'When did he ask you?'

'At the cocktail party,' Kristin said, wanting to say, 'His eyes are like sailboats and his hands are brown and very beautiful'—wanting to say it aloud but not to anyone.

'You've known all that time and you've only just mentioned it?' Her mother's eyes were incredulous, holding little shafts of surprise in their corners.

Kristin turned to the glass and knotted a handkerchief over her hair. May I please him, she thought, looking hard at herself. Oh, God! may I please him! And she felt young, so young; a stranger to herself.

'There he is,' said her mother. There were steps on the veranda, steps in Kristin's heart. In one minute, one second even, she would leave the bridge behind her.

Her mother slipped out of her smock and smoothed her hair. The door had opened. 'Could I see Miss Kristin, please.'

'Just step inside,' said Mary, the maid, her mouth sounding tight with astonishment. 'This way, please.'

Carl was in the doorway. Kristin could not move. His neck is brown like his hands, she thought. There, where his shirt is open, it is brown.

'Mr Bridges!' Her mother was beside him, holding out her hand, drawing him into the room. He was quiet. His voice came softly.

'Good morning,' he said.

'You know we never *actually* met yesterday although I did speak to you. I'm so glad it's such a lovely day for your walk. Kristin's looking forward to it so.'

'Are you?' said Carl. She felt stupid, suddenly.

'Of course,' she answered.

'I've rather changed the plans,' Carl said. 'I've brought the car. I thought we might drive into the country and then walk. There's a place I like particularly. Unless you have other ideas I thought we might go there.'

'Where?' asked Kristin.

'Little Cove,' he said, 'do you know it?'

'Oh, lovely, I'll get my bathing-suit.'

'Kristin, you will be careful. You know I've never liked that place. Kristin got sunstroke there when she was a child, Mr Bridges, and since then I've never really enjoyed going there. Kristin,' she called, 'get a hat at the same time as your bathing-suit. You'll need it.'

But Kristin danced up the stairs. Carl and Little Cove—together. They were part of each other—the rocks and Carl.

'What about food?' asked her mother. 'You can't get it there, you know. Shall I have a basket put up?'

'I had them do it at the hotel,' Carl said. 'Thank you just the same. If I remember, rightly, there's no restaurant for miles.'

'And such a pity! Someone could make a fortune down there if they'd start something like that.'

'Oh, but it would spoil it,' said Carl, 'completely.'

'I suppose, from the artist's point of view, yes,' she handed him a cigarette. 'But I must say I've reached a point where I enjoy a meal in comfort. Sand in the sandwiches is no longer a pleasure to me. You have to be young to smile on inconvenience.'

'I'm ready,' said Kristin from the door. She held her bathing-suit and hat in her hands. She crossed to the cigarette box near Carl. Please, said her eyes, please. He got up.

'I'll take good care of her,' he said. 'Don't worry.'

Her mother smiled. 'Do be careful, Kristin,' she said. 'I shall never forget how ill you were when you were young. Never! It frightened me to death.'

'Good-bye!' Carl called.

I'm stepping off the bridge, Kristin thought. It has held, strong and straight. It has led me to now, to this moment.

Carl opened the car door.

'We are here,' he said as he got in, 'Kristin, we have reached today safely. I thought we never should.' He stared at her before he turned on the ignition.

Her mother waved from the veranda as the car started. They waved back.

'It was a long way,' said Kristin settling herself comfortably, 'a very long way.'

The drive down was easy. Words were ready waiting to be spoken. Kristin was happy, completely at peace in the wonder of loving.

'I love to look at you,' Carl said, 'you are like a child.'

'But I am a child. You'll laugh at me—I still read fairy stories. Truly.'

'So do I, sometimes.'

'Oh, Carl!'

'"The Three Feathers" and "Hansel and Gretel." That frightens me still. I often feel just like Hansel—poking chicken-bones instead of fingers through at Life.'

'And Oscar Wilde. Do you know his fairy stories? They are the best of all.'

'I did illustrations for them when I was an art student. How I worked on them! I'll show them to you some time. The one for "The Nightingale and the Rose" I was very proud of. That seems a long time ago ...' he trailed the sentence off.

To talk like this, thought Kristin, is heaven. To be close to him saying these things. He is so tranquil, so wonderfully still underneath. And the thought of it overwhelmed her so that she had to say:

'Carl, you are like the prairies—still and even for miles and miles—or like a sailboat. When I saw you yesterday I thought, he is a sailboat in a harbour of little tugs.'

He didn't laugh at her. 'Did you?' he said. 'Do you know what I thought when I saw you? Here is the only person I've seen at this party who is not distorted. You were standing quite quietly, each line right. What were you doing there, anyway?'

'I was taken.'

'Oh, taken,' said Carl knowingly.

Kristin lapsed into silence. There was so much to be said. So much to be heard. But she wanted to spread it out. Wanted to leave something for the succession of tomorrows that stretched out before her. For surely, there must be a succession. If it were to end … fingers closed around her neck. If it were to finish today—or after the portrait even …

'Carl,' her voice came in a cry. 'Carl, you won't leave, will you?'

'Leave? When, Kristin?'

'Ever. I just thought—perhaps tomorrow or after you'd done my portrait, that you might leave.'

'Don't worry, Kristin, if I leave I'll take you too. You can be my professional model. I'll paint you sitting and standing and clothed and nude and awake and asleep and—'

'You are teasing now,' Kristin's voice was tired.

'Only a very little,' said Carl.

If he were to leave without me, Kristin thought, if he were to say, suddenly one day, 'I am going,' I think I should die. To live on without him … She covered her eyes and turned her face away, fearful that he would see her with the pain drawing her cheeks.

'We are nearly there. Look, to the left. Surely that beach is the one below Little Cove.'

'Yes, yes!' And Kristin forgot Carl for the moment and remembered only the rocks. 'Soon we'll see the rocks,' she said. 'My rocks. The only things that really belong to me.'

'Why your rocks, Kristin? Why yours more than most things are yours?'

'One day I'll tell you.' She couldn't now. Although she was sure of Carl, not yet was she sure enough that he was steady in his knowledge of her. To tell of the rocks was to give herself to him, complete. And I don't know if he wants me yet, she thought, feeling all in that moment, older and strangely guileful.

'One day—you promise?' He had slowed down and was watching her.

'One day, if you still want to know.'

But he was not content. 'Promise?'

'I promise.' It was an oath, an oath that bound her to him. She could not escape him now. Oh, this sweet terror that held her, this terrible joy! She clutched her knees and rocked a little on the seat, feeling the thrill eating her flesh, dissolving her brain.

He slowed again and turned. 'We are here,' he said. 'Look, Kristin, the island.'

She didn't dare speak. The road was bumpy. It lifted her up and flung her against him and tore her away again. She felt the roughness of his jacket graze her cheek and she held her fingers against her face and laughed.

'I am jolted to death,' she gasped through her laughter. And he laughed too.

He drew the car to a stop at the edge of the bank and she was out, out, before he had pulled on the emergency brake, out and down the bank to the sand.

Oh, the wind in her hair and the sound of it rushing past her ears! The mad glory of it as it flattened against her sides!

'Kristin!' He called to her from the bank, but she didn't turn. If she looked back now, if she called in reply, if she joined with him for one minute even, before she had time to recreate herself as an entity, it would be too late.

Escape! Escape! Down across the sands to the sea.

At the edge she stopped and took off her shoes and socks. She would not turn yet. The feel of the salt water was sharp on her ankles and feet. She swung around to wave.

'Oh, Carl,' she called as she saw him, tall and thin, with the wind whipping the rug he had slung over his shoulder and his hands full with a thermos and picnic basket. 'Oh Carl, I should have stayed to help you.'

She hurried back. He was on the beach now. The thick white sand was almost hiding his shoes and the wind had blown his dark hair over his face. How could she have left, how run away for a moment?

'I'm sorry,' she said. 'I left you. I should have helped.' Will he believe me? Will he know that I mean it? She wished there was some way, other than words, to prove her words. 'Carl,' she gripped his elbows. 'Carl, I had to go. Believe me, I had to leave you.'

'I know, Kristin.' He set down the picnic basket.

'You didn't mind?' She knelt beside the basket, looking up into his face.

'No, of course not. But,' he paused, 'it's just that I have the feeling that it will always be so.'

He knows so soon, she thought. How could he know it? She sifted the sand through her fingers.

'Am I right?' he asked.

'Carl,' she started. But because she could not frame her lips to words of her own, she repeated, 'Yes, it will always be so.' She wanted to cry out, to deny the truth, but she couldn't. If she refused to accept her own truth she faced destruction. If not ... She could not follow it through.

Carl smoothed the rug. 'There,' he said, 'now we have staked our plot. Not that we need to, the beach is practically deserted.'

Kristin rolled on her back. 'If you lie flat,' she said, 'you can't feel the wind and the sun is strong.' She covered her eyes with the back of her wrist.

Carl felt in his pocket for his dark glasses, lifted her hand and put them across the bridge of her nose and behind her ears. She smiled, a little half moon of a smile.

'You look like an owl,' he laughed, 'a smiling owl.'

'And upside down, you look like—I don't know what you look like. Look at me upside down. Isn't it silly!' She pulled a face, reached for her bathing-suit—and began to change, slipping her dress over her head and sitting for a moment in her slip, with the sun beating on her bare shoulders.

'Oh, I love the sea,' she said fiercely, 'love it, love it!' But feeling his eyes upon her she was suddenly self-conscious. What did she mean by changing in front of him? She blushed and covered herself with her dress. She was aware, for the first time, consciously and terribly aware of the shape of her own body; the lift of her breasts, not fully covered by her slip, and the smooth line of her leg above her knee. Carl picked up his trunks and walked back into the bushes.

What happened, she thought, that made it seem wrong and wicked?

What have I done to myself, to myself and Carl? And she changed quickly and moved slowly to meet him, shy all over again as she had been at the cocktail party, but body shy, wanting to hide herself, trying to hide herself behind her skimpy towel.

'Race you,' said Carl, starting off across the beach. 'I'll race you into the water,' and she watched him as he went, saying aloud to herself, 'Thank you, Carl,' before she too, ran down to the water's edge and followed him into the sea.

'You're like a porpoise,' he said, diving for her ankles. But she kicked out in time and was beyond his reach and she lay on her back and laughed at him as he came up dripping, the water emphasizing his dark skin.

Oh, it is good to be here, she thought. It is good, good, good, but the water is cold—and she splashed through the shallows to the shore.

'Oh, Carl, my shoes!' There they were, a little way off, with the water lapping around them. 'They're soaked!' She picked them up and poured the water from them. 'And my socks, like little drowned mice!' She wrung them out. 'How silly. I forgot them when I ran back to you.' And the memory made her thoughtful. 'If they'd gone out to sea,' she said, pushing the thoughts away from her, 'I'd never have remembered where I had left them.'

'Scatter-brain!' He took her arms and raced her along the sands. 'Let's go to the rocks, your rocks,' he said.

Her rocks. She would not let it happen again today. Not today. She would stretch out on them and feel their warmth but this time she didn't want more of them than that. She would not let them steal her away from Carl.

He gave her his hand. It was cool from the sea as he pulled her up.

'Listen!' she stopped and held up her hand, 'you can hear the river. Over the sound of the sea you can hear the river.' They clambered on, the heat of the rocks burning the soles of their feet.

'Here!' Kristin flung herself down on her stomach, her head jutting over the rock cliff that fell down to the water. Carl joined her. They lay like that, in silence, watching the swirling, pounding water flung high in foam.

I am here again, thought Kristin. Their warmth is my warmth, their muteness is my muteness. I have returned to my own. She began to feel the slow penetration of them, the gradual infusion of their substance into her flesh and she fought against it. Not now, not now, she thought, but her will had gone. Already her body refused to obey her mind.

'I'm getting dizzy,' said Carl. 'That water is almost hypnotizing me.'

It was a queer floating voice in Kristin's ears.

'Kristin, I have a surprise for you.'

She couldn't answer. He rolled her over and lifted her to a sitting position. 'Kristin, are you all right?'

She was back now. It hadn't happened. Just in time he had come to her—another minute and it would have been too late. His face looking down was worried.

'Yes, I'm all right.' She spread out her socks to dry and propped up her shoes so the sun could reach their wet insides.

'What's the surprise?' she asked, the echo of his words coming to her from far back.

'A cigarette. Like one?'

'Yes, please.' She held out her hand for it.

'I've at last discovered a waterproof pouch that *is* waterproof. Look.' He undid it and produced the cigarettes. '"A miracle of dryness,"' he said, 'unquote. So runs the ad. Why does a cigarette always taste better after a swim?'

'Is it a riddle?'

'No, just a question.'

'It sounded like a riddle. I hate riddles. They do though, don't they—taste better, I mean.' If she stretched her fingers out to full length she could touch his leg, just below his knee. But she kept them curled, terrified of spoiling the moment by some too-quick movement, of breaking from her life the first moment of reality, the first swift wonder of loving. She watched him instead, his hands brown and firm and supple, economical in their movements; and his dark eyes that looked golden when he smiled. She watched the smoke lift from his cigarette and half hide his face from her, then drift away to leave it showing clear in the sunlight. And she wondered at her complete ease, her feeling of having been used to this always, she who had never felt comfortable before except when alone.

'Do you mind if I stare at you, at your queer half-enchanted face? If it worries you, pretend it's professional interest, the artist viewing his subject.'

'I'd sooner not pretend.' She felt the blood rise in her cheeks as she spoke, felt his personality rush over her, desired only to know the shape of his lips on hers and to hold the smooth stretch of his shoulder blades under her hands. But he came no nearer and she feared that her flesh would rush out to him as steel to a magnet.

She stubbed her cigarette, needful of a definite gesture and ran her fingers through her hair. I am no longer a child, she thought. I have grown up. I am now part of the adult world.

'You are so right,' he said, 'every gesture, every line. Naturally, as a child would, you show yourself off as a woman.' He held out his hand again as he had to help her onto the rocks. 'Let's have lunch.'

He pulled her to her feet and she noticed his hand was warm now from the sun. Her own looked white beside his.

'Do you never tan?' he asked.

'Never,' she answered. 'I don't even burn. It's very odd. We make a sort of study in black and white, don't we?'

'As the old ladies would say,' he led her across the rocks, 'I think we look rather nice together.' He chuckled as if there were a subterranean joke he did not wish to bring to the surface.

'Oh, my shoes!' said Kristin. 'I've forgotten them again,' and she ran back before he had time to turn.

Lunch on the sand was lovely. Stretched out, heads supported by their left hands, their feet still bare, it seemed to Kristin to have all the romance of a Roman feast.

'Only nicer,' said Carl, 'for if it were truly a Roman feast, you, being mere woman, would be unable to break bread with me. And too, this simple food hardly does justice to the high-living of ancient Rome. A bottle of beer and tongue sandwiches and a banana would hardly be fitting food for those extravagant times.' He rolled up the banana peels in the sandwich paper as he spoke.

He is tidy, thought Kristin. His hands are precise and neat. I should love to see him working, watch the way he holds his brush and the sureness with which he must mix his colours.

'Draw something for me,' she said.

'Come then.' He stowed the rubbish back in the picnic basket and got up. Her eyes rose with his figure. 'Before the tide comes in I'll draw for you on the sands.'

They started across the beach. He picked up a stick, drew swiftly with it as she had imagined, barely erasing a line as he worked—quiet, concentrated; turning to her occasionally to explain or laugh or see if she was interested and then returning to his work, using his hands, building up, scooping away, smoothing, patting and bringing forth from the sands figures in bas-relief running together.

'They are like birds,' she said. 'They have the sweet, swift motion of swallows in flight.'

'You try,' Carl said. And she began, timidly at first, continuing with more courage, delighting in the ease with which figures grew under her fingers, astonished at her own ability. He leaned over and watched her. 'But you are good,' he said, 'really good! You should study.'

She shook her head. Already she had decided that this beginning should also be the end. I am using his talent, she thought, I can feel the current of his talent running through my veins. And her forehead wrinkled. Would that this had never happened. Oh, God! that I should begin to absorb Carl as I absorb inanimate things. And a weight fell through her body, growing and filling her with dread. She stopped working.

'Go on,' he urged. But she wouldn't.

'No, no. The sea will only take them all away.' If only the sea *could* take them all away, could erase forever her knowledge that she had stolen from Carl; stolen against her will the essence of the man she loved.

She held her head, heavy with anguish. That my love should destroy when it should create, like the parasite that destroys the plant it lives upon. I must warn him, she thought, somehow I must warn him, of the danger. But her mind recoiled at the thought. Oh no, not yet. Not yet can I tell the whole truth. I must prepare him first. I must have time before I tell him the whole truth. And then she remembered a poem she had liked without knowing why and learned because something made her. Quietly she began to recite, her face still covered, her lips moving slowly as though it hurt to speak:

> She stole his eyes because they shone,
> Stole the good things they looked upon;
> They were no brighter than her own.
>
> She stole his mouth—her own was fair—
> She stole his words, his songs, his prayer;
> His kisses too, since they were there.
>
> She stole the journeys of his heart—
> Her own, their very counterpart—
> His seas, and sails, his course and chart.

She stole his strength so fierce and true,
Perhaps for something brave to do;
Wept at his weakness, stole that too.

But she was caught one early morn!
She stood red-handed and forlorn,
And stole his anger and his scorn.

Upon his knee she laid her head,
Refusing to be comforted;
'Unkind—unkind—' was all she said.

Denied she stole; confessed she did;
Glad of such plunder to be rid—
Clutching the place where it was hid.

As he forgave she snatched his soul;
She did not want it, but she stole.

As the poem ended, as her lips came together again, in silence, she felt better. The weight had gone a little—she had told half. Whether he knew it or not she was playing straight with him. Already he possessed the open-sesame to the secret she was still unable to tell.

'Kristin, what a queer poem. What made you recite it?'

She couldn't answer. She was crying now. She wanted to say: I love you more than my life. Oh, Carl, believe me. Run away from me now while you are still free, before I have stolen your identity. But she could only sit with the tears streaming down her cheeks.

'Kristin, you're crying.' He moved towards her and put his arms around her. 'Darling, don't cry. There is nothing to cry about. What has happened?'

As he held her she felt better. The comfort of his nearness crept over her and washed away her fear. Already she had grown into the conscious-ness of his flesh and hers, warm and touching, and the fierce joy of it was like a fire sweeping through her, purifying as it went. She looked up at him. 'I've been a silly little girl,' she said. 'I'm sorry. I shouldn't have spoiled the day.'

What could she say now to rebuild the day's perfection, what do, to delete the last few minutes of pain? She shut her eyes. She wouldn't think any more. Lying in Carl's arms she couldn't think. The desire, the ability to reason left her as Carl bent her backwards and lowered his face to hers and closed his lips over her mouth. She knew nothing but the throb of blood in her veins almost tearing her body and the terrible passion with which she clung to him and the gradual ebbing of strength as she relaxed under his kisses so that she would have fallen back if he hadn't held her.

'I love you,' he said, 'you know that, don't you? I love you so much that it is an agony to be with you and not touching you. And until you cried I felt I had no right. Oh, my darling, if you hadn't cried I might have gone to bed tonight still not knowing how sweet you are.'

I shall die from very happiness, thought Kristin. Such bliss is almost more than I can bear. 'I love you, too,' she said, tracing his eyebrow with her finger. 'From the first moment I saw you I loved you. Carl, I feel so young and so old all at once. And so—so secure.' She smiled, a slow smile.

'Little Mona Lisa,' he said and kissed the hollow in her neck and brushed the hair back from her face with his brown hands.

'Your hands,' she said. 'They made me cry when I saw them yesterday. I'm an awful cry-baby, Carl. Oh look,' she leaned on her elbow, 'the fog's coming in—and the tide. The fog's rolling up like smoke. Damn!' She got up. 'It's coming quickly. We'd better get dressed.'

They walked hand in hand up the beach. 'I am drunk with it all,' she said, reeling and laughing, 'drunk as a tar. I want to climb to the topmost peak of the world and call "I love him, I love him. He is like fire in my throat, like white flame lapping me round."' She turned. 'Look, the fog has come in. Already the sea is hidden. And it's nibbling your outline, too. We're figures in a mist, fading and forming.'

'Come, you'll get cold.'

Is it real? she thought. In the mist, like this, it seems like a dream. But it must be real, it has to be. She reached out for Carl, touched his shoulder, afraid to find his flesh unresistant, but it was firm.

'It is really true,' she said.

'Yes, Kristin, it is really true, unbelievably true.' He held her to him and kissed her again. This happiness is a pain, she thought, that will devour me. And I want, above all else, to be devoured by it. She laughed under his lips.

'What are you laughing at?'

'Love,' she said. 'That love could be like this. I never knew what it was like before.'

'Nor did I.'

'You?' She drew away and looked at him. 'But, Carl, you must have known.'

'Not that it was like this,' he said, 'I promise you.'

'Thank goodness for Mrs Lothrop,' said Kristin. 'Wouldn't she die if she could see us now? Fat, silly old Mrs Lothrop—but I thank her for her party—I like her better than I ever have.' She hugged herself and shivered. 'We must get dressed.' She ran to her clothes and began pulling them on, shivering as she did so, not knowing whether the fog or the excitement rippled her body and made her teeth chatter. She wrapped the rug around her after she dressed, tense in the knowledge that Carl had touched it, smoothed it out; feeling a sweet satisfaction in the fact that it was his rug.

A dark speck appeared in the fog, grew longer and wobbled as it moved—like a nine-pin teetering before it falls.

'Carl, you look like a nine-pin, so silly. Watch me.' She walked off into the fog and came back. She heard his laughter as though it were her own, deep within her.

'There is tea in the thermos,' he said. 'Like a cup?'

Tea, with Carl. 'Oh, yes, let's have it in the car.'

So in the car it was. She held the cups and he poured the steaming tea into them. Ah, lovely, there together, their hands curled around the warm china. The two of them alone in a car that floated in a white world. They were silent. Kristin tucked her feet under her and leaned back. She could feel, without looking at Carl, that he was watching her and she could keep her eyes away no longer. She smiled at him over the rim of her cup.

'Happy?' he asked.

Happy? Could this be happiness? Could happiness be so large a thing as this joy that possessed her?

'I could stay here for ever and ever without a complaint,' she said.

He had finished his tea. They sat together, her head against the tweed of his coat. Curiosity gnawed her. Who was this man she was with? She knew nothing. Less than nothing. Sitting there she longed to ask him and yet recoiled from asking him about himself. To know more all at once would destroy the keen delight of piecing together little by little the fabric of his being. So she asked nothing, more anxious to learn as he told her.

The waves pounding on the shore were the only sound.

'It is high tide,' she said, 'it sounds like wind in the trees.'

'The sea has claimed the figures we modelled,' he said.

Yes, yes. The sea had them. They had gone. She was glad. She wouldn't think about them again, would forget that she had stolen from Carl. There was nothing to worry about. It was enough to be here with him, her head rising and falling with his breathing; the silence being broken occasionally with words bright and swift as a school of minnows, flashing upon the moment and going again. This is what I have been looking for always, thought Kristin, without knowing it. And now I have tumbled upon it by chance and am still breathless from the discovery.

The drive back was slow. At first the fog was so thick that it was impossible to hurry. But as they drove inland it disappeared. With each mile of the road, thought Kristin, a part of me, a part of my happiness is being left behind. She did not want to return, to go back to the eyes of her parents searching out her face; to their questions. She could hear her mother carefully choosing her words, 'Did you enjoy yourself, dear?' And then, 'And Mr Bridges? He is an attractive man—quite the most attractive man we've had here for some time.' And her eyes would wait for the remark Kristin must make, the remark that would tell all or nothing of the afternoon. But she felt equal to it now; she had grown older since the morning. She could speak with the surface of her mind, saying words that told little more than a silence.

'Tomorrow,' said Carl. Kristin waited. 'Tomorrow,' she formed the word in her mind.

'What would you like to do tomorrow?' She couldn't think. To be with him was enough.

'How about driving up the river? I'd like to see more of the country.'

The bridge is built again, thought Kristin. 'We can drive to the Rapids and swim and have lunch. It's lovely there.'

'And I'll call for you about the same time.' He stopped the car. 'We're nearly into town,' he said. 'We'll stretch out the return a little longer.' He put a cigarette between her lips, took it out again and kissed her. 'You're very sweet,' he said, 'so unafraid to be generous.'

She didn't understand. Generous? How could she be anything else? But he didn't explain. Instead, he held out his lighter for her. She watched him, watched the stoop of his head as he leaned forward, the tightening of his lips as he drew the first puff of smoke into his mouth, the lift of his thumb as he released the lever to snuff the flame and the bend of his elbow when he returned the lighter to his pocket. She was greedy for knowledge of him, greedy to know where he lived, where he studied, who his friends were. She wanted to be able to think of him as a student—in Paris perhaps, or Italy. Wanted to see him in his home, tall Carl, having lunch with his family, sitting with them in the evenings. But where and what were they like?

'I want to know your province, Kristin,' he said. 'Want to see the places you have grown up in, the background of your life. It's strange,' he said, 'I somehow never expected to come down here. But it's a beautiful province and now I shall see it with you; you showing me, not like a guide, but as though you were showing me yourself. We shall have a week together and then I'll paint you.'

A week! Seven days stretched out one after another with Carl. And then the painting and ... then? But she didn't ask.

'Don't make promises,' she said, 'don't make plans. Something may happen. You may grow tired of me. Anything might interfere. And if there are no plans it will be easier.'

He took her hand, laughing at her, and stroked it. 'All right, we won't plan, then, but it will happen just the same; you wait and see, nothing will go wrong.'

She could hardly hear him. Her hand had turned to satin under his touch. Her whole body was satin with little breezes playing over it. He held her again, his arms around her, his lips taking hers. Nowhere was there an ecstasy as sweet as this.

'Oh, Kristin, Kristin,' his voice was muffled, 'we must go back.' He drew away. Kristin smoothed her hair.

'Yes, we must go back.' She wanted to be alone, to give herself up to thinking of Carl, almost more than she wanted to be with him.

He started the engine. Once again they were on their way back.

'Till tomorrow then.' That was what he had said last, standing on the door-sill, his hair still untidy from the wind. Kristin drew the curtains in her room hardly knowing what she did. Till tomorrow.

Her mother had greeted her as she came in, 'Kristin, surely you asked Mr Bridges in to dinner?'

'I never thought,' she said.

'Rush out and see if you can stop him.'

Kristin moved to the hall window. 'He's gone,' she answered, watching his car move out of the driveway.

'But if you hurry ...' She hadn't wanted to hurry. She hadn't wanted Carl across the dinner-table. She knew so well how jovial her father would be as he stood weighing the carving-knife in his hand and how her mother's staccato voice would have risen above the dishes. 'Don't you like him?' her mother had continued, 'I'd have thought you would have enjoyed having him to dinner.'

Questions, questions, leading questions and all she wanted was to be alone. She turned down the covers of her bed and undressed. As she stood in her nightgown before the glass she felt a fierce joy in her own figure. It was slim and supple and straight, hardly hers. She felt as though she was looking at someone else—this white skin, not hers at all, the skin Carl loved. She moved closer. And this face. She examined it closely, tracing the outline of the lips, the lips Carl had taken for his. Her fingers moved over them in a dream, as though half expecting to find the ghost of his kiss still there. Oh Carl! She was a living wire with awareness of him. Somewhere, in a hotel room, perhaps, he moved and she could not see him; moved in surroundings she did not know. Her body tightened with the desire that possessed her, the desire for him to be with her, folding his lips over hers, whispering, 'Kristin, it is true. I love you.' How could she bear this loneliness, sweet as it was with thoughts, how bear a life not linked to Carl's forever?

The wonder of it all. Oh, the wonder! Her mind went back to the beach, to the moment when she had feared his closeness, wanted him closer and yet dreaded the actuality. And the eventual blind surrender of her lips followed by a surprise that it was possible to be touched as she had been touched; possible to be harbouring, unknown to herself, this new creature within her which could sweep aside the other, the known self, in the ecstasy of Carl's kisses.

Oh, Carl, Carl. She turned over. Sleep was farther from her than the tomorrow she struggled towards; the moment when once again the sea of his caresses would break on her body.

But the thought of the bas-relief figures on the beach drained her to a hollow stem holding a thin fear. It must not be, she thought, shutting her eyes in an agony, it must not, must not be. She could feel the tears under her eyelids and she fought them back. I love him too much, she thought, surely I cannot hurt him, loving him so. But she was not convinced and the night stretched out before her—a tunnel of torment that she could not quench; interminable darkness leading to the reality of Carl.

PART TWO: CARL

Carl was waiting. His board was ready. Any minute now Kristin would come. He would hear her steps first on the stairs and then she would stand, framed in the doorway. He walked up and down, lit a cigarette, gazed at the glowing end and leaned on the window-ledge. He was happy and he wasn't happy. The past week, now that it was over, was bright with unreality. The pale child who had grown to become so important to him was like quicksilver—always just when he thought he had her she was gone. And it was that that kept him so alert in his love. When he thought of the women he had known he wondered at himself. Many were more beautiful, certainly most were more intelligent, but none was so fascinating, none had captured him like Kristin. There—her steps sounded on the stairs. He moved forward. She stood in the doorway as he had imagined. Cool, in white, like a lily. She smiled.

'My darling!' He went to her, took her hands. She held up her mouth for him, unselfconscious, simply.

'The stage is set,' he said, 'shall we begin?' He was eager to start.

'Here,' he held the chair. He didn't want to pose her, wanted instead to catch the lines of her own natural position. He waited for her to settle, watched her sit half sideways, cross her long legs and lift her head to look at him.

'How do you want me to sit?'

'Like you are,' he said. 'Just like that.' He drew a chalk mark around the legs of the chair and shifted his easel. It was over a week since he had worked. He picked up a stick of charcoal. It was easy to draw her, he knew her features so well—her small, intense mouth, the wide sweep of her hair-line, the distance between her eyes. His hand moved easily. At this rate, he thought, I'll have finished the sketch at one sitting. Tomorrow, if the varnish is dry, I'll be able to start on the tempera. He worked on, carried away, forgetful of Kristin as more than a model. It was good to be working again, lost in the moment of creation. The sketch was complete.

He stood back, critically, and was pleased; he had caught her exactly. For a background, rocks, her rocks and the line of the sea. Kristin, white and pale against the rocks.

He looked at his watch and frowned. 'You must be tired,' he said. 'I forgot the time. You've been sitting an hour.' He watched her get up, saw from her movements, the stiffness of her body, watched her stretch. 'Weary?' he asked.

'Only stiff,' she said.

'It was selfish of me.' He put his arm around her.

'Oh, no.' She leaned against him, 'I love to watch you work, see you become absorbed in something.'

There is a deathly quietness about her, he thought. It is only in moments of passion that she is wakened to vitality and then it's as if the vitality will destroy her. How can she give herself so completely to love, so unfearfully? She trusts and she follows and she creates all at once.

He could feel her shoulder against his ribs. He turned her towards him, lifted her face to his and stared into her eyes. Her eyes are wide, clean, green, like buds unfolding, he thought, and her body still and clean as if the sea has swept over it. He couldn't help wondering what she would say, how she would react, if he suggested she become his mistress—she so young, so unused to the ways of love, who accepted them without alarm. But she was safe from that. He would never ask her. He was only curious. He didn't want her as a mistress, he wanted to marry her. He stopped in his thoughts, surprised at the line they had taken.

'Carl, what are you thinking of?'

He led her to the sofa and she curled up against him, her hair fanning out behind her head, falling in one piece—sculptured hair, forming a fan, a shell, for her head to rest on.

'What a funny face you have, Kristin. It's not a Canadian type at all. It's Scandinavian, with its high cheek bones and wide forehead. Have you Scandinavian blood in you?'

'Not a drop,' she said. 'My name—that was simply because Mother liked it.'

'It must have affected your appearance. You hear of things like that happening.'

'But what were you thinking of?' She had returned to her question. Like a child again, he thought.

'I was thinking about marriage.'

'Oh.' She said, 'Oh,' and said no more. It was an 'Oh' that gave him nothing. She had a sharp sweet note in her voice as though she held a bird in her throat. Her 'Oh' was the bird's note.

'Marriage,' she said, ignoring the bird, stretching the word out.

'Yes, marriage,' said Carl, the word beginning to sound silly. 'What do you think of it?'

She spread out her arms, one lay over his chest. 'I hadn't thought very much,' she said. 'What can I think, knowing so little?'

He smiled. No theories, so devoid of theories, this Kristin, with her eyes like green buds and her white, still flesh.

'Let's go and have lunch,' said Carl, 'somewhere quiet.'

'There is nowhere quiet,' she answered. But she was animated now. She got up—a swift, silken movement, like a bolt of taffeta moving. Her eyes were unfolding, her mouth drawn up small—silken too—a patch of red satin in her white face, below eyes unfolding to leaves.

'Carl, Carl!' the bird was back. 'Your paintings, I want to see your paintings.'

'I have so few with me.'

'But those you have. How can I know you, not knowing your work; not knowing that which is more you than anything else?' There was a light behind her face, her skin was translucent.

'And I, how can I know you, not knowing the secret of the rocks?'

Her face clouded. 'Not now. Not now.' She brushed it away. He persisted. 'A moment will come,' she said. 'I will know the moment. It will come and I will speak because I cannot help speaking, not because you have asked me but because it will be inevitable.'

He bent over his canvases. He would not persuade her. Perhaps, when she knew him better. He would try. There was a rod between them; he would remove the rod—her way. He leaned his canvases against the wall. There were so few of them. Despite his many moves there was dust powdering their edges. He ran his finger along them and looked at the black smudge on it.

She stood in the middle of the room … quite still … but her mouth was tight again, a little pattern of red satin; and her eyes were bursting to leaves and her hands clenched, clenched. And then, 'That is good,' she said, 'but good.' She pointed, her long pale arm held forward, the white sleeve of her dress hanging straight.

'You know plates and fruit and weight on a table top. You know those things as though you had felt their shapes against your heart. Oh Carl! you know too much to be happy. It is hard for you to escape unhappiness, for even your happiness drains you. It falls like lead through your whole being. And that is why you can paint.'

Kristin! Kristin saying this. Kristin speaking as his being spoke. 'And to be happy, to escape to happiness?'

'To escape to happiness is to run from happiness. There can never be happiness for you, Carl.'

He felt to touch her would be to touch a live wire. What did she know, how did she know, know, that which he was only just beginning to discover as a certainty?

'And there,' she pointed to the portrait of an old man, 'you have been old too. Oh Carl, had you been spared the humiliation!'

'It is over now,' he said.

She smiled a little, sad smile. 'Not really,' she said. 'It cannot be really over. It is there still in your bones, in your heart. You can never be truly young again.' And she came to him, humble, bowing her head. But he couldn't kiss her, nor did she hold her mouth to be kissed.

'Thank you,' she said. 'You have been very generous, you have given me so much.'

It is all suddenly mad, thought Carl. Suddenly it is 'Thank you, you have been very generous.' Party talk.

She linked her arm in his and threw back her head. 'To lunch then,' she said. 'As we cannot go where it is quiet let us go where it is most noisy, so the noise will carry us.'

It was hard to keep up, hard to keep step with her sudden moods. She seemed secure now, different, he thought; all week she has been groping, oh, silently, unobtrusively, but groping. Now she has found; now she knows of me what she wants to know. But I? He felt less sure of her. The more he knew the more she evaded him; it was like trying to catch a cloud in a butterfly net. How could the child know this, or the woman act so?

Over lunch in that crowded room they sat at a table for two and their eyes flew across the table top like moths to meet each other. Carl Bridges, artist, thinking like a poet, he mused, and laughed. Her fork was half-way to her mouth but her eyes were on him.

'You're laughing,' she said. 'Why?'

'I was thinking of Dick.'

'Dick?' She lifted her fork higher and he saw her small white teeth.

'He is a friend of mine,' he said, 'and he watches me like a hawk and makes bald statements, bald personal statements: you are in love; your work has been hurt by a woman—that is Dick.'

'And so you were thinking of Dick.' Her fork was on her plate now and her hands were folded under her chin. 'And laughing.'

'And laughing—because now, if he could see us now he would say to me, "You are in love."' He expected her to follow the conversation up but she said instead, looking very serious, her eyes closing back to buds:

'People—you talk of people, friends. Carl, I don't know people and I have no friends.'

She said it without a trace of self-pity as though she were saying: 'Charles Morgan—I don't know Charles Morgan and I have no books.' He looked at her. There could be no doubt but that she meant what she said. But why, he wanted to know.

'Why?' he asked.

'I've felt no need of people, ever, until now. My life has been like your still-life—plates and fruit and table tops.'

'And rocks,' he said.

'Yes, and rocks.'

'But if,' he was still not clear, 'if you don't know people, Kristin, how did you know about that portrait? How did you know I'd been old?'

'My grandmother,' she answered. 'When I was very young Mother was worried about me. She sent me to stay with my grandmother and I used to sit and watch her, watch her hands, twisted with rheumatism, slowly sewing; watch as she read, her magnifying glass tracing the lines of print. Day after day, day after day, watch her doing little things in slow motion with that dignity that age brings. And I grew old. For a whole month I was as old as my grandmother.'

He was fascinated. The thought of a child Kristin, pale as winter sunshine, sitting as old as her grandmother with gnarled hands.

'Then you do know people, Kristin.'

'No,' she smiled and unfolded her hands and they flew off away from her chin, like two doves and fell into her lap. 'I don't know how they talk or what they talk about; I don't know their anger or their happiness or the reasons for them.'

'But family life,' he kept at it, anxious to know more. 'To live with people as you have, is to know them.'

The doves flew again, to her plate this time, and one flew back to her mouth carrying a piece of lettuce leaf.

'And Dick?' She had returned to Dick. 'Tell me of Dick.'

'He is fair and he can't resist making puns and he ...' But Carl stopped. Damn! he didn't want to talk of Dick. He was stupid to have mentioned him. He wanted to go, get away from the crowd, go somewhere where he could touch Kristin and so prove her reality.

'Ready?'

Kristin nodded and he rose and pulled out her chair, glad to be going from the noise, glad to be going off alone, with Kristin. She let her hand rest on his arm as she got to her feet and he grabbed her harshly almost and pulled her along past the counter.

'Carl,' she stopped him with her voice, 'the bill.'

He felt silly now. The girl at the counter smiled at him as he groped through his pockets and then went back to the table where the bill lay on the plate as it had been when it had been put there. No change, he thought miserably, and rather than go back to the counter again, he left a dollar for a tip and returned, knowing already the half scorn of the waitress who would grab it with eager hands.

She was waiting, a stalk of loveliness, standing still as a shaft of sunlight, wearing friendliness on her face. When they were outside he felt better and when they had reached the corner the anger had died. He turned to her, seeing her anew as a landscape after a storm.

'Tonight, then,' she said stopping, 'we shall see you at seven.'

'You're not going?'

'I must.'

'Kristin ...'

'Yes, Carl?'

He must keep her a moment longer. 'I had hoped we might be alone a little while this afternoon.' But it was no good, she was going. As she went he thought he heard her say, very quietly, over one white shoulder, 'I love you.' He was after her.

'Then stay!' he said, catching her up.

'No, darling. Not now. See you at dinner.' And she went, a slim white figure through the heat and the crowds, alone.

Carl walked back to the hotel, lost. He was a fool to be angry. She loved him, she had told him and he knew. But he wanted to be with her and as the heat of the pavement stung the soles of his feet he grew angrier.

In the hotel room he sat on his bed, hurt. It was stiflingly hot. He flung the window up to the top and took off his coat, sitting in his shirt sleeves, angry. And then he poured himself a drink—a large strong drink of whiskey—and drank it in a rage. Not thinking, deliberately not thinking, just sitting with the drink in his hand, the second drink, while the last of the first one still smouldered in his throat.

There was not enough wind even to lift the silly hotel curtains and beneath, in the square, in the green light, people walked listlessly and the flower beds shone as though planted with jewels, packed tight against each other—rubies and sapphires and diamonds and opals and emeralds, emeralds, emeralds. Hating them, he moved to the window to see them more closely and he leaned on the sill and sipped his drink and the green light of the trees rose up and filled his eyes.

Kristin was—where? If he could only imagine where. Other women, yes, he could see them, any of them, under dryers, at bridge, having fittings. But Kristin? Always she escaped. He turned away from the square, the drink unfinished in his hand, bewildered now, angry no longer. Sitting at the desk, the hotel paper before him, he began a letter to Dick.

It is almost a month since I first arrived in this city. It is a quaint place with a waterfront which should be an artist's delight. Too, the surrounding country, sea one way and dignified rivers the other. But there is no use trying to persuade you that such is the reason for my prolonged visit.

He stopped, ran his pen through it all, lit a cigarette and began again.

It is hot here today. I wish you were here with me to expound your damn silly theories of colour and fling your arguments at my head. No doubt, in the middle of all your talk you would look at me and say, 'You're in love.'

Carl crumpled the paper in his hand and threw it on the floor. It was no good. What could he say to Dick that didn't sound childish and absurd. Love on paper was an infantile thing, to be laughed at by the adult mind. Yet, in reality, he thought, a man's loves are no laughing matter, however puerile; they shaped him to the ultimate man. What would he, for instance, be now, if he had not met Denise, so vulgarly called Student's Delight? Denise, who had, for some unaccountable reason, given him, an angular shy lad, one-quarter of her so valuable time. Denise, the wanton with the kitten's eyes, who drove him to a youthful frenzy in those mad Paris days, so that even now he could not think of Paris without seeing her. Denise, absurdly small, with her little rounded behind stretching her tight dress even tighter; Denise, speaking always so quietly that it was as if her eyes spoke; who could make a shy boy forget his shyness even while she laughed at him for it.

And Marmo—shrill, acquiline—with such an exaggerated sense of the ridiculous, who could not observe the conventions for two minutes together. An *enfant terrible*, striding about hatless with her short, dark curly hair waving like tendrils about her face. To be out with Marmo was to be a brave man, for she delighted in breaking the surface dignity of people. Action, she cried for action and always got it by her unprecedented behaviour. How high her heels were! She was tall but wanted to be taller, wanted to be the tallest woman in any gathering, 'For it is absurd for a woman to be tall,' she would say, 'but it is exceedingly absurd for a woman to be six-foot two, which is what I am with my shoes on.'

Carl lay on his bed thinking. But forever his mind returned to Kristin, Kristin so unlike anyone he had ever met. It would seem, he thought, that the only similarity between the women I have known lies in the fact that they have all had strange names. Never has a Jane or a Peggy or a Mary or a Betty left a mark on my life. Denise and Marmo and Egbert, 'The Egg,' those were the three. 'The Egg' had carried her bad shape courageously and filled the quiver of her mind with stolen arrows, sharply brilliant. He hadn't known that at first.

He had met her in Carnegie Hall … in the intermission. She was standing beside the picture of Wagner, he remembered very clearly, and they had just heard Ravel's *Ma Mere l'Oye*. 'The Egg' was standing there beside the picture, her left hand in the pocket of a heavy sweater that dragged down her low breasts. 'There is Egbert,' Dick had said, pulling him through the people, leaning against the wall by herself.

'Egbert!' Dick had called and coming nearer, 'Egbert, this is Carl Bridges, a friend of mine.'

'Why Egbert?' Carl remembered asking.

She had taken the cigarette out of her mouth with her right hand and looked at him from beneath her half-moon lids. She spoke through smoke.

'It was the christening,' she said.

He felt stupid.

'My father drank,' she went on, 'and arrived at my christening very much under the weather just at the time that the clergyman was asking for my name. Mother caught sight of father at that exact minute and called out in a loud voice, "Egbert!" She was a very unrepressed woman, my mother, and my father's name was Egbert.'

He had felt even more stupid. It served him right for asking personal questions. And then she had smiled, a smile born in the cave of her mouth that forced her lips apart and leaped out.

'You don't believe it either,' she said. 'No one believes that story but myself and even I am sometimes doubtful.' She put the smile and the cigarette back into her mouth. 'Ravel is a very funny Frenchman,' she added, 'and you a very funny American.'

He had wanted to tell her then that he wasn't American but the crowd came between them and they were forced apart. The thought of Egbert had remained with him throughout the rest of the symphony and when it was over he had searched through the people to find her again.

Egbert! They had had good times together before that last night when he had felt the blood rise in him to form another man, a harsh, cruel, irritable man, and he had called out in a voice that astonished him, 'God, God, God! Can you never say anything that you haven't pilfered from other brains? Can you never say anything of your own? When I want La Rochefoucauld or Heine or Lawrence I can read them for myself. A man cannot live on your second-hand conversations presented as your own.'

The half-moon lids had lowered. The harsh, cruel, irritable man within him had died as he watched her face. And he had almost moved to her side when she said:

'Ah, Carl, you have hurt me. But it is all right, all right. "I've always known what it was to accept an enormous emptiness round me, echoing and echoing, and I sitting there in the middle, like a paper doll reflected in hundreds of mirrors."'

Poor child, he thought, starting impulsively towards her. And then he had remembered. That too, he had read. The words suddenly took form on a page and he saw it all. It was blue-covered, the book. He couldn't quite remember but he knew those words. She had thought he wouldn't but he did. The harsh, angry man had risen again and he had walked from the room. As he reached the door he had swung round, ready to speak, seeing the book in his head. '*Wolf Solent*,' he had heard his own words and seen her cover her mouth and sag in her chair. He had opened the door and gone.

Carl glanced at his watch. It was time he changed, time he changed to see Kristin. The thought of her, coming fresh from 'The Egg' was clean and sweet. He turned on the bath water and laid out his clothes for the evening. The thought of seeing Kristin was like a whistle in his mouth.

Standing on the veranda, waiting for the door to be answered, Carl felt caught up in the green evening light thrown out from the leaves of the trees. And he felt for one moment as if he were standing at the bottom of the sea, with marine vegetation growing thick and strong about him. If he moved it would be with the slow movement of flesh against water.

The door was open now; the inside light shattered the sea illusion. He stepped over the sill.

'If you would leave your things in the den, sir,' the maid said.

He held out his hands and shrugged. There was nothing to leave. 'Oh!' gasped the maid, 'I'm sorry, sir.' And he laughed.

'Ah, Mr Bridges!' Mrs Fender came to meet him. Her dress of black was tailored and severe as a man's dinner jacket and the white front of organdie was crisp and fresh about her slim neck.

'Come in,' she said. 'Ralph's mixing the cocktails and Kristin should be down in a minute.'

He liked the room, cool, green, low, with two vases of white stocks.

'I'm glad you're not superstitious about white flowers,' he said, 'I love them.'

'So do I.' She was pleased, he could tell, but her eyes guarded her pleasure. She reached for a cigarette and put it in her mouth. He paused before he lit it for her.

Standing there, slim and straight, with her black plastic hair, the black and white of her dress and her pale face, she made an astonishing figure.

'You look very lovely,' he said, and held his lighter for her. She fluttered just a little and looked up from the flame.

'Oh, Mr Bridges, you flatter an old woman.' She said it with an air of having said it often, the 'old woman' emphasized. But she touched his hand as she bent again to the lighter. And at that moment, he felt, with some extra-sensory power, that he held the key to her in his hands. He knew now more than she could ever tell him of her life. Grace Fender had travelled a long road to this surface serenity. And now that she had attained it her husband ceased to love her. The two things had happened simultaneously, he felt certain. His consciousness leapt to a point of interest—laboriously Mrs Fender had built her own shell. As he thought this, Kristin entered. She was in white again, casual, the top of her dress like a shirt, open at the neck, the skirt plain. But as he noticed, as he took her in, as he said 'Hello!' and she came forward to him, so was he aware of Mrs Fender's shell stiffening. The mother had fortified herself for the daughter's approach.

Kristin sat and hung her long hand over the arm of the chair. 'What did you do this afternoon, Carl?'

'Yes, tell us,' said Mrs Fender. 'What does an artist do in the afternoon?' She said it lightly, scoffing at her own words.

'Nothing, Mrs Fender, I assure you. I started two letters and then abandoned them. It was too hot to follow them through.'

'It *was* hot!' said Mrs Fender. 'I'm told it was the hottest afternoon of the year, though how people know these things I can't imagine. I wish Ralph would hurry with the cocktails. He must be making—oh, here you are, Ralph.'

Carl got up. Mr Fender carried a long tray gay with old-fashioneds. 'Good evening, sir,' Carl said.

'Evening, evening, Bridges. Sorry I've been so long.' Beaded perspiration marked his hair-line. 'The kitchen is hot,' he said, passing the tray.

'It is cool in here, Ralphey; sit down and enjoy your drink.' She prodded at hers with the muddler.

'Always,' said Kristin, 'I think the cube of pineapple is a sugar lump and wonder why it won't dissolve. Always.'

'I should think, by now, you might have learned.' Her father laughed at her. They all laughed. There was something just a little bit strained, as if iron girders held the family together but also held them apart. Carl felt that he alone was free. He could go near or escape entirely.

'I'm very taken with this part of the world,' he said. 'It's beautiful country.'

Mr Fender put down his drink and slapped his knee. 'Don't know where you'll find anything to equal it,' he said. 'Why, take the rivers alone, if we had nothing else here but the rivers it'd be a prize province. And the fishing here! I tell you, boy—why, Lowell Thomas wrote a book about it. Ever read it? I haven't myself, I must admit, but we've got it here somewhere if you want to have a look at it. And the hunting—if you're here for the hunting season I'll take you out. I've a couple of good dogs in the kennels. A little pointer bitch, she's a wonder. If there's a bird in miles Nettie'll find it. And the springer—he's young yet—but a good dog. That dog can carry an egg in his mouth for miles.'

He paused. And this is Kristin's father, Carl thought.

'Get on with your drink, Ralph,' Mrs Fender said. 'We're all ahead of you. Finish it up and mix us another round. The dinner's cold, it can wait.'

'Good idea,' said Mr Fender, draining his glass. He got to his feet quickly for a fat man.

Kristin has hardly spoken, Carl mused. She is sitting, holding silence to her. Mr Fender collected the glasses.

'Not for me, Daddy,' Kristin said, keeping her glass and still exploring it with her muddler.

'One day,' said her mother, 'you'll bite the end off the muddler mistaking it for the cherry.' Her voice had risen a little. Kristin smiled—a smile that crumpled the satin of her mouth to the petal of a Shirley poppy.

'How did the sitting go?' asked Mrs Fender so suddenly that Carl felt the words had come at him from a catapult and hit upon his skin rather than his ears.

'Very well,' he said. 'Your daughter is an excellent model.'

'I must come down and see it some time, that is, if you'll let me. And if it's for sale we'd very much like to buy it.'

'Oh no,' said Carl, feeling thin with discomfort. 'Oh no, there is no obligation. I mean you are under no obligation at all. It was as a favour to me that I asked Kristin to sit, I assure you.'

'But,' said Mrs Fender, 'you don't seem to understand. We should like to have it.'

Carl rolled his cigarette between his fingers. He could feel the warmth of the old-fashioned coursing through him. He looked at Kristin.

'If,' he said to Mrs Fender, 'if it is good, if you like it, let me give it to you.'

He noticed the mother's eyes jump to Kristin's face before she said: 'Mr Bridges, it is sweet of you, but really ...'

'Let's leave it like that,' he said, wanting to escape the subject, knowing that in saying what he had he had given the first real clue to Mrs Fender of what existed between Kristin and himself. He tried to find some indication on Kristin's face as to how she felt at this moment, now that he had given them away to her mother. But Mr Fender entered with the tray. His face was red.

'Here we are then,' he beamed. But the mood had changed since he had left. He looked bewildered.

Carl took his drink unhappily.

'And now,' said Mr Fender settling himself, 'tell me, how is this painting job coming? I don't know much about art,' he said, 'but I'm always ready to learn, always ready to learn.'

Carl winced. 'I'll be able to tell you more about it later, sir,' he said, anxious to hold the conversation away from Mrs Fender. 'It's a slow business, like anything else. You have to have the patience of a fisherman and the eye of a hunter to do a good job of work.'

'Jove! patience,' exclaimed Mr Fender slapping his knee again, scampering off with his own subject. 'D'you know, last year, I sat four hours on a rock above a little pool in my favourite stream, waiting. Four hours,' he said. 'I knew there were trout there, I could see them, great big sleepy fellows. Every so often I'd change my fly and try another sort. And d'you know what fly eventually did the trick?'

'No, sir,' said Carl, looking at Kristin and noticing a flicker of laughter in her face. He heard her father's voice but the words were smudged like the words of someone talking in his sleep. He had done it now, they were safe for the moment. He took a long drink of his old-fashioned and relaxed. Mrs Fender was sitting, her feet under her, disinterested.

'And that was the little beggar,' said Mr Fender loudly, 'that, if you can believe it, was the little beggar that made those trout rise.'

'Was it really, sir?' Carl tried hard to be serious but he wanted to laugh. For no reason that he could possibly name he wanted to give himself up to laughter.

'That was the one,' Kristin's father continued, 'and the funny part is I can hardly get a soul to believe it.' He chuckled.

'No more fisherman's tales tonight, Ralph,' said his wife from the sofa. 'Not until you two are having your coffee, at any rate. Kristin and I are lost. Tell me, Mr Bridges, where were you before you came here?'

'Wandering,' said Carl. 'Just before I came here I was in Montreal, but before that I was up North and before that again, in the West Indies.'

'Ah,' Mrs Fender's face softened, as though remembering something lovely and sad. 'Were you in Nassau?'

'No,' he said. 'Trinidad and Barbados chiefly—and Martinique.'

'But not Nassau?'

'No.'

'It is lovely there,' she said. 'But I suppose the islands are all more or less alike.' She seemed to shake herself with a sudden resolution. 'And now,' she said, 'if you've finished your drinks perhaps we ought to go in to dinner.'

During dinner Carl was enchanted. The two old-fashioneds had done their work. Kristin across the table was like the water-lily that floated in the bowl between them. Mr Fender was very jovial; he brandished the carving-knife like a familiar butcher, thumped the table with his ham-like fist and grew redder and redder so that his fair-grey hairs stood out almost singly against his scarlet scalp. Mrs Fender had tightened up imperceptibly. Carl didn't mind. He was caught up in the stream of his own good humour and opposite him, drifting in a pool of stillness, was Kristin smiling through her eyes.

Mrs Fender wanted to know about places. Throughout the meal she asked him questions about the countries he had visited. It is as if she has a lover wandering through the world and she wants a background for him, he thought. He was glad to tell her, for in so doing, he supplied for Kristin the bare stage-setting of his life. Still Kristin scarcely spoke. There is something unreal in all this, Carl thought—the candlelight polishing the silver, the shiny surface of the table, the two women, as different as the two poles and over all the weight of Mr Fender, the mad butcher, expanding, growing louder as the minutes passed. He could feel Mrs Fender's eyes on him when he turned away from her; so close was her scrutiny that he felt he dare not look at Kristin, for to look was to have the love he felt for her break on the surface of his face and proclaim itself.

'Do you ever lecture, Mr Bridges?'

He laughed, remembering his one and only lecture. 'No-o,' he said. 'I did once, that was all.' But why, he thought, has she asked me that? Surely she is not hoping to book me up to speak at some women's club. Women's faces in rows, as though planted out by the supreme Gardener and then left, without nourishment or sunshine. He had seen them before.

'It's your voice,' said Mrs Fender. 'I like your voice and your hands. I can see you standing on a platform with a pointer in your hands.'

'It would be painful,' he said. 'I can't think how people do it.'

Mr Fender put down his fork with a clatter. 'Nothing to it,' he said. 'Why, it's as simple as just talking here—simpler really, because you know the thread of what you are going to say and you follow it, while in conversation you never know what is going to be said or expected of you two sentences ahead.' He paused, considered his words. 'Why, that's quite a point,' he said, pleased, 'quite a point! I'd never thought of it just that way before. But the important thing about speaking,' he said, 'is to talk slowly, give yourself time to choose your next word.' He wagged his thick forefinger in Carl's face.

'I hope, sir,' Carl said, 'I sincerely hope I shall never have the opportunity to take advantage of your tip. That's the trouble with making any kind of a name for yourself, people immediately expect you to be able to do anything.'

Why is Kristin so silent? he thought. Is she unhappy, is she cross with me for running after her this afternoon? But as he thought she spoke.

'That is true, I think,' she said, 'about people expecting you to be able to do anything if you can do one thing really well. And the opposite is true too. If you have never proved yourself skillful in one thing, people think there is nothing you can do at all.'

'Perhaps.' Carl considered it.

The fact that this had been the first attempt at conversation Kristin had made all evening gave greater importance to her words—as if, he thought, she is saying more than the surface of her thought implies. Is she speaking to me? he wondered, wanting to atone for her lack of talents, wanting to let me know that there is something she can do?—she, the perfect woman, unaware of her perfection, trying to build herself up. Or is she—his mind rested a minute in satisfaction, feeling that this second thought was the right one—is she talking to her parents, warning them of what is to come? He smiled at her across the water-lily. She is mine now, surely, he thought. And the desire to go to her swept over him so strongly that he forced himself to return to the frozen dessert he was eating. He scrutinized it carefully.

'Don't eat it if you don't like it, Mr Bridges,' Mrs Fender said.

'But I do, really.' He began eating hastily to prove his words, too hastily. I am making them ill at ease, he thought, and he looked at Kristin quickly for a clue. She looks golden in the candlelight now that the room is darker. I wonder, he thought, how they would feel if I sold stocks and bonds, whether it would have made a different atmosphere for them, whether they would now be laughing, throwing out small, smart phrases at each other and resting on them?

Mrs Fender lit a cigarette in the flame of a candle and leaned her pointed elbows on the table; Kristin wiped her mouth carefully and gazed long at the smudge of lipstick on the napkin; the only sound came from Mr Fender, who, with a schoolboy's zest, was finishing up his frozen dessert. Each one, he thought, absorbed, complete, and he looked away from them to the candle flames, feeling that in looking at them now he was looking at them exposed and naked as though he were peeping at them alone in their bedrooms. No two out of the three, he thought, share a common ground and he was glad of the knowledge, glad of the further understanding of Kristin that lay embedded in it.

'A cigar?' asked Mr Fender, passing Carl his case. And Carl took it, unwilling to hurt the boy butcher by refusing.

When he looked again at the three of them they had each risen from their moment of isolation. He could look now without feeling ashamed. But the air still rippled like water from the movements of arising.

'Come, Kristin,' said Mrs Fender, 'we'll leave the men together. You and I will have our coffee in the other room.'

As Carl watched them leave he wondered what the two of them would talk about when they were together. Sitting in that low, green, peaceful room, Mrs Fender with her feet tucked under her on the chesterfield, Kristin draped like a length of taffeta on one of the chairs.

But Mr Fender had begun. 'To get back to fishing,' he said, winking, 'now that the wife can't object.' The maid entered with the coffee and liqueurs and Mr Fender stopped.

'We have no choice of liqueurs,' he said apologetically, 'it's Grand Marnier or Grand Marnier,' and his face crinkled with amusement.

'Then Grand Marnier it shall be, sir,' said Carl.

'An excellent choice,' continued Mr Fender, delighted with their make-believe.

With the first sip of the liqueur Carl had the strange sensation that his brain had warmed, swelled and divided. One part was with Kristin, the other part was here with her father, laughing at his obvious and rather crude jokes. Mr Fender had already started his second liqueur and passed the bottle to Carl.

'Kristin,' said Mr Fender, changing the subject abruptly, 'is a very queer child.'

'She is a very beautiful child,' Carl amended.

'Beautiful—' he stopped. 'Hm, I hadn't thought about that. She's put together well ... But beautiful, well, I dunno. Confidentially,' he said, leaning forward, 'Grace and I are almost frightened of her. We wouldn't have her know that, of course, but she's different. Grace sometimes thinks she was a changeling. These hospitals, you know,' he said, 'how they can ever keep the babies identified. God, they all look alike!'

Carl laughed. Mr Fender poured another drink. He is feeling them, Carl thought, they evidently make him fanciful. I wonder if later he'll be sorry for what he is saying now?

'This is very much between the two of us,' Mr Fender continued, curling his fingers around the cigar, 'but Kristin is sometimes queer,' he dropped his head and rolled up his eyes. 'Sometimes,' he said, 'she goes comatose—or so it seems. She won't move or speak.'

'She's just naturally quiet,' Carl said hurriedly.

'You may call it that,' Mr Fender went on. 'You may call it that if you will. But it's queer. Grace and I don't understand her at all.'

Carl could see her with her mother now and he wanted to go to her, the pale child who held his thoughts.

'Well, we may as well join them,' Mr Fender said. 'But don't let on I've spoken to you in this way, I wouldn't have them know I've told you.'

He looks old now, Carl thought. He is worried.

'Ah, here you are,' said Mrs Fender. 'You've been a long time over your coffee. I hope,' she said, 'you've talked yourself out on the fishing subject, Ralphey.'

Kristin stretched out her legs and looked at the tips of her evening shoes, speaking slowly as if to them. 'There's an eclipse tonight,' she said to the left foot, 'an eclipse of the moon. I should love to drive up to the park to see it.' She inclined her head towards the right toe. 'Let's all drive up to the park.'

Carl noticed a look of concern pass between the parents.

'I'm simply too lazy to move,' Mrs Fender said. 'Why don't you two young things go? Ralph and I will stay here.'

'Oh, come with us,' said Carl, 'it's a beautiful night.'

'Not for me,' Mr Fender said, settling himself and lighting another cigar. 'I'm too old for such things. You and Kristin go, as Grace suggested. Have you your car?'

'No, it was such a nice night I walked.'

'Well, you can have mine. I'll go and get it.'

'Let me,' said Carl.

'He never lets anyone back that car out of the garage but himself,' Mrs Fender said. 'You run along, Kristin, and get a coat.'

'You two don't want us butting in,' said Mrs Fender when they were alone. 'I'm only glad Ralph had the sense to realize it. When Ralph gets an idea there's no changing him ... and he does get funny ideas,' she laughed lightly, lightly moving about the room as she spoke. 'Kristin hates a crowd anyway,' she went on. 'You noticed her at dinner. She's a strange child; most people don't understand her. But I have the feeling you do. She comes home happy when she's been with you.'

The father, thought Carl, is trying to frighten me away; the mother, meanwhile, is anxious to encourage me.

Mrs Fender stopped in front of him and put her hands on his shoulders. 'Carl,' her eyes were worried as he looked into them, 'Carl, don't hurt her. I couldn't bear my Kristin hurt. She hasn't the normal defence mechanism. She doesn't know how to ward off blows.'

'Do any of us?' he asked.

'Yes, yes! I do. I've had to. I could walk through hell fire now.'

Is she acting? Carl thought. Why is she talking like this? She walked away; she was just a little bit dramatic.

'I shouldn't speak like this unless it was necessary.' She smiled suddenly, touched the petals of a stock. 'She was born on the night of an eclipse,' she said. 'I was happy that night. But I've learned since that happiness is unimportant.'

'No,' said Carl, 'not unimportant; but not the only importance as so many people think.'

'That,' she said, 'is over my head. And now good-bye.' She held out her hand. 'I hear Kristin coming and the car is in the front, I can see the lights.' She looked young, brave. He wanted to assure her somehow that Kristin was safe with him. He squeezed her hand.

'It's awfully good of you, sir, to let us have the car. I'll try not to bash it up too much.' They were on the steps. Mr Fender was telling him it had the new gear shift and that the emergency brake was under the dashboard.

Kristin snuggled against him in the car. 'Darling,' she said, 'was it a hideous evening? I'm no help at a party. I find it so difficult to talk.'

'It was a very enjoyable evening,' Carl said. 'I know you so much better for it.'

'Do you? You know about them?'

'Your parents? Yes.'

'It's strange,' said Kristin, 'they've been awfully patient. You've no idea how hard it's been for us all. It may sound silly, this talk of not being understood, it's been so overdone. But it's not a case of not being understood or of misunderstanding—there's not enough touching of hands for that. It's more like the stars—from a distance we look part of a pattern, as the stars do, but actually we are miles apart—there is no contact.'

'Do you feel the same way with me—miles away?'

'No, no.' Her voice was suddenly intense. 'Oh, perhaps I do,' she added, 'but differently. It's more as if you're the sun and I the moon; you the strong, vital element and I but a pale thin light—and yet in spite of the difference in quality you are able to eclipse me and ...' she stopped.

'And you able to eclipse me?' He waited a long time for her answer.

'Yes,' she said at length, 'yes.'

'Well, darling, this is evidently my night.' They had reached the park. He turned the car off the road and stopped it. 'But I wouldn't mind being eclipsed by you one little bit.'

'Don't say that!' She clutched his knee firmly. 'Carl,' she said, 'don't say that, or even think it, ever again, will you?'

'Darling, why?'

'I can't tell you. Just *don't*. Please!' She sounded so desperate that under the night he had to smile as he gave his promise—a strange, solemn oath to satisfy her childish whim.

Clouds had rolled up out of the west and covered the sky. 'Damn,' he said, 'we shan't see that eclipsed moon after all.' He expected her to be disappointed.

'It doesn't matter,' she said. 'It doesn't matter a bit. It is there just the same, the feeling's there.'

'Could you tell by the feel?'

'Of course,' she said. 'I was born during an eclipse.' She seemed to think that was explanation enough. 'Let's walk down by the lake.'

'Won't it ruin your shoes?'

She laughed at him. 'You are cautious, darling.'

He caught her hand. 'Only for you,' he said. Why, because she had laughed at him, did he love her more; why because of that laugh, ever so faintly mocking, did he want to hold her, bend her to him, lose himself in the length of her kiss?

A small wind blew her hair across his face like a tent. She drew away, stood stork-like on one leg and began taking off her shoes and stockings.

'See,' she said, holding up her long skirt, 'my shoes will be saved from ru-in.' She threw them into the car.

She moved white against the darkness, like a silver birch swaying. I am in love with a moon-child, he thought. She will never be mine, never. As he started after her he was filled with the same fascination, the same melancholy he felt when swimming at night, following the path of the moon.

The second sitting was not successful. Carl, though eager to begin that second morning, had, as he worked, felt incompetent. With his eyes on Kristin he was sure of what he wanted, but brush in hand, eyes on the canvas, a lethargy crept through him.

'I'm in poor form, this morning,' he said repeatedly. 'Perhaps I'd better leave it. I'll only ruin what I've got.'

But he kept on. I can't give in, he said to himself. If I give in now I only make it too easy to give in the next time, and using every bit of creative energy he could gather he fought against the feeling that someone else had taken over his hands. Perhaps I have tried too hard, he thought. Tomorrow it will be different. Even Kristin is remote this morning; I can't reach her.

At the end of the sitting as she pulled a comb through her hair he said, 'Stay for a minute and talk.' But she only shook her head. And he was half glad. The morning had depressed him. He didn't want to excuse himself to her.

Waiting next morning for her to come he worried at his canvas. God! he thought, I worked with a heavy hand yesterday! But he was confident. He felt enthusiastic. Until she came he would take out, paint over, undo the heaviness of his own work. And when she came he was pleased.

'Darling,' he went to her, holding her with his wrists so that he shouldn't smudge her with the paint on his fingers. 'Look, I've undone it. Yesterday's botches are hidden.'

He began again, working easily, finding a thrill of power in the mastery over paint and canvas. But gradually, imperceptibly at first, the lethargy returned, the stiffness. It is almost, he thought, as if someone is using my faculties, or I using someone else's. And he grew frightened. What was happening? Have I suddenly lost my ability, he thought, am I no longer Carl Bridges, the artist? What strange force is sucking my body's strength?

'Kristin,' he began, but it was no good. Kristin was more remote than ever; if he spoke to her she seemed barely conscious of his words. It is all like a bad dream, he thought. But soon even his thoughts trailed away from him and he worked with a mechanical lack of talent and pitiful lack of power. On and on, on and on, on and on, on and on.

At last Kristin moved. He saw her shift on her chair and get up. The dream-like quality remained, she was on the other side of a veil and he could not move to her or touch her. Then suddenly the veil vanished, the dream was over. He was alive, fresh, energetic. He felt like a dog coming out of the water; he wanted to shake himself. It was all behind him now. Those strange muddled movements, that sick fatigue, the woodenness of his body—finished, ended.

Kristin seemed barely able to move; she said nothing, as if to open her lips was the ultimate in exercise. Walking with the quietness of death upon her, she reached the couch and fell on it.

'Kristin,' he went to her, contrite. Again he had made her sit too long. 'Kristin!' He bent over. Already she was asleep. Her breast rose and fell with deep, regular breathing. Poor darling, he thought as he spread his coat over her, poor little thing.

He tiptoed over to his easel. What had he done, he wondered, in that interval when consciousness slept? He looked at his watch. Two hours he had painted—what had come of those two hours? But as he reached the easel he felt sick. His own eyes mocked him out of the thick mess of paint. He covered his face, shuddering, trying to remember. It was Kristin he was painting. And there, for proof, on the couch, Kristin lay sleeping. Hold to that, hold to that, he thought. It is Kristin you painted, but uncovering his eyes again, staring at the canvas he felt the sick twist in his stomach, the ice creep along his jaw.

Kristin or not—the canvas mirrored him.

Two-inch headlines formed: You are mad, mad.

He had painted Kristin, but instead, crude and terrifying was his own face to contradict him. His own lips shaped, 'Do you not know me? Will you not acknowledge me? You and I—we are one.'

He felt his mind break into hundreds of black pin men, each screaming, 'We are one, we are one, we are one!' If Kristin were awake, he thought, crushing the pin men, she would tell me, she would explain. He would call her. It was all quite simple. He would call her and she would waken and the bird in her throat would say, 'Darling, you're dreaming.

Look—the portrait is me, not you. Look, Carl. It is Kristin.' Yes, yes, Kristin would tell him.

But as he opened his mouth to speak all thought of Kristin vanished in the sudden desperate realization that he was going to be sick.

PART THREE: CARL AND KRISTIN

'Darling, darling, darling! Wake up. It's a beautiful morning and there's a telegram for you.'

'I am awake,' Kristin said, sitting up. And then stretching out her hand, 'A telegram, for me?' Shivers ran down her legs.

'Do you think it could be Carl Bridges?' Her mother was excited. 'Do open it, Kristin.'

Kristin looked at her mother. Certainly she would not leave until the envelope was open, until she knew the message that lay, secretly, behind that opaque envelope. And so I may as well get it over with, Kristin thought. But she wanted to wait. Wanted to hold the envelope in her hand and then very slowly open the flap and all alone read those typed words that perhaps would, surely must, end in the word 'Carl.'

'Hurry, darling.' Her mother was sitting on the bed, her eyes flashing little sparks, her long white hands held together, fingers interlocked.

Carl had been gone a month now—over a month. After that terrible morning when she had awakened on his sofa to the sound of his nausea she hadn't seen him again. And she had only had one short letter:

Forgive me, I had to leave. The cold impact of fear was more than I could face. Another experience like that would send me mad. But my painting's all right now, I've been doing a lot. My work, as you must know, is not only my livelihood but my life. That is why I was so frightened. I love you, Kristin. Try to hold that as truth.

She remembered every word of that letter.

'Kristin, are you trying to pique me? If you don't open it I will myself.' Her mother moved impatiently on the bed as Kristin held the envelope to the light and tore the end off it. 'Arriving at one o'clock Tuesday meet me if you can. Carl.' Kristin tried to hold herself steady.

'It's Carl,' she said. 'He's arriving today.'

'Today! How exciting! Kristin, I believe I'm more excited than you are. What a funny child you are. Aren't you glad?'

Glad! What a word, thought Kristin, stretching her legs straight and thinking her heart would surely break the barrel of her ribs. Glad!

'Yes, mother, I'm glad.' Oh, go now, she thought, please go. Leave me alone with this moment.

But her mother crossed to the cupboard and sorted through the dresses. 'You're going to meet him, of course. What will you wear?'

Wear, thought Kristin, wear? What does it matter what I wear, she thought, what does it matter if I go as I am? What does anything matter beside the reality of Carl returning?

'Why don't you wear this pretty green dress, Kristin? You've hardly had it on more than once and you look sweet in it. I can't imagine why you don't like it.'

'All right,' said Kristin.

The mother looked inquiringly at her daughter. 'You are a funny child,' she said. 'I should think you'd be excited.'

Can't you see, thought Kristin, that I'm so excited I daren't use words? Can't you see that life has begun again for me; that this long, dead interval is finished? Don't you realize that it is true that he loves me? The core of life that dissolved with his going has formed again.

Waiting at the station, pushing through the heavy swing doors, walking onto the board walk of the platform, Kristin could hardly bear it. It is to breathe again, she thought, lungs that were cramped are free again. The tether that staked me to death has snapped.

'Miss Fender,' a crisp voice came over her shoulder. She turned. Miss Gillespie was there with her notebook. 'Are you expecting someone on this train?'

'Yes,' said Kristin, 'Carl Bridges.'

The reporter's eyebrows lifted. 'Is he to be here long?' She was making little marks in her book.

'I don't know,' Kristin replied.

Miss Gillespie stopped writing. 'Perhaps I'd better wait and interview him,' she said. 'After all, he is news. Ah, here she comes now.' Miss Gillespie looked at her watch. 'On time to the minute. I only hope there are a lot of people getting off. The society column's been poor the last few days, no one's entertaining.'

No one's entertaining, no one's entertaining, thought Kristin to herself as the train roared in. She tried to catch a glimpse of Carl in the windows, but saw only a blur of faces. The train stopped. Carl, Carl, Carl! She scanned the people getting off. He hasn't come, she thought, he must have missed it. And the ache in her emptied her, left her drained. Of all the people who are getting off, of all the people who have been waiting, I am the only one left, the only one not feeling happiness surge in me.

'Oh,' she took a breath. 'Oh!' There he was. She began to run. 'Carl!' she called, for he hadn't seen her. 'Carl!' He was in a jumble of luggage and porters and people.

And then he saw her and broke free from the jumble. He pushed the people away. He took her hands. He looked the same—exactly the same—still brown and tall and thin. She wanted to cry again. He was like music, sunlight.

'Darling, you came.'

'Yes, I came.'

'If you knew what I've suffered, wondering, wondering—will she come? What if she's busy? What if she doesn't want to see me? The thousand "ifs" that tormented me, dragged me apart.' He held her hands still.

'Mr Bridges,' said Miss Gillespie, arriving, 'I represent the press. May I say that you are in town?'

Carl hardly turned from Kristin. 'Yes,' he said, 'yes.'

'And are you going to be here long?' Miss Gillespie continued.

'I've made no plans yet,' said Carl.

'Perhaps I could see you later,' said Miss Gillespie, 'when you have decided.'

'Certainly,' said Carl. 'I'll be at the hotel.'

'Thank you.' Miss Gillespie moved off.

'Let's go,' he said. He turned for a porter. 'Those are mine,' he said to the red-cap.

'Will you want a taxi, sir?'

'I have the car,' said Kristin.

They followed the porter. 'It's good to see you, darling.'

'Oh, and it's good to see *you*.'

'Missed me?'

'I've hardly lived since you left.'

'Why didn't you write?'

'I couldn't. I felt dead.'

'Oh, my darling, I was a beast!'

'No, no. I understood.'

They had reached the car. The porter stowed away the bags.

'Just let me look at you,' Carl said, 'for a minute, just let me stare and stare.' They sat together in the car. Kristin wondered if she would ever be able to drive, she was trembling so.

'I had to leave,' Carl said, 'and I had to come back. I had to leave to make sure of my work. I had to come back to make sure of you. Now I'm sure of both. Kristin, I've never been as happy in my life.'

'We must go,' she said. 'Mother's expecting us for lunch.' She stepped on the starter. 'Do you want to book a room at the hotel first?'

'I can phone from your place,' he said.

Mrs Fender met them on the step. 'Carl,' she said, 'how nice to see you again. How more than nice.' She gave him her hand, drew him in. 'You must be hungry,' she said. 'One always has breakfast so agonizingly early on a train. And it's after one now. We won't stop for a drink. You can have one with your meal … oh, and you know where the bathroom is. You'll probably want a wash up.'

'Thank you,' said Carl. 'I think I will, if you don't mind.'

'Kristin, why didn't you wear a hat? I did ask you to.'

'Forgot,' said Kristin, 'simply forgot.'

'I'm sure Mrs Lothrop would like to see Carl,' said Mrs Fender. 'Perhaps I could get her to tea.'

'Oh, Mummy, don't. Wait and ask Carl. He's probably tired.'

Kristin couldn't eat, nor could Carl very much and Mrs Fender looked at the food and at them in despair. But even her glances didn't lower their exuberance. They caught each other's eyes across the table and laughed. Carl kept lighting cigarettes throughout the meal.

He said, 'I've never worked as hard in my life as in this last month. I've brought some of my things with me. If you'd like to see them I'll—'

'But we'd love to, Carl.' Mrs Fender was delighted. 'Love to. Let us see all we can while we can.' She smiled at him. 'For we never know when you are suddenly going to disappear again.'

'That time I couldn't help it; I wasn't well.'

'You look well.'

'I am now.' It is hard, he thought, to remember Mrs Fender when I am conscious only of Kristin.

And Kristin thought, if only mother would realize the ecstasy of this moment and not keep pinning us both down with trivialities. We are like two moths, impaled on the feelers of her curiosity breaking free only to be caught again.

In the hall as Carl untied the canvases Kristin thought, this is as it should have been, as it should always be. This moment is rounded with communion; the ends of the circle are joined; it is complete.

'That,' said Carl propping a canvas against the hall table and speaking for Kristin's ears chiefly, 'was the first thing I did after I left.' A red-headed boy against a background of brick buildings, crude and powerful. Poor Carl, thought Kristin, what an effort to escape from me. But she could say nothing.

'It's very queer,' said Mrs Fender, 'not exactly my meat, though I'm certain it's very good.'

Oh, can't you feel, thought Kristin, Carl's terror, Carl's daring? Can't you feel the reassertion of his masculinity?

Does she understand? Carl thought. I hope she knows. I want her to know, want her to see that I am all right now and this is my only means of telling her.

As the other canvases were unwrapped, propped up, Carl felt better. He had told her everything now—his fears and his ultimate triumph. And as he watched her, he saw her eyes return again and again to the red-headed boy.

'I like it,' she said. 'I like it so. It is not as good but it's more courageous than the others—like the beginning of a journey.'

She knows, she knows, he thought.

'How strangely you talk, Kristin,' said Mrs Fender. 'I don't even know what you mean—like the beginning of a journey.' They laughed then. 'Do you understand her, Carl?'

'I think so, Mrs Fender.' Of course I do, he said with his eyes to Kristin, of course.

The maid appeared in the doorway. 'The telephone, Mrs Fender.'

'I wonder who it is?' said Mrs Fender as she left.

'Darling, you know.' Carl went to her, tipped up her face.

'Carl, how you've suffered!' And I can never tell him, she thought, how I've suffered. Can never tell him I stole his identity. 'Kiss me,' she said, 'quickly, Carl. Mother will be back.'

'Oh, my sweet, it's been so long. Kristin, I want you to have the painting—that first one. I feel somehow that you must have it. Would you like it?'

'More than anything you've ever done; more than anything in the world.' Having that I am safe, she thought, it is the part of Carl I cannot touch, the upspringing kernel that I cannot destroy.

Carl thought, how did I ever live away from her? How can I bear to be separated from her again? He led her out of the door onto the veranda.

'If everything were to stop now,' she said, 'if the bells tolled out the end of the world and darkness fell upon us and washed us into oblivion I should not care. I am happier now than I have ever been.'

'It is exactly two twenty-five,' said Carl, 'to the minute. Remember that time, Kristin, for on such a minute do I ask you to marry me.' He looked out across the lawn. She must say 'Yes' he thought. Surely, she will say 'Yes.'

At two twenty-five exactly, he wants me to be his wife—his wife, she thought. Oh, Carl, is it true? It all feels unreal. She turned to him, looked at him. 'What is the time now, Carl?'

'Two twenty-seven,' he said.

'At two twenty-seven,' she said, 'exactly, I answer that I will.'

'Oh, my darling!' He kissed her. 'Now all that's left is to ask your father for your hand, in the time-honoured custom.'

'Really?' She laughed. 'It seems so silly—as if it's any affair of daddy's anyway.'

'I'll ask him tonight. We'll look at rings this afternoon.'

'Oh, Carl.' She looked at her hand. 'I never dreamed that I'd be engaged. Isn't it funny?' He kissed her fingers.

'I suppose everyone can see us. Does it matter very much?'

'Children, children!' Mrs Fender's voice called, 'That was Sarah Lothrop, she wants us all to go to tea this afternoon.'

Carl and Kristin looked at each other and laughed. 'What does it matter,' said Carl, 'what does anything matter now?'

'Did you accept?' asked Kristin as they returned to the hall.

'Why, of course, darling. You know it was through the Lothrops that we met Carl. It would be very ungracious to try to monopolize him now, wouldn't it?'

'Well, Mummy, Carl wants to get a room at the hotel and take his stuff down. Would it be all right if we went and saw to that now and then collected you in time for tea?'

Mrs Fender eyed them both. Does she know? thought Kristin. And Carl bent down and began to strap his canvases together, not daring to trust his eyes under her probing.

'That'll give you a little over an hour,' she said. 'Sarah likes tea promptly at four o'clock.'

Kristin couldn't help laughing—what did Sarah and her stupid 'on the dot of four' matter? How absurd to regulate life by hours when life was a flower unfolding, unfolding in the face of time.

'You haven't packed *The Boy*,' Mrs Fender said.

'He's given him to me, Mummy.'

'How good of him.' Mrs Fender's voice showed she was glad he had not given it to her.

Good, thought Carl, good! When I would have given her wings, given her the world if only I could. It is a poor substitute, he thought.

'Don't forget a hat this time, Kristin.'

They packed the car again. It is as if, Kristin thought, we were off, as if we were leaving for good. And Carl thought as he stared at Mrs Fender on the veranda, she is sad, her happiness has ebbed from her. I hope she will find a new happiness in our delight. I should like to feel that somehow she will know happiness again through us. But as the car turned out of the driveway he forgot her, forgot everything in the miracle of knowing Kristin for his own.

'Darling, there's so much to talk about.'

'I know,' she said. 'I know.' How queer, she thought, that I know nothing about him, where he lives, his early life; but it hardly seems to matter.

And he thought, the rocks—surely she will tell me about the rocks now.

'The world goes on just the same,' she said, braking the car. 'The policeman at the corner holds up his hand to me and the square is full of people. But the gods are smiling on us a little,' she added, drawing into the curb. 'Look, we have parked right in front of the hotel.' His hand closed over hers as she pushed the gear into neutral.

'Don't,' she said. 'Don't touch me or tell me you love me until we are in your room.'

The bell boy took the bags. Carl carried his own canvases. He's tall and straight and slim as a weir pole, thought Kristin, in the dim light of the hotel.

'Ah, Mr Bridges, nice to see you,' said Mr Seely at the desk. And then, 'Good afternoon, Miss Fender.'

'Are we going to have you with us again?' Mr Seely asked.

'If you can give me a room that overlooks the Square,' said Carl.

'I think we can, I think we can—yes, there we are.' Mr Seely slid the key onto the counter. 'I hope you'll be comfortable,' he said, beckoning the bell boy with a backward shake of his head. 'Room 810,' he said. 'Take Mr Bridges' things up.'

They walked behind the boy, their steps making no sound on the carpet. It is like a dream, thought Kristin, everything feels new. It might be a hotel in a strange city; familiarity is gone. She could say nothing.

But Carl chatted to the bell boy. 'Were you here earlier in the summer?' he asked.

'No, sir. I'm new.'

'I didn't remember your face,' said Carl.

Kristin hardly heard. Carl, Carl, Carl, she thought. Carl's wife. Mrs Bridges. Kristin Bridges.

And Carl thought between the chatter, her green eyes, the satin of her mouth, the bird in her throat; and his hand tightened on the canvases.

Along the corridor, dark and heavily carpeted; the clatter of the key in the lock, loud in the quietness; the sudden burst of white light as the door swung open.

The bell boy put the suitcases on the stands, looked about him to make sure everything was in order. 'Will that be all, sir?'

'Yes, I think so, thank you.' Kristin watched Carl's brown hand move against the pale city flesh of the boy's as he tipped him. She watched the boy turn and go to the door and she moved toward Carl, unable to stay away a minute longer, as though she had been separated for years.

Oh, sweet, sweet, this moment as he held her, this poignant flight, this upsurging miracle of loving.

'I hate this,' said Carl, 'kissing you in a hotel bedroom. There's something sordid about it.'

'Oh, no!' Kristin exclaimed. 'There's nothing sordid in loving. Already the room is beautiful.' She closed her eyes, swaying a little before him.

'You have made it so,' he said, looking only at her, at the pale star of Bethlehem on its slim green stem. And he drew her to him again, feeling the pulse in her white throat under his lips, tracing the long ivory column of her neck.

She sighed. 'I am complete only when I am with you. Only in these minutes alone with you do I know myself to be three dimensional. Carl,' she said, 'to be loved is to know rebirth.'

'If that's the case you'll be born again and again. I'll never stop loving you, Kristin.'

She pulled away then, her fingers on his collar, her eyes serious. 'Don't say that, Carl. Don't make promises. Love me now as I love you, don't think of the future.'

'But if it's true, wise one?'

'Truth is a changing thing. We only know the truth of the moment. Love me at this moment completely.' She moved away. 'Your bed,' she said, sitting on it. 'Oh, my darling, if this moment could be forever.'

'What a funny wife I've chosen,' he said. 'And now, what sort of a ring do you want?'

She looked at him suddenly then, in surprise. 'I hadn't thought,' she said.

'Try to think now. They probably won't have what you want. We'll have to order it.'

'I think a moonstone,' she said. 'Something pale and cool.'

He had started to unpack. His brushes and comb were on the dressing-table and his dressing-gown on the chair.

'Not diamonds?' he said.

'No, not diamonds. They flash. I hate things that flash. I like to look and look at things and feel no splinters in my eyes.' She ran her hand over the counterpane as she spoke.

He leaned over her then, laughing. The square line of his shoulder jutted against the light. She smiled up at him, slipped her hands under his coat to know the strong line of his back beneath his shirt.

'Carl,' she began, but he covered her words and she sank back under the eagerness of his lips, hungry as he from the long time they had been parted. But in the back of her brain a bell tolled out:

> She stole his mouth—her own was fair—
> She stole his words, his songs, his prayer;
> His kisses too, since they were there.

And a small voice answered the tolling, 'How can I steal what I am returning? It isn't true.'

'We must go,' she said, 'or we'll be late for mother.' She got up and stood before the mirror, running Carl's comb through her hair. And he stood behind her watching her movements in the glass, watching her fill in the small patch of mouth with vivid lipstick and smooth her hair to the texture of gold satin.

'Sweet,' he kissed the top of her head and she leaned against him, their eyes meeting in the mirror. 'When can we be married?' he asked.

'Oh, soon,' she said. 'It must be soon.'

'Come then and we'll look for that ring.'

She picked up her hat and walked out into the dark, silent corridor and he, shutting the door on the strange room already grown familiar, said, 'And they celebrated their engagement with a tea party at Mrs Lothrop's! Kristin, how we'll laugh about it later—"Well, Mr Bridges, how nice to see you again and you've brought little Kristin with you."'

'"Yes, Mrs Lothrop, little Kristin *would* come along."'

'"Well, how sweet; how pleased we are you returned to us."'

Their laughter echoed in the corridor, making the hotel sound inhabited, gay, in spite of the darkness. But in the jeweller's their gaiety was subterranean. Kristin held her laughter in check as she heard Carl telling the shop girl confidentially that he was wanting to buy a ring for his sister as a birthday present; and she listened with grave eyes when the assistant suggested that perhaps her birthstone would make a nice gift.

'No,' said Carl, turning to Kristin. 'Hasn't Mary always said she wanted a moonstone?'

And Kristin heard herself replying, 'That's what she always told me. I remember her saying the last time that I saw her—moonstones, moonstones—over and over.'

'We've not a very large choice in that particular stone,' the girl continued, 'but I'll show you what we have.' She bent and scooped out a tray from the case, staying out of sight just long enough for them to turn to each other with ghost laughter on their faces.

'There,' said Carl, picking one ring from the tray—a large moonstone set with small diamonds in a thin white-gold band. 'Do you think Mary would like that one?'

'I don't see how she could help it,' Kristin said, knowing that of all rings, she could like no other better.

'I do so want to get her something she'll really like.'

'If she doesn't,' Kristin said, 'she's not the Mary I thought she was.'

'That decides it,' said Carl to the shop girl.

'You don't know her ring size?' the girl asked practically.

Carl showed mock annoyance. 'I am a fool,' he said. 'Now what can I do?'

'She could always have it made to fit, of course,' said the girl, but Kristin rushed into the breach just in time.

'I think her hands are about the same size as mine. We could wear each other's gloves anyway, if that's anything to go by.' And she stretched out her right hand and slipped the ring onto her fourth finger. 'I'm certain it'll fit,' she said, 'quite certain.'

'So that is that,' said Carl as they left, 'easy as can be. Do you really like it, darling?'

'Carl, I love it! But love it!'

In the car he opened the box. 'Oh,' sighed Kristin, seeing it again, 'let me hold it, Carl.' It was like a soap bubble in her hand. 'It is beautiful, beautiful!'

'Try it on,' he said, pushing it onto her engagement finger.

She sat staring at it, turning her hand right and left. 'I wish I didn't have to take it off,' she said. He bent, kissed the palm of her hand. 'After tonight, after the formalities are over you need never take it off again.'

'After tonight!' She put it back in the box and started the car. 'Are we late?' she asked.

'We'll just make it.'

Mrs Fender was waiting for them on the steps. And Carl thought, as he opened the car door, always she is on the steps; my mind holds a myriad images of Mrs Fender standing just here, welcoming us, waving us off.

'How punctual you are,' she said, 'and I'm ready. Kristin, your hat?'

'It's here,' said Kristin.

'Well, put it on, darling.'

Carl held the door for Mrs Fender. 'No, no,' she said. 'I'll sit in the back. You two sit in the front.' She got in; there was no time for persuasion, already she was settled.

The drive over amused Kristin. She couldn't help thinking how, two months ago, she had driven this route exactly, but driven it with a heart filled with fear and discomfort. And now, two months later, she was driving it again, this time with a heart almost too heavy with happiness. Where before there had been insecurity, now there was security.

Carl talked over the seat to Mrs Fender and Kristin heard him only partly, heard his voice which she loved but failed to hear the words he was speaking. And as he talked, Carl thought, I can see Kristin in the mother. Kristin is what the mother might have been and has sacrificed for propriety and conventionality—sacrificed it to such an extent that she refuses to recognize herself in Kristin—refuses to acknowledge her old basic self.

The lawns are less green this time, Kristin thought as she brought the car to a stop, and the flowers in the border have changed. The air of festival has gone. It is nicer this way. The sweet tang of surprise will not be here today, but sweeter than surprise will be the awareness of a familiar Carl, the Carl I know, the Carl I'm engaged to.

As they walked up the path Mrs Fender lingered over the dahlias that flanked it. 'Ours are so poor this year,' she said. 'And these—look at them. Beauties!' But Kristin was barely conscious of anything but Carl. Even tea with Mrs Lothrop was important, with Carl there.

'Sarah, dear!' said Mrs Fender as Mrs Lothrop came forward to greet them, the spider again in her parlour. But Sarah wasted no time on Mrs Fender, rushing instead into a profusion of greetings for Carl, her fly.

'Ah, Mr Bridges, how charming to see you again. I quite thought you had gone out of my life for good. Ah! Ah!' She sidled around him, fluttered and exclaimed. Kristin was laughing, remembering Carl's conversation in the hotel. 'And Kristin,' said Mrs Lothrop, hardly glancing at her; realizing Kristin's amusement as she turned away and turning back to say, 'Is there a joke, Kristin?' But she didn't wait for a reply. Instead she went on, 'I have invited a few of your old friends, Mr Bridges; just a few. They're so anxious to see you. Of course at this time of day it's almost impossible to get men, but I knew you wouldn't mind. You don't, do you? Now let me see—that's right, Grace, help yourself to a cigarette and get Kristin to pass them to Mr Bridges for me.'

'Let me,' said Carl, anxious to get away from the tirade of words and thinking he had spoken the truth in the hotel when he had said, 'We'll laugh about it afterwards.' It would obviously be much funnier in retrospect.

He lit a cigarette for Kristin. Her hand trembled and his did too, a little, both of them aware so fully of each other's nearness, a nearness unbridgeable. She knew he was amused because his eyes were golden. To touch his fingers was to touch dry ice.

The doorbell rang. Mrs Lothrop was up, fluttering to the hall. 'Ah, ah,' she said, 'I expect that's dear Katie Steen.' And over her shoulder, 'She admires you *so* much, Mr Bridges. I know you'll be nice to her, she's such a *sweet* girl.' And Carl, sitting in a sudden silence, thought, today I can be nice to anyone.

Mrs Fender seemed far away. She watched the smoke of her cigarette float upwards in the still air of the room. Carl and Kristin were unspeaking, as if by mutual consent, hating to interrupt the stream of her thought. But the room shifted to a swift attention, an alertness that provoked a quality of geometrical precision as Katie Steen's excited, confidential voice came like a snake into the room.

'D'you know, you'll never guess, but Tiny phoned just before I came out and said that she was buying a wedding present this afternoon and who should she run into but Mr Bridges and Kristin—Kristin of all people!—and they were at the ring counter.'

'Sh!' said Mrs Lothrop; whispering followed.

Mrs Fender turned her head with a jerk; Kristin, feeling the blood rising to her face, reached for an ashtray behind her. Carl crossed his legs very carefully and thought, damn gossiping women. Damn them! They'd have known tomorrow, surely they need not have interfered with our secret of today.

'Carl,' Mrs Fender's voice was small. He looked at her, trying to read the expression on her face. 'Carl?' her voice rose, a young bird trying to fly. She said no more. It was a question and he didn't know how to answer it. Mrs Lothrop ushered Katie Steen into the room. The question was suspended.

'You remember Katie Steen, Mr Bridges?'

'Of course,' said Carl. 'How do you do?' She held out her hand to him.

'How very nice to see you again,' she said. 'I do so hope you'll stay longer this time than you did last. Are you down on business?'

'A painter is always on business,' Carl said. 'That's both one of the joys and one of the drawbacks of my profession.'

'Ah, Mr Bridges,' Katie Steen answered, 'how elusive your replies are.'

'Simply because, in a sense, my job is elusive too.' He smiled.

Kristin listened to him and was glad Katie wasn't questioning her. At this moment, she thought, I am defenceless; my joy is as exposed as a wound. But Carl would manage. He would be polite and charming and evasive and Katie would soon fall under the spell of his charm and forget.

More people arrived. The room grew thick with them. They built a wall between herself and her mother, herself and Mrs Lothrop, herself and the curious eyes. If she sat still no one would bother her. Carl, poor Carl, would take the brunt of the questioning faces. He was passed round the room, from one pair of hands to another, from one woman to another; the only shuttlecock among hundreds of bats. She saw him again as she had at the cocktail party—his shoulder up-pointing, the tenseness of his whole body concentrated in that shoulder—the sailboat in the harbour of tugs, holding stillness in his eyes.

And Carl, talking, moving his lips to repartee, remembered the cocktail party, remembered as he caught a glimpse of Kristin how she was the only person free from distortion, the only person complete within the confines of her own form. He could bear it all—the words, the flattery, the brittleness of women's voices and conversation, when he looked at Kristin. Kristin, whom soon he would take away from this world to his own world; the world of Birchlands, of Dick, of solid people following a pattern built securely upon the rock of their own integrity.

When people grouped together beyond the hearing of Carl and Kristin they talked quietly, excitedly, and their eyes darted towards Kristin or Carl. She could feel the current of excitement that ran through the room—a forked, electric current unlike the steady stream of her own happiness. Soon, she thought, soon, we shall be able to leave. Her mother came towards her. She looked tired, older than usual.

'Have you asked Carl back to dinner?' she looked at Kristin, but there was a curtain across her eyes.

'No,' said Kristin, 'I haven't.'

'I think you'd better,' she said.

Kristin put down her cup and took a cigarette. She stared long at the end of it. What does mother know, she thought, and what does she think? There is no happiness in this secret. I don't like it. I should like to stand up now and tell all these whispering women that I am going to marry Carl. All my life I've kept secrets but these women have made this one seem wrong. She wanted to go to Carl and feel his arm strong about her and together with him walk out of the house and down the path to the car. If he would only come to her now! But she couldn't even see him, he was hidden by women, women's voices covered his deep voice. She got up then and crossed to her mother. I must tell her, she thought, out of fairness I must tell her. All these people are certain of the truth of our engagement. Mother, alone, is not sure.

Forcing her way through the people she realized that she felt a sudden affection for her mother, a feeling she never remembered before. She went to her, took her arm instinctively but awkwardly; gradually she turned her away from the conversation she was involved in.

'Mother,' she said, speaking close into her ear, 'it's true. I can't have you not knowing when all these people have discovered it. We were going to tell you tonight.'

Mrs Fender gave no indication that she had heard; her face kept the same expression but the curtain was drawn back. She pressed her daughter's hand. 'Thank you, darling,' she said, 'I'll say nothing.'

Kristin felt better. The party seemed almost normal now. Nothing that these old friends of Carl's could say mattered.

'Perhaps we can escape,' said Mrs Fender. 'You collect Carl.'

Walking through the room, dodging elbows and cups, she felt indifferent to the atmosphere. She was walking to Carl; surely, happily, she was walking through chaos to peace. He was in the thick of a small circle; Katie Steen was flapping her long eyelashes and looking up at him. 'Oh, Mr Bridges, you're so modest. Now if I were an artist I'm certain I'd make the most fantastic demands on everyone.' She ended her words with a streamer of laughter.

'I shouldn't,' said a woman Kristin didn't know, who was obviously taking advantage of this opportunity to appear spiritual. 'I should shut myself up all alone and let my divine talent pour through me uninterrupted by the demands of society and responsibility.'

'And for stimulation?' Carl queried.

'Ah, stimulation!' the woman breathed. 'Stimulation would come from within. Stimulation would issue from the fount of my talent.'

It was then Carl saw Kristin. He raised his eyebrows.

'Mother's thinking of leaving,' she said.

He turned to the women about him. 'I'm afraid I must go,' he said.

A protest went up:

'Oh, Mr Bridges!'

'Why don't you stay and I'll drive you home?'

'Such a pity to cut short this delightful conversation.'

'Surely you could stay a little longer.'

Carl smiled at them all. 'It's awfully good of you, but I'm afraid I must go.'

The spiritual woman came forward. 'We must meet again,' she said. 'Perhaps dinner some night. You know I've always felt that I have a talent and it only needs drawing out. Colour means so much to me. I'm fascinated by colour, aren't you?'

Poor Carl, thought Kristin, what a lot of talk. How silly women are! He smiled away from them, tossing them phrases as he went, little empty phrases especially designed for the occasion.

'Need we ever do this again?' he asked Kristin as they fought their way through to Mrs Lothrop.

'Never!' said Kristin, so violently that he was surprised.

'I am jealous,' Mrs Lothrop announced when, at last, they reached her. 'You've hardly spoken to me all afternoon. I had so hoped that we could have a nice talk.'

He was suddenly deflated; he could think of no answer. He had used up his supply of pretty speeches. 'I'm sorry,' he said, 'but it's been a lovely party and you were far too kind to go to all this trouble.'

She held his hand. 'Mr Bridges, Mr Bridges; why didn't you reserve just a few minutes for your hostess?'

He knew no way out. Kristin, watching, felt, I must help him, somehow I must set him free. She moved forward, stretching out her hand. 'I'm sorry, Mrs Lothrop, but we really must go. Mother's waiting for us.' She almost forced her hand between the two locked ones. 'Good-bye,' she said, 'and thank you so much.'

'I knew no escape,' he said, 'every exit seemed blocked.'

They were free now. Mrs Fender had joined them and they were in the hall. It was quiet by contrast and cool.

'Really, Sarah might have warned us,' Mrs Fender remarked as she went down the steps. 'I wasn't prepared for such a mob.' But Carl and Kristin had no words to speak; they were bursting with the spate of other people's words which must form in them, sink and fall away before they could find their own vocabularies again.

'Did Kristin remember to ask you to dinner, Carl? because we want you to come.' Mrs Fender spoke from the back seat; her voice sounded smoother than it had in the house; ironed out like a long sheet of ribbon.

'Thank you,' said Carl. 'I'd love to.'

'You can come right back with us now,' she said, 'there's no need to change.'

And then Kristin remembered the ring. How could she have forgotten for so long the small, square box in Carl's pocket? The symbol of their love. She wanted to see it again, feel it firm between her fingers; she wanted to know that it had not evaporated as it looked as though it so easily might. That so small and frail a thing could be subjected to that noise and heat and still remain whole astonished her. But if symbol it is, she thought, it is intact still. Heat and noise can never destroy the texture of our love ... it will be silence and the ice of fear. Her fingers tightened on the wheel as she thought—silence and the ice of fear. Surely, surely—she fought against the thought, tried to build a door in her mind to shut against her self-knowledge. But like ivy, like morning glory tendrils the knowledge twined up and over the door, forced their way through the slits of its faulty structure until the door was shut behind the thought; the thought locked into her consciousness.

'Kristin, dear,' her mother called, 'you must be more careful. You drove right through a stop light.'

The sinuous green growth was cut down. The moonstone, pale and beautiful, filled the cavern of her skull, shone in her head. Carl watching her, thought, she has gone through a pain and come through to beauty. Peace of mind shines like a jewel in her forehead.

Traffic was thick. They crawled slowly through the old streets with their close-packed houses but as they climbed the hill across the bridge and drove round past the convent it was possible to accelerate, possible to breathe. Turning at last into their own drive a restraint seemed to fall on them all, so that, even when the car had stopped, they sat as they were for a few minutes before they opened the doors and faced the new scene. Mrs Fender moved first. 'I must go in and speak to Mary about dinner.' Carl opened the door for her. And then Kristin moved with a sudden concentration of movement, frightened of the thick foliage of her fear growing up again.

She stretched out on a veranda chair and held out her hand for Carl's, gazing at him long and steadily as he took it, feeling love leap through her like a white panther and curl up, live but momentarily stilled, at her side.

'Carl, I told Mother. I had to. All those people at the tea whispering and pointing. Mother looked dazed and uncertain. It was awful for her.'

He didn't answer. She knew and yet she had said nothing. Uncertainty touched him, like a finger on his heart. Parental disapproval; he had not allowed for that.

'Are you annoyed?'

'No, darling. It's just—I was wondering what she thought.'

'Do you mind?'

'In the final instance, no. But for the moment, yes.'

'I think she was pleased, Carl. How could she be anything else?'

'And then there's your father. You know I've never approached a father before about such a matter.' He passed her a cigarette. She looked at him through the smoke, opening her eyes very wide. And then he told her about Denise and Marmo and 'The Egg'—sketched them into his life with wide strong strokes.

She listened like a small girl, seeing Paris, London, New York for the first time; seeing Denise, Marmo, 'The Egg,' less vividly, unable to picture women so different from those she had known; seeing them only as the smile on Carl's face, the curl of his lips, the movement of his hands. Seeing them as part of him.

His story only ended when Mrs Fender joined them, stood uncertainly beside them and said, 'As Ralph's not home yet, I wonder if you'd mix us a drink, Carl? I'll show you where the things are.' He got up then and Kristin sat still, living over Paris, London, New York; feeling that a strong net of knowledge had formed about her, about her and Carl, holding them together. Soon, soon, she thought, we will know each other so well that our love, a wiry little plant, will grow tall. For, she thought, love thrives on knowledge—my knowledge of Carl, his knowledge of me. As long as we are still discovering each other the growth is slow.

She moved. The white panther at her side rose from his sleep and followed her into the house and upstairs, waiting beside her as she tidied herself for dinner. *The Boy* was in her room, Carl's boy. She had forgotten him in the excitement, the multiplicity of the day. Her mother must have brought him up for her. He looked strong and virile and masculine against the pale femininity of her bedroom. Here we have it, she said to herself, the sun and the moon together, and she looked from the painting and felt secure. Carl will predominate, she thought, as he does here; but as she thought the apple-green curtain billowed out with a sudden gust of wind, billowed out and over the picture and left the room untouched, free of Carl. Ah, she said, forcing the curtain back and seeing the painting dark as old brick against plaster, ah Carl, I love you so. The white panther stirred at her feet. She dipped her fingers into the cold cream, made up her face and then stood, hands crossed over her breasts, leaning a little to one side, saying, 'Ah, ah,' over and over.

'Kristin!' It was Carl's voice in the upstairs hall. 'Kristin, the cocktails are ready.' Oh! she went to the door. He was standing there. The white panther leaped. 'Sweet, sweet, sweet!' he said. He kissed her lightly and held her to him. 'I must wash up,' he said, 'I'll see you in a minute.'

She walked down the stairs and into the living room. 'Daddy not home yet?' she asked.

Her mother ignored the question. 'Kristin,' she said, 'are you happy?'

'Terribly!'

Her mother was holding her elbows and looking at her with no smile in her eyes. 'You love him?'

'Oh, yes!' Her mother's grip relaxed.

'You are very lucky, Kristin. Your Carl is a darling.'

'Oh, Mother, you're glad, then?'

'More glad than you'll ever know. I've not been so happy in years.'

'Don't tell Daddy, will you,' Kristin pleaded, 'Not until Carl has spoken to him.'

Her mother went back to the sofa. 'No, darling,' she said. 'This is the very first secret you've ever trusted me with and I won't let you down.' She laughed then. Carl came into the room. 'To happiness,' she said, lifting her glass, and then, 'Carl's made Planters' Punches, darling, see if you like them.'

It is nice sitting here, thought Carl, jutting into the smooth circumference of family life again, feeling a part of the old formal pattern of the family. For Mrs Fender has accepted me, he thought, and Kristin, sipping her drink, with a faint line of nutmeg on her top lip, watches me over the rim of her glass as I watch her.

'Mother,' said Kristin, 'Carl knows you know.' She lifted her glass again to hide as much of herself as she could.

Mrs Fender's face lit to a city of lights. She patted the seat beside her, looking at Carl, and he went to her. 'I feel young,' she said. 'A grown-up daughter makes me feel like a child instead of an old woman. But Carl, I'm terribly happy—truly.' She took his hand. 'I could never have wished anything more for Kristin, or for myself,' she added. 'Of course,' she said, 'it's rather sudden. You've not known each other very long.'

I've known him all my life, thought Kristin. Carl is bound up in the knowledge of the rocks, in the knowledge of stillness.

'Long enough to be sure,' Carl said.

The room was out of focus with restrained excitement. They felt strange to each other, these three. Carl faced his wife and mother-in-law; Kristin her husband and mother; Mrs Fender her daughter and son-in-law. It was a new arrangement—an arrangement the heart had accepted but one which still knocked on the surface of the mind; and the mind, prompted by the heart said, 'Come in, open the door and walk in,' but the door was barred. To speak with the heart, thought Carl, and disregard the shyness of the mind is something we have not been trained to do, something which we have always been led to believe verges on the maudlin; something we have been brought up to consider not done, slightly indecent. And yet, and yet, he thought, what can we speak of at such a time? What can we say with the white-livered mind, the anaemic brain, that the full-blooded heart will tolerate?

'You think Daddy will approve?' asked Kristin breaking the long disordered silence.

'I know he will. He'll be as thrilled as I am.'

But it wasn't as easy as that, thought Carl later. After dinner, closeted with Mr Fender, Kristin and her mother in the living room, Carl sat in the utmost discomfort, waiting a chance to broach the subject. Mr Fender, unaware of what was to come, talked on and on. And Carl, at last, in desperation, interrupted him—driving through the seaweed of his words and saying loudly, briefly, 'I want to marry Kristin, sir.'

Mr Fender continued with his story and then suddenly pulled himself up. 'What's that?' he said astonished, hearing the words after they were spoken. Carl repeated it, this time more graciously. Whatever reaction I had expected it was certainly not this, Carl thought, as Mr Fender jolted forward in his chair, mouth open, eyes startled. Carl felt ill at ease, but Mr Fender collected himself, stopped long enough to light a cigarette slowly and take one or two puffs before he spoke. When words came Mr Fender was transformed. He was the business man. Carl could see him sitting behind his desk, highly efficient, quick as a trap.

'You want to marry Kristin,' he said.

'Yes,' Carl answered.

'Why do you want to marry her?'

'I am in love with her, sir.'

Mr Fender took another puff, blew the smoke out in a thin swift stream. 'No doubt you've been in love before?'

'Yes,' said Carl, 'I have.'

'Then what makes you think that this time you want to get married?'

'Because,' said Carl, watching Mr Fender's demanding eyes, 'this time I'm in love with the sort of girl I'd like to have for a wife and because I'm in the position to give her the sort of life she's been used to. And,' he added, thinking of the years Kristin had lived remote from human contacts, 'I think I could make her happy.'

'How much have you a year?'

Mr Fender was not making it easy but Carl began an account of his finances. 'To begin with, sir, I make with my painting alone enough to keep us comfortably. I am lucky in that; my work is popular. And quite apart from my own earning capacities I have a private income. My parents are dead. They left me ...' He continued, explaining in detail his financial situation. Mr Fender's face relaxed a little, Carl thought, but he spoke brusquely still.

'There is Kristin,' Mr Fender said. And Carl saw her—pale, slim, generous—saw her when he had proposed; saw her at the station, her face alight, her eyes unfolding, her bright satin mouth; and he said, 'I have spoken to her, sir. She wants to marry me.'

'That is as it may be,' said her father. 'She may think she does, but had you ever stopped to consider that Kristin is barely eighteen? She has never in her life before had a man take any interest in her whatsoever. No doubt she is flattered by your attentions, she is attracted by your glamour. How is she to know, with no experience to help her, if she is in love?'

Carl felt exasperated. 'How is anyone to know, for certain, sir, however much experience they have had before?'

'Then you are not certain?' Mr Fender shot the words out.

'I am certain enough to know that living apart from her is not worth the food I eat.' He wanted to say, can't you remember being young, can't you remember that to be in love is like exposing your cuts to salt water? Can't you try to make this easier for us all? And then he thought: he doesn't approve of me; in his eyes I'm not suitable. And the words 'Kristin is barely eighteen' made him feel helpless. If Mr Fender chose he could refuse to allow Kristin to marry. Carl lit a cigarette himself. He was silent during the first puffs too; he used Mr Fender's tactics.

He said, 'I am thirty-seven. I am old enough to know my own mind. Kristin needs an older man, she is wise beyond her years. As to my family—my father was a well-known Montreal lawyer—you may have heard of him—R. C. Bridges.' He thought he detected a flicker of recognition in Mr Fender's face but he kept on. 'He was raised to the Bench and he died four years ago, leaving me a house in the Laurentians. You needn't fear, sir, that I'll take her to a life of bohemianism. I'm hardworking. I paint, I don't talk about painting. But most important of all, I love Kristin and she loves me.' He stopped. Mr Fender's face was inscrutable. There is nothing more I can say, Carl thought, I have no trumps left.

Mr Fender crossed his legs carefully, pushed his coffee cup away from him and said, 'That is all very well, all very well, but you forget Kristin.'

Forget Kristin! thought Carl, forget her, when she is my only thought; when I would go through this for no one in the world but Kristin. He wanted to cry out, wanted to sweep the dishes from the table in a large desperate gesture. But he sat silent and concentrated movement to the precise flicking of his ash in the saucer of his coffee cup. He heard Mr Fender's voice continue, building obstacles, forming hazards.

'You forget that Kristin has never been trained to do anything. She has no more idea how to run a house than to fly. She can't cook or mend or manage money. And on top of all that, she's queer. In no way is she a normal child. I believe I've mentioned this to you before—she has comatose periods.'

'I know what you mean, sir, but it makes no difference. I still want to marry Kristin.' Whatever you say will be of no use. His mind set to a letterpress: I still want to marry Kristin.

Mr Fender looked at him through half-shut eyes. 'Nothing I say will change you?'

'Nothing, sir.'

'And Kristin? You say she wants to marry you?'

'Yes, sir.'

'You've not known each other very long.'

Does he not know, thought Carl, that you recognize the qualities you love in a person immediately and that the length of time you know them only verifies those qualities, shows them up as true?

'I know, sir,' he shaped his lips to understatement, 'but we've seen a great deal of each other and I promise you we know each other well for we've seen each other alone and so know one another better than we should had we been meeting at parties for months.'

Carl felt that he was losing ground with every word. Somehow, he thought, I must win him over. But how, and how long will it take? How can you convince a man of the insistence of love when he has long since forgotten the sound of its clamouring voice in the night? What a topsy-turvy social system that demands that the young man must approach the middle-aged on a matter they no longer know of themselves. He looked up from his thoughts to find Mr Fender smiling. He had the smile on his face that proclaims a successful business deal, well handled, well carried off, to his advantage.

'Well, Carl,' he said, passing him his cigarette case, 'the opponents always shake hands after a battle, don't they? And the loser takes his defeat with good grace.' His smile was broad and Carl, watching him, listening to his words, felt the sickness of failure gnaw at him.

'And the winner, sir,' he couldn't help saying, for fury rose in him like a long, high tide, 'takes success with modesty.'

'That,' said Mr Fender, 'is for the winner to decide.'

Carl wanted to punch him, wanted to stand up and show him who was the better man, which of them was most fit to look after Kristin.

'I think,' Mr Fender went on, 'if I were the winner it would be hard for me to take this success modestly. If I had had to go through this to marry Grace I doubt if we should ever have been married.'

'I thought,' Carl began, but Mr Fender waved him quiet. 'However,' he said, 'this is a strange battle, for there is no loser, is there? It's the old story—I don't lose a daughter, I gain a son.' He laughed immoderately at that and thumped Carl on the back. Carl laughed too, laughed because his heart was light, laughed with surprise, laughed with delight, laughed, laughed until his throat ached.

Kristin, hearing the laughter, sighed. 'Mother,' she said, 'I think it must be all right. Listen.' And then, 'Oh, mother, I was so frightened, they've been so long.' She dropped onto the sofa then. 'How awful this part of marriage is,' she said, 'and how much you have to love a person to bear going through it.' She found it easier to talk to her mother than she ever had and she remembered how the first time she met Carl she had felt that he linked her with humanity. Now he had managed to link her with her own family. Carl, Carl, she thought, how much you have given me. Oh, my darling, oh, my very dear!

'I'll take your father out,' her mother said. 'You and Carl will want to be alone.'

'Thank you, Mummy.'

'Kristin, I'm so happy, darling.' She slipped her arms around her and held her close. 'My funny little daughter,' she said, 'to be Carl's wife.'

'You do like him, don't you?' She knew but she wanted to hear it again. It was important beyond importance to hear her mother say, 'I think he is perfectly sweet.' And it was comforting to sit there with her mother, knowing that for this minute at least, they had met on a common ground; that she had not been alone in the long agony since dinner and was not alone now, in this delirious happiness.

They opened the door then, Carl and her father, laughter still ringing in their voices.

'We must celebrate,' said her father, 'Celebrate the happy occasion.' He carried a decanter and glasses. The talk flew about her head; her father kissed her; everyone kissed everyone else—she and Carl didn't kiss; the room seemed to hold many more people than it actually did. Glasses were raised: 'To Carl and Kristin. Carl and Kristin.' She smiled, she laughed, she talked, she lifted her glass to her lips. Noise was loud about her, but Carl, like the thin, clear note of a wood-wind, sounded close to her; it was all she heard.

'When do you plan to be married?'

'Soon, soon.'

'But the arrangements, the invitations, the trousseau?'

'Soon, soon.'

'And your linen and china and silver?'

'And fittings and parties and showers?'

'Soon, soon, soon.'

The clatter of glasses; voices falling to a diminuendo, rising again, falling; smoke in the room and a space in Kristin's head where the wood-wind played and she added her own accompaniment—soon, soon, soon, soon. And then silence—silence stretching out like a sea about her, her glass empty and Carl saying, 'Darling, they have gone, we are alone.' Alone and close to Carl and engaged. 'Was it very awful?' she said. 'Was Daddy difficult?'

'Very cautious,' he said. 'I didn't enjoy it very much.'

'Poor darling, You were in there so long. I didn't think I could bear it. I was so sure he was finding a hundred and one objections.'

'He was. I wish you could have seen us. But it's over now and, oh my darling, it won't be long before you're my wife.' He felt in his pocket for the ring and Kristin waited for the sight of it again, waited to have him put it on her finger, waited solemnly upon the ritual, the white panther rampant at her side.

Kristin wakened. He is here, she thought, for a week now he has been here, under this roof. She held up her hand and looked at the moonstone on her finger. For a week he has been here and we have been like mad things, going to parties and coming back. We have seen each other only in little intervals, intervals short and sweet as cointreau. But this morning, she thought, we have claimed for ourselves. And the thought was like waking again. She got out of bed, she got dressed; she could lie there no longer when Carl, perhaps now, was up at breakfast, listening for her coming. 'The day is lovely,' she said aloud, pausing a moment at the window, 'So we must get away early and have every possible moment together.'

The morning is sweet as hay, she thought, as she went downstairs, sweet as hay. She hummed a little, a tune that came out of the air and settled on her lips. By the time she had reached the bottom step the words joined the tune—'Upon the shore I fou-ound a shell, I he-eld it to-oo my ear.' And then the words went off into the air again and she was at the dining room door and Carl was there alone.

'Was that you singing?'

'Yes.'

'I've never heard you sing before.'

'I don't very often but sometimes songs just—come.'

'You look sweet, darling.'

She pushed him back into his chair. 'I'm excited—a whole morning with you and no one to say, "Ah, Mr Bridges," and tear you away from me.' She poured herself coffee. 'Where is the family?'

'Your father has gone to work and your mother went with him—had an early appointment with the hairdresser.'

'Oh.' The sunlight fell in a shaft across the table, lighting one side of Carl's face. She buttered a piece of toast.

'Where shall we go?' he said.

Ah, what were places, what did it matter? 'Anywhere, anywhere,' she said. Like foam, she felt, like cow parsley blowing in a field; Carl the wave behind the foam, the wind in the meadows. He passed his cup for more coffee, his brown hands moving like wings. For a moment their minds united; they saw the foam and the wave, the cow parsley and the wind, the sun and the shade, brown wings flying against the sky, the breakfast table and then their own breakfast table; they saw the trees change, the leaves fall like gold wafers thick about them, the snow gather in the grey sky and drive to earth, bright as fireflies; they saw, with one mind, their lives revolve like a merry-go-round, the dark horse, the white horse, following on each other to the sound of a thin tune—-a wood-wind and a humming voice. They saw—but Carl thought, I have seen a vision—and saw nothing more. And Kristin thought—I have seen a lie—and the shutter fell. They looked at each other then and Carl smiled and noticed the concentration of Kristin's mouth; the patch of red satin was a ruby.

'Let's finish our coffee on the veranda.' They took their cups into the sun and sat together, the smoke from their cigarettes forming similar patterns on the air, joining and disappearing.

'I wish,' said Kristin, 'we could be married without all this fuss. I wish,' she said, 'there need be no parties, no bridesmaids, no invitations, no wedding—just marriage.'

'I wish it too.' I hate, he thought, this long period crammed with unimportance that holds us from each other. But, he thought, it's worse for Kristin than for me and after all, and after all … but the thought faded, went up with the smoke as he looked at Kristin.

'Let us go,' she said. 'Carl, let's escape from telephone and doorbell. Let us waste no more minutes here, lovely though it is.' She got up; when he turned she was gone.

They drove to the country. He had hired a car again as he had earlier in the summer. As soon as he had checked out of the hotel he had made arrangements for it. For, he had thought, if we are dependent on the Fenders we shall never be alone.

Kristin was gay, the child Kristin today, exclaiming, delighting in everything; holding the world in her hands for her joy.

Stopping at last by the river where the water fell deep away from the bank and the trees hung over the river and stared at their own reflections she gave a long anguished sigh. 'Carl, Carl,' she said, 'we shall never be happier than this, never.' She clung to him then with a desperate finality, so that happiness ebbed within him and he knew only the awful melancholy of love.

'But darling,' he tried to soothe her, 'we shall always be as happy.'

She covered her face. 'It is awful,' she said through her fingers, 'to have reached the peak, to be able only to stare at the stars from this perilous position or slip down; slowly, perhaps imperceptibly lose ground, fall away.'

'It's only that you're tired,' he said. 'This last week has worn you out.'

'No, no,' she said, 'it's not that—it can't touch me. There is a centre within me the rush of people cannot approach.' I am frightened, she thought. Even holding Carl close is not enough—even feeling the strength of him under my hands and knowing his love is not enough. She shuddered. For a long time he felt her against him, shivering and then she became still. He was relieved, but Kristin feeling the peace steal over her knew with a dreadful certainty the danger of this moment.

It's happening again, she thought. Carl, save yourself from this, run away from me, leave me. She felt the change come over her gradually—the change of texture—and she couldn't speak. Carl, Carl, she screamed out, but no sound came; she struggled but her body didn't move. Before it reaches my mind I must set him free; now that it is only my flesh, while I still have a chance, I must, must, must. But each moment it became more difficult, each moment the sensual pleasure of absorption coursed through her more strongly. I love him too much, she thought, too much, too much. He moved, he shifted her. It was like a shock striking her nerve ends, it was like sunlight after darkness striking her eyes. Now, she thought, now. She shaped her lips to speech, it took all her concentration.

'Carl,' she said, 'take me swimming.'

They were safe now; it was over. She drew a long breath and moved as in her sleep; the crisis was past. She looked at the water and shook her head.

'Kristin,' Carl's voice behind her made her turn. 'Kristin, did you feel anything queer happen then?' She didn't answer. What could she say to him, how explain? 'It was funny,' he said, 'almost as if I didn't exist.'

'What a silly husband I'm going to have!' She held up her face to him. Oh, if only she could tell him, if only she could share this old ecstasy that had turned to misery since she had met him. Instead she went for her bathing-suit. 'Look at the water,' she said.

But Carl, as he began to change, felt that somehow he had come through a queer experience. It was as if, he thought, as if I were a—he felt for the word in his head—a Zombie. Just body. As if my mind, my soul—he rejected the word as it formed—were sucked from me, the essence gone, the container alone, remaining; useless, empty. But, he thought, why should such a thing have happened? I've probably imagined it. And he dived into the smooth surface of the river and forgot.

Splashing together, laughing, Kristin's memory was washed clean like a slate in the rain. They raced; Carl with his strong overarm fighting to keep up with her minnow side-stroke. And when they arrived breathless on the small beach and flung themselves down, dripping, in the sun, they looked at each other with water-clear eyes, free from the shadow of doubt or dread. Kristin took off her cap and ran her fingers through her long hair. 'Like corn tassels,' said Carl, touching it, 'corn tassels damp in the early morning.'

Ah, to lie here beside Carl, to hear his voice, to hear him saying, 'We'll go to Birchlands for our honeymoon, unless there's anywhere you'd sooner go.'

'No, no,' said Kristin. 'To Birchlands where it is quiet and we can be together—like this, always.'

'You'll love it,' he said. 'The lake, the woods—it's a gorgeous place.'

They lay in the sun a long time. Carl talked. He told her of his early life, of his mother and father and sister. And Kristin, listening, pieced together the jigsaw of his life.

'My father was quiet and infinitely patient,' Carl said. 'He never told me to do anything or not to do anything but when I behaved badly he would call me into his den and we'd discuss it, just like a law suit. He would line up all the aspects of the offence and then he would say, pointing with a long forefinger at an old ink-stand, "There is the prisoner. I shall defend him, you will prove to me he is guilty." And so we would haggle—he putting forth marvellously lucid arguments why I was not wrong—I pitting all my intelligence to prove I was. No punishment ever followed. But I always left his den feeling wise and grown up and very responsible. He did the same with my sister too until he learned that these "cases" as he called them, upset her far too much. She would leave the room so cowed with the thought of her own wickedness that she turned with a sort of fanatical desperation to religion and sang hymns constantly and read nothing but the Bible. He was frightened that the small print would ruin her eyes and he didn't believe in burdening her with such an overwhelming sense of sin so he had to stop. But for me he applied the same tactics until I was more or less grown up. I think he always had a secret hope that I would follow in his footsteps; but at seventeen, when I left school, I knew I wanted to do nothing but paint. He took me into his den—we had moved by then and the den was a veritable study, large and booklined. The old ink-stand was still there.' Carl paused to light a cigarette.

Kristin opened her eyes and watched the trees blowing a little in their top branches. They seemed woven together, Carl's story and the movement of the leaves.

'My father sat for a minute and then pushed the ink-stand into the centre of his desk. "There," he said, pointing, "is the boy who wants to be an artist. The case is open." He began. He stated the joys of a life given over to art, the joys of creation. He was very generous. When it came my turn to speak I could hardly think of anything to say. I remember the light hitting the glass of the ink-stand and flying like splinters into my eyes. I said, "An artist may work for years and get nowhere." I said, "Popularity fluctuates. Even when an artist is accepted he may suddenly fall from favour." I said, "He must suffer more than a man should and then perhaps have to prostitute his art—turn commercial to keep alive." I don't remember if I said anything after that. It was like pricking my own toy balloon. I do remember wanting to cry and being disgusted with myself. And then my father said, "It means a lot to you, boy, doesn't it? Where do you want to study?" I knew then from the tone of his voice that he had agreed. Fortunately he lived long enough to see his faith in me part way justified.'

'And your mother?' Kristin wanted to know, wanted to know all about the family.

'Mother? I don't know how to describe her. She was someone who never seemed quite real to me and now that she's dead I find it hard to believe she ever lived. Not,' he said, 'because she was insignificant. She was more alive than any person I have ever known. She flashed. She moved like lightning. She laughed unexpectedly and the world seemed like a chandelier; she cried and all of life was misery. She was the vital core of the family and yet father was the skin, the binding whole that kept the family together. She died when I was in Paris. I didn't hear until a month afterwards, but during that month I felt incomplete. It was a wretched feeling—and quite apart from my actual life and work, for during that time I had my first picture accepted for exhibition. I should have been happy. Father sent my sister over to join me then. She was terribly upset. I was glad to have her near me; glad to have someone to talk to about Mother. And it was fun showing her Paris. But she was there so short a time. She met a chap—Henri Bateau—and married him. He was home from the States on holidays. As soon as it could be arranged—for she had to become a Roman Catholic—they were married. She lives in Boston now. If only she weren't having a child she'd come up for the wedding.' Carl stretched. 'What a lot of talk,' he said. 'Am I boring you?'

How could he ever bore her? No matter how small, how ordinary, the details of his life, she wanted to know. But they weren't small, they weren't ordinary. It was like having someone read aloud to her. Another family—a family as unlike hers as any could be and he spoke of boredom! What can I give him, she thought, to compare with what he's had? How can I make life a gay and a sad thing for him as his mother did, or a steady and just thing, as his father did? All I can do is love him as I've never loved before; not even, necessarily, she thought, as he's never been loved before. And she wanted to cry out at the bar of her own horizon and knock down the city limits, the signs that marked her boundaries. 'Do you think,' she said, for she wanted to know badly, badly, 'do you think they would have liked me?'

He caught her then, pulled her to him. 'Silly darling,' he said laughing, 'they'd have loved you even as I do. Through me they love you now.'

Ah, she thought, this is security, this is happiness, this is fulfilment, and she lay for a moment, complete in her love. He raised himself on his elbow and looked down at her. The pattern of the leaves dappled her face. 'Oh, darling,' he said, 'my own darling!' I hate, he thought, to leave her even for a week, as I have to, to get ready for the wedding. 'Look,' he cried, jumping up suddenly, 'I'm going to do a painting—of the river—this part of it where it's deep and the trees bend down to meet themselves. The light's perfect.'

He went to the car and collected his things. She watched him as he tacked paper onto a board, unscrewed the top of his paint jar and laid out his paints.

'I haven't done a water-colour for ages,' he said. 'I'm quite excited.'

Once again she was fascinated by the way his fingers moved cleanly, economically; brown and certain from paint to paper. This, she thought, will never weary me—to watch Carl at work. As long as I live I will find delight in watching his hands and the magic that lies under his touch. She saw him sketch in the bank and the huge bole of the tree, rising like a monument from the river's edge and then she saw colour grow on the paper, the trunk brown, but not brown, solid, twisted, holding up its green crown. And though he painted loosely, each leaf was there and the wind too. His brush moved to the palette; her mind moved with his hands—back and forth, back and forth, caught in the rhythm, carried by the rhythm, until thought dissolved in motion and swam like a fish in the current of a stream.

Carl mixed the colours for the water with an insensitive eye. For the second time this morning, he thought, I feel queer. I feel—invaded, he thought at last. Invaded. There is no other word. It is as if I have surrendered my being to an alien force and it has made me less. He looked at his painting and groaned. 'Something is wrong,' he said aloud, 'the invader has ruined it. It's a case of too many cooks, too many cooks. They are spoiling the broth.' He laughed then, a hysterical laugh. 'The broth,' he said, 'that's good. It's the river they're spoiling—the broth.' And then the sensation left him. He painted quickly, unconsciously. The invader marched in, stormed his defences, hoisted the invading flag, took possession smoothly and entirely. The city that was Carl knew foreign leadership; foreign colours waved from the ramparts; foreign primitive workmanship ousted the easy-running talent. Night fell on the city that had been Carl, dark and still—a silent abyss—but the fingers moved on relentlessly, unwittingly.

Kristin stretched. He turned to her and her eyes were ugly with terror.

'Kristin! What is it?' Her face was whittled with fear—sharp and white. 'Are you ill?' She rolled over, burying her face in her hands, unspeaking. He saw her body heave, but she made no sound. 'Kristin, my dearest,' he bent down to her, his arm across her shaking shoulders.

She forced her voice to come, struggled to keep it steady. 'Carl, do something for me.'

'Anything, darling.'

'Get the lunch things and go up the river about two hundred yards and light a fire. I brought sausages. They'll need cooking. I'll join you later.' Don't question me, she thought. Oh God, don't ask me why! 'Please Carl. I wouldn't ask you if I didn't love you.'

Kristin, he thought, what has happened? What has come between us twice today and kept us from each other? But he went, went without questioning, feeling that in some way, his obedience to her wish might close the gap.

Oh, oh, wailed Kristin when he left. Why must this happen, this power for happiness turn to destruction, turn inward upon my love and destroy Carl's identity? Why, why?

She walked to the river and dangled her legs over the bank; the water on her feet made her feel better, brought her back to reality, smudged the horror of her metamorphosis. If only, she thought, I turned into trees or stones or earth when I'm with him it couldn't hurt him. But this way, this way I am like a leech, a vampire, sucking his strength from him—the moon eclipsing the sun. Oh God! And the more I love him, the more perilous the danger. I cannot be with him without stealing into him and erasing his own identity. Why should it be, she asked, why, why, why? But the leaves above whispered in the wind of their high branches and the river flowed past and the world was still. My love is like a blight, she said, lowering herself into the water to wash away the pain from her face. Insidious, evil, she thought as she trod water, like an octopus, like a cobra; like a leech, like a vampire, she repeated. Oh Carl, what can I do, my darling? She swam with the current, letting it carry her. If I were brave, she thought, I would let it carry me out to sea. But the thought of it made her struggle towards land and as she felt the shore under her feet she knew safety again. It will be like this always, she thought—the surrender to the water and dry land emerging just in time. It will be so; it must be. The texture of our love cannot be destroyed.

She walked back to the car and rubbed her face and hair with a towel. There will be interludes, she thought, but they will pass and perhaps, eventually, they will cease altogether. We shall come through them. How little my love is worth if we give in now—if I give in, she amended.

The vision of *The Boy* in her bedroom reminded her of the male mind of Carl that would not tolerate submersion; that would rise up again strong as a weed and as swiftly, no matter what she did to him.

Still rubbing the water from her hair she ran along the path by the river calling, 'Carl, Carl! Oh, my darling, I'm coming, coming.'

She saw him tending the fire, squatting before the teepee of wood that rose in a spiral of blue smoke. He is invincible, she thought, I cannot hurt him, and she slowed her pace, waiting for him to meet her, waiting for the agony to be finally over as they linked hands, and standing together she searched his eyes for the reassurance that she knew lay hidden there.

PART FOUR: KRISTIN

Kristin held her arms above her head and slipped into the dress. It is lovely, she thought seeing herself full length in the mirror.

Her mother, looking her up and down with critical eyes, said to the fitter, 'It doesn't hang quite right here.' She pushed Kristin in the small of the back with her fingers. The fitter grunted. Her mouth was full of pins. She used her hands to speak with, her hands and movements sharp as the pins in her mouth.

'It is so simple,' her mother said. 'Long and slim and plain. You will look as if you are taking a vow of chastity.' The fitter snorted and the pins shot out—bright projectiles from her tight lips.

Kristin was tired of it now. Tired of being pulled and pushed. The dress was a dream. If she had to have a white wedding, well, she was pleased with the dress. But the fittings exhausted her. She wanted to go home, back to her own room and write to Carl. For he has gone, she told herself. Gone, gone. The form of the word in her mind was a hollow echo. It is the loneliest word I know, she thought.

The fitting finished, there was still no escape. As they opened the door of the house piles of presents and letters greeted them. Her mother was excited.

'Oh, Kristin!' she said, 'look. Come and open them. See who they're from.'

And Kristin obeyed. She sat surrounded by tissue paper and excelsior.

'Don't get the cards mixed, whatever you do,' her mother warned. 'What a pity Carl isn't here to see these lovely things.'

The letters came next.

Dear Kristin,

I'm so happy for you. Although I've never met your Carl Bridges I know he must be perfectly sweet. And what a lovely bride you'll make. I wish it were possible for me to get to the wedding to see you both. They say he is very attractive …

Dearest little Kristin,

I've not seen you since you were a strange, tiny girl and it seems impossible to imagine you a bride. What an interesting life you will have, married to an artist! I am sending you a little gift—getting it off tomorrow—and it carries all my wishes for your future happiness …

They were all alike—on and on—it was hard to tell where one stopped and another began. Kristin put them in a pile.

'You'd better write more thank-you notes,' her mother said. 'Once you get behind, you're done for.'

'How I loathe it all,' Kristin complained.

Her mother looked hurt. 'Oh, darling, don't say that. When we're doing everything we can to give you a lovely wedding.'

Kristin couldn't answer. What can I say? she thought. I can't tell her the truth—that if they had asked me I should never have considered even for one moment this sort of a wedding. 'I'll go upstairs and begin,' she said. She marked a description of the presents on the cards. 'I'll try to get all these done this morning.' And her mother smiled.

'Write to them nicely, dear. People have been so kind.'

Upstairs at her desk, Kristin stared at the pile of cards and shuddered. Thank you so much for the cake plate, it was just exactly what I wanted. The sugar tongs are the prettiest I've ever seen. I don't know how to thank you for the … She pulled the paper towards her and sat for a long time, pen in hand. Then,

'Darling,' she wrote,

How I wish you were here. I realize now that it is only when you are with me that I can bear all the fuss of marriage. How much sooner would I go with you into the woods and stand beneath a tree and be married by a solemn squirrel than go through this endless business that is before us. Don't for one minute, imagine that I don't think it worth it. I'd go through death first if I knew I could live with you for a week even. But the letters! Oh, Carl, the letters people write! For all *they* know of you I might be marrying an idiot.

This is a silly letter, darling. I didn't mean to write like this but it all came over me with a rush. What I meant to say was I love you and miss you.

This morning I had a fitting for my wedding dress.

Come back as I remember you. Oh, Carl, Carl, I can't believe it was only yesterday that you went and that it will be eight days more before I see you. When I get terribly lonely I look at *The Boy* and feel better. *The Boy* is more comfort to me than your photo even. The photo is something you can give to anyone, something that anyone might have seen—*The Boy* is yours and mine.

When I think that soon now we'll be at Birchlands together, with no interruptions, no parties, no people, I get almost dizzy. I feel like a very young child one minute and so terribly grown up the next. Do you think I seem older than I did when I first met you? I *feel* so different. I seem to fit into the world in a way I never did before. I lie awake at night thinking of you and hoping and hoping that I can make you happy. I'd love to know what you are doing at this exact minute.

I love you,

Kristin

She read it over and sighed. I wish I were a writer, she thought, so I could really say what I want to. But now, she twirled the pen in her fingers, I must start on the letters. Her whole being revolted at the thought, massed together, became heavy. She addressed Carl's envelope and sealed it, chose a fresh piece of paper and began: 'Dear Mrs Eliot.' She held her pen tightly and wrote with the deliberate care of a child who is learning to write.

The sunlight fell in a pool on her desk and she sat there, pale and fair, her mouth tight and concentrated. But it is hard to focus the mind, she thought. I feel swimming in a pool of light, no part of me touching anything—just adrift in sunlight. She tried to gather her thoughts again—loose threads swaying in the sun—tried to draw them together with her fingers and knot them, so, to form a solid cord. 'Dear Mrs Eliot. Thank you so much for the beautiful …The lampshade is lovely … Carl and I are so grateful …'

The cord had formed. The pile of letters grew; the sunlight thinned to a single beam that fell, steady and strong, on the paper before her. The rest of the room disappeared and Kristin at the desk knew nothing beyond the white squares of paper marked with small, carefully shaped black hieroglyphics, that she pulled towards her, pushed away. She worked at the desk in silence and *The Boy* watched over her shoulder.

The week passed. Letters came and went. Parcels arrived, were unwrapped and placed on the tables in the living room. People called, exclaimed over the presents, drank tea and sherry and left again. Fittings continued: dresses were taken in, let out, smoothed over the hips; lingerie chosen, hats tried on. The clergyman called and Kristin dashed from party to party. But all the time, though too busy to stop and relax, Kristin's heart said, Carl, Carl, come back and take me away. Her mother moved through the days, smart and two-dimensional as a fashion-plate, loving the people, the clothes, the fuss; dealing with the caterers, arranging about the church, inexhaustible, smiling, capable. And her father, returning at night, signed cheques, complained that his chair was moved from the living room and chided her self-consciously and constantly.

At night, in her room, Kristin read her letters from Carl, scribbled notes to him in bed and lay tossing and turning in the darkness, calling for him, crying out against this life in which she had no time to be quiet, no time to be still. But the week passed, passed at last, like the traffic passing from the high street in the early hours of the morning.

'Today,' cried Kristin, wakening, 'today he comes!' She hugged her knees, shut her eyes and moved to music. 'Today,' she cried, jumping from her bed. 'And in less than a week,' she said, leaning on her dressing-table and gazing at herself in the mirror, 'in five days time we shall be married! And then …?' she questioned, 'and then …?' It rushed over her then, the fear, the fear that the busyness of the week had quelled, pushed under. But if I fall like a shadow on him, blotting his personality, destroying his work? 'What can I do,' she called to the mirror, 'to keep him safe from me? Where can he turn to escape? And who can help us, who but ourselves? I am the enemy,' she said, 'with a love in my heart more dangerous than hate.'

But she was torn from herself, drawn into the tempo of the house.

'Kristin!' her mother called, opening the door, 'Oh, you *are* awake. We've a busy morning,' and she stopped. 'Do you feel all right?' she asked. 'Kristin, you look ill.'

'I'm tired,' said Kristin, 'that's all.' She tied the belt of her house-coat.

'I've turned on your bath,' said her mother. 'So hurry, darling, there's so much to do.'

Yes, hurry, hurry; sink thought into the whirlpool of speed, sink like a rock away from reality, disappear in the eddying light and darkness of motion. Allow the wings of your imagination to be bruised and broken by the actuality of things to be done. Forget, forget!

She bathed, she dressed, she ate. She moved like a swirl of wind, brushing aside the partitions of her mind, mounting the morning which, like a wedding cake, rose before her, tier upon tier, until she stood, high on its topmost layer, waiting for the train to come in.

'Carl!' He was off first this time, his brown neck hidden, his brown hands gloved; but like a rocket of light behind her eyes he came to her over the platform. 'My darling!' The world can go hang, she thought as he kissed her, die out from the sterility of its own restraint, fall with a splash upon the still surface of conventionality.

'This,' he said, 'is the last time we shall ever be parted. The worst is over; the best waiting upon our readiness. You are as lovely as I remember you. Oh, my sweet!'

To look into his face, to look at the firm brown lines of his face, the stillness of his eyes. I am at peace again, she thought. What has been jarred is mended.

'What have you done? Tell me, tell me,' she said as they walked through the station.

'Missed you and missed you again.'

'Ah,' she laughed. 'But seriously.'

'I was serious.'

'But all these days—?'

'I went to Birchlands,' he said, 'to get the place ready. It's looking lovely. The trees are turning. The lake is blue.'

'And then?'

'I spent the rest of the time in Montreal. And you?'

'Parties, fittings, thank-yous. Terrible!'

'But now!' he said.

'Yes, but now!' Oh, to be with him again, to know the long ache ended. I can hardly speak, she thought, such is my happiness, such my delight, when I am with him. The white panther is attendant and no fall frost can touch us.

'Let's,' she said, stepping out from the station, 'let's buy a sandwich and eat it in the park. I'd hate to share you with the family so soon and I couldn't bear the noise of a restaurant.'

'We can buy food here, at the station counter.' He supervised the loading of his suitcases and then left her. She watched him push through the swing doors ... her Carl, tall and straight. He burns, she thought, with the steady flame of an Aladdin lamp and I am a candle beside him, to be puffed out by the first gust of wind, inconstant beside his constancy. But no! She swept the words away with a little gesture of her hand. That is not true, she said. The truth, she thought, running her finger around the steering wheel, is not so easy. We both are constant to ourselves, both faithful to the form of our own lives, but my faithfulness is like a drum, sounding at intervals and his is a whistle, steady and endless. But importance lies, she thought, not in the drum or the whistle so much as in the combination of both; the combined sound falling upon a still air through the years ahead. She leaned on the wheel. Now, she thought, watching the people passing before the car, he is saying to the girl at the counter, 'Thank you very much,' and perhaps he is turning with the sandwiches in his hand and coming to me. And I, she thought, am like a small animal behind the wheel, stiff with desire for him, bearing this moment only through the tenseness of my body, holding myself like a shield against the day, until he returns to me.

And here he is, she said to herself, here he comes with the sunlight falling on him and his hands full and his eyes golden. He was beside her now. She moved along the seat. 'You drive,' she said. 'I simply don't dare trust myself at the wheel. I'd probably run over everyone in sight.'

'I'm no more sure that I won't, myself.' He gave her the parcels. 'Sandwiches and two pints of milk and chocolates and cigarettes. All right?'

'Lovely! Oh, Carl.'

'Yes?'

'Just, oh Carl. I can't get used to the idea of you really being here, can't believe that it's not just imagination. When the house was at its maddest I've sometimes told myself, "He is here now," and for a moment believed it and felt the weight lift, only to fall again, heavier than ever, realizing you to be in Montreal.' She sat sideways in the seat so that she could watch him—the tilt of his head—the way he signalled definite clear signals to the cars behind.

'When we meet,' she said, 'it is like fashioning a new building with turrets rising; endless turrets rising up clean and tall and white.'

'Sometimes,' he said, 'you almost take the words out of my mouth. It's as if you know me from the inside—an empathetic knowledge of me.'

'What is empathetic?' She sat up straight.

'Well,' he hesitated. 'It's a psychic term really. An inner knowledge resulting from the projection of the mind of the observer into the thing observed.'

'Oh!' Why are we talking like this, why already are we on the subject I dread? She raised her hand to her mouth to hold it steady. 'Is there any cure for it?' she asked.

'Cure?' said Carl. 'No, I don't think so, darling. It's a sort of extra sense that leads to a fuller understanding. I don't think it's a thing people try to cure.'

Oh, but they do, she thought. Carl, they do, they do.

'At any rate,' he said, 'I was only joking—about you, I mean.'

She covered her mouth again. It's no subject to joke about, for it's true, true, terribly true. But he interrupted her thoughts.

'I've brought you a present, Kristin. See if you can guess what it is.'

'Another painting?'

'No-o-o. Not altogether.'

'Oh, Carl, I can't guess. I was never any good at guessing. Tell me.' She was excited. 'Please.'

'I'll show you when we have lunch. I have it with me.'

'But tell me now, please, Carl.'

'Don't be so impatient.' He laughed at her.

'Will I like it?'

'I hope so.' They had turned into the park. 'Where shall we go?'

'Left here. To the place we were the night of the eclipse. On the little hill that overlooks the lake. Oh,' she said, 'the trees are turning, I haven't had time to notice. How lovely it is.'

He stopped the car then and she leaned against him. Before he had pulled on the brake or turned off the engine she cried, 'Kiss me, kiss me, Carl.'

'Oh, Kristin. Little Kristin.' He held her close and they sat together, forgetful.

'Pity the poor city lovers,' she said at last. 'Oh, Carl, to have nowhere to be together except in the dark shadow of some house. How can they bear waiting until the darkness falls? How can they bear it—people who love each other as you and I do?' She curled her fingers around his neck. 'You look so different, up close, like this. Isn't it funny!' They laughed and they kissed and grew serious again.

'Kristin, I do hope you love Birchlands. I want you to so badly.'

'But I will. How could I help it? With you I could love any place.'

'But I want you to love Birchlands for itself—apart from me.'

She smiled at him. 'Darling, when all my love is centred in you I could only love it *through* you. I couldn't love separately. You see,' she said, with her head in his lap, looking up at him, 'I'm so very one-track.' She sat up then. 'Oh, show me the present. Carl, please!'

'Shut your eyes,' he commanded.

She obeyed him and waited, wondering what the present would feel like in her hands, wondering what it could be, as she heard him rustling through his suitcase.

'Here,' he said.

It was in her hands now. It felt hard. She opened her eyes. *Fairy Stories*, by Oscar Wilde. 'Oh Carl!' She could feel him watching her as she opened the covers and turned through the pages. 'And pictures,' she said. 'Carl, how beautiful!' And noticing CB at the bottom of the illustration, 'Darling, they're yours. But Carl ...?' She couldn't understand. She looked up at him and saw him laughing. 'How,' she said, 'how did you—?'

'You remember that first day I spent with you I told you I had done illustrations.'

'Yes, yes.' She was impatient.

'Well, I found them when I was at Birchlands. So I bought a copy of the book and had an old bookbinder I know rebind it and put my illustrations in.'

'Oh, darling!' She touched the pages as if they were velvet, then reached for his hand. 'Carl,' she said, 'how I love you. How sweet you are.'

'You like it then?'

'Like it! You couldn't have given me anything I like better. Thank you, thank you.' She pulled him to her and kissed him, feeling the sweetness of an ebbing summer live again. 'Thank you for so much—for everything. If I live to be eighty I shall never be able to thank you properly for—yourself.'

'Nor I,' he said, 'for you.'

She clung to him. He is my strength, she thought, my strength and my happiness. Let the world crumble and we, together, will know it for bliss. Oh, my love, my love that grows like a flower in my heart, unfolding the curve of its petals like the loved hand opening; unfolding to beauty throughout the years. But the thought was dammed.

'Carl,' she said suddenly realizing, 'you must be starved. What a selfish wretch I am.' She reached for the parcels and carried them under the trees. But for the moment she couldn't eat, herself; she was content merely to sit there, beside him, watching him eat, while the lake stretched out below like a great arc of blue and the knowledge of Carl fell about her, surrounded her, held her to a composite entity, aware only of her love for him, her love for him and his nearness.

Kristin sat in the garden alone. Alone for the first time since—she couldn't remember. She felt numb. The effort of thought was too much. It meant prising through the cotton-wool wrapping that swaddled her brain—layers and layers of it. But she had to think, had to make the effort now that she had the chance. The last hours had been a nightmare—fear rising upon fear and growing too large to hold within her. It hurt to think, hurt with the physical pain of an incision in her scalp.

The sun is quite hot on my face, she thought, and the strap at the back of the deck chair is firm across my back. These things I can feel, as acutely, more acutely than usual. If I start from here, start from this consciousness of the physical, perhaps, she thought, I can work through. The sun and the strap of the deck chair and the pressure of my knuckles on each other as my hands are twisted together. These things are all quite clear. But, she thought and she sat upright, straightened to a rod with the realization, I can't marry Carl. Loving him as I do I cannot marry him. She held her hands to her head.

'I met him,'—she spoke out loud to keep her mind concentrated—'I met him at the station three days ago. I met him and my love rose like the flight of a bird. We took sandwiches to the park and had lunch there and I remember the shaft of my love on the air; his laughter and his lips; the blue of the lake and the golden trees. All that, I remember,' she said, as though it were etched on my mind. 'And then,' she said—and the fear rose like a mad thing in her head—'it happened. I felt it happening and fought against it but the waters of his being closed over me quickly,' she said. 'I was drowned in him. And this morning,' she went on, forcing herself to follow the course of what happened, 'this morning I came to the surface, I emerged from the sea and reclaimed myself.' She shut her eyes, trying to shut away the sight of Carl's face that floated before her. He looked like death, she thought. When he came to me after breakfast he was an old man. Carl! Her hands went out for him as she thought, and touched nothing but the air. Carl! She held her hands together, then pressed them palm against palm. 'He is not here,' she cried. 'He is'—she narrowed her mind to touch the thought—'he is at the railway office buying tickets for our honeymoon.'

She saw him then, tall and brown, leaning slightly on the desk in the great shiny room and she began to cry. If I could forget his hands and his up-pointing shoulder, she sobbed. She turned in her chair and pressed her fingers against her eyelids. If only I could forget. All my joy has gone, all my happiness. I am left with only my fear and my anguish. Drawing her hands from her eyes she saw her mother coming across the grass and Mary behind her carrying a tray.

'I've had Mary bring a cup of tea out here, darling.' Her mother sat beside her and Kristin could feel her gaze searching out her face. She watched Mary put down the tray and arrange the cups and saucers. Watched her hands moving, turning the silver teapot, putting the blue plate with the thin bread and butter on the table, saw the little cakes.

'That will be everything, Mary, thank you.'

It is all remote, Kristin thought. It has nothing to do with me. She tried to centre herself, to hold reason in her head and stand steady.

Her mother poured the tea and passed her a cup. 'Feeling better?' she asked and Kristin stared at her tea, finding no words.

'I've phoned the people who are giving parties and told them you're simply too tired to go. Carl doesn't mind and they all understand. You'll get a chance now to rest. Two days with nothing to do and you'll be all right.'

If only it were as easy as that, Kristin thought. And she wanted to scream out against her mother's phrases that treated her despair like the neurosis of an hysterical woman. Anyone seeing us, Kristin thought, sitting here having tea on a green lawn that stretches out about us to the tall trees, could never guess at the panic this moment holds.

She watched her mother light a cigarette. She took one too, puffed at it and stubbed it out. There was no consolation anywhere. Like a record in her head the words of the poem repeated themselves over and over.

> She stole his eyes because they shone,
> Stole the good things they looked upon;
> They were no brighter than her own.

On and on, verse after verse.

As he forgave she snatched his soul;
She did not want it but she stole.

That would come. Unless she could hold herself apart from him, know the end of her love, she would steal his soul too. She could see the inevitable stealthy approach; she could see him standing, an empty thing, possessor of nothing but his physical shape, while she, unhappy, laden down with him, hugged his soul to her and could not let it go.

Light stirred through the words in her head, cut them up, destroyed them. He was coming across the grass, dragging his long shadow behind him.

'There's Carl,' said her mother, her words announcing her relief in his coming. 'Carl,' she got up, 'you're just in time for a cup of tea. Come along.'

He was beside the tea table. 'No sugar,' he said, and her hand holding the sugar-tongs paused. 'Of course not, how silly of me.'

'Feeling better, darling?'

She nodded. He is trying so hard to be natural, she thought. Oh Carl, my darling, if only we need never have met.

'I must run off,' her mother said. 'There are still a thousand and one things to be done.'

Carl sat down. 'I have the tickets.' He took them out as he spoke. 'Just think, in two days' time we'll be at Birchlands.' He stretched his legs and took a piece of bread and butter. 'In two days' time,' he went on, 'the hell of this last week will be over, forgotten.'

She pushed the words that formed away from her. 'It has been hell, hasn't it, darling?'

'Your tiredness has, in some way, affected me too. The last few days have been like a mad dream in which I've had no control over myself. I suppose I must have been more tired than I realized. But soon it will all be behind us.' He looked at her but she couldn't meet his eyes. Numbness rose in her again. My brain is bruised she thought, beaten with worry.

'Kristin.' He was reaching across to her, trying to build another bridge; but she couldn't help him. She gazed at her moonstone until it grew large and blurred. He took her hand, lifted it to his cheek. 'Oh my God, Kristin, I love you!' His voice was sharp. He hurt her hand as he held it. The panther moved from the darkness to her side, her veins were studded with light, fireflies moving in her blood stream.

'Oh, love, love, love!' she cried in a voice so shrill it startled her. But calling out against it as she did, mocking it with her mind, the long tide reached out and drew her to Carl. Sitting in his lap, her face against his, knowing his delight and her own, the thin wail continued in her head, like a fire siren against the night: it is over, this is the end; Carl, Carl, this is an interlude only; love me and turn your head away.

Her father was in high spirits at dinner. Carl, in his happiness, was talkative and gay. Kristin watched them all. Her father grumbling good-naturedly, Carl telling stories and her mother's words, like mice, running in and out of their talk. 'The wedding cake has come. Darlings, you must see it.' And, 'Ralph, did you know Lucy Smart sent a cheque for a hundred dollars?' And, 'I wonder why my dress hasn't come yet? They promised to have it here by six.' The door-bell rang and the phone rang and when Mary called Kristin to answer either her father said 'No. We must have our meals in peace.' And then, 'Perhaps it's something important, you'd better go.' Kristin was glad of the phone calls and the door-bell; glad to escape from so much happiness she could not join; glad to be alone for the few minutes in the hall, coming and going; glad even of the letters that still had to be written, which released her from Carl's eyes.

As dinner ended her mother looked at her watch and said, 'Well, children, we must get ready for the rehearsal.'

Kristin had forgotten. The party after the rehearsal had been cancelled and she had forgotten. They got into the car, Carl finding her hands and holding them, no one saying very much. At the church the bridesmaids were already there and Johnny, the best man—a makeshift for Dick who couldn't get away. They were talking in the porch. Some of the ushers had arrived. The church was grey and cold inside. It was too early for lights and just dark enough to be depressing and dreary. Kristin wanted to run away. But the colour of the stained glass windows seemed peremptory, demanding, and held her there. The clergyman arrived, grey and sanctimonious. He said, 'My dear, my dear, this is a beautiful moment in your life, the moment when God sanctions the love in your heart and makes it a sacred, holy thing.' He said it several times and Kristin wanted to cry out to him, scream that her love was evil. He showed them how they walked up the aisle. The ushers were referring to lists and plans, learning the seating arrangements; the bridesmaids were excited, pretending already to be in their dresses, holding their hands as though carrying flowers. Her father was enjoying it all, walking up the long aisle with her, doing it a second time to make sure. Carl looked nervous. Kristin could see him, standing apart, the light from one of the windows just touching the end of his nose, turning it purple, like an amethyst set in the end of it.

The clergyman explained the wedding service to them. He intoned the phrases, 'Love, honour and obey.' 'In sickness and in health.' 'Till death us do part.' 'I plight thee my troth.' And Kristin heard them with a sick heart. Till death us do part. It is only, she thought, death that can part the awful unity of us, the unity that must destroy our love. She wanted to take off her hat, run her fingers through her hair, block her ears to the sound of the clergyman's voice and her eyes to the tall figure of Carl standing apart from her, yet within her. She wanted to cry out to them all: 'I cannot go through with it; I cannot marry Carl, marry a man in whose eyes I only see my own when I look; marry a man to destroy him.' But the harsh words within her evaporated, lifted. For he stood there, complete, strong, virile as *The Boy*, contradicting her thoughts—something apart from her, a rock—steady, self-reliant—something she could not destroy.

The rehearsal was over. The bridesmaids and ushers joined together, called to Kristin, 'Come to the party after all. We're having it anyway.' But it was her mother who answered, 'No, really, I must be firm. She's too tired.'

'Carl, then,' they called. 'He could come.'

Kristin watched him smile at them and refuse; watched them tumble into the cars; heard their words flung across the half-light, 'We'll see you at the wedding.'

'Get a good rest, Kristin.'

'It's a pity to miss such a good party.'

She took off her hat, reached for Carl, feeling that now, at this minute, he was safe from her and she could turn to him. He pressed her fingers, whispered, 'Oh, darling, how I wish that had been the wedding.' They got into the car, her parents still talking to the clergyman on the steps. He kissed her then, quickly, touched her hair. They were apart, Kristin thought, quite apart from the rest of the world, sharing a strange vacuum that no one else could approach with words or gestures. For the moment she was happy—the fear gone—safe in the knowledge that Carl shared this dislocation of life with her, the wrenched moment that was apart from all normal living; this sudden right-about-face of being. He stroked her hand, holding her close to him. Now we are Hansel and

Gretel, she thought, holding to each other. But as the moments passed she grew so light that she felt they were both floating, flying high above the world, knowing only the wind and the clouds, detached from the solidity, the squareness of an earth life. We are Peter Pan and Wendy, she mused. Hansel and Gretel are gone.

'Good night, good night,' her mother called on the church steps. They could hear her heels as she moved on the pavement; they drew apart.

'Such a good man,' said her mother getting into the car.

'He's too serious for me,' her father added. 'I must say I enjoy a laugh and a joke.'

As they drove home through the tree-lined streets, watching the night settle about them, the fear returned to Kristin. Nothing is secure, she thought. Everywhere there is change. The hand stretched out to give is refused; the hand stretched out to receive finds ashes in its palm.

Her father stalled the car at a crossroad and swore loudly. Her mother said, 'I wonder if my dress has come yet?' Carl whispered in the darkness, 'Dearest, dearest!' and then they were home again and her mother was hustling her off to bed. All of time is cut up into pieces, Kristin thought, little lengths of this and that; the reel never unrolls to full length. The images in her mind faded as she lay down. Fear, bright as a sword blade in the sun, dimmed and grew grey; the moment of happiness in the car that shone like the cup of a buttercup grew grey; everything grew grey as the inside of the church. She was sleepy; she couldn't think any more. Falling off to sleep she saw Carl with the purple light like an amethyst set in the end of his nose. She sighed and slept.

The next day was over like a promise broken. No sooner were jobs done than others cropped up that called for attention and Kristin threw herself into the work despite her mother's pleading. Only this way, she thought, can I bear it. Only this way, too busy for Carl to touch the core of me, too busy to think, too busy to question, can I cross the endless chasm. By night-time she was exhausted.

'You look pale and tired, darling,' her mother said. 'No way for a bride to look. I suggest an early bed.'

Yes, Kristin thought, yes. She was willing.

Her father kissed her self-consciously. 'I hope it is nice tomorrow,' he said. 'There are storm clouds in the west.'

'It's sure to be,' her mother announced. 'We'll all concentrate.'

Upstairs, saying good night to Carl, Kristin felt the tears forming in her eyes.

'I've only seen you in little flashes,' he whispered. 'All day long—little glimpses. Oh, my darling!' She leaned against him, holding him tightly, still unwilling to look into his face. 'Tonight,' he said, 'is the last night I'll kiss you outside your bedroom door.' He held her chin and kissed her. The whole world was alight. If it could always be so, she thought, Carl always dominant … She left the words suspended in her head, forgetful now of all but Carl, all but the blind magnificence of him.

'Ah, my love!' He let her go then, leaned her backwards, and stared at her. 'Little Kristin. Dear heart!' She held him again, loathe to leave him at this moment, frightened of turning her back and going to her room.

'Whatever I may tell you after we're married,' she spoke slowly, carefully, 'remember that now, at this moment, I love you more than my life.' She held up her lips. 'Kiss me again,' she said, 'and then I must go to bed.'

He kissed her. She turned then, not looking back, and opened the door of her room. She heard his footsteps move off and she sank on her bed and sobbed into clenched hands, 'I love him, oh God, I love him and our love is nearly over; married, our happiness will be a torn and finished thing.'

She looked up at *The Boy*. It is no good, she thought, he is not strong enough. Even *The Boy* can't convince me now, and she turned the picture to the wall.

She undressed, stared at the boxes in her room lying open still for last-minute things to be thrown in, looked at the tags she had written—red tags with 'MRS CARL BRIDGES' printed on them carefully. Her room looked empty. Empty cupboard, empty drawers—empty of everything but her wedding dress, long and pale in her cupboard and her going away suit; her drawers empty of all but her wedding lingerie and her make-up and accessories. She couldn't look at them; they were part of Carl's destruction.

She walked to the bathroom. In sickness and in health, she thought, turning on the tap. I plight thee my troth, I plight thee my troth. She leaned out of the bathroom window. The sky was dark with clouds, not a star showing. The wind sounded large and angry. Storm clouds in the west—she remembered her father's words. Little Kristin, dear heart. Oh, oh! She held her face-cloth to her eyes, seeing light and colour form beneath her lids as she pressed her eyeballs; feeling the slow white pain creep into the tissue of her eyes.

She could hear the wind howling as she returned to her room. The storm is a symbol, she thought, getting into bed—a pointer predicting the course of our love. Lying in the bare room, the room stripped of her personality, *The Boy* turned to the wall, she felt alive with the reality of Carl. Everywhere she looked Carl was there, like a ghost, filling her with terror. She could bear it no longer. She reached her hand up for the light switch; the room opened to darkness, large, with Carl all about her. She felt his hands, saw the lift of his half smile, heard him whisper. Terrified, she drew the covers about her neck, covered her face. No blind was permanent; each shutter she drew down was nothing more than the slide of glass in a phial which held two acids apart—a slide that was destroyed by the acids and ultimately brought them together to react.

Desperate she lay there, checking the desire to cry; knowing that before tomorrow, tomorrow that loomed like a giant, so immense that she couldn't see it as a whole, she must find a solution that would protect Carl from her. For, she thought, as we are, the steady whistle of Carl's integrity will be torn to tatters of sound by me. As we are, if I marry him, it will mean the complete merging of two personalities. But the truth rushed to her out of the night: it will mean the obliteration of two personalities. That is, she thought slowly, the words like heavy sacks that had to be carried together to form a sentence, that is, if I have a personality of my own. For I am a chameleon, she thought, absorbing the colours about me and our marriage will submerge us, wipe us out as sun obliterates the markings of water on a stone.

Fear sucked her down.

One plus one will equal nothing, she cried, clutching her pillow until her fingernails ached. Mathematicians know nothing, nothing at all. There is another field, a field beyond the realms of accepted mathematics where allowances are made for figures. They can and do add up quite differently. One and one equal two is a truth no longer—it is an instance only.

She felt calmer for a minute, considering her discovery and she heard the wind again, increasing now, like a gargantuan bellows blowing outside her window. The wind held the house and dropped it. Quite suddenly the world was still, suspended in a void—for a second only—and then the rain came, released like cattle into the corral of the roof—wild, flint-shod cattle tearing the structure of the house.

She listened. She could hear the wind again, pulling at the trees, whipping their branches. The night had risen for the furious stampede that held the sea and all emotion in its intensity. And she felt part of it, like a branch torn off and carried by the wind, hurtled through the air, drained of emotion—a chance body that the night had taken and robbed; empty now, left on her bed, tranquil, at peace. No worry could touch her. The problem was solved though the answer was still not in her possession. She lay immobile, a branch the night had tossed and forgotten. She slept, knowing sleep, conscious of it, aware of its quality of slow germination, of gradual growth. She remembered nothing before it, nothing more than the stirring, the easy evolution of the seed that was herself.

And then suddenly she was awake, knowing her strength to be in jeopardy; knowing she must put forth every effort to stay alive. The wind was like a mad creature tearing at her branches and the strain on her roots made her entire being ache and throb. She knew only an instinctive desire to stay standing, to battle with the wind and so remain upright and invincible, to dig her roots into the earth, clutching at the soil, bracing the trunk that was torn and twisted with the force of the wind. Muscular soreness wrenched her, surged through her, but with it a joy in living, a fierce happiness. She was pitting her strength against the wind in a battle for existence and she was winning. For a moment she cried out, remembering something undone. She cried, 'Carl, I've never told you about the rocks,' but the wind stopped her mouth, caught her branches, swung them out, stripped off the leaves and she was forgetful again of all but the fight; conscious of the deeper grip of her roots in the earth, the greater bracing of her trunk against the air. Exultant, she fought, knowing her supremacy; knowing the re-creation of self in the united forgetfulness of self; she pitched her strength at the night and her strength was returned to her.

Gradually the wind weakened, the rain lightened and died and the air fell like velvet about her—soft and sweet. She released her grip and submitted herself to a peace, a peace more surely permanent than any she had known. She was strong, upright and intact. The long night was behind her, the fight over.

As the morning sun dropped honey on her leaves and fell in warm patches on her trunk, so, too, did it creep through the Venetian blinds of the bedroom and stripe the waking shell on the bed that had once contained her. The sun touched them both, the past, the future, equally.

Graceful, swaying slightly, she faced the calm of the day and drank from the rich, wet earth—steady in the security of her fibre and bark; content in the sweet uprising form of her growth, holding her branches up to the sky in the simple, generous gesture of the victor who knows victory to be within.

The day settled to warmth. A breeze lifted the fallen leaves at her roots. Two sparrows perched on a branch and pecked at the clustered red berries she held out for them, turned from their eating and preened the brown and grey of their bodies with their small beaks. One soft feather floated downward to the bronze leaves below. Mary, at the back door shaking the mop, said, 'My, but the leaves sure fell in the storm last night, but it's a lovely day for the weddin'.' The shadows shortened and the sun grew hot.

PART FIVE: EPILOGUE

The sun and a small wind broke the surface of the lake to glinting sword blades. On the far side, where the trees marched unchecked, right down to the water's edge, there the lake was a shifting pattern of scarlet, vermilion and burnt orange—but bright, bright, so that it hurt the eyes and the pain crept like a thin red line of infection through the whole body.

This was beauty to a happy heart. A wild, intense kind of beauty and the red line became a current of recklessness, no mean stream of fierce pain.

Beyond the trees and the trees' reflection hills ranged higher and higher like the backs of large amethyst elephants and camels. A fantastic and gargantuan circus parade, monochromatic, motionless.

Kristin sat in the glassed-in veranda that hung out practically over the water. Beside her on the window-sill was a bottle of nail polish. As she dipped the brush in the varnish she lifted her eyes no higher than the neck of the bottle. She knew no need of the view; she knew no need of shutting the view from her. She knew nothing but a pallid desire to perfect each oval nail and leave each in turn shining, smooth and vivid as a rowan berry. As vivid as an autumn rowan berry.

The whining groan of wet wood brushed against wet wood made her lift her head. Below, at the wharf, Carl was getting out of the row-boat. She watched him a moment and returned to her nails.

Nine were finished.

She dipped the brush in the varnish again, as relentless in her continuance as the lake shifting, eddying and rippling.

Ten were finished.

She placed her hands in her lap and sat gazing passively at the coloured tips of her fingers. A small unamused smile nipped the corners of her mouth. The veranda door opened. Kristin continued to stare at her nails.

'Hello, Kristin,' said Carl.

'Hello,' she answered. Only her lips moved.

'It's beautiful on the other side of the lake,' he went on. 'I cut through the woods, blazing a trail as I went. It's a splendid walk. Takes you clean up to the top of Old John's Hill. We must clear it some time—scrap the cedar that grows as fast as the mushroom—'

'Cedar?' said Kristin.

'Yes. Lop off some of the lower boughs of the maples and spruces and we'll have a fine path.'

'Maples and spruces,' said Kristin.

Still she hadn't raised her head. He crossed to her and lifted her face so that she looked at him. The small blank smile still played about her mouth. His hand was under her chin. He could feel the young firm flesh of her throat and the steady pulse in her jugular vein. Her face presented only a mask for him to look at. It was like living with an idiot. His fingers tightened and he felt her pulse strengthen under the pressure. By God! he would make her feel something, force an expression into her face, if only one of loathing. He bent her to him. He would kiss her until she struggled to escape from sheer exhaustion. He would pit his manhood against her aloofness.

Emotionless, passive, she accepted his prolonged kiss. When he released her, longing for some show of feeling on her face, she turned back to examine her nails, as though merely interrupted by some trivial thing which neither annoyed nor pleased her.

He drew away. Thick with anger he moved with the jerkiness of a puppet over to the windows. The colour and brilliance of the lake cut into him until he hated the place. She hadn't even resisted him. He moved her neither to love nor hatred. She was indifferent; coolly indifferent to his attentiveness and neglect. He forced his knuckles against the frame of the window until pain gnawed at the white blunt joints, hoping that perhaps physical suffering would waken him from this honeymoon which had from the outset been like a hideous nightmare pressing close about him, stifling him, terrifying him.

He'd noticed she was different on the wedding day and dismissed it, thinking she was tired; but a week had passed since they were married and now ... what could he do? His knuckles were numb. In his desire he had treated her always as though she were completely normal, talked to her about little things, pretending that both she and he were interested in them; while all the time he knew that this heightened casualness was but a cloak to cover her unconcern and his distress. The anger had gone now. The waters of his rage had ebbed, leaving him a smooth beach, washed clean of all signs of turmoil. He turned to her again, emotionless as she. Together they could play this game of apathetic living. This was the time when pods burst open, scattering their contents and leaving themselves empty and light. He and she could join in this mad carnival of empty things. They could and should dance frantically, wantonly, to the pipings of September winds. The comparison amused him. With a mind tuned to minuteness he followed the images intricately. Their place in the autumn festival grew to assume importance and with the swelling of this importance his apathy diminished; gradually his vulnerability returned.

Kristin was apparently immovable. She sat as before. As Carl looked at her again he sensed, rather than saw, a certain grossness smudging her almost translucent features. It was as if the flesh had murdered the spirit and risen triumphant from the scene of the crime. He shuddered. The Kristin he first knew had seemed to have been hugging to herself a personal spiritual ecstasy.

He remembered their meeting at the Lothrops' party. He hadn't wanted to go. It wasn't shyness—rather an awareness of the ridiculous—his own particular sense of the ridiculous, admittedly. It had, in the end, been a splendid, garish affair. Shrill *soigné* women had laughed with tense, immaculate men after the initial gush of enthusiasm over the painting. And he had been tossed carefully and quickly from guest to guest by a hostess adept in the arts demanded of her by society.

'And this is Kristin,' Mrs Lothrop had eventually said, considering it unnecessary to mention her last name. 'Kristin, I want you to meet Mr

Bridges so that you can always remember that you met a very great artist in the year you came out.' And she had dragged him on unmercifully, eager to show him off to her guests, careful to monopolize him herself.

'Now, Mr Bridges, another cocktail. I think we both deserve one.' Mrs Lothrop was thick through the waist, Carl had observed, with a fine black hair line on her top lip. Anything, anything would serve to think about until he could escape to Kristin. He must get back to her. He could see—that is, if he turned and passed the olives to Mrs Lothrop he could see—the curve of Kristin's shoulder and the long, lean line of her arm. Something important happened to him when he saw her. He wanted to return to her quite unbeautiful face and discover what it was about her that he liked. He wanted to arrange to have her sit for him. He wouldn't leave tomorrow after all. Damned if he would! 'Oh, yes, Mrs Lothrop, thank you so much, I believe I will.' He held out his glass automatically. He'd get her onto canvas first. The cocktail party was an excellent institution. 'Yes, Mrs Lothrop, a splendid party. Oh, I'm quite certain people are enjoying themselves—take you and me, for example.' He passed her the olives, again, unimpressed by her consumption capacity, seeing only Kristin as he turned with the dish. A fellow-guest joined them. Carl saw his opportunity and escaped. Kristin was still there. He had seen to that.

'Hello,' she had said to him as he came up to her. God, this queer child—but—she's not child nor yet woman, he realized next minute.

'I s'pose I should think of something chatty to make you at ease. I never can.' She smiled, unembarrassed, friendly. She had a pale wedge-shaped face, too pale, wide clear green eyes and a small tight mouth which suggested extreme concentration. It was an ugly mouth. Her hair fell solid to her shoulders, fair, uncurled, shiny as the coat of a horse. He took her all in and afterwards cursed his observant artist's eye. Not for him, the excruciating joy of lying awake wondering about the colour of her eyes, the shape of her mouth, or the look of her hands. For him instead, the detailed, photographic image that most men in love desire but cannot recall. Jove, he would do a fine painting of her, a sort of modern Mona Lisa.

'Carl.' He came back to the present. She was saying his name, not calling him. Her voice was empty of inflection as if she was merely seeing how she liked the sound of his name on her lips.

'Yes, Kristin?'

She held up her hands. 'Carl, do you like my finger nails?'

He paused. 'Yes, dear, they are lovely,' he said, and waited for the satisfaction to mount to the surface of her eyes. The smile nipped the corners of her mouth tighter, but her eyes didn't change. They were pebbles which had seen neither water nor sunlight.

A low white mist covered the lake. Carl, looking down from his bedroom window felt he might be looking up into the sky. It was early yet and perhaps the sun would burn through by mid-day. If the mist was as bad on the road as it was on the lake he'd have to allow a good hour for the drive to the station. He hated driving blind. It made him panicky and God knew he was panicky enough as it was. No one but a panicky man would have sent a wire to Dick two days ago. He had tried to appear casual, yet feared in so seeming that Dick might consider the invitation unimportant and refuse. Carl had waited, coiled like a powerful spring, for the answering wire, and then it had come. 'Delighted meet me noon train.' There was nothing facetious, sniggering, suggestive. Just a simple acceptance. How he hated the supposedly humorous digs at marital relationships!

Carl took off his pyjamas and wondered to himself what, just what, he would do with Dick when he came. Until now his coming had been enough. But at this moment, as he walked naked into the bathroom and turned on the tap, he realized that even Dick might make a burlesque of a tragedy. Perhaps he should have barred any intrusion into this very personal sorrow. Perhaps he should have wired to the Fenders instead of Dick. Perhaps ... perhaps ...

Carl flung the bath mat on the floor as though he had a long-standing hatred for it. God! God! God! He felt about fifteen years old; unable either to control himself or see any clear path away from what tormented him. Living with Kristin was worse than the agony of a love spurned. Living away from her would mean the partial surrender of the all-important undivided mind. Apart from her he could never again know the complete absorption that so far had been vitally necessary to him. His path lay in either of two directions, both of which were cul-de-sacs. He recognized this to be the end of his love; but what was more important still—for no woman could ever possess him entirely—was that it might possibly be the end of his work. In her withdrawal from him she had taken more of him than she could have in completing and renewing the love he offered her.

With superb contempt for what might be self-dramatization Carl continued to think, warily, as he washed himself. And the conflict of a superficial defence with a very real and deep pain made the intensity of his hidden struggle greater.

Should he prepare Dick on the drive back from the station for what was to come? Should he say, 'Kristin and I are at odds,' easily and wait for Dick's reaction? Or should he take him back as if all was normal, delightful and let him find out for himself?

I must not jump so far ahead, Carl thought drying himself with exaggerated care. The thing to do is be but one jump ahead, that is all. I must dwell in the minute to come and the minute that is simultaneously and completely—stretch out the area of my 'now' to include one small portion of what would normally be my future. Thus and thus only can I avoid confusion. Stepping meticulously into the footprints of this plan Carl covered the morning. He dressed, breakfasted alone. Kristin was not yet up. He sprayed the charcoal sketch of his new painting—a pattern of intertwined bodies. When one finger of a friend is laid upon your flesh, he thought, then is responsibility manifold. He felt within him that the picture would remain unfinished. But at this moment his 'now' had already extended to giving it its initial wash of ochre paint and so he prepared his colour and rag and turpentine. He knew that in some way he had stolen a march on time; that somehow, in the trivial things at least, he was preparing his own fate. And the upper layer of his mind smiled, though the lower layers writhed in mortification. In this self-imposed detachment he could find a momentary peace from the large worry that possessed him. It was as if he were two separate entities, working toward a common end, each with individual unconcern for the other.

The mist lay heavy on the lake. The trees and hills were veiled in nun's veiling when he walked down the gravel walk to the garage. The gravel had colour today—the stones proclaimed themselves personally; the lack of a brighter contrast brought them out in their inescapable pastel display. The red roof of the garage shone through the mist—a glowing patch.

The drive to the station took even longer than he had expected. Opaque rolls of mist swirled out at him on the road, slowing him down to walking speed, stopping him at times. The train was in when he arrived and he was thankful. Waiting on the edge of the track was unendurable. Dick, subdued in the respectable Burberry, stood under the shelter of the stationhouse roof. As Carl saw him he forgot everything but a joy in the familiar outline.

'Heigho!' he called.

'A fine friend, a fine friend, I must say,' said Dick. 'Drag a fellow all the way down to this god-forsaken corner of nowhere and then leave him standing on the platform holding the bag. Please pardon pun,' he added, partly from habit, mostly because Carl seemed to be smiling with his flesh only.

Dick was good, Carl considered. Punster or no he was a clean solid kernel. There was a sharp pleasure in merely contemplating the brilliance of his dark eyes and the contrasting stringently fair hair. Carl, long-faced, sallow, of El Greco proportions, felt a dull dog beside Dick.

'How was the trip?' asked Carl.

'Oh—as usual. How are you Carl, happy?'

Now, thought Carl, now is your moment. Here is the opening. 'Yes,' he said. 'Why?'

'I just wondered.' Carl's answer was too evasive. 'You—look like hell.'

'Right,' said Carl, forgetting to keep the 'now' extended beyond itself. 'Something is wrong. Something has happened to Kristin.'

Dick, watching Carl's face as he spoke, noticing the hard line of the tense jaw said, 'And I had hoped to have a nice restful week-end. Well, well!'

Thank you, Dick, thought Carl. Thank you for keeping this conversation level. Thank you for staying in the realm of simple things.

And Dick thought, what has happened? There is something here more dreadful than I know. Carl never speaks quietly like this. Something has hit him below the belt and left him winded. He has broken his own pattern. Dick lit his pipe and gazed out at the white cocoon of a world he was driving through and then launched into talk of the city: of this play, that concert, this book and the ever impudent Tony and his gatherings. He had not seen Carl for weeks. He wanted to talk to him in the old way, effortlessly. He wanted to hear of Carl's work and, too, talk of his own.

The house peered out at them suddenly. The mist had lifted a little. The mallards could be seen clearly now, floating on a lactescent lake; the blue curve of the row-boat was a flute note of sound in the misty silence.

'I've not been here for a year or more,' Dick said. 'It's good to be back.'

Carl turned impulsively. 'Whenever I'm not here you can use Birchlands, you know. I'd love you to ...'

'Thanks,' said Dick hastily. Carl seemed to have forgotten Kristin.

'I mean it,' he went on, picking up Dick's suitcase. 'It's a crime to leave it empty. This place needs living in. It's seen little of life except its own wild life of ceaselessly growing things.'

Inside, Birchlands had a smell peculiarly its own, dependent not upon the meal in process of preparation or the soap or perfume currently popular by its owners. It smelled of old pine panelling and an open wood fire.

Dick hesitated in the doorway. From now on he must be prepared to face it; from now on he must be ready to help Carl, help Kristin, whom he'd never met; help them both, if necessary.

Carl opened the door. The old smell was there, at the far end the fire blazed in the large stone fireplace. It was just dark enough for the flames to dance in the copper and pewter of attending plates and kettles.

'Hello, Kristin,' said Carl. A child with a strange dead face looked up from an armchair. 'This is Dick, Kristin, whom I've told you about.'

God, thought Dick, he's uncanny. He frightens me more than she does. He's too calm. Something will happen. It can't last.

'Dick, my wife.'

'How do you do?' said Dick. I must try to be casual, pretend this atmosphere is one of normality. Not for one moment must I betray the cold fear that prickles in my jaws. 'Carl, your taste is flawless and, Kristin, I commend you on your choice of a husband. Take it from me, an old friend, he's not as bad as he looks.' Damn, thought Dick, there is something here which stilts me, makes me talk like a book. This is awful. This child is terrible.

A long silence drew the room about them, caught the three of them together and held them, so. Dick clenched his hands in his pockets and knew the weight of Kristin heavy on his heart. He could not speak. And then Carl, easily, spoke again and the weight lifted little by little and Dick's hands unclenched.

'We've just time for a swim before lunch. The water's cold but—'

'Invigorating?' suggested Dick and Carl laughed. 'Will you join us too?' Dick asked, turning to Kristin. She didn't even raise her eyes.

'Come on,' said Carl. 'Kristin won't go unless she's thrown in—will you, darling?' He didn't wait for an answer, Dick noticed, but started up the stairs with the bags, saying as he went, 'I'm going to keep you busy, Dick. I want to make a path in the upper woods. How are you with a hatchet?'

'Second only to Washington.'

'Right, I'll make you prove it.' He was gone. Dick lit a cigarette as he undressed and felt happiness evaporate. He must wait, he knew, until Carl volunteered further mention of Kristin. As he went downstairs and passed her chair on the way to the lake she sat as motionless and unaware as though he had passed in spirit form. And he shuddered and suddenly felt too cold to swim.

Carl was already in the water. A voice from the mist hailed him when he came up from his dive and he struck out in the direction of it, glad of the clean sweep of water on his body, finding in it a momentary escape.

'Race you,' said Carl as Dick drew near.

Figures in a mist, figures in a mist, swimming freely but blindly they know not where. Two bodies elongated in water, moving and splashing and the splashing sounding like a watermill—loud and endless.

Dick, for those moments, was conscious of a strangeness but not a fear. It was not until, dressed and tingling, with moisture still clinging to his hair that he knew again the drag of Kristin.

'Scotch and soda?' asked Carl. And Dick accepted eagerly, hoping stimulation would shut Kristin from him and smudge the wedge he seemed to see in Carl's eyes. As they drank, as they smoked beside the fire, Kristin sat still, a shadow between them. By silent, mutual consent she was excluded from the conversation as are the deaf.

'Done any painting?' Dick asked.

'Yes,' said Carl. 'Not much though. And it's pretty bad—unrelated to the moment, in a way. It seems remote, as if I were painting in a dream. It's,' he laughed, 'a product of the imagination.'

No remark was pointed with sufficient excitement to carry interest; banter fell short of its mark, bringing only pale smiles to their lips, or worse still, hearty laughter that crumbled as it came.

Plates and knives and forks looked out of place swimming in the polished lake of table. Nothing bore the conviction of reality except Kristin, now set in the pattern of eating. She sat at the head of the table, filling the place bodily, gracelessly. Occasionally Dick's eyes met Carl's and immediately he flipped a remark to him—his contribution to the rapidly sinking fund of happiness.

The sun burned through during lunch and when they had coffee on the veranda it had turned into a hot Indian summer day. Carl drummed his fingers on the window-ledge. 'We'll start that path,' he said. 'See, Dick, across the lake, that silver birch by the water?' Dick scanned the shore for the landmark. 'That is where we go into the woods.' Carl put down his coffee and looked at his watch. 'In ten minutes time,' he said. 'All right? You'll need your oldest clothes.' The path is his connecting link with reality, thought Dick, anxious already to be off, to escape from Kristin who had said no word to him since he had arrived two hours ago and too, no word to Carl.

The sun was on their backs as they rowed across the lake and in their eyes was the figure of Kristin at the window; she was not looking at them, or if she were her interest was elsewhere, for a smile and a wave brought no answer from her motionless body. Dick watched her figure grow smaller and smaller until it had dwindled to a small dot in the distance. The fear within him lessened and when grounding the row-boat they turned their backs on the house, Dick felt the weight of her spirit had lifted.

'Here,' said Carl, slashing at young willows, 'is the beginning of the path. This is the birch you saw from the house.' He paused, leaning on his axe handle and looked about him. 'One day I mean to clear all the underbrush from these woods so that the trunks of the trees retreat like shadows of themselves.'

'And call it Birchlands Park and you'll retire from the world of art and live the life of a country squire.'

'Come on!' said Carl, feeling the axe blade with his thumb.

It was easy to begin; easy, easy to throw oneself into this rhythmic movement for a short time. They worked hard, hauling moss-covered logs, lopping mercilessly at branches; working with a strenuous determination which, in Carl, seemed to increase as the work grew heavier and hotter.

'Call a halt, call a halt,' cried Dick at last, Carl showed no sign of letting up. 'I come from the city and work at a desk all day—remember?'

'Right,' said Carl, pushing the dark hair from his eyes with the flat of his palm and sitting where he stood. Dick leaned against a tree and patted the moss before lighting a cigarette.

'God,' he said, with the first puff, 'that's the way to smoke—occasionally. This might be a Pall Mall—first time in years a smoke has tasted like anything but straw.' He tossed his packet to Carl, watched him light up. And then suddenly Carl said, looking over Dick's head and hardly moving his lips, 'She's—strange, isn't she? Like a ghost. She moves like the old and her eyes are dead.'

It has come, thought Dick, this moment I've awaited and dreaded. This moment when nothing I say will be right. 'Yes, Carl, she's strange.'

'She was exquisite once. If you could have known her then. Young and so very different.'

Shadows were beginning to fall. It grew cold. Dick put his coat on and cupped his cigarette in his hands as though the small glow might warm the chill which engulfed him. And as Carl spoke to him, explaining the old Kristin, the young Kristin, Dick knew no word that could bridge the gap pity had cut between them. To say the child was mad was to hit out in the dark and strike the defenceless. There was no real indication of madness; it was more a magnified withdrawal of spirit. But Carl wanted help, advice, not vague theorizing and Dick knew that he was no use. The only thing he knew with any degree of certainty was that Carl's restraint was unhealthy; there would come a time when it snapped. And he hated Kristin with a fierce hatred for so destroying the very fibre of her husband; he hated this thin slip of a girl with her long legs and her long hands who was wreaking destruction silently and insidiously in the strong male mind of Carl.

Carl pulled on his sweater. 'We had better get back,' he said. As they walked down the newly made path Carl smiled. 'There's a deep satisfaction in manual labour—deeper than the average man admits—after a certain point a peace is reached. And besides, this path is good.' Dick gripped his shoulder with a blistered hand. It was an awkward self-conscious gesture but at that moment there was nothing else he could say or do.

The sunset burned in the lake as they returned and the face they waited to see at the window was lost in the reflected glory of the burnished glass.

As Carl said good-bye to Dick he felt he was turning his back on the positive side of his nature and he despised the creature that was left, yet knew no escape from it. Normally he would have gone to his picture; but now he was conscious of no desire to paint, only a desire to want to paint and even that was submerged in the thought of Kristin, Kristin, Kristin. Day and night; inside and out; eating and sleeping—Kristin. The cold finger of ice that burned as it touched and was forever touching everything, everything. Deliberately he sought her out. Perhaps this time ...?

She was, as usual, on the veranda. Now he could no longer see her objectively; when he looked he seemed to be seeing only a part of himself. Yet propinquity with her started up a rhythm in his mind, stress the casual, stress the casual. And so he talked of the trivial when he longed to get to grips with the issue.

'It is too nice to be in,' he said. 'Change your shoes and walk with me in the woods.'

Kristin leaned back in her chair. 'Will you?' he asked.

'N-no,' she answered. 'I'm tired.'

'But darling, you've hardly done anything for days.'

'The storm last night tired me. I couldn't sleep. Storms are tiring things.'

'Well then, come and I'll take you in a canoe. You needn't move once you get in.'

'I'd sooner stay here,' she answered.

Carl reached for a cigarette. There was one thing he must know. He must ask. He lit his cigarette and waited until the flame of the match burned down to his fingers before he spoke. 'Kristin, are you happy?' From under his lids he watched her face and for one moment he saw it register something close to pleasure. Her voice was live when she answered, 'Yes, yes. I'm so near to the trees.'

'Then you like it here?'

'Yes.'

Carl flicked the match from him. He could have jumped up and kissed her. But he would wait until he had gone further … wait until he was sure.

'Kristin, I've wondered—you're not sorry to have married me?' She was far off again, the contact had gone. 'Kristin!'

'What?'

'You're not sorry you married me?'

'No.'

There again indifference. The wall of his hope was broken by the shadow of her 'No.' 'Then you don't dislike me, Kristin? I was so afraid, so worried.' Steady, steady, cautioned his mind. But she was not listening. Already she was gone, escaped.

'Kristin, you must answer me—does it annoy you to have me near?' He waited, fearful, ready for the 'No' to fall like a hammer stroke on the air; the 'No' that meant nothing at all.

'No,' said Kristin.

Carl braced himself. Deliberately he was exposing himself for her to mutilate, but he couldn't stop. 'Kristin, Kristin, say you love me a little.'

She looked up, puzzled. 'Love you?'

'Yes, Kristin. Do you love me?'

The puzzled look increased, then as if everything was solved it went again. 'I don't understand,' she said.

'Great God, Kristin, you must understand. What did you marry me for, what are we doing together at all if you refuse to understand the meaning of love?' He wanted to shake her and shake her—this phlegmatic, disinterested woman. 'You told me you loved me, you told me you loved me,' he said, clinging hopefully to her words. 'Kristin, look at me, answer me.'

She shook her head. 'I don't know what you mean.' Then her face brightened. 'Carl, I'm hungry.'

Carl swung from his chair. This was too much. No one should be allowed to hurt another to this extent. He would leave, run away somewhere and hide in a crowd. She didn't want him, she didn't even need him. 'If she had died,' he said aloud, 'if she had died I could have found solace; for this wound there is no comfort.'

He threw clothes into a bag, blindly, desperately. Downstairs in the studio the new painting stared up from its canvas. When one finger of a friend is laid upon your flesh—no painting should remain and tell the world that his knowledge enclosed this truth. No trace should show. No trace.

With painstaking care he cut the canvas to ribbons with his palette knife, turned and left. He had said good-bye to Birchlands and to Kristin. He would never come back. Never.

The sun and a small wind broke the surface of the lake to glinting sword blades. On the far side, where the trees marched, unchecked, right down to the water's edge, there the lake was a shifting pattern of scarlet, vermilion and burnt orange.

(1940–44)

SHORT FICTION

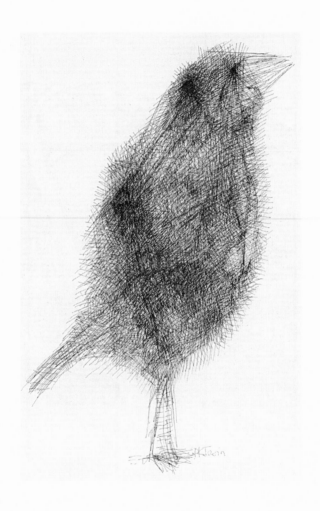

THE GREEN BIRD

I cannot escape the fascination of doors, the weight of unknown people who drive me into myself and pin me with their personalities. Nor can I resist the desire to be led through shutters, and impaled on strange living room chairs.

Therefore when Ernest stood very squarely on his feet and said: 'I'm going to call on Mrs Rowan today and I hope you will come,' I said yes. The desire to be trapped by old Mrs Rowan was stronger than any other feeling. Her door was particularly attractive—set solid and dark in her solid, dark house. I had passed by often and seen no sign of life there—no hand at a window, no small movement of the handle of the door.

We rang the bell. A man-servant, smiling, white-coated, drew us in, took our coats, showed us into the living room.

'So it is this,' I said to Ernest.

'Beg your pardon?' He crossed his knees carefully, jerked back his neck with the abstracted manner of the public speaker being introduced, leaned his young black head on Mrs Rowan's air.

'It is this,' I said. 'No ash trays,' I said.

'But I don't smoke,' said Ernest.

Mrs Rowan came then. There were dark bands holding a child's face onto a forgotten body. She sat as though she were our guest and we had embarrassed her.

Ernest handled the conversation with an Oriental formality aided by daguerreotype gestures. Mrs Rowan responded to him—a child under grey hair, above the large, loose, shambling torso. She talked of candy and birthday cake. She said she didn't like radios.

I said, 'Music', and looked about startled as if someone else had said it, suddenly imagining the horror of music sounding in this motionless house.

She said, 'But you do miss hearing famous speakers. I once heard

Hitler when I was in a taxi.' She said, 'We will only sit here a little longer and then we will go upstairs, I have an invalid up there who likes to pour tea.'

I felt the sick-room atmosphere in my lungs and my longing to escape was a strong hand pushing me towards it. I imagined the whole upstairs white and dim, with disease crowding out the light.

Mrs Rowan said, 'We will go now,' and we rose, unable to protest had we wished, and followed her up the carpeted stairs and into a front room where a tea-table was set up. There was a large figure in a chair.

'Miss Price, the invalid,' Mrs Rowan said, 'insists on pouring the tea. She likes it. It gives her pleasure.' The figure in the chair moved only her eyes, staring first at Ernest and then at me. Her face was lifeless as a plate. Mrs Rowan continued to talk about her. 'She's been with me a long time,' she said. 'Poor dear.' And then, 'It's quite all right. Her nurse is right next door.' She introduced us. Miss Price sucked in the corners of her mouth and inclined her head slightly with each introduction. The white-coated, grinning man-servant brought in the tea.

'You can pour it now,' said Mrs Rowan, and Miss Price began, slowly, faultlessly, with the corners of her mouth sucked in and her eyes dark and long as seeds. She paid no attention to what we said about sugar and cream. She finished and folded her arms, watched us without expression.

Mrs Rowan passed the cake stand. 'You eat these first,' she said, pointing to the sandwiches; 'these second,' pointing to some cookies; 'and this last,' indicating fruit cake. My cup rattled a little.

I pretended to drink my tea, but felt a nausea—the cup seemed dirty. Ernest leaned back in his chair, said, 'Delicious tea.' Miss Price sat with her arms folded; there was no indication of life except in the glimmer of her seed eyes.

'Dear,' said Mrs Rowan suddenly but without concern, 'you haven't poured yourself a cup.'

Miss Price sucked in her mouth, looked down into her lap; her face was hurt.

'No,' I said. 'You must have a cup too.' I laughed by mistake.

Miss Price looked up at me, flicked her eyes at mine with a quick glance of conspiracy and laughed too, in complete silence. Mrs Rowan passed her a cup and she poured her own tea solemnly and folded her arms again.

'Before you go,' Mrs Rowan said, 'I'd like to give you a book—one of mine. Which one would you like?'

'Why,' I said, looking at the cake stand which had never been passed again and stood with all the food untouched but for the two sandwiches Ernest and I had taken, 'Why—' I wondered what I could say. I had no idea she wrote. 'Why,' I said again and desperately, 'I should like most the one you like most.'

Miss Price flicked her eyes at me again and her body heaved with dreadful silent laughter.

'I like them all,' Mrs Rowan said. 'There are some that are written about things that happened in 300 BC and some written about things that happened three minutes ago. I'll get them,' she said, and went.

Ernest was carefully balancing his saucer on his knee, sitting very straight. There was no sound in the entire house.

'I hope you are feeling better, Miss Price,' Ernest said.

I saw the immense silent body heave again, this time with sobs. Dreadful silent sobs. And then it spoke for the first time. 'They cut off both my legs three years ago. I'm nothing but a stump.' And the sobbing grew deeper, longer.

I looked at Ernest. I heard my own voice saying, 'Such a lovely place to live, this—so central. You can see everything from this room. It looks right out on the street. You can see everything.'

Miss Price was still now, her face expressionless, as if it had happened years before. 'Yes,' she said.

'The parades,' I said.

'Yes, the parades. My nephew's in the war.'

'I'm sorry,' Ernest said.

'He was wounded at Ypres. My sister heard last week.' Her arms were folded. Her cup of tea was untouched before her, the cream in a thick scum on the surface.

'Now, here,' Mrs Rowan came in, her arms full of books, like a child behind the weight of flesh—covetous of the books—of the form of the books, spreading them about her, never once opening their covers. 'Which one would you like?' she asked.

'This,' I said. 'The colour of its cover will go with my room.'

'What a pretty thought,' Mrs Rowan said, and for some reason my eyes were drawn to Miss Price, knowing they would find her heaving with that silent laughter that turned her eyes to seeds.

'We must go,' said Ernest suddenly. He put down his cup and stood up. I tucked the book under my arm and crossed to Miss Price. 'Goodbye,'

I said, and shook hands. Her seed eyes seemed underneath the earth. She held on to my hand. I felt as if I was held down in soil.

Ernest said, 'Goodbye, Miss Price,' and held out his hand, but hers still clutched mine. She beckoned to Mrs Rowan and whispered, 'The birds. I want to give her a bird,' and then to me, 'I want to give you a bird.'

Mrs Rowan walked into the next room and returned with a paper bag. Miss Price released my hand and dug down into the bag with shelving fingers. 'No, not these,' she said angrily. 'These are green.'

'They're the only ones,' Mrs Rowan said. 'The others have all gone.'

'I don't like them,' said Miss Price, holding one out on a beaded cord. It was stuffed green serge, dotted with red beadwork, and two red cherries hung from its mouth. 'It's paddy green,' she said disgustedly, and sucked in the corners of her mouth.

'Never mind,' I said. 'It's lovely, and paddy green goes with my name. I'm Patricia, you see, and they sometimes call me Paddy.' I stood back in astonishment at my own sentences, and Miss Price gave an enormous shrug, which, for the moment until she released it, made her fill the room. And then, 'God!' she said, 'what a name!' The scorn in her voice shrivelled us. When I looked back at her as I left she had fallen into silent, shapeless laughter.

Mrs Rowan showed us downstairs and called the man-servant to see us out. She stood like a child at the foot of the stairs and waved every few minutes as the grinning white-coated houseman helped us into our coats.

'You must come again and let Miss Price pour tea for you. It gives her such pleasure.'

Outside, on the step, I began to laugh. I had been impaled and had escaped. My laughter went on and on. It was loud, the people in the street stared at me.

Ernest looked at me with disapproval. 'What do you find so funny?' he asked.

What? What indeed? There was nothing funny at all. Nothing anywhere. But I poked about for an answer.

'Why, this,' I said, holding the bird by its beaded cord. 'This, of course.'

He looked at it a long time. 'Yes,' he said, seriously. 'Yes I suppose it is quaint,' and he smiled.

It was as though a pearl was smiling.

(1942)

MIRACLES

That evening after supper while Madame rocked on the gallery in the slowly settling darkness Annette took us to see her friends. Lights blazed in the windows as we walked with dust muffled steps along the village street and the air was flooded with green as though chlorophyll lit the evening.

Small groups of youths walked by, serious and stolid as moose in their pinstriped suits. '*Salut*,' '*Bon soir*'—the greetings rang out as they passed. Annette was proud in her acknowledgements, walking with a strange stiff-legged self-consciousness. Watching them I was amazed that there were no girls with them—no girls with their heavily powdered faces, extraordinary amateur curls and the stifling smell of cheap perfume.

'They have no girls?' I asked.

Annette was quick to assure me they had.

'But on an evening like this?'

'They are on their way to call,' Annette said.

'But they don't go out together?'

Annette swung horrified eyes to God at the suggestion. The *curé* did not allow it. The *curé* knew what was right for them and what was wrong. *The curé* knew everything and looked after them. The *curé* said it was wicked.

Luke walked, his hands in his pockets, his head back, saying nothing. At first I dragged him into the conversation but when Annette began to talk of the *curé* I forgot. Besides, I needed all my energy to keep up with her, to follow the acrobatics of her speech.

'He is a very great and good man,' said Annette and her words sounded staccato on the long quiet street. 'He performs miracles.' The speed and extravagance of Annette's language made me feel that I was in some way inside a Catherine wheel.

Her face grew long and full of wonder as she recounted her miracle. 'Until I was twenty-one,' she said, 'I was not like other girls. I had been unwell and I was very weak. Mamma was worried about me. All my sisters were strong, they were getting married, but I was not and each month we waited and I was not well. Mamma got the horse and cart from the Pagets' and we drove to the town. It was a long way. And it is very expensive to see the doctor. Mamma had the money in her hand and I was afraid when we arrived. It was hot and my head was full and I was ashamed. We waited for him to come and then we told him. He took the money Mamma had in her hand and gave me some medicine and we drove back home again. All that way, all that money, all that way home again. I took the medicine he gave and waited. Each month I waited. Each morning I went to early Mass and prayed but nothing happened. And all the time I got sicker and sicker. Mamma went to the *curé* then and he came. He said he would perform a miracle. He got a big glass and a bottle of porter and he poured the porter into the glass. Then he added two teaspoons of mustard and he stirred and stirred until it was frothing. He handed me the glass. "Drink it down while it is still frothing," he said. But I couldn't. I shook my head. I could not drink that drink. "Drink it down while it is frothing and you will be cured within five minutes." I saw the big glass. Mamma was crying. "Drink it down," said Mamma and she held her head in her hands and rocked from side to side. "Drink it down, Annette." Then I didn't care any more. I took the big glass and I thought of the face of the Virgin Mary and I made the sign of the Cross and prayed inside me and I drank it down. It was bad, that drink. It tasted bad. I wanted to be sick to my stomach.' Annette paused and gave a great sigh as if she had lived the whole experience over again.

'And it worked?' I asked.

The story finished, Annette nodded her head sagely, smugly. 'Ah, yes. It was a miracle. A miracle in the name of God.'

'And you've been all right ever since?' The tale shocked me. In my own head I saw a black-robed *curé*—Mamma, great fat Mamma, shaking her head and crying and Annette drinking down a devil's brew with its smoking sulphur-coloured fumes that changed her from a child into a woman in five minutes. 'Ever since you have been all right?'

'Ah, but yes, it was a miracle.'

Had the *curé* performed other miracles? I wanted to know. What else had he done?

Annette pursed her lips and shrugged. 'Ah, yes.'

'Tell me,' I said, but we had already arrived at the Simones'. Another time she would tell me. Now her mind was on her friends. They were especially beautiful, Annette informed us, for they were blond. And that was rare. They were the only people in the village who were blond.

On the gallery sat Mme Simone, frail as a Marie Laurençin painting, her high cheekbones dotted with excited crimson, her hair permanented like the fizz on ginger beer. She rocked more slowly as she greeted Annette and was introduced, insisted that we all sit down, brought forward chairs, smiled nervously and moved her white hands across her apron. Noiselessly, as wherever we went, the children collected—stood in silence, pale, alarmingly pale; each with the dot of tubercular rouge on their cheekbones, their uncurled hair smooth on their heads as butter, their legs and arms motionless.

The ground sloped up from the house beside us—grass and apple trees with yellow apples luminous in the leaves, lying in the grass pale as the children's hair—and everything tinged with the green light, washed in it.

While Mme Simone and Annette gossiped I felt bathed in the blond and green incandescence of this family and its garden, and was fascinated and appalled by the still life of the children, the shyness that held them fixed and their flax-blue eyes that looked as shallow and delicate as petals.

'André has bought a truck,' Annette said and her pride sat upon her fat and sleek as mercury, before it broke and scattered in excited description. 'It is big,' she said, her arms enclosing it. 'The whole village could ride in it, it is so big. And it is red.'

'Agathe told me,' said Mme Simone. Her eyelids lifted to hoods and she pursed her mouth to judgement. 'He gets a truck instead of a wife,' she said. 'It is not good.'

'It makes a beautiful noise,' said Annette, like a child. She turned to us. 'It makes a better noise than your car.'

'Where is it?' I asked. 'Why haven't we seen it?'

'André has gone to the city already.'

Madame nodded sagely. 'Soon André will live in the city,' she announced.

Luke knocked the ashes from his pipe, blew through it a couple of times and put it in his pocket.

The greenness grew deeper as we talked—came up and swamped us until it seemed as if we were under the sea. Mme Simone became nervous, rocked rapidly, and suddenly her harsh voice commanded the children: 'Get apples for the English.' But the children hardly moved. A slight tremor of increased shyness rippled them and froze them. Raising her voice to an alarming volume the mother repeated her command and they scuttled then, uncannily green, into the deep grass, picking the globes of fruit from the ground, reaching to the lower branches of the trees, moving with their eyes still on Luke and me; shy, offering their harvest with white-green fingers, smiles making masks of their small faces.

I held out my hand to receive the clusters of fruit with the leaves attached.

'They are flower apples,' the mother said, and Annette, nibbling, explained that they didn't last, but faded like flowers in a few days.

The giant illuminated cross on the hillside sharpened and brightened as the darkness fell. Proudly they nodded at it, Annette and Mme Simone, drew down the corners of their mouths, told how it burned day and night, day and night, and how it was their cross, how each family paid for a light and that light never went out.

In Annette's charge, we left when she gave the sign. The green light was deeper now, the children behind their mother seemed no longer strange, but terrible—tiny and fair and lifeless while Madame rocked unceasingly back and forth in her chair, and beside them, on the hillside, the vegetation crept in closer and closer like a wave.

Leaving, our apples still in our hands, Annette said, 'Eat them. They are good.' But I shook my head, feeling the perfectly formed and infected fruit against my palms—pale apple-green and deadly.

'Are they not beautiful, the Simones?' Annette was anxious to know. 'Are they not the most beautiful people you have seen here?'

'But surely,' I said, sick with alarm, 'surely they are ill. Consumptive?'

'Ah yes,' said Annette in easy agreement, but bored.

'But Annette, it is a dangerous disease. It is catching. It will spread.'

'No!' her voice was incredulous. 'You joke,' she said and laughed.

I felt desperate. I wanted to convince Annette. 'In the city,' I said, 'those people would go away for treatment. Doesn't the doctor see them, Annette?'

Annette was not interested. 'It is nothing,' she said. 'The Bouchards have it and the Pagets and the ...' she listed the family names. 'It is nothing. The *curé* goes and he prays. Sometimes it gets bad and someone dies. Often that happens.'

I wanted to cry out at Annette's stupidity. I grabbed Luke's arm. 'Say something to her,' I said. 'Tell her, Luke.'

'It is a dangerous illness,' Luke said. And the subject was finished. But something violent and terrible was happening inside me. An anger I had not known before, a fury at the ignorance and pitifulness of people. I had hoped for some affirmation of a similar feeling in Luke. But his voice had been factual and indifferent. I let go his arm quickly, and when he felt for my hand in the darkness and tried to hold it I pulled away, even knowing that he too, needed affirming at that moment.

We stumbled a little in the darkness on the dusty road. A smell of salt blew up from the river and the houses were quiet as though deserted. It was as if all the inhabitants were dead—and the faces of the Simone children arranged themselves before my eyes, lying like wax and butter in a row of green wood coffins.

The *curé* goes and he prays. The *curé* is a great and good man. The *curé* performs miracles. But there are no miracles in the consumptive houses, I thought. No miracles there and I was bitter with Annette for her dreadful acceptance of death. Bitter with Annette and furious with Luke.

(1944)

VICTORIA

Victoria claims my memory of the event is not memory at all but imagination. And I wonder. Not only whether she is correct, but about the very nature of the two. Is imagination perhaps a further, longer memory? A remembering outside time, beyond space?

(*Do you remember*, I say to my very old aunt, frail as lace in her hospital bed, *do you remember me?* Her eyes are clear and shining as peaty water. *No*, she says. *Do you remember*, I try again, *your garden at Blythe?* Her eyes narrow, she looks far off and—*No*, she says. *Do you remember...?* But she cuts me short. *I don't remember anything, anymore.* Then, *Perhaps you remember*, I suggest, playful, pressing, *time before you were born?* And, *That would perhaps be easier*, she says.)

Although the question in dispute concerns our first meeting, Victoria would, I am sure, agree that I didn't imagine her. Is she not real enough to argue? To put me straight? Sufficient proof, surely, to her at least, that she is no figment of my imagination. And if not she, then why the others?

I remember her first as a child, pink-coated, plump, glued—as it were—between the angular navy-blue serge figures of her parents. She was small but not altogether young, staring enquiringly through the thick glasses she wore even then. The occasion, a prize-giving for which she had come in from the country, fresh from the butter-and-cream-coloured flowers of her prize-winning painting. Her father, awkward in his best suit, her mother curiously girlish in her pale straw hat. And she, Victoria, short, self-contained, self-centred even; hair cut straight and square above those bright eyes. Dark as a robin's and like a robin's, expectant. Intent. As intent then as now. She panned the room—an intelligent camera—taking in that great warehouse of a studio, its visible walls covered with paintings of nudes and still-lifes, its far walls lost, dissolved by the faint light of the candles.

We were young. Dream-filled. But we must have looked old to her. We smoked. We drank. Neither she nor her parents did either. We had not expected her quite so young, so chaperoned. From so different a world where work was a physical, manual affair that enlarged the hands, lined and roughened the skin.

The group they formed, the three of them standing there in the smoke-thickened air, set them apart. They might have been a piece of sculpture, a painting. In Victoria, the mother's fair colouring merged with the father's features to make a pale, female, juvenile version of the swarthy man whom she would, I felt sure, come to resemble more strongly as the years passed. I saw them very clearly with my painter's eye: the echoing family likenesses, the vivid pink of Victoria's coat repeated—faded—in the flowers on her mother's hat. The two dark forms flanking—protecting?—their bright bud. I saw them clearly then as I see them clearly still. They are printed sharply on my retina—those three short figures outside fashion and city ways, outside pretension, set down in our youthful Bohemia. Real, in a way we weren't.

We presented Victoria with her prize. Pleased, but not unduly so, was the impression they gave—either by her talents or our bounty. One did what one did and took the consequences—good or bad. Such was their attitude. Their presence, alien among us, just happened to be the consequence of Victoria's painting. If they disapproved of us they gave no sign. If they envied us it was not apparent.

And having done what they came to do, they departed, leaving where they had stood a seemingly unfillable space which for a time we walked around as if they were still there.

Victoria insists—certain her memory is more accurate than mine—that she came to the studio right enough, but *alone;* having journeyed by train through the prairie landscape *alone.* (She is firm in her emphasis.) And that she spent the night at the house of one of the competition judges. Damnably, she even remembers her name.

(*Do you remember your name?* I question my aunt, pinched in her hospital bed and cranked up so that she folds in the middle. *Yes,* she replies, looking at me as if I were trying to trick her. *It's Woodhouse. The house I live in.* And, *Do you remember mine?* Eagerly I pursue the reviving memory, close in. She looks at me as if she had never seen me before. Mute. *It's Gail,* I say. *Gail,* she repeats. *Is that the house you live in?* Perhaps it is.)

Victoria laughs at me when I speak of her parents, maintaining that I have always had more imagination than she. She speaks of me with a curious familiarity as if she knows me and my ways. She tells me of our correspondence during the period she spent in the sanatorium. I recall nothing of all this. She says she has my letters to prove it. Then prove it, I say. How otherwise can I know that in what she is pleased to call her memory, my letters are not just as much imagined by her as her parents—so she still contends—are imagined by me?

With age she is longer, leaner, sparer altogether than the child's frame would have led one to expect. The likeness to her father is now striking. Hair cropped and brushed back reveals his high brow, once hidden by her little-girl bangs. The intent glance, in no way diminished, is nevertheless modified by some passivity, some willingness to be observer—a role which, thirty years ago, had already stamped the features on her father's face. If time has so emphasized this resemblance, as indeed it has, was I not—on that prize-winning night—rather more prophetic than imaginative? And if the very model itself was the product of my imagination, how has she now grown so perfectly to match it?

(My aunt has taken her spoon and delicately, incomprehensibly, is working among the petals of the hydrangea on her table. *What are you doing?* I ask, watching her eyes, her fingers, the silver flashing silver-blue in the purple-blue of the flower. She doesn't look at me. *I'm not hurting it*, she replies, defensive. *I am only trying to remove the issue.* She pronounces the word in the old-fashioned way, the double 's' a whistled hiss, the 'u' French. *Is it difficult?* I inquire. *No, it's quite easy but I can't do it. You just very gently force it apart and remove the issue. It doesn't hurt it at all*, she says. *And what do you want it for?* I ask, interested. *To paint the shadow of that star that is shining there.*)

Victoria's paintings—whatever the subject—remain for me like the flowers of her childhood. Innocent, literal, freshly seen. Uncompromisingly honest, the critics say. Honest as far as she goes, I am tempted to amend. For what, after all, is this immediate reality we stub against but the first obvious gate opening onto a further reality? A reality Victoria would undoubtedly call imagination.

We have painted together from time to time over the years on those rare occasions when we are both in the same city—she working from the model before her, the possibility of altering it never entering her mind;

I working from nothing visible, as a spider making its web. Both of us silent, engrossed. *You are more imaginative than I*, she says, and *You've caught it exactly*, I reply.

So here we are after half a century of intermittent meetings, she so sure of the reality before her nose; I like Chuang-Tze, not knowing dream from reality, imagination from dream.

Am I now, at this very moment, no more than the product of Victoria's unremembered dream? Or did I, all those years ago, imagine not only the father she resembles and the mother whose colouring she shares, but the little Victoria—Victoria herself?

(For my aunt, the cosmos has entered her sickroom. The angels crowding her move soft as swans. Their wings are elegantly folded knife-pleat linen, their shining faces, the faces of her friends. They are gentle with her, fingering her worn flesh. *They won't hurt*, I assure her. *They're only removing the issue.* And although I have to put my ear to her lips because there is so little breath left, the words are quite distinct and full of wonder. *Have I an issue to remove?* she says.)

(1976)

UNLESS THE EYE
CATCH FIRE

Unless the eye catch fire
The God will not be seen ...
— *Where the Wasteland Ends*
Theodore Roszak

Wednesday, September 17.

The day began normally enough. The quails, cockaded as antique foot soldiers, arrived while I was having breakfast. The males black-faced, white-necklaced, cinnamon-crowned, with short, sharp, dark plumes. Square bibs, Payne's grey; belly and sides with a pattern of small stitches. Reassuring, the flock of them. They tell me the macadamization of the world is not complete.

A sudden alarm, and as if they had one brain among them, they were gone in a rush—a sideways ascending Niagara—shutting out the light, obscuring the sky and exposing a rectangle of lawn, unexpectedly emerald. How bright the berries on the cotoneaster. Random leaves on the cherry twirled like gold spinners. The garden was high-keyed, vivid, locked in aspic.

Without warning, and as if I were looking down the tube of a kaleidoscope, the merest shake occurred—moiréed the garden—rectified itself. Or, more precisely, as if a range-finder through which I had been sighting, found of itself a more accurate focus. Sharpened, in fact, to an excoriating exactness.

And then the colours changed. Shifted to a higher octave—a *bright spectrum*. Each colour with its own *light*, its own *shape*. The leaves of the trees, the berries, the grasses—as if shedding successive films—disclosed layer after layer of hidden perfections. And upon these rapidly changing surfaces the 'range-finder'—to really play hob with metaphor!—sharpened its small invisible blades.

I don't know how to describe the intensity and speed of focus of this gratuitous zoom lens through which I stared, or the swift and dizzying adjustments within me. I became a 'sleeping top', perfectly centred, perfectly—sighted. The colours vibrated beyond the visible range of the spectrum. Yet I saw them. With some matching eye. Whole galaxies of them, blazing and glowing, flowing in rivulets, gushing in fountains—volatile, mercurial, and making lack-lustre and off-key the colours of the rainbow.

I had no time or inclination to wonder, intellectualize. My mind seemed astonishingly clear and quite still. Like a crystal. A burning glass.

And then the range-finder sharpened once again. To alter space.

The lawn, the bushes, the trees—still super-brilliant—were no longer *there*. *There*, in fact, had ceased to exist. They were now, of all places in the world, *here*. Right in the centre of my being. Occupying an immense inner space. Part of me. Mine. Except the whole idea of ownership was beside the point. As true to say I was theirs as they mine. I and they were here, they and I, there. (*There, here* ... odd ... but for an irrelevant, inconsequential 't' which comes and goes, the words are the same.)

As suddenly as the world had altered, it returned to normal. I looked at my watch. A ridiculous mechanical habit. As I had no idea when the experience began it was impossible to know how long it had lasted. What had seemed eternity couldn't have been more than a minute or so. My coffee was still steaming in its mug.

The garden, through the window, was as it had always been. Yet not as it had always been. Less. Like listening to mono after hearing stereo. But with a far greater loss of dimension. A grievous loss.

I rubbed my eyes. Wondered, not without alarm, if this was the onset of some disease of the retina—glaucoma or some cellular change in the eye itself—superlatively packaged, fatally sweet as the marzipan cherry I ate as a child and *knew* was poison.

If it *is* a disease, the symptoms will recur. It will happen again.

Tuesday, September 23.

It *has* happened again.

Tonight, taking Dexter for his late walk, I looked up at the crocheted tangle of boughs against the sky. Dark silhouettes against the lesser dark, but beating now with an extraordinary black brilliance. The golden glints in obsidian or the lurking embers in black opals are the nearest I can come to describing them. But it's a false description, emphasizing as it does, the wrong end of the scale. This was a *dark spectrum*. As if the starry heavens were translated into densities of black—black Mars, black Saturn, black Jupiter; or a master jeweller had crossed his jewels with jet and set them to burn and wink in the branches and twigs of oaks whose leaves shone luminous—a leafy Milky Way—fired by black chlorophyll.

Dexter stopped as dead as I. Transfixed. His thick honey-coloured coat and amber eyes glowing with their own intense brightness, suggested yet another spectrum. A *spectrum of light*. He was a constellated dog, shining, supra-real, against the foothills and mountain ranges of midnight.

I am reminded now, as I write, of a collection of Lepidoptera in Brazil—one entire wall covered with butterflies, creatures of daylight—enormous or tiny—blue, orange, black. Strong-coloured. And on the opposite wall their anti-selves—pale night flyers spanning such a range of silver and white and lightest snuff-colour that once one entered their spectral scale there was no end to the subtleties and delicate nuances. But I didn't think like this then. All thought, all comparisons were prevented by the startling infinities of darkness and light.

Then, as before, the additional shake occurred and the two spectrums moved swiftly from without to within. As if two equal and complementary circles centred inside me—or I in them. How explain that I not only *saw* but actually *was* the two spectrums? (I underline a simple, but in this case, exactly appropriate anagram.)

Then the range-finder lost its focus and the world, once again, was back to normal. Dexter, a pale, blurred blob, bounded about within the field of my peripheral vision, going on with his doggy interests just as if a moment before he had not been frozen in his tracks, a dog entranced.

I am no longer concerned about my eyesight. Wonder only if we are both mad, Dexter and I? Angelically mad, sharing hallucinations of epiphany. *Folie à deux*?

Friday, October 3.

It's hard to account for my secrecy, for I *have* been secretive. As if the cat had my tongue. It's not that I don't long to talk about the colours but I can't risk the wrong response—(as Gaby once said of a companion after a faultless performance of *Giselle*: 'If she had criticized the least detail of it, I'd have hit her!').

Once or twice I've gone so far as to say, 'I had the most extraordinary experience the other day ...' hoping to find some look or phrase, some answering, 'So did I.' None has been forthcoming.

I can't forget the beauty. Can't get it out of my head. Startling, unearthly, indescribable. Infuriatingly indescribable. A glimpse of—somewhere else. Somewhere alive, miraculous, newly made yet timeless. And more important still—significant, luminous, with a meaning of which I was part. Except that I—the I who is writing this—did not exist; was flooded out, dissolved in that immensity where subject and object are one.

I have to make a deliberate effort now not to live my life in terms of it; not to sit, immobilized, awaiting the shake that heralds a new world. Awaiting the transfiguration. Luckily the necessities of life keep me busy. But upstream of my actions, behind a kind of plate glass, some part of me waits, listens, maintains a total attention.

Tuesday, October 7.

Things are moving very fast.

Some nights ago my eye was caught by a news item. 'Trucker Blames Colours', said the headline. Reading on: 'R. T. Ballantyne, driver for Island Trucks, failed to stop on a red light at the intersection of Fernhill and Spender. Questioned by traffic police, Ballantyne replied: "I didn't see it, that's all. There was this shake, then all these colours suddenly in the trees. Real bright ones I'd never seen before. I guess they must have blinded me." A breathalyzer test proved negative.' Full stop.

I had an overpowering desire to talk to R. T. Ballantyne. Even looked him up in the telephone book. Not listed. I debated reaching him through Island Trucks in the morning.

Hoping for some mention of the story, I switched on the local radio station, caught the announcer mid-sentence:

'... to come to the studio and talk to us. So far no one has been able to describe just what the "new" colours are, but perhaps Ruby Howard can. Ruby, you say you actually *saw* "new" colours?'

What might have been a flat, rather ordinary female voice was sharpened by wonder. 'I was out in the garden, putting it to bed, you might say, getting it ready for winter. The hydrangeas are dried out—you know the way they go. Soft beiges and greys. And I was thinking maybe I should cut them back, when there was this—shake, like—and there they were

148

shining. Pink. And blue. But not like they are in life. Different. Brighter. With little lights, like ...'

The announcer's voice cut in, 'You say "not like they are in life." D'you think this wasn't life? I mean, do you think maybe you were dreaming?'

'Oh, no,' answered my good Mrs Howard, positive, clear, totally unrattled. 'Oh, no, I wasn't *dreaming*. Not *dreaming*—... Why—*this* is more like dreaming.' She was quiet a moment and then, in a matter-of-fact voice, 'I can't expect you to believe it,' she said. 'Why should you? I wouldn't believe it myself if I hadn't seen it.' Her voice expressed a kind of compassion as if she was really sorry for the announcer.

I picked up the telephone book for the second time, looked up the number of the station. I had decided to tell Mrs Howard what I had seen. I dialled, got a busy signal, depressed the bar and waited, cradle in hand. I dialled again. And again.

Later.

J. just phoned. Curious how she and I play the same game over and over.

J: Were you watching Channel 8?
Me: No, I...
J: An interview. With a lunatic. One who sees colours and flashing lights.
Me: Tell me about it.
J: He was a logger—a high-rigger—not that that has anything to do with it. He's retired now and lives in an apartment and has a window-box with geraniums. This morning the flowers were like neon, he said, flashing and shining... *Hone*stly!
Me: Perhaps he saw something you can't ...
J: *(Amused)* I might have known you'd take his side. Seriously, what *could* he have seen?
Me: Flashing and shining—as he said.
J: But they couldn't. Not geraniums. And you know it as well as I do. *Hone*stly, Babe... (She is the only person left who calls me the name my mother called me.) Why are you always so perverse?

I felt faithless. I put down the receiver, as if I had not borne witness to my God.

October 22.

Floods of letters to the papers. Endless interviews on radio and TV. Pros, cons, inevitable spoofs.

One develops an eye for authenticity. It's as easy to spot as sunlight. However they may vary in detail, true accounts of the colours have an unmistakable common factor—a common factor as difficult to convey as sweetness to those who know only salt. True accounts are inarticulate, diffuse, unlikely—impossible.

It's recently crossed my mind that there may be some relationship between having seen the colours and their actual manifestation—something as improbable as *the more one sees them the more they are able to be seen.* Perhaps they are always there in some normally invisible part of the electro-magnetic spectrum and only become visible to certain people at certain times. A combination of circumstances or some subtle refinement in the organ of sight. And then—from quantity to quality perhaps, like water to ice—a whole community changes, is able to see, catches fire.

For example, it was seven days between the first time I saw the colours and the second. During that time there were no reports to the media. But once the reports began, the time between lessened appreciably *for me.* Not proof, of course, but worth noting. And I can't help wondering why some people see the colours and others don't. Do some of us have extra vision? Are some so conditioned that they're virtually blind to what's there before their very noses? Is it a question of more, or less?

Reports come in from farther and farther afield; from all walks of life. I think now there is no portion of the inhabited globe without 'shake freaks' and no acceptable reason for the sightings. Often, only one member of a family will testify to the heightened vision. In my own small circle, I am the only witness—or so I think. I feel curiously hypocritical as I listen to my friends denouncing the 'shakers.' Drugs, they say. Irrational—possibly dangerous. Although no sinister incidents have occurred yet—just some mild shake-baiting here and there—one is uneasily reminded of Salem.

Scientists pronounce us hallucinated or mistaken, pointing out that so far there is no hard evidence, no objective proof. That means, I suppose, no photographs, no spectroscopic measurement—if such is possible. Interestingly, seismographs show very minor earthquake tremors—showers of them, like shooting stars in August. Pundits claim 'shake fever'—as it has come to be called—is a variant on flying saucer fever and that it will subside in its own time. Beneficent physiologists suggest we are suffering (why is it *always* suffering, never enjoying?) a distorted form of *ocular spectrum* or after-image. (An after-image of what?) Psychologists disagree among themselves. All in all, it is not surprising that some of us prefer to keep our experiences to ourselves.

January 9.

Something new has occurred. Something impossible. Disturbing. So disturbing, in fact, that according to rumour it is already being taken with the utmost seriousness at the highest levels. TV, press and radio—with good reason—talk of little else.

What seemingly began as a mild winter has assumed sinister overtones. Farmers in southern Alberta are claiming the earth is unnaturally hot to the touch. Golfers at Harrison complain that the soles of their feet burn. Here on the coast, we notice it less. Benign winters are our specialty.

Already we don't lack for explanations as to why the earth could not be hotter than usual, nor why it is naturally 'unnaturally' hot. Vague notes of reassurance creep into the speeches of public men. They may be unable to explain the issue, but they can no longer ignore it.

To confuse matters even further, reports on temperatures seem curiously inconsistent. What information we get comes mainly from self-appointed 'earth touchers'. And now that the least thing can fire an argument, their conflicting readings lead often enough to inflammatory debate.

For myself, I can detect no change at all in my own garden.

Thursday...?

There is no longer any doubt. The temperature of the earth's surface *is* increasing.

It is unnerving, horrible, to go out and feel the ground like some great beast, warm, beneath one's feet. As if another presence—vast, invisible—attends one. Dexter, too, is perplexed. He barks at the earth with the same indignation and, I suppose, fear, with which he barks at the first rumblings of earthquake.

Air temperatures, curiously, don't increase proportionately—or so we're told. It doesn't make sense, but at the moment nothing makes sense. Countless explanations have been offered. Elaborate explanations. None adequate. The fact that the air temperature remains temperate despite the higher ground heat must, I think, be helping to keep panic down. Even so, these are times of great tension.

Hard to understand these two unexplained—unrelated?—phenomena: the first capable of dividing families; the second menacing us all. We are like animals trapped in a burning building.

Later.

J. just phoned. Terrified. Why don't I move in with her, she urges. After all she has the space and we have known each other forty years. (Hard to believe when I don't feel even forty!) She can't bear it—the loneliness.

Poor J. Always so protected, insulated by her money. And her charm. What one didn't provide, the other did ... diversions, services, attention.

What do I think is responsible for the heat, she asks. But it turns out she means who. Her personal theory is that the 'shake freaks' are causing it—involuntarily, perhaps, but the two are surely linked.

'How could they possibly cause it?' I enquire. 'By what reach of the imagination...?'

'Search *me*!' she protests. 'How on earth should *I* know?' And the sound of the dated slang makes me really laugh.

But suddenly she is close to tears. '"How can you *laugh*?' she calls. 'This is nightmare. Nightmare!'

Dear J. I wish I could help but the only comfort I could offer would terrify her still more.

September.

Summer calmed us down. If the earth was hot, well, summers *are* hot. And we were simply having an abnormally hot one.

Now that it is fall—the season of cool nights, light frosts—and the earth like a feverish child remains worryingly hot, won't cool down, apprehension mounts.

At last we are given official readings. For months the authorities have assured us with irrefutable logic that the temperature of the earth could not be increasing. Now, without any apparent period of indecision or confusion, they are warning us with equal conviction and accurate statistical documentation that it has, in fact, increased. Something anyone with a pocket-handkerchief of lawn has known for some time.

Weather stations, science faculties, astronomical observatories all over the world, are measuring and reporting. Intricate computerized tables are quoted. Special departments of government have been set up. We speak now of a new Triassic Age—the Neo-Triassic—and of the accelerated melting of the ice caps. But we are elaborately assured that this could not, repeat not, occur in our lifetime.

Interpreters and analysts flourish. The media are filled with theories and explanations. The increased temperature has been attributed to impersonal agencies such as bacteria from outer space; a thinning of the earth's atmosphere; a build-up of carbon-dioxide in the air; some axial irregularity; a change in the earth's core (geologists are reported to have begun test borings). No theory is too far-fetched to have its supporters. And because man likes a scapegoat, blame has been laid upon NASA, atomic physicists, politicians, the occupants of flying saucers and finally upon mankind at large—improvident, greedy mankind—whose polluted, strike-ridden world is endangered now by the fabled flames of hell.

We are also informed that Nostradamus, the Bible, and Jeane Dixon have all foreseen our plight. A new paperback, *Let Edgar Cayce Tell You Why*, sold out in a matter of days. Attendance at churches has doubled. Cults proliferate. Yet even in this atmosphere, we, the 'shake freaks', are considered lunatic fringe. Odd men out. In certain quarters I believe we are seriously held responsible for the escalating heat, so J. is not alone. There have now been one or two nasty incidents. It is not surprising that even the most vocal among us have grown less willing to talk. I am glad to have kept silent. As a woman living alone, the less I draw attention to myself the better.

Our lives are greatly altered by this overhanging sense of doom. It is already hard to buy certain commodities. Dairy products are in very short supply. On the other hand, the market is flooded with citrus fruits. We are threatened with severe shortages for the future. The authorities are resisting rationing but it will have to come if only to prevent artificial shortages resulting from hoarding.

Luckily the colours are an almost daily event. I see them now, as it were, with my entire being. It is as if all my cells respond to their brilliance and become light too. At such times I feel I might shine in the dark.

No idea of the date.

It is evening and I am tired but I am so far behind in my notes I want to get something down. Events have moved too fast for me.

Gardens, parks, every tillable inch of soil, have been appropriated for food crops. As an able, if aging body, with an acre of land and some knowledge of gardening, I have been made responsible for soybeans—small trifoliate plants rich with the promise of protein. Neat rows of them cover what were once my vegetable garden, flower beds, lawn.

Young men from the Department of Agriculture came last month, bulldozed, cultivated, planted. Efficient, noisy desecrators of my twenty years of landscaping. Dexter barked at them from the moment they appeared and I admit I would have shared his indignation had the water shortage not already created its own desolation.

As a government gardener I'm a member of a new privileged class. I have watering and driving permits and coupons for gasoline and boots—an indication of what is to come. So far there has been no clothes rationing.

Daily instructions—when to water and how much, details of mulching, spraying—reach me from the government radio station to which I tune first thing in the morning. It also provides temperature readings, weather forecasts and the latest news releases on emergency measures, curfews, rationing, insulation. From the way things are going I think it will soon be our only station. I doubt that newspapers will be able to print much longer. In any event, I have already given them up. At first it was interesting to see how quickly drugs, pollution, education, Women's Lib., all became bygone issues; and, initially, I was fascinated to see how we rationalized. Then I became bored. Then disheartened. Now I am too busy.

Evening.

A call came from J. Will I come for Christmas?

Christmas! Extraordinary thought. Like a word from another language learned in my youth, now forgotten.

'I've still got some Heidsieck. We can get tight.'

The word takes me back to my teens. 'Like old times ...'

'Yes.' She is eager. I hate to let her down. 'J., I can't. How could I get to you?'

'In your *car*, silly. *You* still have gas. You're the only one of us who has.' Do I detect a slight hint of accusation, as if I had acquired it illegally?

'But J., it's only for emergencies.'

'My God, Babe, d'you think *this* isn't an emergency?'

'J., dear …'

'*Please*, Babe,' she pleads. 'I'm so afraid. Of the looters. The eeriness. You must be afraid too. *Please!*'

I should have said, yes, that of course I was afraid. It's only natural to be afraid. Or, unable to say that, I should have made the soothing noises a mother makes to her child. Instead, 'There's no reason to be afraid, J.,' I said. It must have sounded insufferably pompous.

'No reason!' She was exasperated with me. 'I'd have thought there was every reason.'

She will phone again. In the night perhaps when she can't sleep. Poor J. She feels so alone. She *is* so alone. And so idle. I don't suppose it's occurred to her yet that telephones will soon go. That a whole way of life is vanishing completely.

It's different for me. I have the soybeans which keep me busy all the daylight hours. And Dexter. And above all I have the colours and with them the knowledge that there are others, other people, whose sensibilities I share. We are invisibly, inviolably related to one another as the components of a molecule. I say 'we'. Perhaps I should speak only for myself, yet I feel as sure of these others as if they had spoken. Like the quails, we share one brain—no, I think it is one heart—between us. How do I know this? How *do* I know? I know by knowing. We are less alarmed by the increasing heat than those who have not seen the colours. I can't explain why. But seeing the colours seems to change one—just as certain diagnostic procedures cure the complaint they are attempting to diagnose.

In all honesty I admit to having had moments when this sense of community was not enough, when I have had a great longing for my own kind—for so have I come to think of these others—in the way one has a great longing for someone one loves. Their presence in the world is not enough. One must see them. Touch them. Speak with them.

But lately that longing has lessened. All longing, in fact. And fear. Even my once great dread that I might cease to see the colours has vanished. It is as if through seeing them I have learned to see them. Have learned to be ready to see—passive; not striving to see—active. It keeps me very wide awake. Transparent even. Still.

The colours come daily now. Dizzying. Transforming. Life-giving. My sometimes back-breaking toil in the garden is lightened, made full of wonder, by the incredible colours shooting in the manner of children's sparklers from the plants themselves and from my own work-worn hands. I hadn't realized that I too am part of this vibrating luminescence.

Later.

I have no idea how long it is since I abandoned these notes. Without seasons to measure its passing, without normal activities—preparations for festivals, occasional outings—time feels longer, shorter or—more curious still—simultaneous, undifferentiated. Future and past fused in the present. Linearity broken.

I had intended to write regularly, but the soybeans keep me busy pretty well all day and by evening I'm usually ready for bed. I'm sorry however to have missed recording the day-to-day changes. They were more or less minor at first. But once the heat began its deadly escalation, the world as we have known it—'our world'—had you been able to put it alongside 'this world'—would have seemed almost entirely different.

No one, I think, could have foreseen the speed with which everything has broken down. For instance, the elaborate plans made to maintain transportation became useless in a matter of months. Private traffic was first curtailed, then forbidden. If a man from another planet had looked in on us, he would have been astonished to see us trapped who were apparently free.

The big changes only really began after the first panic evacuations from the cities. Insulated by concrete, sewer pipes and underground parkades, high density areas responded slowly to the increasing temperatures. But once the heat penetrated their insulations, Gehennas were created overnight and whole populations fled in hysterical exodus, jamming highways in their futile attempts to escape.

Prior to this the government had not publicly acknowledged a crisis situation. They had taken certain precautions, brought in temporary measures to ease shortages and dealt with new developments on an *ad hoc* basis. Endeavoured to play it cool. Or so it seemed. Now they levelled with us. It was obvious that they must have been planning for months, only awaiting the right psychological moment to take everything over. That moment had clearly come. What we had previously thought of as a free world ended. We could no longer eat, drink, move without permits or coupons. This was full-scale emergency.

Yet nothing proceeds logically. Plans are made only to be remade to accommodate new and totally unexpected developments. The heat, unpatterned as disseminated sclerosis, attacks first here, then there. Areas of high temperature suddenly and inexplicably cool off—or vice versa. Agronomists are doing everything possible to keep crops coming—taking advantage of hot-house conditions to force two crops where one had grown before—frantically playing a kind of agricultural roulette, gambling on the length of time a specific region might continue to grow temperate-zone produce.

Mails have long since stopped. And newspapers. And telephones. As a member of a new privileged class, I have been equipped with a two-way radio and a permit to drive on government business. Schools have of course closed. An attempt was made for a time to provide lessons over TV. Thankfully the looting and rioting seem over. Those desperate gangs of angry citizens who for some time made life additionally difficult, have now disappeared. We seem at last to understand that we are all in this together.

Life is very simple without electricity. I get up with the light and go to bed as darkness falls. My food supply is still substantial and because of the soybean crop I am all right for water. Dexter has adapted well to his new life. He is outdoors less than he used to be and has switched to a mainly vegetable diet without too much difficulty.

Evening.

This morning a new order over the radio. All of us with special driving privileges were asked to report to our zone garage to have our tires treated with heat resistant plastic.

I had not been into town for months. I felt rather as one does on returning home from hospital—that the world is unexpectedly large, with voluminous airy spaces. This was exaggerated perhaps by the fact that our whole zone had been given over to soybeans. Everywhere the same rows of green plants—small pods already formed—march across gardens and boulevards. I was glad to see the climate prove so favourable. But there was little else to make me rejoice as I drove through ominously deserted streets, paint blistering and peeling on fences and houses, while overhead a haze of dust, now always with us, created a green sun.

The prolonged heat has made bleak the little park opposite the garage. A rocky little park, once all mosses and rhododendrons, it is bare now, and brown. I was seeing the day as everyone saw it. Untransmuted.

As I stepped out of my car to speak to the attendant I cursed that I had not brought my insulators. The burning tarmac made me shift rapidly from foot to foot. Anyone from another planet would have wondered at this extraordinary quirk of earthlings. But my feet were forgotten as my eyes alighted a second time on the park across the way. I had never before seen so dazzling and variegated a display of colours. How could there be such prismed brilliance in the range of greys and browns? It was as if the perceiving organ—wherever it is—sensitized by earlier experience, was now correctly tuned for this further perception.

The process was as before: the merest shake and the whole park was 'rainbow, rainbow, rainbow.' A further shake brought the park from *there* to *here*. Interior. But this time the interior space had increased. Doubled. By a kind of instant knowledge that rid me of all doubt, I knew that the garage attendant was seeing it too. We *saw the colours.*

Then, with that slight shift of focus, as if a gelatinous film had moved briefly across my sight, everything slipped back.

I really looked at the attendant for the first time. He was a skinny young man standing up naked inside a pair of loose striped overalls cut off at the knee, *Sidney* embroidered in red over his left breast pocket. He was blond, small-boned, with nothing about him to stick in the memory except his clear eyes which at that moment bore an expression of total comprehension.

'You …' we began together and laughed.

'Have you seen them before?' I asked. But it was rather as one would say 'How do you do'—not so much a question as a salutation.

We looked at each other for a long time, as if committing each other to memory.

'Do you know anyone else?' I said.

'One or two. Three, actually. Do you?'

I shook my head. 'You are the first. Is it … is it … always like that?'

'You mean…?' he gestured towards his heart.

I nodded.

'Yes,' he said. 'Yes, it is.'

There didn't seem anything more to talk about. Your right hand hasn't much to say to your left, or one eye to the other. There was comfort in the experience, if comfort is the word, which it isn't. More as if an old faculty had been extended. Or a new one activated.

Sidney put my car on the hoist and sprayed its tires.

Some time later.

I have not seen Sidney again. Two weeks ago when I went back he was not there and as of yesterday, cars have become obsolete. Not that we will use that word publicly. The official word is *suspended.*

Strange to be idle after months of hard labour. A lull only before the boys from the Department of Agriculture come back to prepare the land again. I am pleased that the soybeans are harvested, that I was able to nurse them along to maturity despite the scorching sun, the intermittent plagues and the problems with water. Often the pressure was too low to turn on the sprinklers and I would stand, hour after hour, hose in hand, trying to get the most use from the tiny trickle spilling from the nozzle.

Sometimes my heart turns over as I look through the kitchen window and see the plants shrivelled and grotesque, the baked earth scored by a web of fine cracks like the glaze on a plate subjected to too high an oven. Then it comes to me in a flash that of course, the beans are gone, the harvest is over.

The world is uncannily quiet. I don't think anyone had any idea of how much noise even distant traffic made until we were without it. It is rare indeed for vehicles other than Government mini-cars to be seen on the streets. And there are fewer and fewer pedestrians. Those who do venture out, move on their thick insulators with the slow gait of rocking horses. Surreal and alien, they heighten rather than lessen one's sense of isolation. For one is isolated. We have grown used to the sight of heli-copters like large dragonflies hovering overhead—addressing us through their P.A. systems, dropping supplies—welcome but impersonal.

Dexter is my only physical contact. He is delighted to have me inside again. The heat is too great for him in the garden and as, officially, he no longer exists, we only go out under cover of dark.

The order to destroy pets, when it came, indicated more clearly than anything that had gone before, that the government had abandoned hope. In an animal-loving culture, only direst necessity could validate such an order. It fell upon us like a heavy pall.

When the Government truck stopped by for Dexter, I reported him dead. Now that the welfare of so many depends upon our cooperation with authority, law-breaking is a serious offence. But I am not uneasy about breaking this law. As long as he remains healthy and happy, Dexter and I will share our dwindling provisions.

No need to be an ecologist or dependent on non-existent media to know all life is dying and the very atmosphere of our planet is changing radically. Already no birds sing in the hideous hot dawns as the sun, rising through a haze of dust, sheds its curious bronze-green light on a brown world. The trees that once gave us shade stand leafless now in an infernal winter. Yet, as if in the masts and riggings of ships, St. Elmo's fire flickers and shines in their high branches, and bioplasmic pyrotechnics light the dying soybeans. I am reminded of how the ghostly form of a limb remains attached to the body from which it has been amputated. And I can't help thinking of all the people who don't see the colours, the practical earth touchers with only their blunt senses to inform them. I wonder about J. and if, since we last talked, she had perhaps been able to see the colours too. But I think not. After so many years of friendship, surely I would be able to sense her, had she broken through.

Evening...?

The heat has increased greatly in the last few weeks—in a quantum leap. This has resulted immediately in two things: a steady rising of the sea level throughout the world—with panic reactions and mild flooding in coastal areas; and, at last, a noticeably higher air temperature. It is causing great physical discomfort.

It was against this probability that the authorities provided us with insulator spray. Like giant cans of pressurized shaving cream. I have shut all rooms but the kitchen and by concentrating my insulating zeal on this one small area, we have managed to keep fairly cool. The word is relative, of course. The radio has stopped giving temperature readings and I have no thermometer. I have filled all cracks and crannies with the foaming plastic, even applied a layer to the exterior wall. There are no baths, of course, and no cold drinks. On the other hand I've abandoned clothes and given Dexter a shave and a haircut. Myself as well. We are a fine pair. Hairless and naked.

When the world state of emergency was declared we didn't need to be told that science had given up. The official line had been that the process would reverse itself as inexplicably as it had begun. The official policy—to hold out as long as possible. With this in mind, task forces worked day and night on survival strategy. On the municipal level, which is all I really knew about, everything that could be centralized was. Telephone exchanges, hydro plants, radio stations became centres around which vital activities took place. Research teams investigated the effects of heat on water mains, sewer pipes, electrical wiring; work crews were employed to prevent, protect or even destroy incipient causes of fire, flood and asphyxiation.

For some time now the city has been zoned. In each zone a large building has been selected, stocked with food, medical supplies and insulating materials. We have been provided with zone maps and an instruction sheet telling us to stay where we are until ordered to move to what is euphemistically called our 'home.' When ordered, we are to load our cars with whatever we still have of provisions and medicines and drive off *at once.* Helicopters have already dropped kits with enough gasoline for the trip and a small packet, somewhat surprisingly labelled 'emergency rations' which contains one cyanide capsule—grim reminder that all may not go as the planners plan. We have been asked to mark our maps, in advance, with the shortest route from our house to our 'home', so that in a crisis we will know what we are doing. These instructions are repeated *ad nauseam* over the radio, along with hearty assurances that everything is under control and that there is no cause for alarm. The Government station is now all that remains of our multi-media. When it is not broadcasting instructions, its mainly pre-recorded tapes sound inanely complacent and repetitive. Evacuation Day, as we have been told again and again, will be announced by whistle blast. Anyone who runs out of food before that or who is in need of medical aid is to use the special gas ration and go 'home' at once.

As a long-time preserver of fruits and vegetables, I hope to hold out until E. Day. When that time comes it will be a sign that broadcasts are no longer possible, that contact can no longer be maintained between the various areas of the community, that the process will not reverse itself in time and that, in fact, our world is well on the way to becoming—oh, wonder of the modern kitchen—a self-cleaning oven.

Spring, Summer, Winter, Fall.
What season is it after all?

I sense the hours by some inner clock. I have applied so many layers of insulating spray that almost no heat comes through from outside. But we have to have air and the small window I have left exposed acts like a furnace. Yet through it I see the dazzling colours; sense my fellow-men.

Noon.

The sun is hidden directly overhead. The world is topaz. I see it through the minute eye of my window. I, the perceiving organ that peers through the house's only aperture. We are one, the house and I—parts of some vibrating sensitive organism in which Dexter plays his differentiated but integral role. The light enters us, dissolves us. We are the golden motes in the jewel.

Midnight.

The sun is directly below. Beneath the burning soles of my arching feet it shines, a globe on fire. Its rays penetrate the earth. Upward beaming, they support and sustain us. We are held aloft, a perfectly balanced ball in the jet of a golden fountain. Light, dancing, infinitely upheld.

Who knows how much later.

I have just 'buried' Dexter.

This morning I realized this hot little cell was no longer a possible place for a dog.

I had saved one can of dog food against this day. As I opened it Dexter's eyes swivelled in the direction of so unexpected and delicious a smell. He struggled to his feet, joyous, animated. The old Dexter. I was almost persuaded to delay, to wait and see if the heat subsided. What if tomorrow we awakened to rain? But something in me, stronger than this wavering self, carried on with its purpose.

He sat up, begging, expectant.

I slipped the meat out of the can.

'You're going to have a really good dinner,' I said, but as my voice was unsteady, I stopped.

I scooped a generous portion of the meat into his dish and placed it on the floor. He was excited, and as always when excited about food, he was curiously ceremonial, unhurried—approaching his dish and backing away from it, only to approach it again at a slightly different angle. As if the exact position was of the greatest importance. It was one of his most amusing and endearing characteristics. I let him eat his meal in his own leisurely and appreciative manner and then, as I have done so many times before, I fed him his final *bonne bouche* by hand. The cyanide pill, provided by a beneficent government for me, went down in a gulp.

I hadn't expected it to be so sudden. Life and death so close. His small frame convulsed violently, then collapsed. Simultaneously, as if synchro-nized, the familiar 'shake' occurred in my vision. Dexter glowed brightly, whitely, like phosphorus. In that dazzling, light-filled moment he was no longer a small dead dog lying there. I could have thought him a lion, my sense of scale had so altered. His beautiful body blinded me with its fires.

With the second 'shake' his consciousness must have entered mine for I felt a surge in my heart as if his loyalty and love had flooded it. And like a kind of ground bass, I was aware of scents and sounds I had not known before. Then a great peace filled me—an immense space, light and sweet—and I realized that this was death. Dexter's death.

But how describe what is beyond description?

As the fires emanating from his slight frame died down, glowed weakly, residually, I put on my insulators and carried his body into the now fever-hot garden. I laid him on what had been at one time an azalea bed. I was unable to dig a grave in the baked earth or to cover him with leaves. But there are no predators now to pick the flesh from his bones. Only the heat which will, in time, desiccate it.

I returned to the house, opening the door as little as possible to prevent the barbs and briars of burning air from entering with me. I sealed the door from inside with foam sealer.

The smell of the canned dog food permeated the kitchen. It rang in my nostrils. Olfactory chimes, lingering, delicious. I was intensely aware of Dexter. Dexter immanent. I contained him as simply as a dish contains water. But the simile is not exact. For I missed his physical presence. One relies on the physical more than I had known. My hands sought palpable contact. The flesh forgets slowly.

Idly, abstractedly, I turned on the radio. I seldom do now as the bat-teries are low and they are my last. Also, there is little incentive. Broadcasts are intermittent and I've heard the old tapes over and over.

But the government station was on the air. I tuned with extreme care and placed my ear close to the speaker. A voice, faint, broken by static, sounded like that of the Prime Minister.

'... all human beings can do, your government has done for you.' (Surely not a political speech *now*?) 'But we have failed. Failed to hold back the heat. Failed to protect ourselves against it; to protect you against it. It is with profound grief that I send this farewell message to you all.' I realized that this, too, had been pre-recorded, reserved for the final broadcast. 'Even now, let us not give up hope ...'

And then, blasting through the speech, monstrously loud in the stone-silent world, the screech of the whistle summoning us 'home'. I could no longer hear the P.M.'s words.

I began automatically, obediently, to collect my few remaining foodstuffs, reaching for a can of raspberries, the last of the crop to have grown in my garden when the dawns were dewy and cool and noon sun fell upon us like golden pollen. My hand stopped in mid-air.

I would not go 'home'.

The whistle shrilled for a very long time. A curious great steam-driven cry—man's last. Weird that our final utterance should be this anguished inhuman wail.

The end.

Now that it is virtually too late, I regret not having kept a daily record. Now that the part of me that writes has become nearly absorbed, I feel obliged to do the best I can.

I am down to the last of my food and water. Have lived on little for some days—weeks, perhaps. How can one measure passing time? Eternal time grows like a tree, its roots in my heart. If I lie on my back I see winds moving in its high branches and a chorus of birds is singing in its leaves. The song is sweeter than any music I have ever heard.

My kitchen is as strange as I am myself. Its walls bulge with many layers of spray. It is without geometry. Like the inside of an eccentric Styrofoam coconut. Yet, with some inner eye, I see its intricate mathematical structure. It is as ordered and no more random than an atom.

My face is unrecognizable in the mirror. Wisps of short damp hair. Enormous eyes. I swim in their irises. Could I drown in the pits of their pupils?

Through my tiny window when I raise the blind, a dead world shines. Sometimes dust storms fill the air with myriad particles burning bright and white as the lion body of Dexter.

Sometimes great clouds swirl, like those from which saints receive revelations.

The colours are almost constant now. There are times when, light-headed, I dance a dizzying dance, feel part of that whirling incandescent matter—what I might once have called inorganic matter!

On still days the blameless air, bright as a glistening wing, hangs over us, hangs its extraordinary beneficence over us.

We are together now, united, indissoluble. Bonded.

Because there is no expectation, there is no frustration.

Because there is nothing we can have, there is nothing we can want.

We are hungry of course. Have cramps and weakness. But they are as if in *another body*. *Our* body is inviolate. Inviolable.

We share one heart.

We are one with the starry heavens and our bodies are stars.

Inner and outer are the same. A continuum. The water in the locks is level. We move to a higher water. A high sea.

A ship could pass through.

(1979)

BIRTHDAY

After the effort of dressing—and it was an effort these days, quite exhausting, in fact—she needed to pause a little, compose herself, before beginning the day. The chair she sat in, like a burnished throne, shone brightly in the sun and there she rested, burnished too, and the glitter of her rings transformed the morning. Sometimes she wondered if the chair and the sunlight ... perhaps especially the sunlight ... contributed to or even hatched, the fragments of knowledge which slipped into her head from the side, glancing through her, leaving a trace like the silvery trail of a snail or which, more directly, arrived head-on—shooting stars, illuminating but transitory.

So far she had been unable to attach meaning to these glimmerings and flashes, palely glowing; she might even say 'burning sweetly,' in the space in her head where her brain had once been but where, now, it was as if her heart were tenant.

What was she to make, for instance, of the knowledge that she was awaiting an event, one which—she now realized—she had been awaiting since birth? Perhaps before. Possibly even before. As to the nature of the event or what prompted its knowledge, she hadn't the least idea.

Was its source, she wondered, some quickening in the air—the same quickening one feels as the old year draws to its close? Or, perhaps she had been programmed—she was amused by her change in vocabulary, for surely, she once would have said 'influenced'—by images from all her forgotten dreams. Were her changing cells simply bypassing the 'operator' entirely and dialling direct to the 'listener' within? Here, she could only speculate.

But she knew time was short. Knew it certainly. Knew the event near and beyond question. And even though it had no form, no detail, and she possessed no clues as to what it was, she couldn't rid her mind of it. It was there that her thoughts centred—electrons circling a nucleus. At times it was as if the electrons were becoming an entity in themselves and gradually replacing what she had always thought to be—for want of a better word—herself. For surely it was not she who, yesterday, threw out the eyedrops that control glaucoma? Even less would she have refused, stubbornly refused, the analgesic which eased the pain of arthritis. Something other than herself must be in control.

Was it simply that she was old and scatty? For she was old, after all, and strangely changed, on the surfaces at least. For proof she need look no further than her rheumaticky hands, wrinkled and blotched like snakeskin, the fingers swollen and twisted. The knuckles shiny. But as she examined them in the bright sunlight, she knew quite clearly that in no time at all they would be the tiny, soft, rubbery, red fists of a baby. Involuntarily her stomach jerked. It was rather as she had felt when first she knew that she was something other than her body; that although it was flesh that made her visible, she was not that flesh. No wonder her stomach jerked: flesh objects to playing so secondary a role.

And then she remembered the dream. Those little red fists had brought it back. It was bizarre, of course. One's dream scenarist tends to be antic.

Head foremost, she was forcing—and at the same time being forced—down a long book-lined corridor. Books on both sides. How tight it made the passage! Painful. Cramped. Intolerable, actually. And an area between her shoulder blades—not usually one of her more sensitive spots, though she had many these days—was unbearably tender. But as she struggled, constricted, half blind, she was comforted by a series of brilliant images: butterfly; bird; man; angel. Her own joyous laughter had wakened her that morning. She remembered it now with a matching lightness of heart.

Suddenly curious, she tried to touch that spot between her shoulders. The pain in wrists and elbows hindered her movements. But when the fingers of a persistent right-hand finally succeeded, she was rewarded by the discovery of two protuberances—ridge-shaped—one on either side of her spine, and agonizingly sensitive to the touch. For, added to the accustomed pain of arthritis, was the suddenly remembered torture of teething and the unique realization of the distress and ecstasy of the unicorn as a foal when, cutting his horn, he perceived that he was not the young horse he had thought himself to be.

A long arm of sunshine reached out from where she sat and fell upon the glinting aglets of a pair of narrow shoes. Her brother was standing just inside the door—thin, aquiline, smiling. How many years was it since she had seen him? 'Robert!' she cried, 'how good of you to come.'

'It's Victor,' a voice answered. 'Your son and heir. You've forgotten, Mother. I was here yesterday.' Yesterday? Ah Robert, Victor, time does bear thinking about, doesn't it. Passing without notice when it wishes or travelling at the speed of light. And what day was it, that she should be lying here in her bed? What time of day? She reached out to the sun's pale, fine dust which lay like a ribbon on her blanket, and with the jolt that she had come to know as certainty, she realized that this was her last awakening in this bed, this room, this ... 'place.' Could the wintry sunlight, starting with her fingers, dissolve her flesh, her bones, all matter? For, light as thistledown, she and the material world were suspended, painless, totally detached. The cord that had bound her to all she loved was severed, she thought, forever. What possible links could survive this atomization?

Yet links survived. Her sight—better today than usual—took in the bare boughs of trees, their colour a nameless dark against the sky. It was as if she had never seen them before, yet their diffuse forms were as familiar to her as the bed she lay in. Her mind was clear too—startlingly clear—for she actually saw the two contradictions arise as one and separate and become two as if they had passed through a prism or fragmenter. 'But it's not only opposites which are born single and become dual,' she thought excitedly. 'More complex still, any image, at a certain point will splinter and multiply.'

Eager to test this new perception—'tree,' she thought, and immediately it was sawn into planks, hammered into coffins, shaped into violins, pressed into paper. She could not hold 'tree' in her mind singly, simply. The one became two, three, four or even more. And this propensity to fragment had been, she now knew, central to her life. Not her life only, of course. It was in the nature of humankind. And she was on the brink of controlling it. All she had to do was allow a stop to occur at exactly the right moment—no more difficult than releasing the shutter of a camera when the light, speed, focus and subject were all correctly aligned. But the art of doing it vanished along with a certain radiance the room had contained and there she was again, an old body on a bed, faced with the imminence of the event and shaky. Shaky.

'Oh I would go back on the whole thing if I could,' she said, knowing that she couldn't, but not why.

'When was the decision made and by whom?' she demanded. 'Was I a conscious party to it? Was it my wish?'

'I suppose it's like waiting to die,' she thought. 'The same uncertainty about what is to come, the same fear of pain, the same wrench from the known. But,' she queried, 'being born where? In what country? With what planets rising? And what colour?' she asked herself idly. But as to that, she was only mildly curious, for no part of her cared whether or not she continued white.

'The same with size,' she went on, 'although that, I suppose, might embrace differences other than those measurable in feet and inches. But I'd adjust,' she said, confident. 'Alice did, after all. Took her changes with remarkable *sang froid*—a reflection of the age and race to which she belonged, perhaps.'

'But sex,' she thought with a stab, 'is another matter.' Appallingly repellent, the mere idea of being male. Not that she hadn't loved male flesh well enough in her time. 'Too well,' she thought, nostalgically. But the prospect of being it … the stubble, the muscle, the hair on the chest … the Adam's apple … No! 'I wouldn't know how to be male,' she exclaimed aloud. 'I'm so at home in this female body.' But as she spoke she realized that she wasn't at home in it any more. Nearly all of it was painful to her—a stricture—especially in that area between the shoulder blades. In fact, since the appearance of those two new ridges, it was impossible for her to lie on her back, and her bed was a rack and a harrow.

'More important,' her thoughts were racing now, reminiscent of the descriptions of the speed of flying saucers—'vastly more important even than gender … or nationality or colour or size … is kind.' What if she were born in the body of a dog, for instance? Not that there weren't exceptional dogs. But it would be disappointing and repetitive, for on the evolutionary scale she must already have been a dog or its equivalent, must already have managed four hairy legs and a tail, and it would be a matter simply of doing it all over again.

But curious dislocations were occurring within her and without. Reassemblies. She was no longer … in place. From this great height, she could barely make out towers or steeples and geometry, which she had studied so eagerly as a girl, was now either pre- or post-Euclidean. Its angles altered. 'Michael, Raphael, Gabriel,' she said. 'All male. And Uriel. Male also.' And despite the fact that her mind surged and flowed and she seemed able to draw upon the whole of creation as if from a meticulously indexed encyclopedia, she couldn't recall a single female angle.

Such vast accessibilities without. So great a condensation within. A gathering together, a coalescence. Heightened inertia. 'Bend back thy bow, O Archer ...'

'What matter,' she asked, 'if I die female and am born male? Through the alembic of this giant eye, male/female are won.'

And as the fragmenter or prism in her mind reversed direction, all multiplicity without—the trail of the snail, the shooting stars, the baby, the tree, her brother, her son—was, through its unifying beam, drawn into her to become again what it had always been and was still—hole, won; and this same reversal made possible the contraction of all her particles as if in preparation for rising—a spacecraft taking off. And through one supra sense she heard the rush of air, and through that same sense—upstream of the five now left behind in a fractured world—she felt the exquisite movement of its currents stirring the small down on her incredible wings.

(1985)

MME BOURGÉ
DREAMS OF BRÉSIL

Is it the hot wet air that lies like a sheet on Paris, or the *confiture de Brésil* in its little pot, placed by *l'inspecteur* on her bedside table? Whatever the reason, Mme Bourgé sleeps a tropical sleep, casting aside a tumble of ecru lace, her torso glistening white as magnolia soap.

Marmoset faces form and shift in the reflecting crystals of chandeliers; glittering jewelled macaws peer from sconces.

Mme Bourgé walks in the black-green jungle, calling, calling. Who is loosed and lost among unfamiliar trees, odours of tree-moss, scents of Shameless Mary? Is it Mme Bourgé herself, now pocked with shadows, trailing leaves and the conjugations of Portuguese verbs?

Marmosets swing in the branches, chatter and wheeze, their faces the size of her thumb's top joint. In their eyes she sees the points of their tiny dreams. Brilliant and noisy as silk umbrellas opening, vast birds rise from her feet.

Za Za is very secretive, busy with *macumba*. She models discarded lovers—waxen homunculi jabbed full of pins—forgetful now of their shapes, their given names. In a day, in a week, their beautiful strength will fail them. Mme Bourgé scolds, 'Oh, heartless, heartless Za Za, leaving the pin box empty, the candle guttering wax.'

Late afternoon sun fills the *sala* with zebras, casts palm-frond stripes on sofas and chairs. Tree orchids split the baroque legs of tables, erupt in delicate durable blooms.

Green light stains the white octagonal tiles of the *copa*, stains Augusto's hornet jacket, his lifted hands. Augusto, coffee maker to the Pretender, wears the royal coat of arms on his golden sleeve. Water, metallic, furious as quicksilver, falls through the green air like a school of trout; is caught in a flannel funnel, a vertical windsock, as if in a landing net. 'Like molten lead plummeting down shot-towers, it is the length of the fall that counts' ... Augusto is offering some simple lesson, but Mme

Bourgé is falling too. 'When or where?' she cries, and 'where or when?' But Augusto, nimble, bearing a polished tray with pie-crust edging, pours her a *cafézinho* black as tar.

Still half asleep in the stifling morning, Mme Bourgé stretches a lazy arm. Into the pale trumpet of the house phone she calls Augusto. 'A windsock for the equatorial winds,' she sighs, 'and little suits for the marmosets—of satin.'

How can she grasp an air that has no hand-holds, cling to this curve of space? Mme Bourgé waits, ear pressed to the receiver, for the reassurance of Augusto's voice.

(1987)

EVEN THE SUN,
EVEN THE RAIN

Robert, looking frail and old after his last illness, collected her nevertheless and they drove up to the lookout.

They had not been there since they were young lovers and today the snow was still on the ground around them though the city itself was through with it. They peered at the maquette of buildings below. Those that had been giants when they were young were now hidden by massive plinths.

He talked of the death of the city and she thought how they were dying together—he and his city. She could give him no comfort by her long view—that another city would rise up, was rising up, to replace this one; that the young who were having to leave because work was no longer available would go elsewhere and that *that* elsewhere—or those—would surge and grow.

They walked over to the great neglected building that had once housed a restaurant. Couples lay about on its steps in the sun, the first warm sun of the year, and he walked carefully between them, she following.

He said, 'Have you ever seen the steps of the Capitol in Washington, on a fine day?' and the contrast was painful to her in a way she was unable to understand.

They walked into the vast, empty, unswept hall. Two dispensing machines against the far wall provided the only colour, were the only objects. He offered her a chocolate bar which she refused, thinking of calories. He put coins in the slot and pulled the plunger.

'A little energy,' he said.

He was pale and there were small hair-line veins in his cheek that she had not seen before. His mouth fell open as if it cost him too much to keep it closed. The lower lip was slack but the skin was stretched taut and shiny. It was an old man's mouth.

They sat on the steps in the sun and she talked about the three brains—reptilian, mammalian, the neocortex—and their possible functions. He questioned her on the biological soundness of the theory and, laughing, she told him she thought there were three brains, all right. But there was some niggling unease between them. After all, just because they had known each other for forty years and loved each other for forty years it didn't mean they could fall into step immediately when they met. It always took time. Not a lot of time, but time, especially after so long an interval as this one had been.

They walked slowly back to the car past the piles of dirty snow and drove down to the city where he parked recklessly in a no-parking area. 'A calculated risk,' he said, and she knew it was a matter of energy.

Lunch was delicious—*doré amandine*, green salad, white wine. He grew flushed with the martini—'the first since my illness'—and easier.

'I was frightened of seeing you,' he said.

A young man passed their table, stared hard at Robert, was about to speak, saw her and stared harder at her. Stared at Robert again, introduced himself and moved on.

'He wondered if we were the right couple,' Robert said.

'How could you *ever* be frightened of seeing me?'

'The mountain is so enormous it's hard to be anywhere but the top.'

'Take it as it comes,' she said. 'Wherever we are will do—even on the slopes.'

His usual high spirits returned. But he ate very slowly, so she talked to give him time to eat.

'Extraordinary to be so slow. But it won't go down faster.'

Quite suddenly they were in step again. They were holding hands tightly under the table.

'Had you better put your feet up?' she asked. 'You can drop me wherever you like.'

'How about 203?'

She was surprised. Enough for her eyes to go a shade lighter. She had expected him to go home.

He had a ticket, of course. He pocketed it without a glance. 'Well worth it,' he said.

Once in the car they wanted to buy each other books—all the books they had talked about. It was an old pattern. He headed towards a book shop but the streets were thick with traffic.

'Too complicated,' she said. 'Let's buy them later and send them.'

He drove to her hotel—careful in all those roaring cars. Parked, again illegally. Inside her hotel room they took off their clothes and lay beside each other on the bed.

'Even the sun is not like this,' he said.

'Or the rain. Rain is also something.'

'Even the rain ...'

The old joy filled them.

'I call it subliming,' she said. 'Funny that all these years I've never told you.'

(1999)

FEVER

Baroque furniture, the colour of cinnamon bark. Black-and-white drawings—di Cavalcanti's line as wide as if done with his little finger. Portinari's small purl-purl-purl on thin needles. It is all of a piece with his house but disconcerting to find it here in his office where we must talk, once again, of my uterus. I had thought that finished. The di Cavalcanti seated nude is drawn in an almost continuous line.

Why are we sitting here hand in hand? How did it happen? Did he see my hand across a mile of air or was it close, almost already in his? If it was taken, without my knowledge, why is it now so difficult to withdraw? The two hands play together as we talk—much as children play, separate from their mothers having tea. Playing so prettily that withdrawal becomes a kind of surgery. Not painful—not painful at all. Just violent.

It is done. Without looking. Disengaged.

I know that hand of his as well as one of my own. It is firm, unfleshy—oval nails large in proportion to the fingers. I've seen it so many times changing my dressings, pressing liquid out of the small drain—that practically colourless tube so like the veins one finds in liver.

His hands were surer than the nurse's and so, hurt less. 'Gentler than a woman's.' Such phrases do not belong to this world, this modern world where women are wanting to be men.

The examining room has a bed in it. A bed, not a table. Baroque. Single. It has a scarlet leather mattress and a small green pillow. (And beautiful 'purple shoes with crimson soles and crimson linings,' if I correctly remember my *Little Black Sambo*.) Two sheets folded and very white.

'Will you help yourself. I have no nurse today.'

'What do you want me to take off?'

'Everything.'

'Everything?' This is absurd.

I took trouble getting dressed. Now I am having trouble getting undressed. My dress is over my head, caught by the keepers that prevent shoulder straps showing. Trying to undo them I get very hot. I end by having to put the dress on again and start once more. I hear the door open as I am stepping out of my pants—back-view to him.

'*Não estou pronta.*'

'Good,' he says, entering. I had forgotten he was deaf. He goes out. I spread the sheet on the bed and hide its scarlet. I lie down very straight. Feet together. I cover myself with the other sheet and lie motionless.

He examines my incision—his incision. It is barely discernible. That dreadful fresh scar like a large painted mouth now healed and minus its mercurochrome, half-hidden in the pubic hair.

His movements are purposeful. He is quite solemn as if listening for a far sound.

'Menstruation?'

'Not yet.'

'No?' He is surprised.

You are the only man who has ever stopped my periods, I think.

'It will return,' he said. 'I was very careful.'

That was not why I had come. 'And the pain?' I asked.

'It will pass. It sometimes happens during healing.'

I rush into my clothes when he leaves. I don't dare look at the bed.

As I go he kisses my hand. We are suddenly quite gay and glad, as if after a catastrophe, which has mercifully spared us. He sees me to the elevator and our voices are loud and inane in the hall.

I move in a dream. Move lazily in the roaring street. He is a tiny image—the size of a reflection in a pupil. Totally secret. Small enough to recur and recur. Immobilizing.

✳ ✳ ✳

My upbringing taught me to associate sex with love. 'And if two people love each other very, very much …' Then, by obverse reasoning? How difficult to be a parent. Is it better to tell a child the two things can be, and frequently are, quite separate? I cannot hold my parents culpable. I would probably have done the same in their place. Certainly *then.* And nine times out of ten it would have been all right.

Can one do exercises in loving? In not loving? Can one direct and teach one's passions?

Let me try.

* * *

Stuart looks at me with such wonder and love. But the small image leaps. I feel the smile of the genitals.

'We need an extra man,' he says. 'How about Henrique?'

'No.'

'No?'

'He'd fit in better with the de Mellos.'

'Then who would you suggest?'

Who? Oh, who? Somebody help me think.

* * *

That small image refuses to leave. Like a jack-in-the-box it pops up—stops me in my tracks. So much for giving myself lessons! Nothing has changed. I have not seen him again and have decided I shall not, of myself, try to see him. Our chances of meeting are rare. We met only three times before I went to him professionally. But the first time had an uncanny element to it that disturbed me even then.

Stuart was ill—too ill really to go to a dinner, yet we went. Just before we were to dine my hostess said, 'Your husband asked me to tell you he had to go home. He will send the car back for you.' And then, 'Do you want to stay? I will so well understand if you want to be with him.' But I had no car and Stuart, I knew, would want only a quiet dark room and to be left alone. 'No,' I said, 'I'll stay—unless it is easier for you if I go.' It *would* have been easier, as it turned out, for we were thirteen at table and she was superstitious—but how could I have known?

After dinner I sat on a sofa with him. We had been introduced just before dinner—'How d'ye do?' 'How d'ye do.' A small man with a red nose. The sofa held two and was placed apart, with no chairs nearby. We were on a desert island in a sea full of people and there we sat until protocol permitted me to leave. I liked him. He was a surgeon. He had recently been to my country to study our methods of deep freezing patients, so he said. He talked of Portinari, of science, of art. We were a long time in the hands of an inexpert hostess, marooned together. He offered to take me home. I refused.

Stuart was better in the morning and I told him about the party. 'He's nice,' I said, 'and bright.'

Then most unexpectedly a book of Portinari paintings arrived with a semi-legible note. I enjoyed the book and in due course returned it to him with a semi-legible note.

I saw him next at the Cabrals. He was with his fiancée—or so it was rumoured. An ex-actress full of mannerisms and affectations. I sat beside him at dinner. He described his ideal life. 'With friends all evening. In bed all morning. Operating all afternoon.'

Then a Sunday lunch at his house. A beautiful old colonial house behind a wall. Deep veranda vines. Thick walls. So tropical, so beautiful. What a wonderful world. A whole book of Debret. But I was uneasy. I found the other guests difficult. And I watched him attempting to juggle them. He served the drinks himself. Delicious food: *Vatapá*. *Lombo de porco*. I loved his house, disliked his party, and felt nothing about him either way.

His daughter, as a child, painted by Portinari. Wearing green shoes. The Portinari of many flecks of light against a dark ground. People—those bright flecks. Are we so bright?

* * *

The gynecologist said, 'I recommend an operation. Have you a surgeon?'

'No.'

He gave me three names.

* * *

'It's not serious,' I told Stuart afterwards, 'but it is surgery.'

He pulled a face.

'And the sooner the better.'

'Who will do it?'

'He gave me three names. I would prefer Henrique. I know him and like him. It's already a beginning.'

* * *

My appointment was at the hospital. Like a sheep on its back I greeted him, infuriated at not being allowed to see him first, dressed and on my feet.

In the small examining room he behaved as if he didn't know me. 'I find a cyst. It is best to remove it.' The telephone rang. He spoke Portuguese. He used the familiar *você*. He looked at his watch. 'At noon,' he said. 'At your house or on the corner?'

I thought of that woman and wondered about her. Was he really going to marry her? It interested me as it would interest a novelist.

He turned to me again. He was in a hurry. 'I have no choice but to recommend surgery.' He stood up, extended his hand. 'Goodbye,' he said. Brusque.

'But wait a minute. I would like you ...'

'In that case.' He sat down again. 'I was asked only to give an opinion.'

It was decided quickly. Next week. As simple as an appointment with the hairdresser.

'Not Tuesday, I have a luncheon.'

'Wednesday I'm operating.'

'Thursday?'

'Thursday.' That's settled then.

Although he saw me in the hospital before the operation, I have no memory of it. He was not in the operating room when they rolled me in.

The nurses were in awe of him and so was I—a little. In the reversion to infancy which accompanies illness, I found him stern. His jokes at my expense did not amuse me. And there was too big a language problem. He really didn't understand English very well—certainly not the rather high-flown language of metaphor I am inclined to use under any stress. And I still spoke a kind of child's Portuguese.

He took to entering my room in a small explosion of bad English that so confused me I frequently forgot to say the things I had been planning for hours.

I found myself night after night opening my eyes and seeing him standing by my bed. 'I have a very sick patient in the hospital and I just looked in to see you on my way.'

The night superintendent of nurses said, 'He certainly looks after *you*.'

'Nonsense, he has another patient here who is very sick and he ...'

'He has no other patients here.' Her pretty blue eyes grew round and full of a sudden comprehension. She put her cupped hand over her mouth in alarm.

'*Don't* tell him I told you. *Please!*'

'Perhaps not on this floor,' I said.

'Not on this floor, not on *any* floor. You're the *only* patient he has anywhere in the building.'

As related, this seems to have more significance than it had then. I remember it now. Then it was unimportant. I don't even recall trying to

183

figure out his reasons for coming. Perhaps I was very sick. But I don't think I felt any undue concern over my condition. It was all just part of the slightly surreal life of illness.

* * *

He discharged me from hospital and said he would see me in a month.

It was wonderful to be home. The house was quiet and very beautiful. A slightly hushed staff greeted me. They were self-conscious seeing me in my dressing gown walking on the terrace in the sun—slowly, peacefully. I was very happy. There were no pressures on me. The household ran smoothly. For a few days I even had a child. The laundress's daughter attached herself to me—a soft little cross-eyed girl who wore a perfume that smelled slightly of urine. We drew together and she was very patient with my Portuguese. Quite wonderfully she drew fingers like ribbons growing out from arms. The weather was hot. Day after day of sun. The mountains still as a painting. A green world.

The days passed smoothly, peacefully. Stuart came and went. Friends dropped in for coffee. The house was filled with flowers. I read and I drew.

At month's end Henrique paid a house call. He examined his 'signature', as he called it. Said I would carry it with me for life. Proclaimed me '*ótimo*'. Said yes, of course I could swim and anything else I liked.

'Golf,' he suggested.

'I don't golf.'

'*Bom*,' he said. He told me he was going to his *fazenda* for two weeks, gave me the name of his partner in case I needed a surgeon in his absence.

'I dismiss you,' he said. 'You are no longer my patient.'

He took my hand, leaned towards me. I was in turmoil.

'Kiss me.'

I turned my face away.

'As you wish,' he said. He kissed my hand. '*Boa tarde*.'

I rang for a servant to see him out.

And I could not bear it.

* * *

'What did he say?' Stuart asked, business-like, on his return. 'Have you passed muster?'

I nodded. 'He said I can swim. Play golf!'

'Did he say we could make love?' Stuart said. 'Now?'

* * *

Then the pains began. Not bad pains—but bad enough to waken me and keep me awake. Bad enough to make me limp slightly. At the end of the week, bad enough to make me feel worn out and wretched.

'Get in touch with the other surgeon,' my husband said, but I preferred to wait. It was an unreasonable kind of loyalty. If something was the matter—and I had by now begun to think there was—I would sooner Henrique's partner was not the one to discover it.

The morning he was due back I phoned. His servant could not understand me or I her. At noon I tried again. Only with the greatest difficulty did I reach him then. He arrived on the phone in an explosion of Portuguese. '*É um prazer falar com você. Como vai, como vai?*'

'*Não muito bem.*'

'*Muito bem? Ótimo!*'

'*Não, não—eu disse não muito bem.*' I was close to tears. The pain had gone on too long.

The appointment, this time, was in his consulting room.

* * *

The decision to lose one's virginity is very different from the decision to cuckold one's husband. In the first instance one has only oneself to consider, which alters the nature of the decision. Looking back I am surprised to find the first decision was not made in the height of passion. *That* I had withstood. I made a deliberate intellectual choice. 'Next time,' I had said to myself. Meaning it.

This comforts me a bit for I find it difficult to believe that intellectually I could decide to cuckold my husband.

But I wanted to see him. I scanned the parties ahead, wondering. Might he possibly be at dinner at the de L's on the 12th? I found myself on the night of the 12th taking special pains with my appearance. And it was then, looking at myself in the mirror, that I made a decision: *I will do nothing to further the relationship.*

Only as we went into the dining room, when I realized for certain that he was not there, did I know how much I had counted on seeing him. The evening became insufferable. The enchanting young man beside me had to work far too hard. He had, indeed, got out his drag nets. Young man, young man, I am sorry, but I am not here.

Now a new panic develops. My physician has insisted I see Henrique again. A urinary problem. I postpone phoning. In two days, God be thanked, my symptoms have lessened. I tell Stuart. He says the GP would not have asked me to go without a reason. We argue mildly and I am suddenly overcome with the need to tell him what he is doing. But I say nothing. Instead, I phone the physician.

'My symptoms have gone. It is not worth bothering Henrique now,' I say firmly.

He is obdurate. But still I do not make an appointment.

'Have you phoned Henrique?' asks my husband.

'No.'

'Why not?' He is slightly irritated.

Why not have a gynecological examination by a man …!

We are dressing to go out. Perversely, knowing I cannot see him tonight, I allow myself the complicated luxury of dressing for him.

'Why don't you phone him now?'

'He'll be having dinner.'

'Oh, God!' says my husband.

I don't use the upstairs phone. I go downstairs, dial as if guilty, my hands trembling. The smell of my perfume is strong on the air.

He answers. Is jovial. The appointment is made. For Thursday. Tonight is Tuesday. 'At three—no, wait a minute. At four-thirty.'

'Yes,' I say but I am beside myself. I cannot possibly go through with it. If he were to examine me I would have to make a confession I do not intend to make. I am a fool to have agreed to the appointment. Tomorrow I will call and cancel it. Yet how can I? How do I explain myself to the physician? To Stuart? 'I am so infatuated that the mere thought …' Let me pretend to feel nothing. Nothing. Strange word, nothing. But now, of course, I am overwhelmed by him. He is with me every minute. I fling myself at life with a kind of madness.

'I will do nothing to further the relationship,' I had said. And what have I done?

Stop thinking. Turn him off like a light. Many years ago my older half-sister had astonished me by saying, 'I shall destroy my love for my son. It has only become destructive to him, so I shall destroy it.'

'But how?' I was genuinely curious.

'I shall turn it off as one turns off a light.'

'Turn it *off?*'

Turn it off, then.

* * *

There are times when I am semi-detached, only to be obsessed again. Moments when I am so plunged in the implications of it all that I wonder Stuart has not noticed.

Absurd how I long to say, 'Help me, Stuart. You know I love you. Our life together is good. We have worked through to this—not without difficulty for us both. Help me, now. Help save us.'

Why must I make so much of everything? Why must an infatuation of very short duration already assume such giant proportions, such earth-shaking dimensions?

If I could say to Stuart, 'It is nothing. It will pass.' But if it doesn't pass? If it doesn't?

* * *

The afternoon has arrived. Good God, how many times have I washed? I wear a blouse and skirt. I had my hair done this morning and it is hideous. Hideous. Then, all the better.

A male nurse greets me. There is a patient inside. I can hear her voice.

If someone were to stand me on my feet, my skeleton would not support me. I would fall, a pile of clothing and flesh, to the floor.

Think of something else.

The door opens. I don't look up. Out of the corner of my eye I see a woman pass. He is framed in the lighted door. He is wearing his white coat—arms bare to the elbows.

'*Boa tarde.*'

'Hello.'

'*Momentinho.*' I hear the water running in the far room as he washes.

I am calmer already.

'Tea?' he says. And we have tea together in his beautiful baroque room. But it is not safe. The stillness of danger is here. I cannot keep my body still enough. Nor my mind. With all my might.

So much of our conversation is misunderstanding. Often I cannot understand him in either language—or he me. He is full of formal compliments which I disregard. And then I press him to get on with the examination. I must leave soon. We are due out at seven.

He leads me to the little red bed. And leaves me. I take off my clothing and lie, so I imagine, like a dead virgin in my slip and pearls on the red bed, my head on the green pillow. The sheet comes only to my waist.

When he returns his manner changes. He is quite open.

'You look lovely,' he says. 'The green looks wonderful under your hair.' And quite frankly he stares, admiring.

Is the ear of the male nurse pressed against the door?

'Cough,' he says and he palpates my incision. 'Cough,' he says again. 'Cough.' I cough and cough.

'Philipe was afraid part of your bladder was caught in the incision. But it's not.' He kissed the back of my hand. Then its palm.

He got up. There was only a slatted wall between the two rooms. He withdrew behind the slats while I dressed.

'So *that* was why he insisted I come to you. I didn't want to, you know.'

'Which only shows that Philipe is my very good friend and you are not.'

'Yes?'

There is an enormous relief in me. I was not forced into any confession. For the moment I am safe.

He catches my hand and perhaps because I am so filled with relief I am off guard. His next remark falls like a hammer on my heart.

'I was very pleased when we met—very happy to have met you. You knew that, didn't you? You remember the occasion. And I was very angry when you came to me as a patient. Very angry indeed. You put me in an impossible position. I was in love with you. Surely you knew. Yet you asked me to operate. For a surgeon to cut into the flesh of someone he loves ...'

I could hardly bear what he said. I had not known. Why had I not? Had I ignored the signs? But what signs were there—the loaned book? the invitation to luncheon? Surely not.

* * *

I drove home by the sea, the beautiful warm extravagant night soft on my skin. A tremendous fatigue and a great slow sadness filled me. A kind of ultimate melancholy—as if I had suddenly learned the meaning and the terrible poignancy of 'forever'.

Our house glowed in the darkness. All its windows as if lighted by candles. Stuart was already home. I went into his study. He was not there.

I went upstairs, calling his name.

He was in bed reading. He looked up, glad to see me.

'Have you seen the surgeon?'

I sat on the side of his bed. 'Yes.' He pulled me to him.

'What did he have to say?'

'Apparently Philipe wanted to know if my bladder was caught in the incision. It isn't.'

'Is that all he told you?'

'Yes.'

'What else happened today?'

'Nothing much. And you?'

'Just a series of small annoyances.'

'We must dress, I suppose.' I was so tired. So filled with despair. 'Must we really go?'

'You'll enjoy it when you get there.'

I was astonished to find I looked quite nice as we left—quite Brazilian. In black, with mink and pearls.

I pitched myself into a group where I had to speak Portuguese, where my total concentration was needed. And then I saw his partner. 'Every doctor in town is here tonight,' he said. 'A medical convention.' He laughed. I doubted Henrique's presence. I simply didn't feel it.

But suddenly, as if a torch were ignited, he was beside me, looking all crossed sticks. Quite fierce.

* * *

That night I had a snake dream. The first of my life. Common though they are said to be, I had not had one before. Our driver was holding a large one. Someone I do not remember had a small black one. An immense venomous one miraculously pushed through the tightly woven Caucasian carpet. I was delighted. Awakened laughing.

'What's so funny?' Stuart asked.

'A dream.'

We leave by car for Lages. I am glad to be away. Glad of the distractions of new things. But—I am not distracted. I am a sleeping top.

I don't understand why things have moved so fast. Why already I suffer such pain. It all seems back to front like the New Guineans' introduction to transportation: first the plane, then the truck, then the horse. For me the plane has come long before the horse.

189

In our hotel room twin beds. On a dressing table opposite are two vases of flowers. In the morning all the flowers in 'my' vase are dead. Stuart's are fresh as ever.

Before breakfast I picked a pomegranate from its tree and ate it. Found a strange pleasure as the clear red crystals broke into bitter-sweet juice and left only savourless pithy seeds. As if I were acting out the entire course of love.

* * *

During the night I come to the overwhelming realization that I cannot hurt Stuart. How strange this delicate balance between us. He is already compensating for my withdrawal—a withdrawal I swear he cannot consciously feel. There is a certain panic in his love. A pressing towards me, a greater enfolding of me in his heart. In the night he wakened me with cries of terror. Were his dreams telling him what I wasn't? I renounced Henrique at that moment and as I did so realized that with that decision I had left my youth behind and I wept at this, the most terrible renunciation of all.

* * *

Tuesday he called. 'Come to tea. I must talk to you.'

After some thought I accepted. It is playing with fire, but I lead from strength, or so I thought. I must work out with him what I should do if I were to need a surgeon. And, too—out of vanity, I fear—I would like him to know that I had no idea he was in love with me when I asked him to be my surgeon. Well, we shall see if it *was* strength!

Miraculously I slipped into a kind of emotional side street. Quite tranquil there. The furious physical desire abated. Was it because of a conversation with his partner's wife?

'Do you know Henrique?' she asked, out of the blue.

'Of course. He operated on me.' Why did she ask?

'Don't you find him a very lonely person?'

'I don't know. What's happened to the woman he was going to marry?'

'There have been a succession of women. The first was one of the most attractive Brazilians I have ever met. He had an affair with her and was on the point of getting a divorce to marry her when she made a fatal mistake. She told him that his wife was having an affair. So then he did a thing of great character. He divorced his wife and didn't marry his mistress.'

I was bewildered by this. 'But why did he divorce his wife?'

'Because she was having an affair.'

'But…'

'I know. It seems absurd. But they're *Brazilians*.'

I suddenly felt quite sick and very tired. I wanted to go to the sea and let a great wave break over me.

* * *

On Tuesday I shall see him. I shall say … but there seems almost no need to say anything now. It no longer matters that he know that I didn't know, etc., etc.

Perhaps I am through this. Safe out the other side. And no one hurt.

* * *

Tuesday. Portuguese lesson rather depressing. I have hit a plateau. Will I ever master the subjunctives, which are used in the most colloquial of conversations by quite uneducated people? An extraordinary language. My *professora* was moody and abstracted. She must be in love. Perhaps everybody is—the heat keeping us all at fever pitch.

There is time to spare between my lesson and tea with Henrique. I look for material for a new dress and suddenly I can barely walk with tension. Going up to his office I lean against the wall of the elevator, put the back of my wrist against my forehead, catch myself doing it and am half amused.

I am early. I hear through the door the harsh voices of Brazilian women. His male nurse is not there. I start to leave but the waiting room fills—an older woman and a younger, possibly her daughter, and Henrique. He sees the women to the door and we are together in the consulting room.

He takes my hands. 'Your hands are wet.'

'The result of a wish I made as a child. And the gods were kind.'

'I love you.'

'This is not love.'

'What is love then?'

'I don't know.'

'Isn't this a part of love?'

191

'Perhaps yes.'

'I miss you so much. I ...'

'Don't.'

'There are tears in your eyes.'

'You're wrong. It's my hands, not my eyes that are wet.'

But he is right. What am I doing sitting crying?

He goes back to the days of the hospital. 'I had to be so strict with myself. I think I was sometimes almost rude to you.'

'Almost!'

'You noticed?'

'It would have been hard to miss.'

'Forgive me.'

There is no pleasure in this. I survey the vast desert of my life as he talks.

I get up. 'Goodbye.'

'When can I see you?'

'You can't.'

'When can I phone?'

'You can't.'

'Why be strong when it is so sweet to be weak?'

I give no answer.

'Look at me. I am going to my *fazenda* on Thursday. I am coming back on Monday.'

I am grateful to know that from now until Monday I cannot meet him or hear from him. 'I shall phone you Tuesday.'

'No.'

'Then meet me here.'

I get up. He tries to kiss me but when I turn my mouth away he lets me go.

'Goodbye.'

'Don't say that.'

'*Até logo*, then.'

'Better.'

He opens the door to his waiting room and I am faced by two young men. I am caught completely off guard. I had thought we were alone, the office empty. I turn back. Drop my keys.

We start again. He sees me to the elevator. 'All my love.'

I press the button for the ground floor and the elevator goes up.

* * *

On Monday at the concert he passes me during intermission. He is with the 'actress' and walks almost right through me.

'There's Henrique,' Stuart says and makes an attempt to catch him. The crowd closes like a door between them. Momentarily I am upside down and glad of its support and its screen.

* * *

'We must have him to dinner,' Stuart says. 'Soon.'

I don't answer. Henrique at our long table among the silver and glass.

'Let's make a list. The de Mellos, Henrique ...'

I cut him short. 'A reception,' I say.

Stuart brushes the idea aside with his arm as if it were an object. 'The de Mellos, Henrique, and how about that architect and ...' And. And. And. The list is made. The date chosen.

* * *

That night as if I had a rigour, I shook and shook. Stuart so tender, so inarticulate, so loving.

'I think you should see a doctor,' he says.

'It is nothing. It will pass.' But I want to say, 'Fight for me. Please, please fight for me. I need your help.'

* * *

The morning of the dinner, the papers announce the death of two prominent politicians. We must cancel our dinner. The government is in mourning. But the pre-party flowers have been ordered ahead. A boy walks slowly up the long drive, an enormous *cesta* on his head. Flowers like birds. My heart pounds. From Henrique? I reach for the card. No. And later, dozens of red roses. Surely from Henrique. No, once more.

Is he stingy? I play with the idea. Perhaps he is. All this love and no celebration of it in presents. He said he would send me Bandiera but he has not. He says he is waiting for a new edition. I decide he *is* stingy and comfort myself.

I expect him to phone—*saudades*. But no.

So?

And then his partner's wife phones. 'Did you hear about Henrique?'

193

I don't want to talk to her about him. Don't like her gossipy tongue. Don't trust her.

'No,' I say, sharply perhaps.

'Well, he's dead.'

'But he was coming to dinner with us,' I say inanely as if that changed things.

'He won't be now. He was on the same plane as the ministers. They were all killed.' Her voice broke suddenly. 'Isn't it awful!'

I put the phone back in its cradle with intense concentration.

Dead? Henrique? It cannot be true.

The phone rings again. Henrique, I think. But it's Stuart. His voice is grave.

'I have sad, bad news. About Henrique,' he says. 'I am coming right home.'

(1999)

A KIND OF FICTION

Veronika saw the old woman fall. She couldn't prevent it. She was as helpless as if she were falling herself. She felt with excruciating clarity the old
woman's foot slip inside her shoe, saw her pitch forward, extend her
arms, and crash down the steps. Slow motion. The sight was horrifying.

Veronika was there when the old woman lay extended on the
driveway. 'If I can get her up,' Veronika thought, 'we'll know how badly
she is hurt—whether or not she needs to go to emergency.' Veronika
didn't like the responsibility. Wasn't sure she would know what to do if
the old woman's leg were broken or her collar bone or hip. Wasn't this the
sort of thing that happened to old bones? They grew brittle and cracked.

And these must be old bones. Veronika guessed her to be in her late
sixties. She watched as the old woman slowly pushed herself into a sitting
position; noticed the quite beautifully set moonstone ring on her engagement finger. Veronika thought the old woman behaved as if she were
entirely alone in the world—unobserved. As if the driveway on which she
had fallen led only to an empty street in an empty city. In fact, except for
Veronika, there was no one about. The old woman looked dazed.
Veronika wondered if she had suffered a slight concussion or a small
stroke for she didn't seem to be aware of Veronika.

She was talking to herself. 'Hurt,' she said, and then, 'Badly?' she
asked herself as she stretched each leg … her stockings in ribbons. Her
expensive shoes were Italian, Veronika thought. She felt she had seen her
before somewhere. At the symphony or on the bus. Veronika couldn't be
sure which, and as she continued observing she felt the old woman had a
slightly familial look. Would her mother have looked like that if she had
she lived so long?

The old woman rubbed her shins and then, slowly again, got to her
feet, shrugged her shoulders, turned her head side to side, testing.
Veronika noted the excellent cut of her coat.

She noted again that the old woman seemed unable to see her. Didn't want to see her perhaps. Who enjoys such moments of humiliation? Veronika watched her take a step, then another, and set off down the street, slow, but very erect.

* * *

It was some months before Veronika saw her again. Actually saw her. She had dreamed of her often enough and thought of her daily. Had become quite disproportionately preoccupied with her. She was leaving an afternoon concert. Alone. Using a cane. And moving carefully. Veronika wanted to speak to her, but as before the old woman didn't seem to see her, seemed in fact to give her powers of invisibility. Powers she didn't necessarily want.

Veronika followed, on the verge of speech, but somehow silenced. What could she say? 'I've seen you before'? 'I hope you're OK'?

Preferably, perhaps, 'Did you enjoy the concert?' Less personal. But Veronika knew the old woman had enjoyed the concert, had a feeling for this music as she herself did. Perhaps the old woman had played the violin in her youth, even performed the difficult Beethoven B flat quartet they had both just heard. Veronika felt she knew what the old woman had thought of the performance. Could she, by some form of thought transference, get into the old woman's mind? If she were to say, 'What did you think of the *presto*?' would the old woman reply that it should have been played faster? Veronika thought she would.

Even so, she felt it would be an impertinence to speak to her. There was a kind of inviolability about the old girl … an impenetrability, perhaps. Veronika felt she actually knew the old woman from the inside … knew her self-containment, knew it was not an aloofness, as many might think, but a mask for a too-warm nature which, in her own best interests, she had to control and direct.

Who were her friends? Veronika wondered. Elderly women, for the most part … women usually outlive men. Gardeners, probably. Or were they faceless companions found on the Internet? It would not surprise her if the old woman had a computer. Even though most of her generation had not. She looked, in a kind of a way, contemporary.

Veronika, lost in her ruminations, suddenly realized that the old woman had disappeared, or that she had misplaced her, the way she misplaced papers on her desk. She must have caught a bus, or picked up a cruising cab, for she was nowhere on the street where she had been in full sight only minutes before.

So easily and completely had she disappeared that Veronika began to wonder if she had imagined her. But why, under heaven, would she imagine such a person? Surely if she were capable of inventing, she would have invented the perfect companion ... male, antic, musical; someone who would make her laugh, pour her a drink when she was tired, draw her a bath. No, she could not, would not, have invented her.

She had read somewhere that characters in fiction very often took on lives of their own, got out of hand and surprised their creators. She had never quite believed that. But she was in no position to argue now. For that was exactly what was happening. The old woman was a kind of fiction, one she could not erase from her mind, one who was absorbing more and more of her time and thought. One who had a provenance. A history. And Veronika knew it, was privy to it in some way she could not understand but which interested her deeply.

Perhaps she should see a shrink, Veronika thought, in parenthesis. For surely this was not a normal preoccupation ... but then, what was?—get right down to it. Just *exactly* what was?

Veronika knew the old woman was comfortably off ... or had been once, at any rate, before inflation. And married ... most certainly. But what did he do ... the husband? Veronika questioned briefly. Was he not away most of the time? That perhaps accounted for the children ... a girl and a boy. Outrageous children. The girl had been stage-struck since her first school play and, to everyone's surprise had, in her teens, been cast in a production of *Hair*, mainly because ... it was commonly thought, 'That girl would do anything!'—she had been perfectly willing to stand on stage bare naked, something her mother had not been overly enthusiastic about, but neither had she been exactly shocked or critical, having known her daughter 'from the egg', as it were. Unlike Trik, who had been affronted ... darkly affronted. Their son, on the other hand, was a right-wing journalist and that she had found far harder to contend with. It hadn't occurred to her that rebellion would take such a form. Rebellion was surely a swing to the left, or so it had been in her day. So when he had supported the extreme right ... publicly, in his column ... she had had difficulty discussing it with him. And as his columns became bigoted, prudish, fundamentalist even, it was painful for her ... exceedingly painful, as if she herself had made a humiliating *gaffe*.

Jimmy had been quieter than Sylvie ... taken to books as other boys take to baseball, despite Trik's valiant efforts to play catch with him, take him camping. That male-bonding that had become so popular and, in some way, so phony. Not that Trik had been phony. He had genuinely wanted to play with his son, but Jimmy had other interests. He wanted Superman comics, but more importantly, children's histories about the fur trade or the wreck of the *Titanic*. They thought he might take a history major but he took political science and got a night job on a newspaper while still at college. They hadn't worried about Jim the way they had about Sylvie. He was unlikely to take drugs or stay out all night or do any of the things that Sylvie was almost certain to do ... once, at any rate.

But neither child had turned out quite as expected ... not for *her*, Veronika, for what could *she* expect?—but for the old woman and the dead husband who had dreamed it differently. And now that Trik was dead ... yes, Veronika said, that was the husband's name without any doubt ... it was not the first time she had said it ... now that Trik was dead and she couldn't discuss it with him, or look at it with his objectivity, for he was discerningly objective in the realm of ideas ... it was difficult indeed. Although, Veronika thought, the old woman had lived long enough to have seen much diversity in her life and was sufficiently knowledgeable to know how huge the gene pool was, she felt sure that ... what? Her mind was wandering.

Veronika, on her way home, dreaming in her fiction-writing mode ... a mode she had never explored before, and why now? she asked herself ... knew all this about the old woman, and more, even more, when she could keep her mind on it. That was the key ... keeping her mind on it, as members of the family created themselves for her, seemingly as fast as they could. She was in no way their puppeteer, their activator, could not have changed a hair on their heads ... although Sylvie had done so over and over, dyeing her blond hair black or red or green ... and now she was never to do so again. Dead ... flying too close to the sun, drag racing, of all things. Suddenly Veronika shook with sobs. As if Sylvie were her child ... bright, gilded, now ash-blackened and gone. Unbearable. She thought of her at kindergarten, like quicksilver on the green grass, so far ahead of all the others. Had she been programmed for attention? Needing it so badly and getting it wherever she went. Shining. Buttercups, she thought. And couldn't bear it.

Veronika wept unashamedly as she walked, burdened by grief ... the loss of Trik, of dazzling Sylvie ... who had stamped her feet as a child when they called her Syllie ... Jimmy's attempt at her name. Veronika felt suddenly weak, barely able to walk, and her head was flooded with them all, such a crowd walked with her ... Trik, beloved Trik, and silver Sylvie and Jimmy, poor, poor Jimmy whom she loved ... indeed, loved dearly, but loved from the stone heart he had created for her ... and why? oh why? Oh why?

Dizzy and almost falling, her face wet from weeping, they jostled her ... Trik and the two children ... Sylver Diamond (stage name); James Ormond (by-line). She had not invented them ... Trik, Jimmy and Sylvie ... or their real names ... Patrick, James and Sylvia. Those were their legal names, their baptismal names. She knew them all as if they were members of her family. But the old woman ... the old woman had been nameless. Veronika felt so weak she had to lean against a railing for support. She wondered whether she was ill, gravely ill. Then suddenly, as if struck by lightning, she knew the old woman's name. It was Veronika. Veronika Sylvia Ormond. Her own.

(2001)

A BIRTHDAY CARD FOR
DADDIE

CRAYONS

The house was large and airy with beds of lilies of the valley in its garden and, almost nightly, thunderstorms shook it and made it rattle like a cup for dice, and lightning whitened the sky to a sheet of paper. When that happened her cousins hid their heads and screamed, but perhaps because she had never seen anything like it before, she watched in silence and wonder. She liked the sheet lightning best.

She and her mother didn't live in the house. They had a bedroom across the road. But they spent all day and part of the night with her mother's cousin, the man she married, and their two little girls—one older, the other younger than she was. Her mother's cousin had a flat straight body and yellow hair. No crayon but the yellowest in the pack would do for her hair. And the husband had black hair for which only the black crayon would do. His hair grew in a semi circle from ear to ear and contrasted sharply with his white skin. It was so white it glowed with white rage, and she had to look aside when she saw him. She chose the brown crayon for the little girls' hair and wondered if they were adopted.

The bedroom across the road had a bed and a cot, and a small red table and chair especially for her. The flavour of that table and chair was one she would taste forever. She had only to visualize their small shapes, their bright red, exactly the colour of her red crayon, and the taste rushed into her whole body and filled her with pleasure. And the floor was beautiful, covered with squares of various sizes that fitted into one another like boxes. She had never seen a floor like it. Sometimes she sat and traced their outlines with her finger—the blue, the yellow, the green and then—the green, the yellow, the blue. And sometimes she took out her crayons and made the room over again on paper.

Susie and her mother were to stay there only a short time before they all went to the lake. Her father had just died and her mother's cousin had thought it would be a good idea for them to get away. When the invitation arrived her mother packed a big suitcase and the two of them went to the station and climbed aboard the train.

The night before they were to go to the lake her mother sat with her cousin sorting clothes to take for the girls, and her mother's cousin picked up a middy dress that had belonged to the older one. It was white and had a dark blue collar with braid on it.

'Would Susie like it? It would fit her a treat. Rita's outgrown it.'

'What about Beth?' my mother asked.

'Not yet,' my mother's cousin said. 'Here, take it.'

'Put it on,' they both said.

She didn't like it but she did what she was told.

'Perfect!' said her mother's cousin. It was too long.

Her mother laughed for the first time since her father died and hugged her and said, 'You do look fine! Just like a sailor girl.' She thought of the little red chair.

Next morning when they went across to the house for breakfast she was wearing the middy dress and Rita looked up from her cereal and said, 'That's mine.'

'It's too small for you,' her mother's cousin said.

The man with the black hair was reading the paper and he put it down and stared at them.

'But it's mine,' Rita said. Beth was smearing honey back and forth on her toast.

'Whose dress is that child wearing?' the man said, his face very white and blinding.

'Susie's,' her mother's cousin said. 'I gave it her. So, it's hers.' The sunlight fell like a knife blade across the table.

'Take it back,' he said. 'Beth will grow into it soon.'

'But I gave it to her,' her mother's cousin said. There were tears in her eyes.

'I said, take it back,' the man said and gave his newspaper an angry shake.

Her mother said, 'You shall have it back.'

She and her mother went across the street to the room with the little red chair and she took off the middy and put on her own dress with the cross-stitch which she liked much better. Her mother was very quiet when they returned for breakfast. By then the man had gone. Her mother's cousin was quiet too.

After breakfast Susie went into the garden and picked some dandelions and sucked their stalks until they curled and stuck them into her hair to surprise her mother.

'Do you like butter?' she asked and held a dandelion under her mother's chin. 'Yes! You like butter a lot!' she said.

Her mother smiled at her. 'Run outside and play,' she said. 'We have to get packed for the lake.'

She had never seen a lake and didn't know what to expect. Lake, lake, lake. The word sounded flat and hard.

The man said, 'Hurry up. We haven't got all day.'

It was tight in the car, and hot. She sat between her mother and Beth, and Beth pinched her and she felt sick. Beth pinched her again and she yelled.

'She pinched me,' she said to her mother.

'You pinched me first,' Beth screamed.

'I did not!' Susie said.

'Make those children keep quiet!' the man said.

Her mother put her finger over Susie's lips and squeezed her hand.

'We're nearly there,' her mother's cousin said. Her voice was bright.

They rounded a curve in the road. 'There's the lake,' her mother said. She looked and it was blue—the exact colour of the blue in her crayons.

The car came to a bumping stop. Rita and Beth went racing down to the beach and back. Her mother and her mother's cousin unpacked sandwiches and a thermos of tea and they had a picnic on the veranda. The house smelled funny. It smelled grey. Inside it was dark. Rita and Beth were yelling for their bathing suits.

'Wait a minute,' her mother's cousin said, clicking open the locks on a suitcase, pulling out two suits, one red, one green. '*We*'re going *swim*ming.' Rita chanted and Beth joined in. '*We*'re going *swim*ming.'

'Not so fast!' the mother's cousin said. 'You've only just eaten. You'll drown, if you swim now. Wait for half an hour.' But they were off, Beth trailing Rita, bare feet on the pebbles. Beth screaming.

Her mother helped her cousin tidy up the picnic and Susie sat on the veranda rail, swinging her legs and looking at the lake.

The man said, 'Who's moved my fishing rods? They're not where I left them.' He sounded cross.

Her mother and her mother's cousin were putting things away, opening drawers and fitting things in place.

'Oh, mice!' her mother's cousin said, getting a cloth and cleaning out the inside of a drawer.

'I said, where are my fishing rods?' the man said. This time his voice was loud.

Susie got down off the railing and found a crawl space under the veranda and crawled in. It was just earth and stones and old leaves. It was dark and cool and secret there. She heard her cousins in the lake screaming at each other. She made little piles of the leaves and then she scooped out hollows in the dry earth and filled them with the leaves. And she made little piles of the stones, which were smooth and grey. When she licked them they shone black or brown for a moment until they dried. And then she saw something white. A sharp white stone. And it had a vein of blue through it like fork lightning. It was the most beautiful blue in the world. Not a bit like her crayon blue. And another white stone with a vein of green. Bright bright green. And most beautiful of all—a white one with red. As red as the little red chair. She looked about for more but there were no more. When she held them where the sun came through the lattice, they glinted.

She heard her mother's cousin calling the girls. They didn't answer. Then her mother's cousin called her. She didn't answer either. This was a secret hiding place. When she heard the girls come back from the lake, the screen door bang, and the scuffle of feet overhead she crawled out, the three stones clutched in her hands.

The girls' hair was wet. Their teeth were chattering. 'You look like drowned rats,' her mother's cousin said. 'Go and get changed before you freeze to death.'

'Darling,' her mother said. 'Where have you been? You're covered with dirt. Come and let me wash your face.' In the kitchen there was a pail of water and a little saucepan with a long handle. Her mother scooped some water into a basin and took a cloth and washed and dried her face. 'Now your hands,' and Susie opened her hands and showed her the stones. 'Why, Susie,' her mother said, 'how beautiful! They're truly, truly beautiful! They must be quartz,' her mother said.

Beth and Rita came into the kitchen. They were still in their bathing suits.

'Look how pretty,' her mother said, showing them the stones. Rita grabbed them and held them over her head. 'Show me, show me!' Beth yelled and tried to grab them from Rita and they both began screaming.

'Be quiet!' her mother's cousin's husband said. 'We come away for a holiday at the lake and all we get is screaming children.' He glared at Susie.

Everyone was silent. Then Rita flashed the stones at Beth, who screamed again.

'Would someone tell me exactly what's going on here?' The husband's voice silenced everyone but Beth who said in a pouty voice, 'I want them.'

'They're mine,' Rita yelled. 'Mine. Mine. Mine.'

'Whatever they are, give them to Beth,' the husband said. 'She's the baby.'

'Actually, they're Susie's,' her mother said.

'Where did she get them?' The husband's face was blinding white again and Susie wanted her white crayon and wanted to press down on it very hard.

'I said where did she get them? Did she bring them with her?'

Her mother's cousin said, 'Tom, please. Can we talk about it later?'

'I suggest we get to the bottom of this once and for all,' the husband said. 'To begin with, what are they? Show them to me, Rita.' Rita opened her hands and the beautiful stones shone their bright colours in the room.

'And where did they come from?' the man continued.

'They're mine,' Rita said.

'Mine. Mine,' Beth screamed and began to cry.

'Susie found them,' her mother said and put her arm round her and held her close.

'And where, exactly, did Susie find them?' the man said.

She didn't want to tell about the crawl space.

'Where did you find them, darling? Your uncle wants to know.' Her mother's voice was encouraging her to speak.

'Outside,' she said.

'You mean you found them here, at the lake?' the man said his face very white.

She nodded her head.

'Then they are *not* yours,' the man said. 'They are ours. If you found them here, they are ours, wouldn't you say?' He looked directly at Susie. 'Ours, not yours. Give them to Beth,' he said to Rita. 'She's the baby.'

'I wa-a-ant them,' Rita yelled and opened her mouth.

'Tom,' her mother's cousin said. 'Please, Tom.'

'Let's consider that settled,' the man said and he went out slamming the screen door.

It was quiet again. You could hear the waves lapping on the beach. A gentle lap-lap.

'Let's get the crayons,' her mother said to Susie, taking her hand and leading her to the bedroom.

She lay on her stomach on the bed and opened the beautiful box and looked at the rainbow of colours. Then she took the black crayon and covered a whole sheet of paper with it until not the tiniest bit of white showed. Black. Black. Black.

She heard her mother and her mother's cousin talking in the kitchen in quiet voices as they started to get the supper. Far off she heard Rita and Beth screaming at each other.

Then she took a piece of coloured paper and her white crayon and pressed very hard and made a white stone. By mixing the blue and the green crayons she got nearly the right blue—almost exactly right. Then she made the stone with the green. She was beginning to work on the red when her mother joined her.

She looked at them a long time. 'Beautiful, darling,' her mother said. 'They are a work of art. Perhaps one day you will be an artist.' And she took her in her arms and rocked her back and forth, back and forth. Then she took her hairbrush and began brushing Susie's hair. 'We must both get tidy for supper,' she said. 'And tomorrow we're going home.'

(2001)

EX LIBRIS

Publication date

The book, worked on for years, was finally published the day he was born. It was waiting for him, so to speak, on December 3. Of course he was too young to read, so his mother read it aloud to him—between feedings. The first snow was falling outside and the household was turned upside down—broken nights and nappies and—a baby! With Christmas looming. Reading it exhausted his poor dear mother and it is unlikely that he understood a word. But it was a major influence in his life, none the less. In fact, it was his life.

His mother read the four-volume edition. It has since been edited, hopefully improved, with certain episodes deleted entirely.

The edited version

I was born into a literate family, literate but far from wealthy—or so I thought. Why have I used 'but' where I might have used 'and'? As if wealth and literacy are opposed—as indeed they are, today. But surely not then. Many of my parents' friends were layabouts—bookish and broke—so that may be where the idea came from. Today a so-called education prepares you for commerce, not scholarship.

My parents were such avid readers it surprises me that I was conceived at all. I don't quite understand that 'at all.' Except that it must have been nip and tuck—between the end of *War and Peace* and the start of *The Brothers Karamazov*, perhaps. I think I belonged to the Russian period. It would account for my name.

I was an only, lonely child

Oh, they loved me, I feel sure. But it was a literary love—nursery rhymes and Beatrix Potter, fairy tales and King Arthur. I liked *Mrs Tiggy-Winkle* and *The Tale of Two Bad Mice*. I also liked Merlin a lot. Dreamed I was the young Arthur. Looked for an Excalibur in every stone, thought there might be miniature Excaliburs no bigger than darning needles waiting for the bright-eyed. How I polished my eyes! And I longed to be the youngest son in those fairy tales where three brothers set out to win the treasure. I suppose I was the youngest, but as I was also the oldest and the middle one as well it seemed to cancel me out.

They didn't converse much, my parents—even with each other. 'Brilliant!' my mother would say, handing a hard-cover to my father who would give her a metallic glance through his reading glasses. That was about all that passed between them. And the books kept piling up. Everywhere. In my tiny bedroom a narrow path between stacks of books—read and unread—led to my cot. My nightmares—I was a fire child, and the least fever induced hallucinations—usually consisted of two people building a wall of books higher and higher. No room for windows or doors. No room for the light. Just little me in my sleepers tossing on my cot in a paper canyon.

But it was not a narrow life

I defy anyone to contradict me. What most people didn't know was that I was given to out-of-body experiences. Or, out of *my* body and into that of a dog. Always a dog. Sometimes rough-haired, sometimes smooth-haired. I can still feel the collar of rough hair, the taste of a leather leash. The sleekness of hair as smooth as skin. Even today I cannot see a dog—any dog—without feeling my being enter into its being, rejoice in its being. Feel the difference in the blood—the astonishing difference in the blood. Don't think dogs don't think—you, who have never been one. Take my word for it. They do. Serious long thoughts about bones. A flutter of thoughts about running and jumping and the most extraordinary thoughts about smells—near-epiphanies.

You might have expected me to react against this life of books and parents and dogs' bodies and seek out other kids, tough ones maybe, or at least, jocks. But I suppose genes play a large part, especially before experience has entered the picture. I was pretty much the cat that walked by itself. But there were kids, occasionally. One little girl on our street took down her underpants in her dad's garage and I stared in a kind of bewilderment at her malformation. Thought about it a lot, actually. A sort of pink wall. It stays in my mind mixed with the smell of engine oil. Other than that my world was mainly books, as my parents' was. I believe I was precocious. Used words like 'fenestration' and 'lazaretto' and 'recanalization'. I liked to see the look on people's faces.

I don't remember being unhappy, beyond having spots. All the other manifestations of puberty and adolescence were dealt with adequately by my father. He was intelligent. And scientific in a way, for all his love of literature.

At college I lived in the stacks

Where else? They were just like my bedroom, but organized. Besides, I was bred for stacks. Long legs, long arms. Good eyes that I had polished. I began by reading the A's. It took me a long time to get to Auden. You can imagine. Even with *my* eyes. But when I did, I fell in love. At home I had been immersed in the classics. I knew my Shakespeare and I loved him, even tolerated wordy old Wordsworth. My parents were into modern translations of all kinds—Rilke, Lorca, Seferis. Although translations intrigued me, I wanted the real thing. Auden was it. He was like jazz. I devoured him. Funny, really, because he was dead, for Pete's sake. Long dead.

There are people on earth who are dead and don't know it. Walking about. I read it in a book. Are the dead—Auden, for instance—those who have returned, believing themselves still alive? Slow learners, you might say. Or are they the living—my Mum and Dad? Me? It makes me uneasy. How can I prove to myself I am living?

Dead: having the appearance of death; lacking power to move, feel, or respond; very tired; incapable of being stirred emotionally or intellectually; grown cold; no longer producing or functioning; no longer having interest, relevance or significance.

What if I answer 'yes' to those definitions—am I dead, then? Dead before achieving anything. Unlike Auden. Alack, alas. Alas, alack.

But bless my long arms and legs

I was made for basketball. My game drove spectators wild. In a team I moved slow motion, or so it appeared. People who watched said they were caught in two time streams. It affected the circuits in their brains.

'Ivor moves like slow honey. All the other guys are like bees.'

I didn't know what they meant. I was just playing the game. But as they liked it, I was happy for them. At first I had played unselfconsciously. Then the shouts of the crowd reached me and I began to love those shouts. Soon I played for the shouts alone. Became aware of every move I made. It wasn't that I was actually slow but my long arms and legs made me look slow. I took one step where others took two or three. Then I developed a taste for slowness and began to test just how slowly I could pass and run without actually stopping. A slow dribble drove the crowd mad. It was as if all the clocks had run down, they told me. Dreamy. For me *and* the spectators. Our team was a sensation. We won every game.

We were national champions when a scout got to me and I found myself on an all-black team. The Tall Boys. We matched, the Tall Boys and I. Arms and legs long. Polished eyes. There was no difference in our timing. We were all slow honey. But I was the only white. It was the first time this had happened in the annals of the sport. I was called 'nigger-lover', I was called 'piss-ass'. But the crowd loved me and we took all the games. Slow and dreamy. Even my parents raised their eyes from their books and looked at me with surprise. Between *War and Peace* and *The Brothers*... they had conceived a star.

The year we took the World, I married Esmeralda.

My black orchid, I called her

A cliché, I know. Long arms and long legs. Eyes polished. Like me. Black and white, white and black, our languorous, violent love. Nothing had prepared me for Esmeralda. To love her was my career. I embraced it. My body, her body—I no longer knew which was which. I loved her as I loved myself.

I am not proud of this blatant declaration of self-love. It makes me uneasy. We love ourselves first, our friends second, God last. It should be the reverse. Where had I read *that*? Interesting that friends remain in the middle, either way. If I were to say, I loved myself as I loved Esmeralda, would anything change? The idea is provocative. And let me provoke myself further, blaspheme, perhaps: I loved her as I love God.

An observant reader will notice the tenses: I loved her as I love God. Do I not love her still? I do.

But I cannot go into that yet

I was wealthy, of course. I had amassed a fortune. Basketball became a thing of the past. I didn't even watch the games. I might have coached, I suppose, and without Esmeralda, I probably would have. But with Esmeralda there, in my arms as I wakened—long arms, long legs—what choice did I have? We made love. It was my vocation; my avocation.

On Sundays we went to her church and sang. Holy Saints! She was another Kathleen Battle. And the whole congregation sang too. Lordy! Lordy! There had been nothing like that in my literary childhood. Nothing like that at all. No room for music among all the words. And now I was swamped by it, overwhelmed, in fact. What was this art that demanded your entire lung power—took your breath and gave it back, took your breath and gave it back. It was more like a kind of sport. Writing, painting, sculpture required no special breathing. Only dance. And music. My voice came out of some hidden vault. 'They crucified my Lord.'

I went to see my parents from time to time

Their world didn't change. They had neither computer nor TV. The house was solid with books—a book meat loaf. They couldn't bring themselves to get rid of any of them. Easier they said, to get rid of furniture. They sold the chesterfield, all but two armchairs, and the spare bed. As a concession to me, they read Toni Morrison. Living through books, as they did, with no time for life, nothing had readied them for *Beloved*. Surely, I thought, in all that reading, they would have learned something about racism. But, 'White people don't behave like that,' they said, a questioning note in their voices, as if asking me to agree. I replied that white people do. All people do. We are half animal and half angel. A very difficult mix. They could only shake their heads—my father's, now, a shock of grey, my mother's turning white at the temples. They were old.

As for me …

I was putting on weight—thickening through the waist. Even my once so muscular thighs were becoming flabby.

One morning Esmeralda wakened, and instead of turning to me lazy and drowsy as usual, she sprang out of bed and turned on the shower. The scent of her gel, heavy as gardenias, filled the air. Oh, Proust, do I not know what you mean? That smell would come to conjure up my whole life with Esmeralda.

'What's up?' I asked, unbelieving.

'I've got a job,' she said. 'Modelling.'

'Modelling! A job! What the heck? We don't need the money, honey.'

'Somebody in this family's got to work. It's only right.'

The logic of it was absurd. I saw, in a flash, that I didn't know Esmeralda—how her mind worked, what her thoughts were. It was terrifying. I went into the bathroom and pulled her beautiful black naked body to me. 'Honey,' I said. 'Don't leave me. We've got to get to know each other.'

'No talk of leaving,' Esmeralda said. 'I just need to find myself. I don't want to be a sex object all my life.'

A sex object! Esmeralda? 'You are my love, my life,' I said. There were tears in my eyes.

'*Yours*,' she said. 'That's the whole point.'

If I were to tell you my world fell apart …

It did. Morning to night, my life was a vacuum. Her hat box, her cosmetic case, her beautiful long arms and legs, her polished eyes. She had no place left in her heady, hectic life for her lover. With those looks, with that voice, she was destined for stardom and she knew it. Something any fool could see. And now I was any fool. Every fool. Why had I not seen it before?

I took to pacing back and forth like an Alzheimer's patient. As if the very action of my feet could heal my heart. I saw Esmeralda less and less. Photo shoots, fashion shows, beauty parlours. New York, Paris, Rome, Singapore. She bought a pale Afghan hound—her perfect match, even as I had been—who walked at the end of a golden leash. They modelled together. Sometimes she phoned, sometimes she was too busy. Lonely, I sought her on TV. She was on shampoo ads—her long shiny black hair lifted by a fan. Tampons, pantyhose, face cream. Sometimes because of the lighting, the camera angle, the hairdo, I barely knew her. Recognized her just as the image faded, and my heart broke.

I spent more and more time in front of TV. Took to drinking beer. Alone.

When she came home with the dog after months abroad, I was waiting for her, avid for her. And the dog. I had begun to see the dog as me—or me as the dog. Which? Those long legs, that pale fur. I wondered if that was why she bought it.

She was astonishing. I could hardly believe her. Always dazzling, she was now perfect. I wanted to fling my arms around her but as soon as my eyes fell on the dog I had an out-of-body experience.

I was that dog. And hostile. I strained at the leash. 'Heel, Holly, heel,' she said firmly, and yanked my collar. It was a choke-leash and she almost strangled me. 'This is Ivor. Nice Ivor,' she said, and patted me. But Holly hated 'nice Ivor' and lunged again. *And I was Holly. Holly was me.*

It lasted no longer than a minute or so. I don't think Esmeralda even noticed but it unnerved me. Of all the dogs I had ever been, I had never been a dog that disliked me.

'He usually loves people,' Esmeralda said and I felt accusation in her tone. Then her eyes looked me over. My thick waistline had become a paunch. It was not disguised by the new Armani jacket I had bought especially for her. With my unmanicured hands I reached out to her. 'Don't touch me!' she said in a sharp voice I had not heard her use before. And Holly lunged again.

In short, her homecoming was a disaster

We never made love. That dog wouldn't let us. And the telephone, the fax machine, the e-mails all interfered. A steady stream of beauticians came to the house. She worked out.

'I have to tell you,' she said, between appointments, 'I'm leaving for Hollywood.'

'Hollywood!'

'Yep. I'm going to play Josephine Baker. They tell me I'm made for it.'

'Josephine Baker!' I could only repeat what she said. I had no words of my own, apparently. 'Josephine Baker,' I said again.

'The great jazz singer!' She was impatient.

'Can you sing jazz?'

'I can sing anything, honey. Just you watch.'

I didn't know this Esmeralda. I had never seen this confident metallic woman in my life before. Where had she come from? 'Esmeralda …' I pleaded. But she was on the phone again and that goddam dog was between us, always between us. A canine wall.

Before I knew it she had gone

I looked at the desolation of the house. Garment bags, tissue paper, cardboard boxes. Our bathroom full of lotions and creams and gels. There was barely room for my razor.

When the telephone rang I didn't answer

I was not going to be her appointments secretary. Let it ring. She isn't here. Let it go on ringing. But the persistent bell in the empty house was intolerable. Just to shut it up, I lifted the receiver. It was my father's voice.

'Ivor, I've been trying to reach you. Your mother is dying.'

My head was so full of Esmeralda I couldn't take it in.

'Ivor, did you hear me?'

'Mum?' I said. Mum couldn't die. He must be wrong.

'She had a stroke and they say … Oh, son, can you not come home?'

And so I went

Threw my razor into a bag along with my pyjamas and a change of shirt and shorts and caught the first plane out.

I hardly knew my father. He was a stick of skin. Small, grey, broken. He led me through walls of books, up the dusty stairs and into their bedroom. There was barely room for both of us beside the bed. My mother lay, her right side paralyzed. Her face twisted. Unrecognizable. But on the floor beside her bed, open and face down, as if she had put it there before turning off the light, lay Emily Dickinson's poems.

'She wouldn't have been able to read,' I said, looking at the book and then at her.

'What? What's that you said?' Perhaps my father was deaf.

'Left hemisphere,' I continued, not believing my words, my mother, the crypt of books we stood in.

'Speak to her, son,' my father said.

I didn't know what to say. Then, 'It's Ivor, Mum. Ivor.' My voice sounded like a kid's.

'Mum. Mum!' Her left eyelid flickered. 'Oh, Mum!' But her face closed again into that contorted mask.

I thought my chest would break. I had to get out of there. I pushed past my father, past all those piles of books, looking for a place to sit down. The house smelled like an antiquarian book store. At last, in the kitchen, I found a chair. My chest broke. I began to sob. I sobbed for my mother, for my father, for Esmeralda. And I sobbed for myself.

Oh, I looked after what had to be done

Hired a nurse. Cleared a wider passageway to the bedroom between the books. Got some order in the kitchen. Bought some eggs. And settled in to wait. There is a lot of waiting in a house of death. A lot of standing, hands hanging helpless. Useless rearranging of sheets and pillows. 'A little jelly, Mum? Some mango ice cream?'

I had picked up the Emily Dickinson beside her bed and now I opened it. It had been read and reread, marked in pencil with stars, asterisks, underlinings. Poems about Death.

> Because I could not stop for Death
> He kindly stopped for me.

Did she suspect, in her pell-mell race through literature, that He was about to stop? Probably not. More likely it was the poetry she loved. The turn of phrase. Dickinson's unique turn of phrase.

When I began basketball I forgot books. Really didn't miss them. And then Esmeralda wiped my tapes completely. Now, suddenly, I longed for literature. A spring of fresh water gushed as I read. Plants bloomed. I read hungrily.

> The manner of the Children—
> Who weary of the Day—
> Themselves—the weary Plaything
> They cannot put away

How did she know all that—that spinster Emily in her white house behind white curtains? How could she possibly know what I felt? A weary Plaything. Weary to death.

I was astonished by my grief. This old lady who had conceived me between books, given birth to me between books and read to me, sometimes at great cost to herself, would read to me no more. But as her farewell present she gave me Emily Dickinson.

My father and I were the only mourners

My father a little stick figure clutching a bunch of summer flowers. Delphiniums, daisies, roses—yellow and pink.

We returned, drained, from the crematorium to that comfortless warehouse he called Home. With the nurse gone, my mother gone, the place was dust and debris. We hardly spoke, my father and I. I poured us a whisky. Later, I scrambled us some eggs. Then we crashed.

What to do now? I thought, as I wakened. The books towered above and around me, stacked helter-skelter. I heard my father moving about downstairs. I thought of Esmeralda, beautiful Esmeralda in Hollywood with that goddam dog. And I wondered where I—the star, the guy with the beautiful wife—had vanished to? The whole tone of my life had altered. No longer a figure to be envied, I was a deserted husband with a father bereft, in a house of despair. Psychologists have a name for it: mid-life crisis, they call it. Damn them.

Then my father died

I found myself the sole inheritor of a surprising amount of money, an old house in a run-down neighbourhood, and thousands of books. My first thought was to call in a second-hand bookseller and get rid of them all. But I moved slowly, hobbled by inertia. Esmeralda's absence, the death of both parents—the enormity of my inheritance ...

Little by little, book by book, I got sucked into that dust-filled vortex. A most eclectic library—if a jumble could be graced by such a name. I was interested to see that the largest single category was poetry. Art books were perhaps second—the surrealists from Bosch to Ernst and Carrington—and the whole history of art. Folk tales, science fiction: Verne and H. G. Wells and Abbott's *Flatland* as well as Clarke and Sturgeon and the inner space fiction of Lessing, plus people I had never heard of. Their astonishing thoughts about time and space turned me upside down. The literature of ideas. I had read nothing like it in contemporary fiction—a genre noticeably absent in my parents' collection, as far as I could see. 'If you don't read the best-sellers when they first come out,' my father had said, 'you don't need to read them at all.' Perhaps he was right.

Had my parents absorbed this wealth of ideas, I wondered? And if so, what did it profit them? Why had I not spent more time at home, asking them questions, instead of goofing off with Esmeralda? But that was what I thought with Esmeralda gone. What would I have thought if she had suddenly appeared?

Did I say I loved her?

I do.

Books, books, books

They became my life, even as they had been my parents' life. Lethargy and inertia were things of the past. I was on fire.

I found an unemployed librarian and together we began the

interminable work of sorting and cataloguing. I installed a computer and the software required for itemizing what, at times, felt like the contents of the city dump. We wore masks against the dust of decades. We found treasures and learned skills I could not have dreamed of. And although, originally, I thought we should construct a special building for the books, I soon discovered that the house was well enough built for us to renovate. So I hired carpenters and designers. Shelves rose in all the rooms. Floors were reinforced. Temperature and humidity controls installed.

When not working on the project, I was reading. I became a vessel for all that print to pour into. And the hallucination of my childhood—of book building upon book and blocking the light—was now reversed, and book building upon book was letting the light in. I had had no idea how many combinations and computations of words there were, no idea of the extent of human thought—psychological, philosophical, spiritual. I began to sense space/time, stretching back to the beginnings of language and beyond, and forward beyond my imagination's reach. The world that had seemed large enough to me when I had Esmeralda—a bed-sized world—was now, without her, immense. A vast glass-house, light-filled. A night sky by day, if one can conceive of such a thing.

I had calls from her occasionally. The filming was going well. She was 'a natural', they told her. Everyone loved Holly. And what did I think about a divorce?

And then it came to me. A vast glass-house was exactly what I wanted—an atrium with a glass ceiling—UV glass, of course—around which the books … How my thoughts raced. The property next door was for sale. I snapped it up. And hired an architect, the best I could find. To hell with the cost. I wanted the space to reflect the contents. A glass bomb.

The work was a wonder

Even before it was finished—half-finished—librarians and architects beat a path, as they say. The architects were stunned by the cantilevered extension which took in the property next door. And the light pouring in. The librarians didn't quite know why I featured Auden so prominently. Not only did I include his complete works, but all books with references to him—*The Changing Light at Sandover*, for example, in which he comes back as a shade, conjured by Merrill. And the David Hockney drawing, blown up, life size, of his raddled face—the only face I know with actual runnels in it. I told them I planned to do the same with certain other authors—chosen in a somewhat idiosyncratic manner, or seemingly so. Persian miniatures for Hakim Sanai, perhaps, or elegantly handset, a quotation from him: 'The human's progress is that of one who has been given a sealed book written before he was born.' The Modigliani drawing of Akhmatova for her section, of course. What would I use for Immanuel Velikovsky and his *Worlds in Collision*? Something from an observatory—the heavens blazing. Or I could hire an artist, for Pete's sake. Why not? And why Velikovsky, come to that? Was he one of my faves? Actually no. He may have been a nut. But that Immanuel shook things up—questioned all those scientists locked in their certainties. I like doubt cast on conventional wisdom. I guess I like doubt a lot.

The librarians shook their serious heads—this was not according to the book, ha, ha—but they took notes.

Meanwhile

The neighbourhood altered. Old houses became boutiques and delis. Were remodelled for the wealthy young. What a change-about. And at its centre, at its very heart—the library. It shone.

A phenomenon, not a folly

My parents' obsession, now an idiosyncratic collection of paintings and books, was written up in the press, in architectural journals, in librarians' bulletins. It attracted worldwide attention.

And that attention generated work—more than our small staff could handle. We appointed a board, a chairman of the board—me. We hired experts. And we had an official opening where speeches were made and ribbons cut. There had never been such an event. Artists and writers, bureaucrats of culture—celebrities of all kinds—fought to attend.

Esmeralda swanned in—a creature from another planet. All jewels and line. 'Where is Holly?' I asked. Her beautiful eyes swam with tears. 'Dead,' she said. 'Run over.' I put my arm around her. 'Ivor,' she said, 'you are like a brother,' and for the briefest moment her glittering body relaxed against me. But then she was on stage again, camera men crowding, flash-bulbs popping. And before I knew it she was gone.

Do I still love her?

I do.

I had built my shining palace

Out of tears, perhaps. It was dedicated to the memory of my parents, to Emily Dickinson, and W. H. Auden. Their names were engraved on a tablet in the foyer. The foyer that had once been our small book-jammed hall.

The days after the opening were crammed with appointments—the Ministry of Culture, the International Commission on the Arts. No time to read. Once again, no time to read. Exhausted, I dashed from interviews to meetings, from hotels to board rooms.

Because I could not stop for Death

I was late for my last appointment of the day—a TV appearance. It was rush hour. I stood on the curb waiting for the light. And then I saw a dog, a terrified dog, running in and out between the cars. In a flash I was out of my body and into that dog.

He stood on the curb waiting for the light

He had no idea he was approaching death. But as he entered the body of the dog, he suddenly remembered what his mother had read him when he lay in her arms—a babe, newborn—tiny; squalling, wanting to be fed.

(2001)

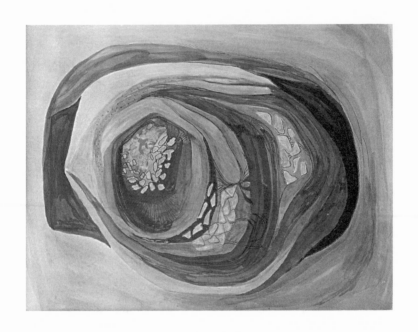

STONE

There was nothing she could do about it.

'It' was a piece of marble weighing 312 pounds—which had been shipped to a show in a presumably reputable gallery in the depths of Los Angeles from the northerly point of—well—who has ever heard of the name? The work was entitled, *What Marble Remembers*, and the problems it had caused its sculptor, a slight girl in her late twenties, to have it crated and dispatched—let alone to have conceived it in the first place, or carved it in the second—were beyond description. The gallery had accepted it on the basis of slides—also a problem. For the marble was polished to a high shine and the sculpture's irregular shape meant that whatever angle you shot it from did it an injustice, also in her cramped studio you could not get far enough away to convey its size, or—magnitude, she felt was a better word. But the gallery to which she had sent what she thought were two unsatisfactory slides had been ecstatic. Subsequently, so had she. And no problem is too great for ecstasy. Not the crating, the forms in quadruplicate, or the miles of red tape that would get it across an international border. Ecstasy, unlike despair, always wins.

For the artist, C.D. Stone—had her name forced sculpture upon her?—known to her friends as Cass, who had never exhibited internationally before, it was a matter for celebration. She could not afford to go to the opening. And, as it turns out—just as well. What money she had, had gone into the marble—not much; and the shipping—a great deal. But she celebrated, you may be sure, with her friends Ruby and Joe. Joe had informed the local paper, which had sent a reporter and a photographer to see her. They had run a picture of her in her goggles as if working, and a poor reproduction of a slide of the work. The night of the event they drank God-knows-what mixture of drinks and all of them ended up very drunk indeed. The hangover lasted for days.

In fact, for Cass, the hangover went on. And on.

Ruby was first to be concerned. 'Come out of it,' she said, 'you're famous. The first famous person ever seen round here.' Ruby was a painter—a part-time painter. She used acrylics and painted small lichens and tiny plants. But she knew she was out of the loop. She knew paintings and sculpture were being replaced by installations, so for Cass to have made it into a show in L.A. was an event.

But had she? It soon became evident that more than geography separated Cass from the gallery. When no literature about the show came to her, as promised, she blamed the mails. But as day followed day and her trips to the post office produced nothing but flyers and the monthly letter from her mother, she grew anxious. Hadn't they said they would send a catalogue? They had. She phoned the gallery, at the number she had used before. A recorded voice announced the number was no longer in service. She must have misdialled. Calls on the hour throughout the day and the night brought the same reply. She got help from Ruby and Joe. She got operator assistance. Finally, the unbelievable truth dawned: there was no such gallery. But if there was no gallery, where was her sculpture?

She contacted the Canadian Consulate in L.A. That was Joe's brilliant thought. The Canadian Consulate agreed the phone number was no longer in service. It had been disconnected. And the address was nothing more than a mail drop. She could write. And she did. No answer. No gallery. No show. No sculpture. It had all been a scam. There were no tracks to follow. Nothing to do.

Cass felt she had been raped. In her studio she stared and stared at the space where *What Marble Remembers* had been born and grown to maturity. The fact that its loss reminded her of her reasons for leaving home only added to her misery. She had never before worked as hard at anything—not that hard work means good work. But rarely had she been as excited, and for her excitement was often a fairly good gauge of quality. Nor had she worked on such a scale or with such material. It was her best work.

She had been surprised to find that the texture of marble was unlike granite—surprisingly much softer. More like wood, or hard limestone. Working on it, it glowed as if there was a presence in the room—a celestial presence. The stone was alive.

It had been nearly a year of backbreaking work and during that time she had not only greatly improved her carving skills and mastered the art of sharpening chisels, but had learned to be compliant. On granite she imposed her will, carved the shapes in her mind's eye, or better, her eye's mind. But with marble, majestic marble, it was master; and her job—merely menial—was to free the mass she sensed within it.

The sea and all its shells were in it—shells like those she collected as a child: mother of pearl and molluscs and cowries and clam shells and cone shells and little sea horses—which, over eons of time, the sea had made smooth as sucked candy. Then, it had ground them like a mortar and pestle, and its great weight had pressed them into each other, layer upon layer. She wanted to recreate those shells. Not as they had been, but as the marble remembered them, rather in the way that ice might remember water.

She could discuss the idea with no one—didn't want Joe and Ruby to see what she was doing or say, 'marble remembering!' and shake their heads and look at each other.

Weeks went by with Cass so absorbed in her work that no one saw her. She was carving all the shells of the sea—transmuted—that was the key word. And her arms and legs and back ached as if the weight of the sea were pressing on her. She began each morning as soon as it was light, spent a meditative time making sure her chisels were sharp, and then—the moment she had waited for!—confronted that beautiful mass.

Had it not been for Mann's Monumental Works shutting down she would never have had such a chance. The young Mann, into whose hands the business had fallen—the old Mann unable to hold a chisel, the bones of his fingers having been destroyed by a lifetime of carving, his eyes unable to read a balance sheet—had gambled his inheritance away. All his stock and equipment was to be disposed of. Joe heard of the bankruptcy sale and tipped her off. And there, in the dust and litter of the neglected Monumental Works, among the slabs and chunks and lumps of granite and limestone was this one block of marble. It must have been there for years waiting for the day when someone rich enough would order a marble gravestone—an angel, perhaps. Young Mann when questioned as to where it came from could only answer 'me dad must've bought it and it must've just laid there iver since.'

Young Mann was a trembling wreck. His eyes were bloodshot and the stubble was rough on his chin. He had never been the carver his old man had been. He had carved as a job, without passion, doing only what was needed. Not even keeping his tools in shape. And with his father's retirement, he became more and more slovenly.

Respectable burghers or bereft widows who entered his shop and found him standing among the stone chips, a nicotine-stained cigarette hanging from his lip, would have gone elsewhere for their headstones had there been an elsewhere. And before long there was. A new Memorial Works had opened down the street, nearly next door for godssake, with a showroom full of angels and gilt and finely carved lettering in gothic script, and salesmen in three-piece suits as slick as undertakers. And Mann's Monumental Works was bypassed.

Coincidentally, with this march forward, a casino had opened in a nearby town and there the young Mann decided to recoup his losses. With a couple of cronies at first, but finally on his own, he played the machines. It wasn't only a wish to make money, although that started it. The larger and more important part was that it fed a craving, a craving for life. He felt fully alive only at the moment he passed the bouncer—an enormous woman bursting out of her tatty tuxedo—and walked up to the wicket with a wad of notes to exchange for a cup full of loonies. That full cup acted upon him like a sugar rush. And the noise of the machines, the lights, the music were to him as the Hallelujah Chorus is to a singer. He fed two machines at a time—right hand, left hand, right hand, left hand. He barely saw the cherries and berries whirling and spinning. And also, alas, he rarely heard the whirr and clash of coins spilling. But he knew that one-day he would hit the big time.

After some weeks he became suspicious of the machines. Looked at them sideways. Although apparently all alike, he knew they were as different as people are different. He developed a fine sense for knowing which ones would give him a fair chance and which were set against him. One by one they were all set against the young Mann.

By the time he had lost nearly everything he owned, Cass was able to get the tools and the marble for little more than the asking. Joe helped her move it all to her studio—a shed out behind a dry cleaners where the almost lethal smells of cleaning fluid hung in the summer air, and where, in winter, she worked in parka and gloves. Far from ideal. But hers. And once the block of marble was in there, an iceberg in a grey sea, she could have believed herself Michelangelo.

The day of the move was a day of ice and gold—the purest autumn day—when Joe pushed the dolly through the narrow door and heaved the marble onto the turntable. It was astonishing how the room changed, accommodated itself to the presence of marble. Marble from Italy? Marble from Vancouver Island? She had no idea.

Joe produced a bottle of sparkling white, but as he began to cut the foil with his pocket knife, she put her hand over his. 'Not now.' She wanted to be alone with the marble. He folded the open blade back carefully, gave her a long look and left.

She was barely aware of his departure. She pulled out the stool and sat and stared. Kicked the turntable with her toe to turn it, turned it again. When her eyes could take in no more, she touched the marble with her fingertips, with her palms, put her arms around it to feel its bulk. But bulk is not what she felt. What she felt was amplitude. The space it occupied was an amplitude of space. Like a perfume, it filled the room. And her heart swelled with it. She fell in love.

This, as it turned out, was hard on Joe, for although there was no formal arrangement between them, they slept together from time to time and, on Joe's part at least, there was the unspoken belief that one day not too far off, they would become full-time lovers. If he didn't press his case it was because he believed in inevitability. And there was no hurry. Neither wanted children in a world hurtling towards extinction. Neither was gainfully employed. Joe, when he had moved north, had taken any job going—bartender, waiter, truck driver. He had lost any sense of the importance of work beyond that of keeping himself alive. The idea of a career, such as his father had envisioned, was absurd. He planted a vegetable garden and sold what produce he and his friends could not eat. He ran an intermittent jitney service and worked as a handy man when occasion arose.

The day he first saw Cass, he had just delivered a pile of merchandise to Ginty's General Store. An early snow was blowing and the wind was bitter. Knitted cap pulled down over her ears, shoulders tight, she was standing on the street corner waiting to cross. He offered her a ride.

'Where to?' she asked.

'Wherever you like.'

They drove to her studio.

'I'll make you a coffee,' she said, lighting the small butane stove and adding a spoonful of Nescafé to each mug. A large table was littered with chisels, mallets, and instruments that looked as if they had belonged to a dentist.

'Right,' she said. 'I had a friend who was a dentist and he gave them to me. They're great for clay.' She turned on a small electric heater. 'Sit, if you can find somewhere.'

He pulled a stool out from under the table, dusted it off, looked around him. She worked mostly in wood. Some of it was stained, some painted. He had never really looked at sculpture before but he felt a vitality and uniqueness about her work. Strange forms that might be organic stood on roughly built shelves. He didn't know if they were animal or vegetable but felt they were pre-language.

'They can't speak,' he said.

She looked at him with surprise. 'No.'

Larger pieces carved from some kind of stone took up floor space. Rough, grey, heavy enough to break your toe. Joe saw them as unformed, embryonic creatures from the mineral world. Not exactly unnerving but weird.

He drank his coffee, got up, pulled on his mitts. 'I better be off.'

'You know my address,' she said. 'And thanks for the ride.'

The room was so bitterly cold she wondered if she wanted to work after all. She rubbed her hands and breathed on her fingers. Maybe she'd go back to her apartment over Ginty's and read her mother's letters. Or settle down to the bookkeeping she did for Ginty in lieu of rent. On the other hand, perhaps she might look for something better in the way of space heaters. The thought of warmth so cheered her that she pulled on her parka and headed for the hardware store.

That evening as she was struggling with plugs and wires, there was a knock on the door.

'Saw your light and just wondered ...' Joe's voice trailed off.

'You are exactly what I need.' She pointed to the two new space heaters, the one wall outlet, and shrugged.

He wasn't sure he liked the 'what' but he surveyed the set up. 'I'll need some stuff. Back in a minute.'

He worked in silence as she watched. Wires, pliers, plugs, switches. His movements were sure, the way hers were.

'You may burn the place down, but you won't be cold,' he said finally. And the blast of heat from the two little fires was immediate. He glanced round at the walls, ceiling. 'What you really need to do is insulate.'

'Insulate me,' she said.

He didn't know if this was a personal invitation. He moved

tentatively towards her but she was already staring at one of her painted wooden objects and oblivious of him.

Later he took her request impersonally, installed a false wall, and blew in cellulose. She didn't seem to mind him being around but mostly she was absorbed in what she was doing—hacking and scraping and pounding. Fair enough, he felt. He had forced his presence upon her, after all.

Then one particularly cold day when he had arrived with a bottle of brandy expecting nothing more than that she accept the warming drink, she had impulsively thrown her arms around him and things had changed for the better. It was almost as if she saw him for the first time.

'You've got a good head,' she said. 'If I did heads I would like to do yours. For some reason I can't make your profile and your full-face match. Have you ever noticed that with people? With some people they are perfect matches. With others … turn sideways again.' He did so. 'It's a much more aquiline profile than your full face could imagine.'

'Imagine?' he said, surprised. 'Surely you're the one doing the imagining.'

She laughed, took a sip of brandy. 'I guess I'm imagining all the time.' She glanced at the carved figures on the shelves. 'What do you imagine, Joe?'

'Since meeting you, being in bed with you is about all.'

'All?' she asked.

'It's enough.'

And so began a new phase in their lives together, one he had not exactly anticipated. At times she was happy to be with him day and night, at others he seemed invisible to her. Sometimes he felt it would be easier if she expressed irritation or anger, but she showed no signs of either. She didn't suggest he move in with her, but he had his own key and spent much of his time over Ginty's.

'Do you have parents?' she asked one day, and before he could answer, 'Do you like them?'

'Yes, to both—in a relative way. That is, I respect my dad. But talk to him … mm mm. He doesn't know about the world, doesn't know there's been a change in kind, not just in degree. He's a royalist and a capitalist. His whole world is a shambles and he doesn't know it.' Joe hit his head with his fist. 'He spends long hours with his grandchildren, whom he sees as his legacy. I am the youngest of ten and he feels I owe him another grandson. He believes in big business and hates the NGOs. So I am a piker and a rotter and a whole lot of other old-fashioned pejorative words. Mother has been his slave, no mind of her own, and now no mind at all or so bizarre a mind no one can follow its inconsistencies.' He shook his head. 'And you?'

'I hate my mother.' She stared into space. 'Is that a terrible thing to say? Look,' she took a packet of unopened letters out of a drawer. 'All from my mother. She writes once a month. I haven't read them. Don't even open them—or haven't yet. I left home because she drove me out. I couldn't stand it. Why didn't I behave like a normal girl? wear a skirt? go to the skating club? go to the tennis club? Boy, was she born bourgeois to the bone!'

She laughed, but he could see she was agitated. 'I was taking a book-keeping course in the mornings because I like figures and am good at them. That pleased her. But the only thing I wanted to do was sculpt.'

She took a deep breath and went on, 'I managed to get some clay and I kept it in the attic under wet cloths. I was working on a head—well over life-size. It was high realism. I really needed a turntable for it but I was too ignorant to know that. Those dental tools would have been ideal too. I worked with my nail file and orange sticks and knives. It must sound absurd but I think I loved that head more than I ever loved a human one. Maybe a mother feels that way for her child. I had created it, after all. Then one afternoon I went up to the attic to work and the head was gone. There was no sign that it had ever been there. I couldn't believe it. The attic looked the same, smelled the same, but the only thing that mattered was the head, and it had disappeared. I confronted my mother. She was sitting in the sun, doing a crossword.

'Where's the head?' I said.

'She barely looked up from her puzzle. 'I won't have you wasting your time on such rubbish.'

'I said, 'Where is it?'

'I threw it out,' she replied as if she were referring to used kitty litter.

'At first I couldn't speak. I thought I might kill her. 'OK,' I said, 'if you want war, this is war.' Her expression was unchanging. Stone, I thought. She married a Stone.

'I went up to my room, grabbed a red felt marker and wrote on her pillowslip, "I am a sculptor!" Then I filled two garbage bags with my pos-sessions—mostly books. Epstein, Michelangelo, Brancusi, Giacometti, Hepworth, Moore. And I walked out.'

'It may explain why I don't do heads,' she added, after a pause.

Joe knew he couldn't fix this in the way he had fixed the lack of heat in her studio. Or could he? Was it not, *au fond*, the same thing? He would try. Perhaps he could make it up to her with the support she had never had.

'And father? Siblings?'

'I didn't know my father. Or anything about him. And I learned early on not to ask questions, as my mother wouldn't talk. She never had other men as far as I know. And as I was the first born, there were no siblings.'

'And the rest?' Joe asked.

'Is history.'

He could see she didn't intend to tell him more. And there must be more. She couldn't have come directly here when she left home. But he didn't ask.

'And you?' she said.

'If you can believe it, I was an assistant to a parliamentary assistant as a student. Then, one day I saw government with new eyes. I wanted no part of it. My father was disgusted. He thought I had a future in the civil service, or even politics. Before too many weeks had passed, I discovered that words were turned into their opposites and I was very afraid that if I stayed I would become more corrupted than I already was. I was sorry to disappoint him but I had to leave.'

He stopped, his gaze distant. And then he continued in a different tone of voice. 'I read a story once about the waters of the world becoming poisoned and how one man who knew in advance filled a reservoir with pure water. I can't remember the story in detail, but the rough cut, you might say, was that the poisoned waters made those who drank them go mad. Finally, the one man who drank the pure water was so unbearably lonely that he, too, drank the poisoned waters. I felt like that man. I could see that I would have to drink the poisoned waters if I stayed on—or more accurately, that I was drinking them. So I left.'

'Just like that?'

He nodded. 'Just like that.' After a pause he said, 'Up here I feel safer. Oh, I know it is far from lily-pure, but whatever happens will happen on a smaller scale. There's no chance of a really big hornswoggle. The only thing big here is the land. And as for words reversing their meanings, well, this is a world of small vocabularies.' He laughed.

'I'd have thought prevarication was worldwide,' Cass said.

'That even *yes* and *no* can change places? True. But what I saw happening was different from lying. It was as if the bones of the language were being destroyed.'

* * *

The loss of *What Marble Remembers* and the destruction of the clay head were two cavernous holes that Cass couldn't come to terms with. Wearing her goggles as if they gave her comfort, she sat in her studio day after day mourning the two most important works of her life. She knew the head was not a work of art. But she couldn't help believing *What Marble Remembers* was. Otherwise why would the people in L.A. have accepted it? They must have liked it and kept it. She assumed the whole thing from start to finish was an ingenious way of acquiring art at no cost.

She could still feel the marble beneath her hands—its silky finish created by hours of rubbing—and the great stylized wave—so stylized that it wasn't a wave, with its small shells that were only in her head. No one looking at it could guess that was what she had in mind. She hoped it would make people think of the sea.

'Why not do another one?' Joe asked. 'We'll find another piece of marble and—'

She cut him off. 'I can't copy myself!' There was a kind of wail in her voice.

Looking at Joe's face she regretted her words. How could he be expected to know about the process of art? Know that it is the original idea that provides the energy and the growth of a piece. For it does grow, very often unexpectedly, rather like a child.

She told him the story of the gringo in Mexico who came across a beautiful chair with a woven seat and painted ladder-back. On being asked if it was for sale the craftsman quoted a price that was absurd for the amount of work involved: five dollars U.S. The American was overjoyed, bought the chair and took it home. There, one of his friends saw it and asked where he could find the craftsman, for he too was going to Mexico and he would like to buy two. The American was surprised when the Mexican asked twenty dollars a chair but as the price was still low for such beautiful work, he agreed. A friend to whom he showed his purchases thought how wonderful it would be to have a dozen, so when he next went to Mexico he, too, sought out the craftsman. Thinking he was giving the man a good order and believing things are cheaper by the dozen, he couldn't understand the craftsman's reluctance to accept.

Twelve?—he didn't know that he could make twelve. But finally after much arguing he capitulated. And the price? the American asked. One hundred U.S. each, the Mexican said. The American was astonished. Why should the price go up? Well, the Mexican replied, 'One chair is a pleasure to make. For two I have to charge more, to pay for the boredom. To make twelve, *señor* ...' He threw up his hands.

'In my case, of course, price has nothing to do with it, but the boredom and drudgery would be identical. I couldn't do another.'

At least she had taken off her goggles and was talking again. But not yet working.

'It's the absence of it,' she said. 'I don't know how to express it. I suppose if you had a perfect baby and it died—no, I'm not equating the two—but it is a parallel experience. And then, where is it? It's the "I know Daddy's dead but why doesn't he come home for supper?" syndrome. And it isn't as if it's the first time. The head was a kind of dress rehearsal. That's what makes it so freaky.'

'We'll find a piece of marble, anyway,' Joe said.

* * *

'Where's Ruby?' Cass asked, a day or so later, and Joe realized she was recovering.

'She had to go home. Her father was ill.'

'Poor Ruby. How long has she been gone?'

'Three weeks.'

'No way.'

'Time passes,' Joe said. He noticed she was whittling a piece of wood and rubbing it with the palm of her hand, contemplatively.

'I think I'm going to do a lot of small pieces. You know when you're in a swarm of midges how molecular it is.' And then, 'I've missed her,' Cass ended.

'You couldn't have missed her. You didn't even know she wasn't here.'

'I've missed you, too,' she said.

'Oh Christ!' Joe exclaimed. 'Put that damned knife down and I'll come back.'

* * *

Ruby's return was joyful. Her father had not died. ('Saved only to die again,' Joe thought.)

Ruby had taken advantage of being in the city to go the rounds of the little galleries. And when she saw the 'swarm of midges' Cass was whittling and painting she knew how the two of them might exhibit together. They would call the show 'Molecular.' Joe would make the slides, take on the business end of it.

As it happened, Joe too began to carve.

It began the day he picked up a piece of pine from the floor of Cass's studio, looked at it a long time, opened his pocket knife and started to whittle a spoon. He discovered he had a three-D eye. He also had a computer and was able to track down a variety of woods—basswood, ash, cedar, pine. Before he knew it he had an assortment of tools, including a burning tool. His head held a museum of images—small rodents, birds—all of which he could reproduce in miniature with astonishing accuracy. He bought acrylics, and his eye for colour was as true as his eye for form. A menagerie of small creatures proliferated. Discrete small creatures, utterly complete in themselves—unlike Cass's small forms which had to be grouped to make a whole.

'Did it ever occur to you that creativity is catching?' Joe asked one day as the three of them were sharing a pizza. 'I am told there are whole villages in Mexico where everyone is a potter or everyone a weaver. Is it a case of genes or proximity?'

'Or destiny?' asked Cass. 'Someone I knew—who had lived in Mexico—told me she had a house boy from a weaving pueblo and when she asked him why he slaved away in her house when he could be a weaver, he replied with the utmost gravity, "*Es mi destino, señora*."'

'Which leads us to God,' Joe said, solemn after the laughter the remark had evoked.

'It isn't an age that believes in destiny—or maybe it's just this country that doesn't,' Cass said.

'Do you?' Ruby asked. She had never thought of it until this minute and didn't know what she thought.

Joe spoke slowly. 'I believe the small details of our lives are in our hands.'

'And the big ones?' Cass asked.

'Are not.'

'How do you determine which is which?' Cass asked. 'Would you consider my losing *Marble* big or small?'

Joe was nervous. It was the first time Cass had referred to it. But Ruby rushed in. 'If Joe's right, it has to be big,' she said, 'because it was not in your hands.'

'But the making of it was, the shipping of it was ...'

'Oh, come on,' said Joe, still anxious. 'Let's go, and I'll buy you both a beer.'

'And that,' said Ruby, 'is big!'

* * *

'I've found a place,' Ruby announced one day.

'What kind of a place?' Cass asked. 'I didn't know you were looking for one?'

'A house, where we could have studios and a gallery. And where we could live—you, me, Joe. It would need a lot of work but ...'

It was an old building, as old goes. There were fireplaces in every room. Small windows, great wall space. They'd share the rent.

'Maybe we should get one more person,' Ruby said. 'That way it would be easier.' Ruby's motives were pure enough but it was her boyfriend she wanted for the fourth. A new boyfriend at that.

'But he's not an artist,' Cass said.

'Nor is Joe,' Ruby replied.

'Have you seen his carvings?' Cass asked.

'That's not art,' Ruby scoffed.

'And besides, you hardly know him,' Cass went on, deliberately avoiding an argument about Joe. 'And Joe and I haven't laid eyes on him. And,' she ended a bit lamely, 'maybe he wouldn't want to join us.'

But Chuck, Ruby's boyfriend, did indeed want to join them. A local boy who worked at Smith's Radios, he had sold Ruby a cellphone and been blown away by her. Exotic Ruby was unlike anyone he had ever met. She brushed his shyness aside, thrust her tongue in his mouth when they kissed and drove him crazy. Of course he wanted to join them. He had never met such people before. They laughed easily, teased each other, argued and planned. Drank too much, he thought, not liking to disapprove, but his temperance upbringing made him feel guilty on even those rare occasions when he downed a beer with the boys after work.

'What makes you think it would work?' Cass asked.

'Oh, God,' Ruby exclaimed. 'What makes one think anything'll work? You give it a try and if it doesn't then you deal with that.'

Chuck went with them when they inspected the 'place', walked through its deserted rooms. Empty a long time — as is the way with houses when a town grows and its residential area shifts — it smelled of tomcat, the wallpaper was peeling, some of the floorboards were broken and they didn't even want to think about the roof. But it was well built and had all the space the four of them would need. It also had a large overgrown garden. 'Great for sculpture,' Ruby said, jabbing Cass with an elbow.

They poked about in cupboards. 'Look at this!' A chamber pot painted with roses. A faded calendar with a picture of a small boy in a sailor suit hugging a puppy. A pile of yellowed newspapers.

These leftovers of a life started a flood of thoughts in Joe's mind. How seemingly easy it had been then. Mummy and Daddy and the obedient children. Radio still a luxury, TV undreamed of. A windup phonograph for music. A fiddler maybe and a square dance on occasion. Perhaps he was going back too far. Perhaps this house had had TV — that rusting metal contraption half hidden in the grass outside had probably been an aerial — but even so the contrasts with today were vast. Such enormous freedoms. Or restrictions. It worked both ways. His thoughts were interrupted. Chuck's cellphone was ringing.

'Hi,' answered Chuck. 'Well hi-de-hi, guy! Are ya? Great. OK. See ya.' Chuck grinned at them all. 'That was Sid. Great guy, Sid.'

Joe was irritated. The call symbolized the world he was running away from. On the other hand, the 'place', symbolized the simple life he longed for — the life his grandparents knew. And so he measured and dreamed, and to that end carried a spirit level and tape measure with him at all times.

They were sitting on the steps of the old-fashioned veranda. The early evening sun was colouring pink a few small clouds that drifted in a blue sky. A lilac that neglect had not killed was in full bloom and flooding the air with its sweetness and when they stopped talking the silence seemed to be scented, too.

'How lovely it would be to live here.' Ruby had her arm round Chuck. 'Let's decide tonight. Right now. If we don't, we might lose it.'

'Lose it!' Joe laughed. 'Who but a bunch of idiots would even consider it? Does the owner want to rent? Or is he trying to sell? Do you know, Chuck?'

'I figure he'd take what he was offered,' Chuck replied for it was he who had shown the house to Ruby in the first place. 'He's sure not making anything out of it the way it is.'

'If he'd rent it and put the rent towards the selling price we might be able to swing it.'

'Well, I don't know about the rest of you,' Cass said, 'but my misadventure with *Marble* has left me short of cash. The way things are now I can just manage. I pay nothing for my apartment and in the summer months the studio costs next to nothing. I'll have to think about it.'

Joe took a deep breath. This was the first time she had referred to money.

Chuck volunteered to talk to the owner. His report back was that the old man would rent it for $1,000 a month and his selling price was $40,000, which meant they would own it in some foreseeable future.

It was a silencing thought. None of them had dreamed the price would be so low.

'There you go,' Ruby said. 'We can't afford not to take it!'

'What if one of us leaves?' Cass asked.

'Thinking of going somewhere?' Joe's voice sounded anxious.

Cass replied that one never knew and it made sense to consider all angles. 'Didn't you ever read de Bono?' She was really wondering about Chuck, how he would fit in, how they would get rid of him if he didn't. 'It'll take an awful lot of work,' she said.

'We've got all summer to fix it up,' Ruby offered and Joe said, 'We?'

'Of course. All of us,' Ruby replied. 'You should see me with a paintbrush. I'm the fastest brush in the West.'

'How are you with plumbing?'

'I'm great with a plunger!'

'You're local,' Joe said to Chuck, 'maybe you can get some of the stuff we'll need wholesale.'

'I'll sure try,' Chuck said and Ruby smiled at him as if he were a genius.

Cass continued to have doubts. It seemed so permanent, for one thing, and for another she wanted to work, not to spend months struggling to get a place ready for work.

'You'll ruin it for us all.' There was despair and anger in Ruby's voice. But Cass was not to be moved.

'It'll cost a small fortune before it's finished—if it's ever finished.' And then, as an afterthought, 'Look, as you're so keen, why don't you and Chuck find another couple to go in with you?'

'Another couple!' Ruby was outraged. 'The whole point of it was for you and me—studios, display space. What other couple is there? No. If it's not you, it's not anyone.'

'But I never wanted it. I'm happy the way I am.'

'It's no good,' Cass said to Joe, later. 'Ruby is pushing me into deciding now and the only decision I can make now is no. You and Ruby and Chuck go for it, why don't you.'

'It could be a great place,' Joe said. 'But if you don't want it, there's nothing in it for me. Besides, I'd sooner find a place for just the two of us. The world is breaking down. We'll be back to tribal living soon enough.'

'Ruby will be devastated,' Cass said. And she was.

* * *

Spring gave way to summer. The grasslands turned brown. Indian paintbrush, tiger lilies, bugloss came and went. Cass stewed in her studio behind the dry cleaners and obsessively went on with her carving. A kind of stasis settled upon them all. She saw almost nothing of Ruby who was painting less and spending more and more time with Chuck.

'It won't last,' Cass predicted. 'Chuck's not right for her.' But Cass was proved wrong.

'Guess what?' Ruby burst into Cass's studio.

'What?' Cass said. Then, joking, 'Pregnant?'

'How did you guess?' Ruby was radiant. 'And Chuck and I are getting married.'

'Married?' Cass was unbelieving.

'Aren't you happy for me?'

'Of course.' She was nearly speechless. 'If that's what you want, of course I am.'

As it turned out, a baby was exactly what Ruby wanted. Her paints, her dreams, became things of the past. She had painted because she wasn't pregnant. Cass was as sure of that as she was of the fact that she, herself, sculpted because she had to. Ruby was to settle down into small town domestic life as if born to it.

* * *

'D'you think there were so few women artists in the past because they were having babies or ...?' Cass began.

'They wouldn't have had much time to be artists if they were bringing up kids,' Joe replied.

'I didn't mean that exactly. I was thinking about creativity. Making a baby and then turning it into a human being is an enormous creative act. It satisfied their creative urge and they didn't know … hadn't been allowed to know …'

'But look at all the modern women who do both?'

'That's what I mean, in a way. Somewhere between then and now, we've been given permission. And those who do both are, I guess, the real artists. The ones who can't be stopped.'

They were lying together on Cass's bed. She was quiet for a long time. He wondered if she had fallen asleep.

'I had an abortion,' Cass said. The words blurted out. 'It seems terrible to me now but I felt I couldn't bring a child—especially a fatherless child—into this world and I was only a kid and scared half to death, and Denny—he was my classmate—was younger than me and didn't even shave. And you may be sure, my mother insisted—big time! Now, that loss has become part of a pattern of losses: the baby, the head, the marble. I feel I must fill those great holes in my life by making things. At the same time, another part feels the world itself is a loss—this beautiful dying world. What greater loss could there be than the loss of the world? If it dies, there's no point in anything. So why should I sculpt? I'm not being very clear, am I?'

Joe was overwhelmed by her outburst. Beyond anything in the world he wanted to comfort her.

'I've just had a flash thought,' he said, 'especially for you. The phrase, "Nero fiddled while Rome burned," may not mean that Nero didn't care, it may have meant that as there was nothing he could do to prevent the disaster, he might as well do what he could do—i.e. "sculpt."'

'And,' he added with a big grin, 'Rome is still standing.'

Cass laughed in spite of herself. 'Why am I so pessimistic?' she asked.

'Maybe it's all those absences. First an absent father. You hadn't included him.'

'And a mother, in a way.'

She thought of the letters piling up that she still couldn't bring herself to open. They filled her with horror. No change in the envelopes or the handwriting, month after month. Like a kind of recurring decimal. Why didn't she stop?

'What we have to do is fill the absences,' Joe said. 'We can't, as far as I can see, fill the parent slots. But we could have a baby—'

'No.' Cass was firm. 'You can't mean it? I thought we had agreed on that.'

'I'm just listing the choices. You see, I have read de Bono. Or we can have a show—in your studio. We could fix it up. Make it look really good.'

'Who on earth would come?'

'Or we could contact the galleries Ruby spoke about and those where you've already shown.'

'And ship everything again?'

'It would be a snap this time. We could do it. Believe me. Have you got an up-to-date resumé?' And so Joe, with his astonishing good humour and imagination began to dig Cass out of her misery.

He took photographs of the 'swarm of midges' and his own miniatures. He set up a website showing examples of their carvings and urged Cass to send out her resumé—to paper the world with it.

∗ ∗ ∗

Ruby and Chuck meanwhile were getting on with their lives. They had moved in together despite his parents' disapproval and were busy making preparations for the wedding. To Cass's astonishment it was to be a white wedding and Ruby wanted Cass to be her bridesmaid.

'What shall I do?' Cass asked Joe. 'You know how much I have wanted to escape this kind of life.'

'It will make Ruby happy,' he said.

'But to do things you don't want to do, to make someone else happy … I don't know,' Cass said. 'Isn't that the way the old control the young? In this case Ruby isn't old but she is perpetuating an ancient point of view. And the dress,' Cass complained. 'I can't afford the dress. I don't want the dress. I'll never wear the dress again. Why do dying traditions have such enormous power? You'd think Ruby would be free of them.'

'It's probably Chuck's family. After all they live here and they want to look just as much like everyone else as they possibly can. It's some kind of a law. Look at peas in a pod.'

'So you think I should go along?'

'Well, I guess if it were me she was asking, I'd do it.'

'You'd look sweet,' Cass began to laugh. 'Princess lines? Ruffles? Or bias cut?'

'Bias cut!' Joe said. 'Emphatically, bias.'

'And pi-i-i-nk!' Cass spluttered.

And so, Cass agreed.

* * *

It was a summer wedding. The church was full of flowers. Ruby in her wedding dress—white, with a train—mercifully, did not look pregnant and so, mercifully, the family face was saved. The ceremony was twice interrupted by Chuck's cellphone. The first time he answered automatically and the guests were amused more than shocked. The second time it went off during the 'exchange of rings' and as he didn't have a hand free, it rang on and on.

Chuck looked as if he were choking to death in a rented tux that didn't fit, with a green bowtie and matching handkerchief in his pocket. Like the Mayor of Casterbridge, Joe thought. Ruby's lace was threaded with ribbons of the same green. Cass was in a sheer slim dress and Joe thought if he hadn't been in love with her before, he would be now. There was something to be said for dressing up. 'Clothes maketh the man,' he thought and wondered if he had misquoted. 'Manners maketh the man,' he amended. He couldn't have made up 'maketh'. One of them might be a known quotation. But he didn't agree with either. Perhaps 'Manners maketh the man' was the school motto of a British public school his uncle had gone to, but he wasn't sure. A bit like 'Be toidy, be clean, be noice,' the motto of an Australian girls' school his cousin had attended.

His mind was on anything but the service. What, then maketh man? he asked himself and realized it couldn't be answered without a definition of man. Could man apply to both Nelson Mandela and a child abuser? To Mme Curie and those poor hookers murdered by the pig farmer? Somewhere, something was wrong with our idea of what man is. But his thoughts were interrupted by the shuffle and swish of rising bodies and the blaring forth of 'Amazing Grace' from a CD player as the married couple, for all the world as if they had swallowed a flight of canaries, marched down the aisle.

The reception was in the basement of the church. It was stiflingly hot. At Ruby's insistence they had champagne. It was a great mistake. Her in-laws didn't approve, there was nowhere to chill champagne for so many people and there was a decided air of disapproval from the temperance guests who drank punch. The punch was pink—and cold, at least—for it was poured over a block of ice in a large galvanized tub. Ruby's mother-in-law, in violet polyester, face a near match, was busy with the photographer. Their only son's wedding must be recorded in all its details.

One of the wedding guests was the young Mann. He had tidied himself up a good deal since Joe had last seen him. 'Sid Mann, friend of the groom,' he said to Joe, as if he needed to justify his presence.

'How are things going?' Joe asked. And the young Mann replied that he was working at Smith's Radios with Chuck. And things were going great.

Ruby, radiant Ruby, appeared at Cass's elbow. 'Come with me when I change,' she said. 'I'll give you the high sign when I'm about to go.'

* * *

It was hotter still in Ruby and Chuck's apartment. Ruby took one last look at herself as a bride and began to undress.

'Oh, Cass, I am so happy—here, help me with these hooks, I seem to be stuck.' She sat for a minute on the side of the bath. I never dreamed life could be so perfect. Cass, you should marry Joe.'

'I have married Joe,' Cass said.

'It's not the same,' Ruby said. 'Not the same at all.'

'I suppose by now you've decided where you're going on your honeymoon,' Cass said, laughing.

'Believe it or not, we were still arguing as we fell asleep last night. But we're back to our original plan of following the coast road south. It will be heavenly. And because Mum and Dad couldn't come to the wedding we'll stop over a day or two with them so they can meet Chuck.' She turned on the shower.

'How will that be?' Cass yelled.

'How will what be?'

'The meeting.'

'They'll love him,' Ruby said. 'Who wouldn't?'

* * *

'Promise me that nothing like that will ever happen to us,' Cass said. 'Why on earth does Ruby want it?'

'I'm relieved to hear it didn't give you an attack of wedding fever,' Joe said. 'It would be a high price to pay for the pleasure of living with you.'

He peeled her dress from her hot body. 'You are beautiful,' he said, 'as the lilies of the field,' and, after a pause, 'or the stars in their courses.'

* * *

'What do you think has happened to Sid Mann?' Cass and Joe were packing work for a gallery in the east. To their near disbelief, it had responded to Cass's resumé and offered to take ten pieces from each of them on consignment.

'Last time we saw him he was a big time loser. At the wedding he was all spit and polish.'

'Who knows.' Joe didn't seem particularly interested. He was filling a box with crumpled newspaper and hardly heard her.

'It's so remarkable a recovery, it makes me suspicious.'

'Don't start worrying about Mann,' Joe said. 'He's hardly our problem.'

'But he may be Chuck's,' Cass said. 'He's working with him. And that, in turn, may be Ruby's.'

* * *

But Ruby didn't have a problem. Wherever she looked the world was rose-coloured—hormone rose. Even Joe's carvings had become art in her eyes. And Chuck was Mr Perfect himself, although not, as she had foolishly expected, in the eyes of her parents. Her father had frozen stiff at first meeting and not thawed out before they left. 'Oh, Mum, just because he didn't go to university,' Ruby had said.

Now, back in their apartment, she put them out of her mind and busied herself making curtains and buying cookbooks and behaving in the way she had been led to believe young brides behaved. They bought a living room suite and a bedroom suite and matching china and stemware and towels and linens. Cass felt quite ill at the sight of it, but Ruby was ecstatic.

Sometimes Sid Mann came in for dinner after which he and Chuck played computer games and that excluded Ruby. Sometimes Cass and Joe dropped in with a bottle of wine and that excluded Chuck.

'I can't understand it,' Cass invariably said after seeing Ruby. 'I suppose I understand the urge to procreate. The need was implanted in us in a devious, ingenious way when the planet needed bodies. Now we can't feed the bodies we have and we are still behaving as if the world is new. It's

241

like setting the watering system for drought and the rains come. Surely to God we ought to know enough to turn it off. Or has intelligence been bred out of us? Do you think there's a cosmic script we follow blindly? Or what?'

'The churches were the scriptwriters once,' Joe said, 'and they've let us down. It's all the fault of the Pope. It's all the fault of the Pope.' He did a little dance. 'Actually,' he said, 'it's the boiled frog syndrome and we're the frog. If you put a frog into a pan of cold water and slowly increase the heat, the frog will boil to death before it knows what's happening. It isn't that we're without intelligence, we're just geared to a different...'

'What?'

'We're out of sync with the speed limit—we're biologically driving along at 20 km/hr when the technological speed limit is 80. Here, wrap my mice and wrap them carefully. They're very delicate.'

As usual, Joe addressed her concerns and led her through them into a more open space. She wondered how she had managed all those years without him. And then she thought that actually she hadn't managed. She had merely stumbled along.

'Did you ever read Huxley's *Brave New World*?' Joe asked. Cass shook her head.

'I had to read it for English 100. It seemed too far out to be possible. Now it's not only possible, it's true—super-true. In Huxley's world, consumerism was the highest social duty. In our world, a recent poll reported a large percentage of teenagers (I've forgotten the actual figure) said the most important things in their lives, in this order, were shopping and TV. So it's not a social duty. It's something much more insidi-ous—it's part and parcel of our culture, oh God! Here,' he handed Cass the packaging tape, 'let's get this finished so we can go to bed.'

* * *

Most people, even hardened businessmen are moved by small creatures, and Joe's mice and wrens proved to be real heart-softeners. The gallery re-ordered almost at once. But like the Mexican craftsman with the chairs, Joe couldn't go on churning out identical mice and birds. He had to enlarge his repertoire.

'Why do you think Australian birds are so brightly coloured?' Joe and Cass were eating a leisurely meal with Ruby and Chuck. 'I had always thought colour made them visible to their predators and so, a no-no. Yet in Australia almost all the birds are brilliant. For instance where our wrens are brown, theirs are blue—bright, bright blue. And red. And all the parrots and parakeets. Are there fewer natural enemies down under?'

'Lichens are pretty fluorescent sometimes. I collected them once and some of them looked like they'd been dyed,' Ruby said.

'It's not quite the same,' said Cass. 'They don't have natural predators—lichens, I mean. Or do they?' She realized she knew nothing about lichens.

'The whole idea of colour,' Joe was going on with his own thoughts, 'is fascinating. Look at us—the four of us sitting here—faded jeans and T-shirts. Our generation has made a uniform of colourlessness. Is some unconscious part of us protecting us from the Great Predator in the Sky? Or is it just that a smart advertiser, or series of smart advertisers, are telling us we can have "any telephone we like provided it's black"—although in this case it's dirty blue. And all because some manufacturer bought a shipment of denim at almost no cost at a time when the great masses—meaning us—had had the need to conform burned into us. By whom? And how? What do you think, Chuck?'

'Me? Oh, I guess I never thought about it.' Chuck had grown a moustache since they'd last met, and he was playing with it now, lovingly smoothing the blond hairs with a forefinger.

It had been some weeks since the four of them had been together and Cass was uncomfortable with what she saw. Chuck had changed. Marriage had matured him in an unpleasant way—and seemingly, overnight. It was as if the role of homeowner and husband had been waiting for him and he was filling it the only way he knew—in the manner of his father. He was cocky, confident and dominant. He sat back and ordered Ruby about and waited for her to serve him. Cass raged.

'How about seconds all round?' Chuck pushed his plate towards Ruby. Then 'Get a load of this,' he said, removing a palm-sized gadget from his pocket. 'It's the latest. And the best. A portable computer. You can send and receive e-mails and browse the Web. How about that! Five hundred smackeroos. They're going like hot cakes. With this and a cellphone, you have the world in your pocket.' He was beaming. 'Every kid'll want one.'

'Chuck's doing so well,' Ruby said, 'they're talking of promoting him.' Chuck stroked his moustache again. Cass saw it as a gesture of self-congratulation, self-love, almost masturbatory, and she didn't like it.

A shadow fell across the table.

'As I live and breathe, if it isn't Sidney Mann!' Chuck exclaimed, looking up. 'Hiya guy! come on in. There's a beer in the fridge. Help yourself.'

'Thought you might feel like going out,' Sid said, nodding to the others as he helped himself and sat, legs spread, drinking from the bottle.

'Sure would,' Chuck replied. 'A little business to talk over,' he explained, grinning at them all. 'But you folks feel right at home,' he said to Joe and Cass and then, patting Ruby's stomach, 'and don't wait up for Dad, kiddo. Your Daddy may be late.'

* * *

'I suspect I was right all along,' Cass said as they walked back to her apartment. 'It isn't going to work. Once the baby's born Chuck will ... Chuck will ... well, I guess I don't know what Chuck will do. He is unlikely to dump her, with Mum and Dad breathing down their necks. But maybe, if it comes to it, Ruby will dump him. D'you remember her attitude about the "place"—that you give a thing a try and if it doesn't work, then you deal with that?'

But Cass was depressed. 'Chuck will be a lousy husband and father, I'd bet my last penny on it, and unless he's very careful, he'll be in trouble with Sid Mann. There's something fishy about Sid Mann.'

But Joe was not really interested. He was excited by what he and Cass had going with their carving. And now that Cass had got 'the midges' out of her system she was wanting to work large again. He saw her spending hours poring over Hepworth's smooth, strangely female forms and he suspected she was once again ready for a piece of marble.

* * *

Ruby was happy about the baby, due now in three months. If she was unhappy about the change in Chuck she didn't show it. Cass and Joe were happy with their carving—Cass, absorbed and baffled by a piece of snow white marble Joe had bought for her, and Joe pursuing creatures great and small and creating them in wood. It is possible that Chuck and Sid were also happy ...

* * *

244

Cass was exhausted. With Joe out of town on one of his long distance deliveries, she had spent the entire day working on Ginty's books. When she raised her eyes and saw the leaves on the trees had turned into green numbers that she was trying to add together, she knew it was time to stop.

At the bakery she bought a jelly doughnut and ate it sitting on a bench in the late afternoon sun, dreaming about the marble. So far, all she had seen in it was a blizzard—a blinding blizzard—and how could she sculpt that!

Too tired to work, she couldn't resist stopping at her studio for one last look before going home. And in that last look everything changed. Her sight shifted to a third or inner eye—did crystal gazers feel like this?—and her heart raced. An enormous egg floated before her. Egg of the World: egg *oeuf huevo ovo ei*. Without taking her eyes off it, she reached for a chisel automatically and rolled its handle between her palms. Tomorrow she would begin.

* * *

At the post office on her way home she gathered up the usual flyers. Her head was so full of the egg that she had her key in the door before it dawned on her that there was no letter from her mother. Cass panicked. She felt as if she had missed a period. Surely it was over a month since the last letter. Well over, in fact.

'Mails are no longer reliable,' she spoke out loud as if the sound of her voice would give authority to the statement. The familiar envelope would arrive tomorrow, or the next day, or the day after that. It was absurd for her to react like this but the letters' regularity reassured her. They were like a heartbeat. And now the beat had stopped.

Was her mother ill? Dead? The enormity of the thought overwhelmed her. She had always believed her mother immortal but tonight she seemed as mortal as all of them. Fragile even. Old.

Cass examined the last letter minutely, tried to remember exactly when it had arrived. Why had the post office eliminated date and place from postmarks anyway? Given her mother's unchanging choice in stationery, the last letter looked exactly like the one before, and the one before that. However hard she scrutinized it, there was nothing to indicate when it had come. All she had to go on was her own inner clock that told her it must be five weeks ago or even six.

Should she phone her mother? The thought filled her with fear. Cass realized that if her mother needed help she was not yet ready to handle the situation. She had thought that leaving home would solve everything. It hadn't. It had solved the problem of her being able to sculpt; by a series of flukes she had fallen on her feet. But it had done nothing to solve the conflict between her mother and herself. The two of them were locked insolubly together—like one of those large iron puzzles in which two seemingly inextricable pieces, connected by chains and bars, have to be separated without force.

When and where had this locking occurred? She tried to relive her childhood but found it difficult to remember much before her teens. Green lawns, tended hedges—somewhere she had seen topiary and been intrigued by the shapes that bushes could become. An early response to form, she supposed. And she had had a lavender muslin dress with a velvet ribbon. She had loved that dress. And then there were the shells and the sea. But she had no memory of being happy or unhappy.

Her teens on the other hand she remembered all too well. Misery. She wasn't allowed to grow up. She had to wear knee socks when her friends wore pantyhose, she couldn't stay out beyond eleven or listen to jazz. And on the rare occasions she brought friends home, her mother had been icily polite and frozen them out. No wonder she had interpreted Denny's friendliness as love, she who had no yardstick for love, no memory of ever having been hugged. And no photographs of herself as a child sitting on an adult lap, or snuggled up to another body.

Tonight she knew that if her mother died before they made peace she would forever live a kind of half life. 'Those you love or hate block your view.' Had she read that? Made it up? She also knew that her mother was the only possible route to her father about whom she was curious—wildly curious. Was her story a repetition of her mother's story? Had her mother become pregnant and had to have the baby? Was she the baby? And was that why she was so insistent that Cass have an abortion. Cass's head was blown wide open by the thought. She couldn't imagine her mother in such a situation. But if true, that might explain any number of things. And what if her father had been a sculptor? Mightn't that have given her mother a hatred of sculpture? Cass was astonished by her thoughts. Perhaps they were not thoughts. Had she, 'a little pitcher with big ears,' overheard remarks that came back to her now as if they were her own speculations?

Her head was buzzing. To stop the buzz she thought of the egg. But the egg had lost its lustre. It was now merely egg. No longer transcendent. She remembered a child's book about a codfish. She could hear a voice reading. And with it came a rush of warmth and love. Was it her mother reading to her? 'And one eye was a fairy eye. The other merely cod.' Those phrases, today, had a totally different meaning for her. The codfish was a metaphor for the artist—with one fairy eye and one that bought groceries, cooked meals, went to the laundromat, had moments of bliss and moments of total despair.

Cass was close to the latter now. Tomorrow she might know what to do. But now she was as finished as the last page of a book.

Half undressed, she fell into bed. Pole-axed.

* * *

The morning was rainy. Grainy. Like an old black and white photograph. Cass put on the coffee. Minutely examined her mother's latest letter once again. Nothing new to observe. Thought of egg *oeuf huevo ovo ei.* It was still without lustre.

Last night she had barely been able to wait to get to her studio and start work. Today the carrier wave was broken and, with it, the energy required to begin. Strange that so many of the real barriers in life are invisible.

She was pouring her coffee when the phone rang. 'Joe!'

'When will you be back?' she asked, after the preliminaries.

'My van's broken down and I'm waiting on a part so I won't be back until tomorrow.'

'Oh.'

'You're disappointed.'

'To put it mildly.'

'If the part comes today I should be back before noon.'

She couldn't speak.

'Cass. Cass?'

An unsatisfactory conversation for them both.

She finished her coffee and went down to Ginty's to buy something for lunch. The 'silent' Ginty was behind the till and a couple of people she had never seen were poking about in the tired-looking produce. Whatever she was hoping for she didn't find—nothing at all for the fairy eye, little enough for the cod—so she bought a frozen pizza and left.

Upstairs she looked at her mother's letter again. After some time she picked up her nail file, slipped it under the flap of the envelope and slit it open. She was shaking as she removed the single sheet, unfolded it, and began to read.

Dear Cassie,

If you have read my earlier letters—and it's hard for me to know because you don't reply—you may not be too surprised by the news I am about to send you. On the other hand, if this is the first you've heard of it, you'll undoubtedly be astonished.

I am getting married. By the time you get this we will be in Europe—your father and I.

Cass stopped at 'your father'—her father?—and then continued.

I am still a relatively young woman, although I must seem old to you. I am just forty-six. I had you when I was barely eighteen.

Cass stopped again. Forty-six. And she had been thinking of her mother as old, ill, possibly dying.

I hope this news will make you happy and that you wish me happiness in return.

— Your loving Mum

Cass sat there holding a letter that weighed no more than air. A great burden dropped away from her. Suddenly her life was almost too full. Did her mother mean her biological father? The thought was dizzying. She wanted to talk to her mother, rejoice with her, phone. But if her mother was in Europe, all she could do was write. The letter would be there for her return.

Cass grabbed a pen and piece of paper. 'Dearest Mum,' she began, hardly knowing whom she was writing to. In some astonishing way, her hatred had turned to love. 'I am so glad!' She stopped, and not knowing how to go on, she signed it 'With Love, Cassie'. Then feeling it was inadequate, added, 'So very glad!'

She would take it to the post office at once.

And then she would go on to her studio and to the beautiful white marble in which the egg, transformed once again in her mind's eye, was waiting to be released. She desperately wanted to read her mother's letters, but the urge to work was even stronger. The letters could wait. The egg couldn't. And tomorrow Joe would be home.

(2002)

YOU ARE HERE

IN THE MALL

Mimi is in the mall. She visits it seldom and, as things change so fast she has no idea how to find what she is looking for, she goes to the mall directory. YOU ARE HERE, the directory says. She stares at it a long time.

How does she move away from that dot that holds her? It is as if she is in a board game and until released by some other player she has to stay in place. Standing there she forgets entirely that she was wanting to buy shoes. You are here, she thinks. It is like a deep well that she is falling into. Here.

Where is here? she asks, bewildered for a moment.

And then she remembers the centre of the universe is where you are. There/here. Only an inconsequential T divides the two. She has read that somewhere, she thinks. In a story, perhaps, or was it a dream?

NAME

She was not christened Mimi. In fact she was not christened at all. Does this mean she has no name in the mind of God? She would like to think she has.

Mimi, ignorant about religious orders, supposed that one of the possible reasons why a nun acquires a new name when she takes her vows is to exist anew in the eye of God. Sister Aline, once Arith Smith. Not Metic, she thinks. Mimi cannot resist playing with words. But perhaps there is more to the ceremony than name alone. Baptized with water, she thinks, the only element that can mix with the clay of which we are made, dissolve it even—this too, too solid flesh. Mimi realizes her head is a scramble of facts, half facts, quotations.

She became Mimi at university. She seems to remember it had something to do with *La Bohème*? Just what, she can't recall, but whatever it was, it took. Before that she had been known to family and friends in various ways. Margaret, Maggie, Marg, Meg, even. She can't help asking herself if she had a personality to fit each name. That we are multiple, she has no doubt. She is not questioning her multiplicity. She questions, rather, whether her multiple selves had been correctly aligned with the varying names? Fitted. And how big a jump was it from Marg, for instance, to Mimi? She asks her mother. 'You will always be Maggie to me,' her mother says, a loving look in her eyes. 'Yes, but ...' Mimi attempts to arrive at a clarification. 'Was I different when I was Margaret, for instance?' 'You were never Margaret to me,' her mother replies. 'Besides, why are you so preoccupied with yourself? It's not a good sign.'

Mimi doesn't know how to convince her mother that she is not, definitely not, preoccupied with herself. It is not about her at all. It is about identity, and identity is close to consciousness, or so she suspects. And consciousness is what? A matter of the soul? Perhaps.

Mimi thinks she was any number of little girls: Mummy's girl, Daddy's girl, best friend (many times), a holy terror to those teachers who bored her, and a different child altogether to the teachers who found her bright.

Mimi wonders, too, about the time before she was born. She is not talking of history, of events. She is talking of 'me, myself, and I, the one who's talking', as she used to say as a child. She is asking what entity formed the embryo that became her. Was she a spark from the glowing body of God? Did she exist from the beginning of time? Was she, neither male nor female, floating about waiting for the perfect union of sperm and ovum? Or, as the reincarnationists believe, did she live endless lives before she became Mimi? She searches and searches, trying to reach back to some glimpse of a time before this time, before even Time itself.

MARKETING

When Mimi goes marketing she is always Mrs. It goes with the activity. She can only shop as Mimi when she's buying clothes. She writes her list with a pencil on the back of an envelope that contained a begging letter and thinks of the time when she received letters, real letters. Expensive note-paper and fountain pens. She is reminded of the smell of her mother's chamois gloves.

She chews the end of her pencil. It is a yellow wooden pencil with many tooth marks. After some thought she writes:

> *1 soup bone*
> *pckt dried peas*
> *2 loin lamb chops*
> *celery*
> *cat food*

She doodles a bit as she thinks of her cats. She is working hard not to anthropomorphize them. They are cats, after all. Not variants of herself. When they first came into her life as two white kittens, litter brothers, she fell totally in love. Pure white except for their pink noses, anuses, the pads of their paws and their transparent ears. And their lemon-coloured eyes. I mustn't spoil them, she had said to herself. And what had happened? She had spoiled them. They would only eat the most expensive cat food. They had acutely sensitive noses. Could smell a pill before it was out of its container.

She goes back to her list. She is Mrs Richardson again.

> *Brie*
> *brown bread*

Why did I write 'brown'? she asks herself. As if they ever ate white. Oh, and

> *Wine*

she adds, already enjoying the thought of it, and seriously considering how much she is prepared to spend.

CATS AND BUCK

When Mimi lets the cats out in the morning a large buck is standing on her lawn. As unmoving as a statue. The cats have never seen a buck before. They freeze. Then Henry, the larger cat, looks at her anxiously. The buck is unmoving. He is beautiful with his suede coat and head held high under its antlers. Mimi's heart is torn, but Margaret can only think that he will destroy her tulips. And he will. He will wait until they are in full glorious red flower and then eat them one by one as if swallowing fire—a flame swallower.

For the moment they are a tableau—buck, cats, herself. She has a fleeting glimpse of the three entities—the three different consciousnesses. For one briefly illuminated moment, she is all three.

The perfect morning light falls on them all evenly. Shows the animals off at their best. Only she looks a little uncombed, unwashed, flawed. This is the price she pays for consciousness, she thinks. But why? Why should humans not be as flawless as animals? As flawless as her pure white cats? They never sweat, they never smell. Their hair never grows. Once having achieved their adult size, growth continues only in the cat's claws and the buck's antlers. Their instruments of defence.

We, of course, have bullets.

PERSEIDS AND TIME

This is the month of the Perseids, when Zeus showers Danae's lap with gold, or so say the Greeks. The Muslims say that angels are throwing spears at devils trying to eavesdrop on heaven. Whatever the truth, year after year, Mimi tries to see them. Not always successfully. Some years the sky is overcast; some years she is so deep in the heart of the city that nothing is visible through the haze of man-made light.

But those years when the nights are clear and she is within driving distance of unobstructed sky, she stays up late, has been known to lie on damp grass for hours. It is as if she needs to see those stars, to *ooh* and *aah* as an 'earthgrazer' comes close, only to be expunged as it is about to touch her. She cannot avoid those involuntary gasps of surprised delight.

This year she goes to the Observatory. They drive up in early evening and watch the darkness gather, bringing with it families, friendly, good-natured families, parents laughing with their children—a golden community—like something from her past. She remembers the glow of her mother under a cone of light, embroidering, and her father under another cone, reading aloud. It is warm in her memory, perfectly retained. The three of them, united, as perhaps they always will be, always have been. A glimpse of the eternal.

Darkness enfolds them on the hilltop. The Big Dipper is immediately overhead. She remembers seeing it as a child on the prairie where the skies were vaster than the ground beneath their feet. She remembers her mother saying, 'Look, Maggie. Look up.' And bigger and blacker and more enormous than anything she could have imagined were the startling starry heavens.

Here, once again, parents were saying the same thing to their children. 'Look up. Up.'

The night is now black, quiet and seemingly still. But whole families have twisted their red glow sticks into circles which they wear on their heads like haloes and groups of these haloed invisible beings move about silently.

She gazes at the Dipper again and the North Star. Cassiopeia, an upended W, is off to the right as it should be and it is from that part of the sky that the shooting stars will come. She loves the Dipper, it is probably her oldest heavenly friend, but it is Orion with his jewelled belt she loves most and it is too early in the season for him.

She is dizzied, as always, by the realization that what she is seeing occurred light years ago. Light years. The very phrase sets her head spinning.

Reaching back to her grandparents' day is struggle enough—a time within living memory. If she goes back as far as her mind will reach, she sees the pastel colours of sugared almonds in a silver dish. She must have been two. Consecutive memory—whole little plays—were later. She sees and hears her grandmother as she says, 'Sweetly pretty, dear,' to a drawing she has done; and later, her grandfather in his smoking jacket dictating a letter that she is painstakingly trying to write.

Why, she wonders, will her mind not stretch further into the past? Perhaps a PhD in history would have provided her with stepping stones leading her back and back—to what? She is equally unable to go forward beyond her youngest niece's graduation. And even here she can only see the child, lengthened into a young woman, not the society in which that child will live. It must already be here, just as the past is. Why can she not bring it into focus?

Vaguely she sees a more automated world. But this is imagination, not truth, although it may well be all too true.

In her darker moments, it is a world in which whole countries are dying for want of water, computers crash, criminals and lunatics escape, banks close, and people get stuck in their virtual realities—for ever.

Then she cheers up. If a Phoenix is dying, then surely a new Phoenix is being born.

A PIECE OF ID

At the airport she is asked for a piece of ID. Photo ID. We are identity-crazed, she thinks. Surely these small plastic cards bearing unrecognizable photos—they could have been forged, after all—are not the identity that has preoccupied her since she was a child. She looks at the appalling photo in which she can identify herself only by her jewelry.

Is her jewelry her identity? Is that what it comes down to? She doesn't want to think so, but can't be sure.

She remembers her mother complaining that she was either her husband's wife or her daughter's mother. Never herself. That was much less likely to happen today when women have careers, or something that passes for education. But it happens. She knows women for whom motherhood is their identity. For men it is more likely to be their bank balance.

She tries to look at herself as if she is a spreadsheet. Daughter, sister, writer, wife, aunt, housekeeper, cook, gardener. But she doesn't think any of those roles constitute her identity. Daughter? She was a reasonably good daughter, she thinks, but it is not her identity, or not now. Certainly not now. 'I am a sister,' she says to herself. She loves her brother but being his sister is not her identity. If he were a famous astronaut, a distinguished actor, would that alter things? No. She can't hear herself saying, 'I am Mimi Richardson, sister of...'

Writer? she asks, getting back to her spreadsheet. And here she deliberates. She identifies with being a writer, but only slightly. Suspicious of her response, she tries another approach: what if she were to learn that everything she has written has been lost, her name as a writer unknown? She feels a slight lessening of herself—as water lightens when it becomes ice—but her identity is still intact. Unnameable, but intact.

And wife? she asks. This is very strange territory, indeed. She has never felt married. That ring on her finger has made no difference beyond telling the world she was not single. But then, if she really thinks about it, she didn't feel single either. Married. Single. Divorced. Those are the categories on any form. None seems to apply to her. This is not a subject she could bring up with her husband, the logical person to discuss it with. Is she his mistress? His housekeeper? His cook? *His*. Her identity goes deeper than that. In fact marriage has not changed her identity. Her personality, perhaps. Her habits, certainly. But not her identity.

JOKE, OR IS IT?

Mimi remembers a story of a man who goes into a store and says to the owner, 'Did you see me come in?'

'Of course,' the owner replies.

'Have you ever seen me before?'

The storekeeper shakes his head.

'Then how did you know it was me?'

WINDOW CLEANER

Today the window cleaner comes with his tall ladder and his squeegee. Did Plath write a poem about window cleaners? They are worthy of a poem. Swish, swish, in the bright air.

She is Mrs. Richardson again. And Mrs. Richardson doesn't write. But she watches the skill of the thin man on the ladder. No soap. No ammonia. Just water and a squeegee and the window is a pane of glass again. Invisible.

And invisibility is attractive, she supposes, because it suggests dematerialization. But why dematerialization attracts her she doesn't know. She wonders, vaguely—she is frequently vague—how many invisible beings walk among us. Here. Now.

Cats see them, she supposes, and that's what accounts for their sudden stops and starts. And she has read that members of the First Nations are surrounded by their ancestors. Perhaps she in other universes—and there must be many—walks about, invisible, too. She has not enough physics to support or contradict these thoughts. They lead her nowhere. But they idle in her mind as quietly as one of the new hybrid cars. Silent but ready to take off.

As Mrs Richardson, she talks to the tall thin man. He is quite young. 'Does one make a profession of window cleaning?' she asks, watching his wrist move the squeegee back and forth with the skill of a professional house painter. He doesn't plan to. He's getting in shape to join the army. He has all the qualifications but lacks a certain level of fitness. He sees a life of adventure ahead. He looks quite dreamy as he talks. Like a man in love. In love with war?

HOROSCOPE

Mimi reads her horoscope in the daily paper. Although she knows there is no truth in it, she is like the friend who cuts a pack of cards first thing in the morning—'Just to get the taste of the day ahead'—a red suit, good; a black one, less so. Did her friend believe it? No. Not really, but …

And that is the way with Mimi. Yes. And no. If the moon can pull tides, control menses, why could the stars not have an effect on a new baby? Even continue to affect it all its life? It seems elementary.

But that doesn't mean the columnists who give a blanket reading for each sign are even as accurate as her friend's cutting of the pack. Mimi knows that. But she also knows this borderline, this area between belief and unbelief, a state that allows her to entertain ideas, or at least not to reject them. A capacity for what-iffing. It is something she was born with, like the colour of her eyes. 'Negative capability' is another phrase for it.

Her sun sign is Sagittarius, a centaur. The Archer, it is called. Jovial, straightforward, philosophical. A fire sign. But as she is almost on the cusp of Scorpio, she is a bit watery. And water can put fire out. Looked at another way, fire can make water evaporate. Perhaps that accounts for her high degree of self-doubt.

For the most part, the writers of horoscopes are masters of ambiguity. Read the forecast for any sun sign and it *could* apply to you.

But even doubters must beware. Once an idea is in your head, it's hard to get it out. Are we hard-wired for suggestibility? 'Don't think of elephants for five minutes.'

'The fault, dear Brutus, is not in our stars but in ourselves.' Well, yes. And, no.

Mimi feels on the brink of something. There are times she feels as if she might break through to a great illuminated space with love as the carrier wave. She has had taste of that love, a love that doesn't originate with her. It was as if she was caught in a great beam of love that included everything in its path. Because she was included in that beam, she loved everything she saw, everything she apprehended. Discrimination was gone.

She wonders where it came from. From her heart? Or does it come from the nöosphere? She thinks not. Nöosphere is mind, not heart. Pre- or post-sleep she is sometimes warmed by this love.

Pre- or post-sleep is a curious region. Hypnogogic, hypnopompic—accessible only when her mind is not active. Those tiny figures on the inside of her eyelids. Those enlarged body parts. Times when her head filled the entire room, an amorphous head, huge, without limit, all-knowing.

And is the nöosphere another word for consciousness? Mimi asks too many unanswerable questions.

THE DREAM

Mimi talks to her husband about her dream in which she looks out to the green lawn and sees it swarming with small people, dressed in red. She doesn't like them. They are mischievous at best. She feels she has had this dream before. They are selling small objects of red and green felt. Her husband is sympathetic but essentially uninterested.

'They were ominous,' she says. 'And all the forces were against me. The friend I was with didn't believe they were dangerous. I couldn't find the telephone number for the police. I couldn't even find the organizing principle for the phone book.'

'What is frightening you?' he asks. 'And, why didn't you call me, not the police? I was right beside you in bed.'

'Oh, dreams,' she said, 'are not life. I needed the dream police, not the real life husband.'

He shakes his head. 'Mimi,' he says. 'Oh, Mimi.'

Mimi's computer is down. And even though she has a telephone and a fax machine, she feels amputated. What can she do to fill this empty space? What did people do, years ago? Her mother for instance. And herself, come to that! What did she do?

She typed, for one thing, first on a portable Underwood and ultimately on an IBM Correcting Selectric. What had been the height of luxury at the time is now as a bicycle is to a Rolls-Royce. Slow. Clumsy. Tiring. All that pounding on the keys. And limited. Only able to type. No e-mail. No Web. (As the young say to their parents, 'When you sat around listening to radio, what did you *look* at?') Once your consciousness has been raised, it doesn't like going back.

She wanders about aimlessly. At a time like this, with a friend coming to stay, her mother would have been cooking a celebratory meal. Cheese straws, salted almonds, meringues. A *Coq au vin* in the oven. Mimi's friend is Hollie. One who calls her Marg. They too will have a delicious dinner. It is only waiting to be picked up at the caterer's.

She rather dreads Hollie's arrival. School friends. In the same class. She can thank Hollie for her lopsided smile. Her face had come down so hard on Hollie's head in basketball that her teeth had gone through her upper lip. Hollie's head seemed none the worse. But Marg's face was permanently altered.

Mimi wonders if Hollie will refer to it again today. 'Every time I see that sideways smile of yours I think of the day we collided in the gym.' It has become the most binding of events. 'Not that the smile is not rather engaging,' she will undoubtedly add.

Mimi wonders why this has to recur over and over. Is this all Hollie has to offer? And if so, why do they go on seeing each other? They are like lines that cross and cross at indeterminate intervals. Apparently without purpose. And Hollie's remark is like the recurring decimal. Is this a taste of infinity?

Mimi thinks you really ought to be very careful about choosing your friends when you are young because they will stay with you for life. And long familiarity somehow equals friendship.

Once again, sure enough, Hollie says, 'Funny how every time I see your crooked smile, I am reminded of the day we collided in the gym. Blood, will you ever forget the blood! I guess it has made us blood sisters.'

Hollie hasn't said this before and she clearly thinks it funny, because she laughs.

Mimi can't quite become Marg again. Marg probably would have laughed.

'Do you remember,' Hollie says, 'your green phase? You said it was the Irish in you.'

Mimi is astonished. Her Irishness has diminished over the years. She no longer buys a shamrock on St. Patrick's day.

'It was my father,' Mimi says. 'He loved his Irish blood and wanted his children to be proud of it. "Wilde, Shaw, Yeats," he would say.' And later she learned of the Book of Durrow, the Book of Kells, one of which had been found only after a cow had eaten part of it. Such intricate Celtic knots and beautiful calligraphy. She wondered if eating beauty alters your molecules. Was that cow different afterwards, special in some way? Did it give better milk? As she thinks it she knows the thought is absurd. She knows it isn't a thought, either. Just a flash from the idiot in her.

MARATHON AND LIFE AFTER DEATH

Today their street has been closed to traffic. The end of it is the half marathon. Those wanting to run the whole 26 miles turn at the end of the street and run back. Mimi watches for a while—hundreds of them running—thousands, actually. They have come from the US, the UK. Every conceivable combination of X and Y chromosomes—small, tall, short-legged, long-legged, fair, dark, long-haired, short-haired, etc., etc., and their strides and styles unimaginably varied. Some waste half their energy swinging their torsos from side to side; some pump vigorously with their arms. Some are already walking. There are blistered feet, bad knees, sore ankles. One, wrapped in blankets, is taken out on a wheeled stretcher. He/she is not in serious trouble because he/she waves like royalty to the passing runners.

Mimi thinks of the origin of the marathon—of Pheidippides, the Greek soldier, who ran non-stop from Marathon to Athens, to announce the defeat of the Persians. He proclaimed his message and dropped dead. It is a wonder, Mimi thinks, that anyone today would want to run that distance. Yet many thousands try. The winners run it in just over two hours. It seems a perfect metaphor for our world: Pheidippides ran for an urgent reason, but today, all over the world, people run simply to win.

She wonders if behind it all is a preoccupation with death, a fear of it. In a godless world there is every reason to fear it. If there is no heaven to look forward to then it is important to keep healthy, to prolong life, to stay for ever.

She thinks of those extraordinary maps of the world at night, showing where artificial light is concentrated and wonders what a similar map of cancer patients would look like.

Why is Mimi so (almost) sure there is life after death? She tries and tries to trace it back. She supposed both parents, unorthodox though they were, considered it a real possibility. But they also subscribed to many beliefs that she has long since tossed aside. What is there about this, besides wishful thinking, that has made it stick? And then it dawns on her.

It was Helen's return.

Mimi was Marg then, in her late teens or early twenties, and Helen her closest friend. They argued about everything, seldom agreeing. Even then, Marg thought death was only another door on the journey. Helen thought it final. Then Helen died. One night lying in bed, grief-stricken, Marg saw small specks of light in the dark room which gradually coalesced until they formed the figure of Helen, radiant, shining, real.

'So I was right after all!' The words were out of Marg's mouth before she could think.

'That's what I've come back to let you know,' Helen replied.

'Then tell me about death.'

Her friend shook her head. 'I can't do that. Every death is personal. Knowing about my death won't help you with yours. You will die your own death.' She leaned forward to kiss Marg and as Marg put her hands on Helen's solid upper arms she felt the flesh change to the consistency of dry rice.

Startled, she pulled back. Helen had become those small specks of light again and Marg watched as they blinked out one by one. What was that molecular dance, that bright augury?

Mimi's life changed. After that, everything was different. She actually *knew* something. Sometimes. Like alternating current she remembers, then she doesn't.

Today, looking at the last straggle of runners passing her window, some barely dragging themselves along, she remembers that they bear within them the promise of everlasting light.

Mimi wonders what it would be like to be a twin. An identical twin. What would happen to one's identity then? she asks.

She has known twins who fought for their own identity. Deliberately did the opposite of their twin, even if it flew in the face of their own wishes.

She has also known twins who bought Christmas presents for everyone but each other. Didn't know the other wasn't herself. And then there are the male twins, grown men, married, who have only one bank account between them.

Say she had a double. Where would her loyalties lie? To herself or her sister?

Mimi feels the strong pull of blood where members of her immediate family are concerned. Would that pull not exist between herself and her twin because they were as one? Or would it double and redouble? They would have identical blood types and identical looks and they alone would know for sure which one was which. Would they not fall in love with the same man? And what would it be like to fall in love with a twin?

LIVING WITH ANIMALS
AND THE APPEARANCE OF ALIENS

Mimi has inadvertently let the little cat out. In the house he is timid, running at the least sign of a caress. Outside he is a tiger. He appears to be stamping on low-lying flies. Very intent, he is bright white against the grass. Blinding.

His brother, older by minutes, is even more timid. He is a house cat and he spends much of his time under her bed, which is about three inches from the floor. When he was a kitten he slipped easily underneath; now, as a full-grown tom, he has to flatten himself into a plate. But it is his safety zone, the only place he is sure of.

Mimi loves these cats with all her heart, but she gets little in return. They sleep in each other's arms in an armchair in the living room like a mound of marshmallows. They are beautiful. When she looks deep into their faces, which they permit from time to time, she feels she is looking into the face of God. And she is, she thinks. It *is* the face of God. Her friends would think her out of her mind. But she is used to her friends.

The cats have brought about major changes in her life. The fact that they are destroying her curtains is something she can't worry about. Once she would have been disturbed.

The fact that they are almost indifferent to her existence is another matter. She is used to being liked by dogs—loved, in fact. The cats' indifference cuts her down to size, if she had a size. She hadn't realized that she is used to—not obedience, but agreement. And no cat agrees.

She wonders—how can she help but wonder?—what they are doing here, these domesticated animals? What is their role? And why only cats, dogs, horses, donkeys—maybe cows and elephants? Could they be training us, far more than we are training them? Are they preparing us for encountering a new species? Opening something in us, stretching a membrane that, when stretched, might perhaps make us able to meet beings from Space?

Mimi wonders about those people who claimed to have been abducted by aliens. Barney and Betty Hill especially, who, cross-questioned by psychiatrists, were found to be completely normal, intelligent people.

She has not heard of any abductions lately. Have people been laughed out of daring to talk? Not so long ago such encounters, imagined or real, were frequent. Mimi had in fact known someone, her dressmaker, actually, who had said, conversationally, as she shortened Mimi's skirt, 'They came again last night—the aliens.' But when pressed for further information, she always said, 'They wipe your memory when they bring you back.'

'Then what was it like immediately *before* the abduction?' Here her dressmaker was better-informed. It was always at night, there was always a curious rise in the temperature.

'Do you mean really a rise?'

Her dressmaker was impatient. 'Of course I mean really. I felt it.'

She has not answered what Mimi was trying to get at, but Mimi hadn't pursued the thought. 'And then?'

'Then you are drawn to the window and you see their spacecraft. It is just hovering there and glowing. Please, turn a bit.'

'How do you mean "drawn to the window"?'

'As if you are being pulled. Bad luck for you if you have something on the stove, because you *have to go to the window.*'

'And?'

'There is the spacecraft, hovering, glowing, and they throw out a drawbridge to your window and come for you.'

'What do they look like?'

'Small. Greenish. Enormous black eyes.'

'Are you afraid of them?'

'Not really. I don't think they are evil.'

Mimi wondered why if they abducted her dressmaker they didn't abduct her. She wanted to be abducted. Or so she thought.

But that was years ago. Lately there has been no mention of sightings. Yet those people who have 'seen' UFOs cannot be budged from their conviction that they are real. Speed usually enters into the description.

Mimi wonders if there is always a rise in temperature or something that gives the experience a different flavour. A flavour other than life, other than dreaming.

THE FACE IN THE WINDOW

Thinking about aliens, Mimi is reminded of the face she saw when she was a child. It hadn't occurred to her before that perhaps it was an alien.

She was about twelve. Her family lived in a bungalow only a few yards from a similar bungalow, occupied by a husband, wife and two girls who were her friends. From her parents' bedroom, if the curtains were not drawn, it was easy to see into their dining room. One early summer evening she was lying on her bed reading when her mother called, 'Maggie, come here a minute.'

Her mother was looking out her bedroom window at the dining room opposite. 'Do you see anything?' she asked. What Maggie saw was a head, slightly smaller than life size, the flesh vaguely greenish, the hair on its head fine, soft—lanugo hair—and its eyes enormous, black and evil.

Big girl though she was, she had thrown herself at her mother, saying, 'Mummy I'm frightened.'

'There is nothing to be frightened of, darling,' her mother said and drew the curtains. 'It was probably just a trick of light.'

But Maggie had known it wasn't a trick of light.

'Could you draw it?' her mother asked, getting pencils and paper. 'Let's both try.'

Maggie drew a head with a rather pointed chin and enormous black eyes. Her mother, who drew better than her daughter, drew a head with a rather pointed chin, soft hair and enormous black eyes. There was no question that they had seen the same thing.

'Let's talk about it,' her mother said. And they talked and talked. 'Was it floating?' her mother asked.

'Its chin was resting on the sill.'

'Then it must have been either child-sized or sitting.'

And so they talked until it began to feel almost normal.

Her mother, practical, enquiring, returned night after night at the same time, trying to see if it was a trick of light. She never saw it again, or anything remotely similar, and the whole episode was played down. But her mother knew and Maggie knew that they had seen a face, as real as they were themselves, but of a different species.

Mimi wonders whether it was, indeed, evil.

To the ignorant, an angel can look like a devil. Or vice versa.

CROP CIRCLES AND FLATLAND

As a long-time reader of science fiction, Mimi is a natural for crop circles. She keeps up to date on the Internet.

The earliest simple circles might well have been created by two men with a plank. But the vastness of the intricate designs that followed—swallows in flight, for instance, or pi—and even more, the patterns of the flattened but unbroken grasses themselves, overlaid and layered, have shown, to her at least, it would be almost impossible for a team of men, however ingeniously clever, to create them.

The opportunities for hoaxes are, of course, endless. To begin with, Mimi has only seen photos of the circles, and what do photos tell you? With software they can be altered flawlessly. Human beings can be added or taken out. A convincing crop circle could probably be made on a computer.

And as for the farmers on whose lands the enormous designs have supposedly appeared, it would be easy enough to pay them to say whatever was required. But then there are the measurements, the inspections. If the whole thing is a hoax it has become an elaborate and expensive hoax.

Mimi knows one person who has been in a crop circle and who claimed to have *felt something* in the air. But Mimi, for all her credulity, is suspicious of feelings, even her own. She has often considered whether Helen's 'return,' those many years ago, was not an excess of feeling on her part, of imagination, or, as the few friends who knew about it have suggested, a dream.

She knows it was none of the three. Its specific gravity was different. It was as feathers are to lead. Unless you have had such an experience you cannot know just how unlike a dream it was. Or unlike waking life. It had its own reality—a hyper-reality; waking-life-plus. The action was consecutive and congruous and, given the original premise, totally logical.

And unlike dreams. Completely unlike dreams. Many years ago Mimi read *Flatland*, and the image of a three-dimensional object entering a two-dimensional world has stayed with her. To a Flatlander anything above or below two dimensions is non-existent. Ergo, says Mimi to herself, for who else will listen? might not the crop circles be all we can see of a four- or five- or six-dimensional object that has entered our three-dimensional world?

Or, a new thought to Mimi, perhaps they are signalling to aliens. If so, what is their message? Help?

Mimi knows the jury is out on this. But was the jury—and a very powerful jury indeed—not out on the theories of Copernicus?

LETTING IN THE LIGHT — OPHTHALMOLOGY AND DEATH

The waiting room at the ophthalmologist's is full of elderly people in running shoes. Most of the men wear baseball caps. Some have walkers. Glaucoma, macular degeneration, short sight, long sight, cataracts. The young ophthalmologist is eager to provide light for those who are approaching darkness.

Mimi finds them a cheerful lot, ready to exchange greetings, unlike the middle-aged, who are preoccupied by divorces, children on drugs, mortgages.

To judge from this particular group, the elderly appear to be past all that. If they are preoccupied with death, they don't show it; they seem to have come to terms with worldly things. Death is evidently less fearful the closer you get to it.

Mimi is not afraid of death. But she thinks she might be when the time comes. She is not afraid of lions, either, but if one came in with a roar, now, what would her reaction be then, poor thing?

THE THIRD EYE

Mimi dreamed she was looking at a field of ripened grain, golden under a blue prairie sky. Racing from it, golden as the corn itself, were two golden retrievers. 'Vegetable/animal,' she thought at the time—evolution occurring in her presence.

As these beautiful, vibrant dogs leaped towards her, she saw that in the middle of each forehead was a human eye, blue as the sky.

Mimi remembers waking and thinking, 'If *their* third eye is human, what, then, is *our* third eye?'

MIMI CONVERSES WITH A FRIEND

Mimi lunches with a friend who talks of mirror neurons.

As far as the friend can tell, they are neurons that fire when an action is perceived.

As far as Mimi can tell, they must surely be the neurons that make empathy possible and that provide proof—and badly we need it—that we are all one. Certainly when Mimi sees a wound, she feels pain. Not true of everyone, she has been told. Have the brutalizing events of the world desensitized the neurons?

Yet surely war, brutal in the extreme, doesn't seem to have desensitized those men she has known who survived it.

She and her friend toss the ideas back and forth, ignorantly. Neither has enough background in science to know the definitions of the words they are using.

MIMI PREPARES FOR WINTER

Until this week the world has been golden. Enough leaves still on the trees to make it golden overhead and those that have fallen make the ground golden, too.

Now that the trees are bare and the streets have been cleaned by the municipality, the world is grey and Mimi prepares for winter. This is a psychological preparation for the big winds that put their trees at hazard, and the rain. The endless coastal rain.

How can the world be short of water? There are times, year after year, when Mimi thinks they should build an ark.

She and her husband bring in the patio furniture, cut back the dying plants, order firewood and brush off their parkas. This is the season of wind and rain but it is also the season of concerts and theatre. Their dates are like small lights on the calendar.

Then, before one knows it, the trees are in flower again, and the snowdrops and aconites are bright against the black water-logged soil of the garden.

Once again the world is innocent. Anything is possible.

MIMI AND HER HUSBAND GO TO A CONCERT

This is not just any concert. This is Philip Glass himself. Solo piano. For Mimi, the ground that is the basis of most of Glass's works is profoundly meditative. For her husband, it is mechanical, so they are not in step as they usually are when they go to concerts.

The theatre is jammed. Scruffy-looking kids, middle-aged hippies, blue-collar, white. He seems to cut across age. Across Life Styles, to use that revolting phrase. Who is he? Mimi asks herself. A prolific composer, reminiscent of Bach. That is her answer. She thinks about *Satyagraha*, the first work she saw by Glass.

Musical theatre. About Gandhi. Magic. Pure magic. When Glass's music repeated itself with slight variations, so did the actions on the stage. So when Gandhi, a newly graduated lawyer from Oxford, arrives in South Africa to open a practice, he is rejected by the white country club. And in step with the music, he enters, is rejected, enters, is rejected. The repetition makes it profoundly moving. Your nose is rubbed in white prejudice over and over again.

It was not only the music that was extraordinary.

The stage magic took your breath away—as magical as a singer holding a note longer than expectation or a ballet dancer doing one more *fouetté*. In those moments you are transported.

Red ribbons joined the builders heart-to-heart in the scene when a building is being constructed. The choreography was astonishing. And as the invisible building grew higher, white ribbons connected the workers' hearts with heaven.

But Mimi's husband didn't see the production; he has only heard the soundtrack and he is inclined to get up and go into the garden when she is in a Glass mood.

But tonight he is carried away. He is on his feet applauding and calling 'bravo.' And there is Glass, a middle-aged man with untidy hair, modest, having filled the hall with something more than music.

IDENTITY THEFT

Mimi reads of identity theft. She is urged to take out insurance against it. 'Identity theft refers to all types of crimes whereby someone wrongfully obtains and uses another person's identifying information for the purpose of fraud or other criminal activity,' she reads.

Identifying information consists of credit cards, social insurance numbers, drivers' licenses, etc. Mimi had not thought of her identity in terms of plastic cards until her photo ID had been requested at the airport.

It appears she can be robbed of her identity at any moment. And then what?

But what they call identity today has nothing to do with her idea of identity. No wonder the world is at odds with itself, if such a serious matter can be so hopelessly confused with one's credit rating.

MIMI REMEMBERS BEING A CHAIR

Mimi wishes she could remember more clearly. Time blurs the edges of things. She had been reading *Wolf Solent* by John Cowper Powys, a book that had a powerful effect upon her. How or why she no longer knows. But something in the book seems to have been the forerunner of her experiencing herself as a chair.

A total change of identity. (Was it perhaps stolen?) She was Marg at that time, a time when she was most hard-headed, or so she thinks. She remembers sitting in her parents' living room and looking at an oak armchair. Looking and looking, as if it were foreground *and* background, the only focal point in the room or, indeed, in the world.

From looking to becoming was, as she thinks of it now, gradual. First she felt a total rearrangement of her molecules, as if she were a blizzard. And as the blizzard abated, the stresses that held the chair together became hers. How the arms joined the back, the legs joined the seat, the rungs supported the legs. She felt the cleats that held the parts together, for this was a beautifully made chair.

She experienced a change of class, even. From middle class to aristocrat.

To begin with, the stiffness was uncomfortable and then she found herself settling with enormous ease into the rigidity. As if it were her destiny. How ironic, she thinks, that she knows the soul of a chair but not her own soul.

MIMI IS IDLE AND ANXIOUS

Mimi is idle. At least, a lot of the time. And it worries her. The world is going to hell and she idle. But at least she is not eating meat any more. Not since reading the manuscript of Noah Sarc's novel *Animals*. How thin the line between animal and human. In no time at all people can rationalize anything.

Her husband thinks she is overreacting. Why not just eat less meat? He doesn't understand it's not a question of more or less. It is none. And so she buys him steak. 'Lips that touch beefsteak shall never touch mine,' she says laughingly.

But something in her doesn't laugh. Soon no lips will touch beefsteak. Gaia will force us to eat berries and nuts—as long as they last.

MIMI'S CLEAREST THOUGHTS
ARE IN THE SHOWER

It has happened before, this sudden illumination. Too strong a word, of course. Mimi is inclined to exaggerate. But it is common knowledge that negative ions are released by running water, updrafts, the sea-shore, waterfalls, fountains. And negative ions increase the serotonin level, provide a sense of well-being, sharpen the mind. That is why monasteries were built on the tops of cliffs or beside the sea. Or both.

Mimi can see this may seem a *non sequitur*, but those old monks were evidently wise, and knew how to obtain the maximum help from the physical world to achieve transfiguration.

Today, Mimi is in her shower, soaped and smelling of lavender, no thoughts at all in her head, when suddenly she sees her mind through the mind of an accountant and realizes how difficult it is for a sequential thinker to understand the mind of an irrational right-brainer.

Then, faster than light, she sees her brain and all the differing brains making one giant brain and that giant brain is the nöosphere, consciousness, an area available to all who are properly in tune. Mimi was clearly in tune for a split second and then she was lost again. She glimpsed the nöosphere like a halo round the earth.

IN THE ORGONE BOX

Years ago Mimi—inexperienced, nervous—was scheduled to give a reading in one of those off-beat lofts where artists gathered to exhibit their paintings or read their work. She arrived early and terrified.

The organizer of the event, jean-clad, bearded, did his best to tell her she'd be fine, just fine, but when he saw his words of encouragement weren't working he suggested she go into the orgone box. The box was rather like a small outhouse with a chair inside. Knowing nothing of orgone boxes she was willing to do anything to distract herself.

Later she learned it was designed by Wilhelm Reich, psychiatrist, who had studied with Freud before arriving in America, and of the theory of orgone energy which the box was believed to concentrate in the genitals. Had she known, she probably would have declined, believing at that moment she needed all her energy in her head.

Mimi entered the box, and the door was shut. She was told she could come out anytime—see, the door opened from the inside. It was dark in there, but not airless. The seat was hard and she sat not quite knowing what to do or expect.

She said, 'orgone, orgone, orgone' to herself a number of times and wondered if it was a word she could find in a dictionary. Then she began to count. Odd how difficult it is to do absolutely nothing.

And then, imagination being what it is—or was it true?—she felt the outline of her body, rather as one does when one goes from a warm house to the freezing outdoors. Except that the air temperature had not changed, or so she thought.

Normally, Mimi is not aware of her shape in the air, has gone through life as an invisible being. But sitting there, in the dark alone, it was as if the darkness was making a three-dimensional drawing of her. Or did it sculpt her? She felt she was sculpture without mass. Only surface.

Engrossed by this new sense of herself, Mimi was unaware of time until she was called to read.

Thinking about the orgone box today, she googled it. To her surprise she learned that the air temperature in the box was twelve Fahrenheit degrees warmer than air outside the box. This difference was verified by Einstein. Had the increased heat limned her?

Poor Reich, in favour of the orgasm as a cure for mental illnesses, was hounded by the FBI and died in an American gaol.

Mimi doesn't understand why she is reminded of the box now. How does it relate to her identity? That she went into it, when others mightn't, is the direct result of her father's telling her, 'You are no daughter of mine if you won't try anything once.'

Perhaps at that stage in her life, her identity was more linked with 'daughter' than she now remembers.

NATIONALITY AS IDENTITY

When Mimi created her identity spreadsheet, she had not included 'Canadian' among the options. It hadn't sprung to mind. But thinking of it now, she realizes it should have.

Perhaps because she has moved so much, she has never had a sense of place. She has felt at home wherever she was. But given the right circumstances, of course she would say she was Canadian.

She tries to imagine a person without a country and cannot. Everyone has a country, a lost country perhaps, but certainly a country. And although she has many quarrels with hers, considers it far from perfect, it is hers nevertheless. Like a husband or a child.

COINCIDENCE

Mimi has wondered about coincidence for a long time without ever coming closer to understanding it. Synchronicity. Serendipity. It teases her.

She realizes she has gone on about it far too long when the friend to whom she is talking, says, 'But think of the numberless times when things *don't* match.' True. But does that make the matching untrue? Mimi wonders, somehow certain that it doesn't.

She thinks back to playing Snap as a child and seeing two matching cards turn up. A coincidence, certainly.

Now that she is older she realizes that if you split a deck of cards in half and you and your opponent turn the cards up one by one, you are bound to have two of the same denomination turning up occasionally. If you are playing by suit, then cards of matching suits turn up more frequently still.

That, she can get her mind around. It is inevitable. So, she asks herself, is all coincidence inevitable?

And what about more complex coincidences—such as the day she saw a Steller's Jay in the garden, far from its natural habitat; read a headline in the paper, 'Symphony gives stellar performance,' and received a letter from Jay whom she's not heard from for months. All within an hour. That surely is beyond the law of averages. And what is *she* meant to make of it, anyway? And why do *they* want her to know? She supposes she plays a role in it all. If she wasn't partly awake, she would miss the connections. Is it a measure of consciousness? Or is it a wake-up call? To a higher reality, perhaps.

Strangest of all is the time-space-defying coincidence. She dreams she receives a letter from a friend in India and the next day it arrives. A kind of psychic coincidence that over-rides the laws of time as we know them. Totally baffling. Nothing but a coincidence. Nothing but! Those nothing-butters have much to answer for.

There are no coincidences, she can't help thinking. But if they aren't coincidences, then what are they?

Such events seem to come in rushes, like shooting stars. Falling in love brings them in showers. 'Why, I have an uncle named Bill, too!' 'Your family had dogs? Ours couldn't live without dogs!' 'Peanut butter! How extraordinary! I *adore* peanut butter!' and, and, and …

It is as if, when the circumstances are right, two or more previously hidden things become visible. What shines that sudden light upon them?

Today she looked up coincidence in a dictionary. Def. 1: the act or condition of coinciding; 2: the occurrence of events that happen at the same time by accident but seem to have some connection. Merriam Webster. She is like the Spanish checking the dictionary to see if *it* is right which, in this case, it isn't. And yet she wouldn't know how to give a better definition. To her, coincidence is more cosmic, more profoundly planned. But by what or whom, she can't even imagine.

STONED AND IDENTITY

Mimi is stoned. Once, many years ago, in a drug house in Haight Ashbury, she saw a roomful of young people sitting about, looking just as she looks now. She sees herself from the outside. 'Stoned.' It is a perfect word. She is stone. Slow as stone. Her specific gravity altered. Her identity and her consciousness b l i s s e d   o u t. She knows what that means, now. It is a kind of evaporation. And slow. Everything slow.

She is in the green armchair in her living room, deep inside herself.

Her companion says, 'It was too strong. Much too strong.'

She is like a stone falling deeper and deeper into infinite space. The ghost of a stone.

I   a m   p e r f e c t, she thinks, not with satisfaction. Just recognizing a truth.

After what seems like a very long time, her companion says, 'Y o u should eat. Let me make you a little omelette.'

'I   a m   p e r f e c t,' she says again, astonished at how long it takes her to speak.

'A   g l a s s   o f   w a t e r?' her companion suggests.

'I   a m   p e r f e c t   t h e   w a y   I   a m.' She gazes deeper into infinity.

'I   h a v e   f o u n d   m y   B u d d h a   n a t u r e,' she says. And as she looks in deeper still she finds that infinity—contained within her, as it is—is Buddha-shaped. Large body, small head. Like a fractal.

She rests in it. The only pure rest she has ever had. The only perfect state she has ever known. Time is stationary. Eternity is stationary. And deep. And far. And here.

Her companion says, 'Mimi. Mimi.' His voice comes from another universe. Quite clear. But irrelevant. A gnat to a lion. Slow as molasses.

'It was too strong,' her companion says again. 'Way too strong.'

'I found my Buddha nature,' Mimi says. 'It was nirvana,' and as she says it, the word is Buddha-shaped—*nir*, the tiny head, and then the swelling Buddha body of *vana*.

'Would you do it again?'

'Never.'

'Why not?'

'It's not what I'm meant to be doing.'

She doesn't really want to talk. She wants to think, to remember. What was her identity then? she asks herself.

'Yes, that's me, alright.' She did know. Her Buddha nature was that part of her that linked her with infinity.

SECOND IDENTITY JOKE

A man goes into a store and wants to pay for an expensive pair of shoes by cheque.

'Can you identify yourself?' asks the storekeeper.

The purchaser pulls a mirror out of his pocket, looks into it and says, 'No doubt about it. That's me alright.'

(2008)

NOTES

THE SUN AND THE MOON

First published, Macmillan 1944; copy-text, *The Sun and the Moon and Other Fictions* (Anansi, 1973). The poem, 'Kleptomaniac', by Leonora Speyer is from *Fiddler's Farewell* (Knopf, 1926), and is reprinted with the permission of the publisher.

– lunar eclipse: A lunar eclipse occurs on the night of a full moon when the sun, earth and moon are aligned exactly, with the earth in the middle, and the moon is obscured by the earth's shadow.

– ether: A general anaesthetic; also, in ancient cosmology, 'an element conceived as filling all space beyond the sphere of the moon, and being the constituent substance of the stars and planets and of their spheres' (*OED*).

– pulps: tabloid newspapers (printed on poor quality paper)

– devil's purses: egg cases of sharks, skates or chimeras

– fisherman's floats: glass bulbs attached to and supporting fishermen's baited lines or nets

– flotsam and jetsam: In law, flotsam is 'the wreckage of a ship or its cargo … found floating on the surface of the sea' and jetsam is 'goods discarded from a ship and washed ashore' (*OED*).

– ecstasy: 'the state of being "beside oneself", thrown into a frenzy or a stupor, with anxiety, astonishment, fear, or passion' (*OED*)

– the year you came out: As a young woman of the upper middle class, Kristen is a debutante, formally introduced into society at eighteen.

– poking chicken-bones instead of fingers—In 'Hansel and Gretel,' each morning Hansel deceived the witch who was fattening him up to eat by presenting her with a chicken bone instead of his finger.

– Oscar Wilde … fairy stories: Irish playwright Oscar Wilde (1854–1900), author of *The Happy Prince and Other Tales* (1888), a collection of stories for children

– 'The Nightingale and the Rose': In Oscar Wilde's fairy tale, a nightingale impales herself on the thorn of a white rose, sacrificing her life to produce a red rose for a lover who does not understand its worth.

– bas-relief: a sculpture in which the figures project only slightly from the surface on which they are carved

– a poem /'She stole his eyes …': 'Kleptomaniac' by Leonora Speyer, from *Fiddler's Farewell* (1926)

– tar: sailor

– nine-pin: skittle or 'pin' in a bowling game popular in Europe and Eastern North America

– your province: New Brunswick

– living wire: a wire carrying electrical current

– board: drawing or drafting board

– varnish: used to set the charcoal sketch

– tempera: 'an emulsion in which pigment dissolved in water is mixed with egg yolk, or any of various gums, glues, or oils' (*OED*)

– not a Canadian type … Scandinavian: The establishment in 1940s New Brunswick was of English or Scottish heritage.

– Student's Delight: (slang) a woman available for sexual experimentation

– *enfant terrible*: 'a child who embarrasses … elders by untimely remarks; … loosely, one who acts unconventionally' (*OED*)

– Ravel's *Ma Mère l'Oye*: *Trans.* Mother Goose; a piano duet composed for children by French composer Maurice Ravel (1875–1937)

– 'I've always known … in hundreds of mirrors': from John Cowper Powys's novel *Wolf Solent* (1929)

– stocks: (*Matthiola incana*) a highly fragrant flowering plant, also called gillyflower

– superstitious about white flowers: In Asian cultures, the colour white is associated with death.

– Lowell Thomas wrote a book about it: *In New Brunswick We'll Find It* (1939) by American broadcaster and travel-writer Lowell Thomas (1892–1981) and Rex Barton

– muddler: a tool used to crush or blend ingredients in a drink

– fly … little beggar: a fishing lure

– changeling: an odd, inhuman child left in exchange for a human child taken by fairies

– pin men: matchstick figures. In 'The Stenographers' (1946), Page writes: 'In their eyes I have seen / the pin men of madness in marathon trim / race round the track of the stadium pupil' (ll. 33–35).

– weir pole: part of a fence or enclosure in a waterway designed to take fish

– moonstone: 'any of various milky, pearly, or opalescent varieties of albite and other minerals … cut as a gemstone' (*OED*)

– streamer: 'a flag streaming or waving in the air' (*OED*)

– trumps: in card games, a card that can 'take' any card of another suit

– set to a letterpress: mechanically repetitive

– 'Upon the shore I fou-ound a shell …': an English children's song. It continues, 'I listened gladly while it sang, / A sea song sweet and clear.'

– Zombie: 'In the West Indies and southern states of America, a soulless corpse said to have been revived by witchcraft' (*OED*)

– two-dimensional … fashion-plate: a printed illustration of fashion trends

– Hansel and Gretel … Peter Pan and Wendy: two, lost children (characters in the German folk tale recorded by the Brothers Grimm), and two children able to fly (characters in the play *Peter Pan, The Boy Who Wouldn't Grow Up* [1904] and novel *Peter and Wendy* [1911] by Scottish writer J. M. Barrie)

– nun's veiling: In a traditional nun's habit, the hair is covered in white, and the head is draped in a black 'veil of profession' that flows over the shoulders.

– Burberry: a trench coat made by the Burberry company

– El Greco—Doménikos Theotokópoulos (1541–1614), known as El Greco, trained as an artist in Crete and Venice before moving to Toledo, Spain. Figures in his paintings are often distorted—elongated and sallow.

– lactescent: having a milky appearance

– stilts: a short form of 'stiltifies': makes seem foolish or stupid

– Washington: Legend has it that, as a child, George was accused by his father of chopping down a cherry tree, and admitted it, saying 'I cannot tell a lie.'

– Pall Mall: a premium brand of cigarettes

– propinquity: physical proximity

THE GREEN BIRD

First published in *Preview* 7 (Sept. 1942): 7–9; copy-text, *A Kind of Fiction* (2001), pp. 137–41.
– daguerreotype: an early photographic process
– Ypres: The second battle of Ypres (22 April–25 May 1915) was the first major engagement of Canadian troops in World War I.

MIRACLES

From an unfinished novel, *The Lion in the Streets*. First published in *Preview* 20 (May 1944); copy-text, *A Kind of Fiction* (2001), pp. 153–8.
– gallery: a covered verandah
– '*Salut*', '*Bon soir*': (Fr.) 'Hi', 'Good evening'
– *curé*: (Fr.) parish priest
– Catherine wheel: St Catherine of Alexandria was tortured to death on a wheel with spikes projecting from its circumference
– porter: 'a dark-brown or black bitter beer' (*OED*)
– Marie Laurençin: (1883–1956) French painter and printmaker active in the Parisian avant-garde; a member of the Cubist movement
– tubercular rouge: the flushed complexion symptomatic of tuberculosis or consumption, a highly infectious respiratory disease
– the English: English-speakers
– consumptive: tubercular

VICTORIA

First published in *Tamarack* Review 69 (Summer 1976): 50-3; copy-text. *A Kind of Fiction*, pp. 81–5. Page identified Elizabeth (Betty) Brewster as the model for Victoria (*Journey with No Maps*, pp. 63–64), and Brewster has said that her own story 'Essence of Marigold' in which 'the handsome "Marguerite," a tall young woman in her twenties, who glowed like a crimson gladiolus as she blew smoke rings and flirted, observed by a much younger girl' was a response to Page's depiction of their meeting in 'Victoria' (*Invention of Truth*, pp. 93–94). The dementia of Page's Aunt Bibbi (and possibly her mother's drifting toward

dementia) are reflected both in "Victoria" and in the poem
"Conversation with my Aunt" (*Journey with No Maps*, p. 239).
– sanatorium: a hospital or nursing home specializing in the treatment
'either of convalescent patients, or of consumptives undergoing the
open-air treatment' (*OED*)
– issue: possibly, an accumulation of sap or mildew
– Chuang-Tze: [Zhuangzi, Zhuang Zhou] (late 4th century BCE),
Chinese philosopher, one of the founders of Taoism. He conveyed his
philosophy in the form of fantasy and parable.

UNLESS THE EYE CATCH FIRE

First published in *Malahat Review* 50 (April 1979): 65–86; copy-text, *The
Exile Book of Dog Stories* (2009), pp. 99–125. The plot is similar to Doris
Lessing's *Memoirs of a Survivor* (1974), but Page wrote to Lessing that it
had been written before Lessing's book appeared. Lessing replied
'Perhaps we dreamed the same dream at the same time? It seems to me
that ideas and stories go floating around in the air and get "picked up"
by sympathetic minds, like radio receivers' (10 Dec 1982) (*Journey with
No Maps*, p. 225).
– cockaded: wearing a cockade, 'a ribbon, knot of ribbons, rosette, or
the like, worn in the hat as a badge of office or party, or as part of a
livery dress' (*OED*)
– Payne's grey: a dark bluish-grey paint 'composed of blue, red, black,
and white permanent pigments, used esp. for watercolours' (*OED*)
– macadamization: paving
– Niagara: 'a deluge, a torrent; an outpouring *of* something'(*OED*)
– cotoneaster: 'a genus of small trees or trailing shrubs' (*OED*), often
used as a hedge
– aspic: a savoury jelly
– moiréed: having the rippled or watery appearance of moiré silk
– range-finder—'an instrument used for estimating the distance
between an observer and an object, e.g. in surveying' (*OED*)
– 'sleeping top': a perfectly balanced spinning top
– constellated: 'studded with stars' (*OED*)
– epiphany: 'a manifestation or appearance of some divine or
superhuman being' (*OED*)

– *Folie à deux*: a shared hallucination

– transfiguration: metamorphosis to another state of being

– borne witness to my God: testified 'by signature or oath' (*OED*)

– Salem: From February 1692 to May 1693, in a famous case of mass hysteria in Salem, Massachusetts, prosecutions for witchcraft resulted in the execution of twenty women.

– Triassic Age: the geological period (0.6 to 0.2 million years ago) which began and ended with major extinction events marked by catastrophic climate change

– axial irregularity: change in the angle of the earth's rotation on its axis

– Nostradamus: Michel de Nostredame (1503–66), author of *Les Propheties* (1555) in which he purportedly predicted many subsequent disasters and major historical events

– Jeane Dixon: (1904–97), a well-known American psychic and astrologer

– Edgar Cayce: (1877–1945), an American mystic who delivered his prophecies while in a trance state

– Heidsieck: a brand of champagne

– Gehennas: 'place[s] of future torment; hell[s]' (*OED*). The name is derived from a valley outside of ancient Jerusalem where human sacrifices were made to the fire-god Moloch (2 Kings 16.3; 2 Chronicles 28.3, 33.6).

– dissimated sclerosis: 'hard external tumour' able to 'kill, destroy, or remove one in every ten' (*OED*)

– rainbow, rainbow, rainbow: from 'The Fish' by Elizabeth Bishop (1911–79)

– faculty: 'an ability or aptitude' or 'in psychology, one of the several "powers" of the mind ...: the will, the reason, memory, etc.' (*OED*)

– pall: 'a cloth, usually of black, purple, or white velvet, spread over a coffin, hearse, or tomb' (*OED*)

– no birds sing: from 'La Belle Dame Sans Merci' by John Keats: 'O, What can ail thee, knight-at-arms. / Alone and palely loitering? / The sedge has wither'd from the lake / And no bird sings.'

– St. Elmo's fire: 'a naturally occurring corona discharge about a ship's mast or the like, usually in bad weather' (*OED*)

– bioplasmic: generated by 'living protoplasm' (*OED*)

– *bonne bouche*: choice morsel

– ground bass: in music, 'a bass-passage of four or eight bars in length, constantly repeated with a varied melody and harmony (Stainer & Barrett, 1876); also *fig.*, an undercurrent' (*OED*)
– desiccate: 'deprive thoroughly of moisture; ... dry up' (*OED*)
– immanent: 'Chiefly *Philos.* and *Theol.* Existing or operating within; inherent; *spec.* (of God) permanently pervading and sustaining the universe' (*OED*)
– beneficence: 'the manifestation of benevolence or kindly feeling, active kindness' (*OED*)

BIRTHDAY

First published in *Malahat Review* 71 (June 1985): 17–21; copy-text, *Up on the Roof*, pp. 89–94.
– The chair she sat in, like a burnished throne: from Enobarbus's description of Cleopatra's first meeting with Antony at Cydnus in Shakespeare's *Antony and Cleopatra* (2.2.191–201)
– atomization: 'the process of reducing to minute particles or droplets, *spec.* of reducing liquids to a fine mist' (*OED*)
– I'll adjust ... Alice did: In *Alice's Adventures in Wonderland* (1865) by Lewis Carroll (1832–98), she drinks and then eats substances that cause her to shrink and grow.
– Bend back thy bow ... O Archer: the opening line of 'The Archer,' a sonnet by A.J.M. Smith (1902–80)
– alembic: '*Chem.* An early apparatus used for distilling, consisting of two connected vessels ... containing the substance to be distilled, and a receiver or flask in which the condensed product is collected' (*OED*)

MME BOURGÉ DREAMS OF BRÉSIL

First published in *Cross-Country Writers* (1987); copy-text, *A Kind of Fiction* (2001), pp. 105–6.
– *confiture de Brésil*: (Fr.) Brazilian jam
– *l'inspecteur*: (Fr.) the housekeeper
– marmoset: a small monkey native to South America

– macaws: large long-tailed parrots (often with vivid plumage), native to tropical and subtropical America

– Shameless Mary: (*impatiens walleriana*). In her *Brazilian Journal*, Page describes 'a low red-flowering plant, *Maria sem vergonha* (Shameless Mary) for it will grow anywhere' (January 21, 1957).

– *macumba*: 'an Afro-Brazilian folk religion or cult combining elements of Brazilian Roman Catholicism and spiritualism with traditional African religious practices' (*OED*)

– homunculi: 'little or diminutive men' (*OED*)

– *sala*: (Port.) room

– *copa*: (Port.) pantry

– hornet jacket: yellow and black striped

– the Pretender: Prince Pedro Gastão of Orléans-Braganza (1913–2007), head of the Petrópolis branch of the Brazilian Imperial House and one of two claimants to the throne of Brazil which had been abolished in 1889

– windsock: 'a cloth cone flown from a mast, esp. on an airfield, to indicate the direction of the wind' (*OED*)

– landing net: 'a net for landing large fish' (*OED*)

– shot-towers: 'tall round tower[s] in which small shot are made by dropping molten lead from the top into water' (*OED*)

– *cafézinho*: (Port.) small cup of coffee

EVEN THE SUN, EVEN THE RAIN

First published in *Malahat Review* 127 (Summer 1999): 103–5; copy-text, *A Kind of Fiction* (2001), pp. 71–73. This story is based on the meeting between Page and her former lover, Frank Scott, in June 1970 at a meeting of the League of Canadian Poets which also inspired Page's poem 'Beside You' (*Journey with No Maps*, p. 225).

– maquette: miniature model(s)

– plinths: square slabs at the base of pedestals (*OED*)

– three brains: In the 1960s, American neuroscientist Paul MacLean argued that the human brain is 'triune', composed of three distinct brains developed in successive stages of evolution. The theory was popularized by Arthur Koestler in *The Ghost in the Machine* (1967).

– subliming: 'elevating something to a higher state of existence or to a higher degree of excellence' (*OED*)

FEVER

First published in *Exile* 23.4 (Winter 1999): 18–44; copy-text *A Kind of Fiction* (2001): 15–34. This story is based in part on health problems suffered by Page in Brazil. In December 1957, she elected to have a hysterectomy for an ovarian cyst (*Journey with No Maps*, p. 169; *Brazilian Journal*, pp. 146–7).

– di Cavalcanti: Brazilian painter Emiliano Augusto Cavalcanti de Albuquerque Melo (1897– 1976)

– Portinari: Brazilian neo-realist painter and printmaker Candido Portinari (1903–62)

– *Little Black Sambo*: The classic children's story by Helen Bannerman (1899) begins with a description of the grand clothes bought for Sambo by his mother and father, including 'purple shoes with crimson soles and crimson linings.'

– '*Não estou pronta*': (Port.) 'I'm ready'

– Debret: French painter Jean-Baptiste Debret (1768– 1848) produced many lithographs depicting the people of Brazil.

– *Vatapá. Lombro de porco*: (Port.) *Vatapá* is a Brazilian dish made from bread, shrimp, coconut milk, finely ground peanuts and palm oil mashed into a creamy paste. *Lombro de porco* is pork loin.

– the familiar *você*: In Portuguese, *tu* is the form of address used with family, friends and minors, while *você* is used between people who are social equals.

– '*ótimo*': (Port.) 'great'

– '*Bom*': (Port.) 'Good'

– *fazenda*: (Port.) farm

– '*É um prazer falar com você. Como vai*': (Port.) 'It's a pleasure talking to you. How are you?'

– '*Não muito bem.*': (Port.) 'Not very well.'

– '*Muito bem? Ótimo!*': (Port.) 'Very good? Great!'

– '*Não, não—eu disse não muito bem*': (Port.) 'No, no—I said not very well'

– '*Momentinho*': (Port.) Just a moment

– all crossed sticks: 'Ill-tempered, peevish, petulant; in an irritable frame of mind, out of humour, vexed. (*colloq.*)' (*OED*)

– Caucasian carpet: rug from the areas south, east and north of the Caucasus mountain chain

- Lages: a Brazilian city in the mountainous state of Santa Catarina
- *professora*: (Port.) teacher
- '*Até logo*': (Port.) 'See you later'
- *cesta*: (Port.) basket
- Bandiera: Italian Baroque painter Benedetto Bandiera (c. 1557– 1634)
- *saudades*: (Port.) longing

A KIND OF FICTION

First published, *A Kind of Fiction* (2001), pp. 9–14; copy-text, *Up on the Roof* (2007), pp. 63–68.
- Beethoven B flat quartet ... *presto*: The second of six movements in Beethoven's String Quartet No. 13 in B-flat Major, Opus 130 (1825). The term *presto* indicates that it should be played extremely fast.
- *Hair*: Hair: *The American Tribal Love-Rock Musical* (book and lyrics by James Rado and Gerome Ragni; music by Galt MacDermot) depicted the 1960s hippie counter-culture and protests against the Vietnam War. The controversial nude scene at the end of Act I was optional for performers.
- *Titanic*: The British luxury liner RMS *Titanic* sank after colliding with an iceberg in the North Atlantic on April 15, 1912, in the greatest peace-time marine disaster to that point in history.

CRAYONS

First published in *Exile* 26.2 (2002): 107–14; copy-text, *Up on the Roof* (2007), pp. 37–44. This story is based on an incident in Page's childhood during a visit to the vacation home of her uncle Frank Whitehouse in British Columbia (*Journey with No Maps*, pp. 15–16).

EX LIBRIS

First published in *Border Crossings* 21.1 (2002): 58–64, and *Best Canadian Short Stories* (2002), pp. 108–24; copy-text, *Up on the Roof* (2007), pp. 9–25.

– *Ex Libris*: (Lat.) 'from the library of'; 'an inscription, label, or stamp indicating the owner of a book (*OED*).

– *War and Peace ... The Brothers Karamazov*: epic novels by Russian authors Leo Tolstoy (pub. 1869) and Fyodor Dostoyevsky (pub. 1880)

– Beatrix Potter: (1866–1943), English author who wrote and illustrated twenty-eight children's books, including *The Tale of Peter Rabbit* (1902)

– *Excalibur in every stone*: The narrator confuses two swords from the legendary stories of King Arthur: Excalibur was the magic sword given to King Arthur by the Lady of the Lake, while the young Arthur learned of his destiny to become king when he alone was able to pull a sword from a stone.

– 'fenestration': 'the arrangement of windows in a building,' or '*Anat*. the process of becoming perforated; the formation of small holes' (*OED*)

– 'lazaretto': 'a lazer-house';'a building set apart for the purpose of quarantine' (*OED*)

– 'recanalization': 'redirection (of energy, emotion, etc.) towards a different object or goal, rechannelling' (*OED*)

– W.H. Auden: (1907–73), Anglo-American poet known for technical experimentation and exploration of political and social themes

– Wordsworth: English poet William Wordsworth (1770–1850) whose masterwork is the 14-book-long *Prelude or, Growth of a Poet's Mind; An Autobiographical Poem*

– Rilke, Lorca, Seferis: Austrian poet Rainer Maria Rilke (1875–1926); Spanish poet, playwright and socialist activist Federico García Lorca (1898–1936); and Greek poet Giorgos Seferis (1900–71), penname of diplomat Georgios Sefeiades

– Alack, alas. Alas, alack: echoes Auden's 'Autumn Song': 'Close behind us on our track, / Dead in hundreds cry Alack, ... / In false attitudes of love.' (ll. 9–12)

– It should be the reverse: This is, in fact, a reversal of Jesus's declaration that '... thou shalt love the Lord thy God with all thy heart, and with all thy soul, and with all thy mind, and with all thy strength: this *is* the first commandment. And the second is like, namely this, Thou shalt love thy neighbour as thyself. There is none other commandment greater than these' (Mark 12:29–31).

– Kathleen Battle: (1948–), American lyric soprano known for her recitals and recordings of a wide range of music from opera to spirituals

– 'They crucified my Lord': The spiritual 'Were you there when they crucified my Lord?' is a staple of Kathleen Battle's repertoire.

– Toni Morrison: (1931–), American novelist, winner of the Nobel Prize in Literature in 1993

– *Beloved*: The novel tells the story of a runaway slave who kills her infant daughter rather than see her experience a life of slavery.

– Proust ... that smell: Marcel Proust (1871–1922), French novelist, author of the seven-volume semi-autobiographical narrative *A la recherche du temps perdu* (*Remembrance of Things Past*). In the first episode, a surge of childhood memories is evoked by the taste of a tea cake—a *madeleine*.

– Armani: Italian fashion designer Giorgio Armani (1934–)

– Josephine Baker: (1906–75), American-born singer, dancer and actress, famous for her erotic performances in *La Revue Nègre* at the Théâtre des Champs-Élysées and the Folies Bergère in Paris

– Emily Dickinson: (1830–86), reclusive American poet

– Left hemisphere: The left hemisphere of the brain is associated with language production and apprehension.

– 'The manner of the Children—/ ...: the final stanza of Emily Dickinson's poem 'The Months have ends—the Years—a knot—'

– A most eclectic library: All of the authors and books mentioned here are in Page's own library.

– surrealists from Bosch to Ernst and Carrington: Hieronymus Bosch (1450–1516), Flemish painter known for his nightmarish paintings of Heaven and Hell; German painter, sculptor and poet Max Ernst (1891–1976); and English-born painter and author Leonora Carrington (1917–2011)

– Verne: Jules Verne (1828–1905), French author of *Journey to the Centre of the Earth* (1864), *Twenty Thousand Leagues Under the Sea* (1870), and *Around the World in Eighty Days* (1873)

– H.G. Wells: (1866–1946), author of *The Time Machine* (1895), *The Island of Doctor Moreau* (1896) and *The War of the Worlds* (1898)

– Abbot's *Flatland*: In *Flatland: A Romance of Many Dimensions* (1884), Edwin Abbott (E.A.) Abbott (1838–1928) imagines a two-dimensional world.

– Clarke: Arthur C. Clarke (1917–2008), author of *Childhood's End* (1953)

– Sturgeon: Theodore Sturgeon (1918–45), author of *More than Human* (1953)

– Lessing: Doris Lessing (1919–2013), author of over fifty books including *The Canopus in Argos: Archives* series (1979–83) of science fiction influenced by the Sufi teachings of Idries Shah
– what did it profit them?: an echo of Mark 8:36 (King James Version): 'For what does it profit a man to gain the whole world and lose his soul?'
– A vast glass-house, light-filled: According to Marilyn Bowering, Page had 'a recurring dream of a book-lined corridor, a kind of hidden room, where she felt complete bliss. It ultimately turned into a light-filled atrium that she liked less because it was more exposed, but the feeling of bliss remained the same' (*Journey with No Maps*, p. 306).
– *The Changing Light at Sandover*: a three-volume poem by American James Merrill (1926–95) incorporating messages transcribed from séances with a ouija board
– David Hockney: (1937–) English painter and photographer
– Hakim Sanai: (1080–1131/1141), an early Sufi poet, author of the epic *Hadiqatu'l Haqiqat* (The Walled Garden of Truth)
– the Modigliani drawing of Akhmatova: As a young man in Paris, Amedeo Modigliani (1884–1920), had an affair with Russian poet Anna Gorenko (1889–1966), pen name Anna Akhmatova, and completed several portraits of her, including the stylized line drawing referred to here.
– Immanuel Velikovsky: (1895–1979), Russian-Jewish scholar who argued in *Worlds in Collision* (1950) that near collisions with Venus in the 15th century BCE and Mars in the 8th to 7th centuries BCE had altered Earth's rotation
– a bed-sized world: an echo of 'The Sun Rising' by John Donne (1572–1631): 'To warm the world, that's done in warming us / … This bed thy centre is, these walls thy sphere' (ll. 26–30).

STONE

First published in *Descant* 34.4 (Winter 2003): 27–57; copy-text, *Up on the Roof* (2007), pp. 95–131.
– jitney: unlicensed delivery truck or cab
– high realism: 'high realist' artists begin with nature, but interpret it in deeply personal ways
– *Epstein, Michelangelo, Brancusi, Giacometti, Hepworth, Moore:* With the exception of Michelangelo, all are modern sculptors: Jacob Epstein

(1880–1959), Constantin Brâncuși (1876–1957), Alberto Giacometti (1901–66), Barbara Hepworth (1903–75), and Henry Spencer Moore (1898–1986)

– *au fond*: (Fr.) at its root

– I read a story once [...]: the parable of the king and the poisoned well (source unknown)

– '*Es mi destino, señora.*': (Sp.) 'It is my destiny, madam.'

– de Bono: Edward de Bono (1933–), Maltese physician and psychologist who popularized the phrase 'lateral thinking'

– the Mayor of Casterbridge: In the 1886 novel by Thomas Hardy (1840–1928), the protagonist is a man of humble origins with aspirations above his station.

– 'Clothes maketh the man' ... 'Manners maketh the man': Mark Twain (1835–1910) observed that 'Clothes make the man. Naked people have little or no influence on society.' The adage that 'manners make the man' is attributed to William of Wykeham (1324–1404).

– 'Be toidy, be clean, be noice': a humorous play on phrases in W.H. Auden's poem 'The Two': 'Be clean, be tidy, oil the lock, / Trim the garden, wind the clock, / Remember the Two.'

– Nelson Mandela: (1918–2013), South African activist. Imprisoned for twenty-seven years for opposing apartheid, he served as president of the post-apartheid government from 1994–99.

– Mme Curie: Marie Curie (1867–1934), Polish-French scientist whose research on radioactivity won her Nobel Prizes for both physics (1903) and chemistry (1911)

– hookers murdered by a pig farmer: Robert Pickton of Port Coquitlam, British Columbia, was convicted of murdering six women in 2007, but confessed to the murders of forty-nine prostitutes and homeless women.

– 'Amazing Grace': hymn by English poet and clergyman John Newton (1725–1807)

– 'the lilies of the field ... or the stars in their courses': In the first phrase, Jesus draws attention to the simple beauty of the 'lilies of the field': 'they toil not, neither do they spin: And yet I say unto you, that even Solomon in all his glory was not arrayed like one of these' (Luke 12.28–29). In the second, the female judge Deborah leads the Israelites in their war against the Canaanites: 'They fought from heaven; the stars in their courses fought against Sisera' (Judges 5.20).

– Hepworth: English sculptor Barbara Hepworth (1903–75), known for her abstract bronzes
– Egg of the World: According to Carl Jung (1875–1961), the myth that the cosmos or a primordial being was hatched from a 'world egg' is shared by many cultures. Page repeatedly returned to the image in her visual art, most notably in *A Kind of Osmosis* (1960).
– egg *oeuf huevo ovo ei*: 'egg' in English, French, Spanish, Latin, German
– 'And one eye was a fairy eye. The other merely cod.': The rhyme continues: 'And with this fairy eye he'd see / The fairies passing by, / While he'd see only fish and seaweed / With the other eye.'

YOU ARE HERE

First published, *Exile* 32.2 (Summer 2008); copy-text, *You Are Here* (Hedgerow Press, 2008).

Marketing
– chamois: 'a soft, pliable leather, prepared from the skin of the chamois [antelope]' (*OED*).

Perseids and Time
– the month of Perseids: Annually in late July to mid-August, a meteor shower caused by debris from the comet Swift-Tuttle appears to radiate from the constellation Perseus.
– 'earthgrazer': a meteor that skims the top of the earth's atmosphere, appearing to move horizontally across the sky
– Light years: a unit of astronomical measurement: the distance light travels in one year—9.4607 x 1012 km (nearly 6 trillion miles)
– Phoenix … dying, … being born: 'In classical mythology: a bird … which was said to live for five or six hundred years in the deserts of Arabia, before burning itself to ashes on a funeral pyre ignited by the sun and fanned by its own wings, only to rise from its ashes with renewed youth to live through another such cycle' (*OED*).

Joke, or is it?
– Author's note: 'The two jokes […] are my retellings of stories from the Mulla Nasrudin corpus, as told by Idries Shah in *The Pleasantries of the*

Incomparable Mulla Nasrudin and *The Subtleties of the Inimitable Mulla Nasrudin*, both from Octagon Press.'

Window Cleaner
– Did Plath write a poem about window cleaners?: an allusion to *The Bell Jar*: 'She stared at her reflection in the glossed shop windows as if to make sure, moment by moment, that she continued to exist.'

Horoscope
– 'Negative capability': the phrase used by Romantic poet John Keats to describe the capacity to accommodate 'uncertainties, mysteries, doubts, without any irritable reaching after fact and reason' (letter to George and Thomas Keats, 21 December 1817)
– 'The fault ... is not in our stars but in ourselves': William Shakespeare, *Julius Caesar* (1.3.140–1)

Hypnogogic or Hynopompic States
– Hypnogogic or Hynopompic: dream-like states of mind related to falling asleep and awakening from sleep (*OED*)
– nöosphere: 'the part of the biosphere occupied by thinking humanity' (*OED*)

Old Friend and Irishness
– the Book of Durrow, the Book of Kells: illuminated gospel books created in medieval Irish monastaries (650–800)

Marathon and Life after Death
– Helen's return: In an interview with her biographer, using almost exactly the same words, Page described the return of her friend Tommy Smith shortly after her death on 22 January 1940 in the form of 'a whole lot of little specks of light dancing, like a molecular dance' (*Journey with No Maps*, p. 60).

Living with Animals and the Appearance of Aliens
– Barney and Betty Hill: An American couple from Portsmouth, New Hampshire, who claimed to have been abducted by aliens on 19 September 1961.

The Face in the Window
– lanugo hair: the down on a human fetus, usually shed before birth

Crop Circles and Flatland
– pi: a transcendental number (3.14159265…) equal to the ratio of the circumference of a circle to the diameter
– specific gravity: 'the degree of relative heaviness … expressed by the ratio of the weight of a given volume to that of an equal volume of some substance taken as a standard' (*OED*)
– *Flatland*: *Flatland: A Romance of Many Dimensions* (1884), a 'mathematical fiction' by schoolmaster E.A. Abbott
– Copernicus: Nicolaus Copernicus (1473–1543), a Renaissance mathematician and astronomer who advanced a heliocentric theory of the universe

The Third Eye
– third eye: In Hinduism and Buddhism, 'the eye of insight or destruction located in the middle of the forehead of the god Siva; hence … the power of inward or intuitive sight occasionally gained by humans' (*OED*).

Mimi and Her Husband Go to a Concert
– Philip Glass: (1937–) American composer whose work has been described as 'minimalist' and is characterized by repetitive structures
– *fouetté*: (Fr.) a pirouette in which the dancer executes a 'whipping' movement with the free leg (*OED*)

Mimi Remembers Being a Chair
– *Wolf Solent*: a novel by John Cowper Powys (1872–1963). Page acknowledged an episode from this book as the inspiration for the empathetic ability of the heroine of *The Sun and the Moon* (*Journey with No Maps*, p. 65).

Mimi Is Idle and Anxious
– Noah Sarc's novel *Animals*: a fictional work; a play on 'Noah's ark,' filled with animals
– Gaia: in Greek mythology, the primordial deity from which all life is derived; the personification of the earth

Mimi's Clearest Thoughts Are in the Shower
– serotonin: a chemical needed for the nerve cells to function
– transfiguration: metamorphosis to another state of being

In the Orgone Box
– Wilhelm Reich … orgone energy: Wilhelm Reich (1897–1957) argued
that sexual energy or life force could be collected and used to treat
mental and physical illnesses (*OED*).
– verified by Einstein: In 1941, Albert Einstein (1879–1955) was one of
several scientists who agreed to assess Reich's experiment.
– limned: painted or embellished

Coincidence
– Steller's Jay: (*Cyanocitta stelleri*) a jay native to western North America

Stoned and Identity
– Buddha nature: A central tenet of Buddhism is that all beings share
the potential for enlightenment.
– fractal: 'A mathematically conceived curve such that any small part of
it, enlarged, has the same statistical character as the original' (*OED*).
– nirvana: (Sanskrit) 'extinction.' In Buddhism, 'the realization of the
non-existence of self, leading to cessation of all entanglement and
attachment in life; the state of being released from the effects of karma
and the cycle of death and rebirth' (*OED*).

LIST OF
ILLUSTRATIONS

Cover: *Jacaranda Door*, 1958.
Felt pen and gouache, 44.3 x 34.2 cm. Private collection.

Page 2: *Triptych*, 1958.
Gouache, 34.3 x 40.4 cm. Collection of Trent University.

Page 5: *Undercover Chairs*, 1957.
Felt pen on paper, 28.9 x 44.6 cm. Private collection.

Page 8: *White Lilies in a Copper Mug*, 1957–58.
Felt pen and gouache, 44.4 x 30.4 cm. Private collection.

Page 18: *Flowers and Railing*, 1957–58.
Gouache, 35.5 x 27.3 cm. Private collection.

Page 129: *Stairwell*, circa 1957–58.
Felt pen and gouache, 31.3 x 44.7 cm. Collection of Trent University.

Page 130: *Crow*, circa 1970–79.
Pen and ink. 47.5 x 31 cm. Private collection

Page 140: *Painting Table*, 1957–58.
Gouache, 34.3 x 40.4 cm. Collection of Trent University.

Page 166: *Angels*, 1957.
Gouache, egg tempera, 29.8 x 34.8 cm. Private collection.

Page 172: *Powder Room*, circa 1957–58.
Felt pen and gouache, 44.4 x 35.5 cm. Private collection.

Page 174: *Black Telephone and Flowers*, circa 1957–58.
Felt pen and gouache on paper, 32.5 x 47 cm. Private collection.

Page 178: *Dining Room*, 1957.
Felt pen and gouache, 53 x 50.8 cm. Private collection.

Page 200: *A birthday card for Daddie*, circa 1920–21.
Pencil and water colour. Collection of Trent University.

Page 220: *Womb Form*, 1957.
Felt pen and gouache, dimensions unknown. Private collection.

Page 249: *Untitled*, undated.
Pencil, 23 x 15.1 cm. Private collection.

Page 250: *I'm Always Bowing*, 1958.
Ink on tracing paper, 32.9 x 20.2 cm. Collection of Trent University.

Page 277: *Flowers of the Upper Air*, 1961.
Oil pastel and watercolour, dimensions unknown. Private collection.

Page 299: *Ficus*, 1957.
Felt pen, 45 x 29.8 cm. Private collection.

Page 300: *Self Portrait*, 1958.
Gouache, 33.8 x 32.3 cm. Private collection.

Page 303: *Plants in Copper Mug*, 1957.
Felt pen, 45.7 x 37.1 cm. Private collection.

ABOUT P.K. PAGE

P.K. Page was born November 23, 1916, at Swanage, Dorset, England, and died January 14, 2010, at Victoria, British Columbia, Canada. In 1919, she left England with her family and settled in Red Deer, Alberta. She went to school in Calgary and Winnipeg, and in the early 1940s moved to Montreal where she worked as a filing clerk and researcher. She belonged to a group that founded the magazine *Preview* (1942–45) and was associated with F.R. Scott, Patrick Anderson, Bruce Ruddick, Neufville Shaw and A.M. Klein. Her first book published was *Unit of Five* (1944), where her poetry appeared alongside that of Louis Dudek and Raymond Souster. From 1946 to 1950 Page worked for the National Film Board as a scriptwriter. In 1950 she married William Arthur Irwin and later studied art in Brazil, Mexico and New York.

P.K. Page is the author of dozens of books, including poetry, a novel, short stories, essays and books for children, and two memoirs based on her extended stays in Brazil and Mexico with her husband, who served in those countries as the Canadian Ambassador. A memoir in verse, *Hand Luggage*, explores in a poetic voice Page's life in the arts and in the world.

Awarded a Governor General's Award for poetry (*The Metal and the Flower*) in 1954, Page was also on the short list for the Griffin Prize for Poetry in 2003 (*Planet Earth*) and, posthumously, in 2010 (*Coal and Roses*), and she was awarded the BC Lieutenant Governor's Award for Literary Excellence in 2004. She had numerous honorary degrees, received the Order of British Columbia and was a Fellow of the Royal Society of Canada. She was also appointed a Companion of the Order of Canada.

Painting under the name P.K. Irwin, she mounted one-woman shows in Mexico and Canada and exhibited in various group shows. Her work is represented in the permanent collections of the National Gallery of Canada, the Art Gallery of Ontario, the Victoria Art Gallery and many collections here and abroad.